A DISTANT SHORE

Other Life-Changing Fiction™
by Karen Kingsbury

Baxters Family Stand-Alone Titles
The Baxters: A Prequel
  (Coming Soon)
Truly Madly Deeply
Someone Like You
Two Weeks
When We Were Young
To the Moon and Back
In This Moment
Love Story—The Baxters
A Baxter Family Christmas
Coming Home

The Baxters—1—Redemption Series
Redemption
Remember
Return
Rejoice
Reunion

The Baxters—2—Firstborn Series
Fame
Forgiven
Found
Family
Forever

The Baxters—3—Sunrise Series
Sunrise
Summer
Someday
Sunset

The Baxters—4—Above the Line Series
Take One
Take Two
Take Three
Take Four

The Baxters—5—Bailey Flanigan Series
Leaving
Learning
Longing
Loving

Other Stand-Alone Titles
Fifteen Minutes
The Chance
The Bridge
Oceans Apart
Between Sundays
When Joy Came to Stay
On Every Side
Divine
Like Dandelion Dust
Where Yesterday Lives
Shades of Blue
Unlocked

Angels Walking Series
Angels Walking
Chasing Sunsets
Brush of Wings

9/11 Series
One Tuesday Morning
Beyond Tuesday Morning
Remember Tuesday Morning

Lost Love Military Series
Even Now
Ever After

Forever Faithful Series
Waiting for Morning
Moment of Weakness
Halfway to Forever

Women of Faith Fiction Series
A Time to Dance
A Time to Embrace

Cody Gunner Series
A Thousand Tomorrows
Just Beyond the Clouds
This Side of Heaven

Red Glove Series
Gideon's Gift
Maggie's Miracle
Sarah's Song
Hannah's Hope

Life-Changing Bible Story Collections
Family of Jesus
Friends of Jesus

Children's Chapter Books Ages 8–12
Best Family Ever (Baxter Family Children)
Finding Home (Baxter Family Children)
Never Grow Up (Baxter Family Children)

Children's Picture Books
Let Me Hold You Longer
Let's Go on a Mommy Date
We Believe in Christmas
Let's Have a Daddy Day
The Princess and the Three Knights
The Brave Young Knight
Far Flutterby
Go Ahead and Dream (with Quarterback Alex Smith)
Whatever You Grow Up to Be
Always Daddy's Princess

Miracle Story Collections
A Treasury of Christmas Miracles
A Treasury of Miracles for Women
A Treasury of Miracles for Teens
A Treasury of Miracles for Friends
A Treasury of Adoption Miracles
Miracles: A Devotional

Gift Books
Forever Young: Ten Gifts of Faith for the Graduate
Forever My Little Boy
Forever My Little Girl

e-Short Stories
The Beginning
I Can Only Imagine
Elizabeth Baxter's 10 Secrets to a Happy Marriage
Once upon a Campus

www.KarenKingsbury.com

KAREN KINGSBURY

A DISTANT SHORE

A Novel

ATRIA BOOKS

New York   London   Toronto   Sydney   New Delhi

ATRIA
BOOKS

An Imprint of Simon & Schuster, Inc.
1230 Avenue of the Americas
New York, NY 10020

First Atria Books hardcover edition April 2021

ATRIA BOOKS and colophon are trademarks of Simon & Schuster, Inc.

For information about special discounts for bulk purchases, please contact Simon & Schuster Special Sales at 1-866-506-1949 or business@simonandschuster.com.

The Simon & Schuster Speakers Bureau can bring authors to your live event. For more information or to book an event, contact the Simon & Schuster Speakers Bureau at 1-866-248-3049 or visit our website at www.simonspeakers.com.

Interior design by Dana Sloan

Manufactured in the United States of America

1   3   5   7   9   10   8   6   4   2

Library of Congress Control Number: 2021932218

ISBN 978-1-9821-0435-1
ISBN 978-1-9821-0437-5 (ebook)

Dedicated to Donald, the love of my life, my husband of thirty-two years. And to our beautiful children and grandchildren. The journey of life is breathtaking surrounded by you, and every minute together is time borrowed from eternity. I love you with every breath, every heartbeat. And to God, Almighty, who has—for now—blessed me with these.

CHAPTER ONE

*Even though I walk through the valley of the
shadow of death, I will fear no evil. For You are
with me; Your rod and Your staff, they comfort me.*

—Psalm 23:4

The long ago moment danced and breathed and lived
inside her.

Mama's voice singing in the warm Belizean breeze,
the way it had every afternoon at this time, calling them
in from an afternoon of gathering eggs and tending to
the chickens. "Lizzie James, dinner! Bring your brother!"

"Yes, Mama!" And Lizzie was shading her eyes so she
could see her mother standing in the distance, just outside their small thatched-roof house. Long brown hair
blowing over her shoulders. Eyes the same pale blue as
Lizzie's. Happy eyes.

And in this, her most precious memory, Lizzie was
grabbing hold of her little brother's hand. "Let's go, Daniel. Rice pudding for dinner. Your favorite."

In the memory, Lizzie was eight and Daniel was six,
the two of them inseparable. Half the day they sat side

1

by side at the village schoolhouse learning their numbers and memorizing Scripture. The other half they worked the fields or played in the grassy school yard.

But in this moment, before their daddy moved away—all they wanted was to be home for dinner. Daniel was running beside her, laughing because their cousins' Labrador retriever puppy, Milo, was galloping out to greet them, and just ahead their mother was waiting for them. Smiling at them, arms wide, and she was pulling them close.

Of all God's gifts, she was saying, *you two are my favorite.*

Lizzie blinked and the images disappeared. Again.

She wasn't in her mother's arms and Daniel wasn't beside her and they weren't about to eat Mama's rice pudding. Milo was long gone and this wasn't her Mennonite village. She hadn't been there in a year at least. Instead she was nine years old, standing on the smallest beach in all of Belize. And no one called her Lizzie Susan James.

She was Eliza Ann Lawrence.

Mennonite men never leave their families. That's what Mama said. But Lizzie's daddy had left them and moved here for his very important job, here to Belize City. Where Mama and Daniel died out in the ocean. And where Lizzie's life had become one unending nightmare.

"Get into the water, Eliza," her aunt Betsy yelled across the sandy beach. She sat on a beach towel, dark red lipstick and sunglasses. Aunt Betsy waved her hand, frustrated. She was always frustrated. "Go! Girls at the Palace need their sunshine. Even you."

Girls at the Palace.

Lizzie turned and faced the ocean. Sixteen girls worked at the Palace, but she wasn't like any of them. No, she was a little princess. That's what her daddy had called her ever since Mama and Daniel died. Eliza had her own wing at the Palace because she was the daughter of Anders McMillan. That's what he called himself now. Not Paul David James like before.

Her daddy was an evil man. That much Lizzie knew, because the other girls always told her. Bad things were happening at the Palace, Lizzie was sure. Things she couldn't talk about or even think about.

"You're a princess, Eliza," Dora told her yesterday. "Men don't visit you at night." Dora lived on the third floor of the Palace. She was fourteen and blond like Lizzie.

Dora was right, the men who came and went from the Palace didn't visit Eliza. Her daddy said they never would. "I'm saving you for someone special, Eliza," her daddy had told her when she moved in after losing Mama and Daniel.

So Lizzie was safe from the men. At least for now. But even so, every day after her time at the beach she was scared to go home to the Palace. Because what if this was the day the men were allowed into her room? Also, Aunt Betsy was mean and sometimes she yanked Eliza's long blond hair if she didn't walk fast enough on the way back.

"Hurry up, Eliza. Your father is expecting you." Aunt Betsy was her daddy's sister. They both had the same angry face. Aunt Betsy's breath smelled like sausage and onions.

For now Eliza had an hour alone in the water. A tear slid down Eliza's cheek and she took a step toward the sea. "You lead me beside still waters . . ." The words were a whisper, something left over from the life she used to live.

Eliza still wasn't sure how everything had gone so bad, so fast.

First, her daddy left and Mama cried for a long time. People in Lower Barton Creek would talk in quiet words and give sad looks at Mama and Daniel and Lizzie. Then her father's sister Aunt Betsy came to visit. It was the first time any of them had met the woman. In front of other grown-ups, Aunt Betsy laughed a lot and used her hands when she talked. And that day, she had a dolly for Eliza. "Come to Belize City to see your father," Aunt Betsy had said before she left. "He's a very important businessman. He wants his family with him."

Mama said the reason they'd never met Aunt Betsy was because the woman had lived in the States, and that she had just moved to Belize. A few weeks later, the three of them did what Aunt Betsy asked. Mama, Daniel and Eliza went to Belize City and visited Daddy. He ran the Palace, a hotel he told them. There were no girls at the Palace back then, but her daddy sold more than hotel rooms. "You're dealing drugs, Paul David," her mother had said one night when she thought Eliza wasn't listening. "We can't be part of this."

Eliza wasn't sure about all of the details. But her daddy got angry at Mama. And something must've happened. An accident maybe. Because one morning Eliza woke up in the room at the Palace where she was staying with Mama and Daniel. But she was alone.

"Mama?" she had cried out. Her heart pounded loud and she felt sick. "Daniel? Where are you?"

And then Aunt Betsy had come into the room. The woman stood there, her hands on her hips. Her eyes looked different than before. Meaner. "It's a tragedy, Eliza."

Who was Eliza? She had blinked a few times. "I'm Lizzie."

"You're Eliza now. Your father wants you to be Eliza. That's your given name." Her aunt didn't say anything for a long time. Then the woman sat on the edge of the bed and shrugged. "There's no easy way to say this, Eliza. Your mama and brother are gone."

Her daddy had come into the bedroom then. "They're in the ocean, Eliza. They didn't make it. You're going to live with me, now. Here at the beach."

Lizzie didn't understand, not then or now. Her mama and brother were in the ocean? What did that mean?

At first, Lizzie would stand at the water's edge and call them. "Mama? Daniel!" But they never called back and they never came out of the ocean. So Lizzie lived at the Palace with her daddy and her aunt.

And eventually Lizzie became Eliza.

The other girls moved into the Palace a few at a time. Some of them were older teenagers and some were young. They wore fancy dresses and every night the men came to their rooms. That's what the girls told Eliza at lunch and dinner.

But Daddy didn't like Eliza talking to the other girls. "You're different, Eliza," he would tell her. "I'm saving you for something special."

A tear slid down Eliza's cheek. "You restore my soul . . ." Her whisper faded. For a long time she believed God had died in the sea with her mother and brother. But here at the ocean she believed she could see Him. Far off in the horizon.

There at the water's edge.

"Eliza! Go!" Her aunt was on her feet, her full face redder than usual. "You're wasting time."

Fear sent chills down Eliza's arms and legs. She ran down the wet sand and splashed her way through the surf. This was where she belonged. Here in the soft blue waves she was free. All afternoon, as long as Eliza played in the water and swam beneath the sunshine, she wished she might stay all day.

Aunt Betsy and the two guards stationed up the path from the beach wouldn't bother her.

But when Eliza couldn't take another hour of sunshine and surf, when she was so tired all she wanted was to curl up and fall asleep on the sand, that's when her aunt would turn her over to the guards. And they would take her back to the Palace.

Eliza dove into the clear gray water just beyond the surf. *I would swim to the other side of the sea if I could.*

She dropped below the surface and pulled at the water. The waves were rough today. The gray sky getting darker. One stroke, two. Three. She lifted her head above the waves and cried out, the way she did every day at this time. "Daniel!" She scanned the watery horizon for her brother. Her best friend. "Daniel, where are you?"

She was too far out for Aunt Betsy to hear her. "Mama! Come back!" Her tears mixed with the salt water on her soft cheeks. "Daniel?"

A few more strokes and Eliza stopped swimming. She was farther out than usual, bobbing about in the salty water. Before her life changed, she and her family would come to the beach four times a year. At the start of each season. A holiday, her parents had called it.

But this was no holiday now.

Clouds grew darker in the distance. A storm was on its way, which meant her time at the beach was about to be cut short. She swam out a little farther. Not yet. She didn't want to go back. Again she looked out across the ocean. If God had her mother and brother, then maybe He would give them back to her. Out here on the waves.

If only she could yell loud enough.

"Daniel?" Eliza caught a mouthful of seawater and she started to cough. "Mama, where are you?"

Suddenly beneath the water something grabbed her legs. Not a fish or a shark, because it didn't have teeth. It was strong and warm and it had a terrible hold on her.

"Stop!" she yelled but her voice got lost on the wind. *What is it? What's happening?* She put her face underwater and opened her eyes. And that's when she saw the terrible truth.

A monster didn't have hold of her legs.

The current did.

Watch out for the undertow, Eliza. That's what Aunt Betsy always told her. *Don't swim out too far or the water will take you away forever.*

"No!" Eliza screamed. "Let me go!" She could kick her way out of this current. She was a strong swimmer. She moved her feet in frantic bursts, and made big grabs at the water.

But the ocean wouldn't let her go.

The fight was too much for her so she stopped. Stopped kicking and pulling at the sea and she turned on her back. Suddenly the scared feeling inside her melted away. "You guide me in paths of righteousness"—her words were quieter now—"for Your name's sake."

Storm clouds moved overhead. Dark gray layers and flashes of lightning. If Aunt Betsy was calling, Eliza couldn't hear her. The only sounds were the wind and waves and thunder. A voice called to her from the horizon. Her mama's voice.

Whenever you're scared, Lizzie, recite Psalm Twenty-Three. God is with you. He is always with you.

"Even though I walk through—" A wave washed over her face and knocked her deep into the water. Again Eliza fought the pull of the current, and finally she pushed her face free. *Breathe,* she told herself. *Breathe while you still can.*

"Even though I walk through the valley of the shadow of death"—each word was a gasp, an attempt at staying alive—"I will fear no evil. For You are with me; You comfort me—"

Another wave.

"Mama!" Eliza clawed and kicked, but it took all her effort just to keep her head above the ocean. "Mama, help me!"

Then she remembered something. If she could see God at the back side of the ocean, if that's where her mother and brother lived, then that's where she wanted to be, too. This wasn't a bad thing happening to her. God was calling her home. *You prepare a table before me in the presence of my enemies. You anoint my head with oil; my cup overflows.*

Yes, that was it. If she gave herself to the current, she could be finished with Aunt Betsy and the Palace and her terrible father. Maybe the thing pulling at her, taking her under was God. Anointing her head. Making her cup overflow.

She cried out louder this time. "Surely . . . goodness and love . . . will follow me . . ."

The sea was rougher, but the current no longer grabbed at her. Finally, she looked back at the shore. Aunt Betsy and the Palace guards were waving their hands at her. Eliza had to finish the Psalm because the best part was at the end.

Other people ran toward Aunt Betsy. Tourists, proba-bly. *Stay away from the tourists*, Aunt Betsy always said.

You're not for sale. A bigger wave knocked her under and Eliza used all her strength to get back to the surface. *Mama, I'm coming for you. God, help me find them.*

She gasped and spit the seawater from her mouth. Her legs and arms were too heavy to move, and her words came out like a whisper now. "Mama! Daniel?" She was too tired to yell.

Eliza raised her face to the stormy sky. "Surely . . . goodness and love . . . will follow me . . ." Never had she kicked so hard in all her life. But she had to finish. Had to get to the end. ". . . all the days of my life." Another wave. Eliza made one last try to breathe. "And . . . I will dwell . . . in the house of the Lord. Forever."

She smiled and a beautiful peace came over her. And there was Mama again in the distance, waving at her, calling her close. *Lizzie James, dinner! Bring your brother!*

"Yes, Mama!"

And I will dwell in the house of the Lord forever. The house of the Lord.

It would be a small house with a thatched roof. The place where Lizzie's mother and brother still lived. The only people who had ever loved her. And now they would be all together. There at the edge of the ocean where they would live in the house of the Lord.

Forever and ever and ever.

CHAPTER TWO

The righteous perish, and no one takes it to heart;
the devout are taken away, and no one
understands.

—Isaiah 57:1

Jack Ryder snagged the football from the warm sand and threw it to his brother, a dozen yards down the beach. "Shane! Keep it low," Jack shouted as he pointed to the stormy sky. "Too much wind!"

Up the sand a ways the boys' parents sat side by side in identical resort beach chairs. Both of them on their cell phones. Thunder rumbled in the distance and their dad looked at Jack. "Okay. Let's wrap it up."

"Yes, sir." Jack caught the football and glanced at his father. *Let's wrap it up* meant they had another five minutes. Maybe ten. Jack threw the ball to Shane. Their dad was too busy to notice their disregard of his order.

Work trumped everything, even his teenage sons. Even here, on their annual vacation to Belize. The beach was just a different sort of office for their parents. Dad was an ambassador, and Mom ran a handful of charities.

They were good people, kind. But Jack and Shane couldn't compete with all that. Which was okay.

Jack caught a spiral pass from Shane and jogged a few steps back. He glanced at his parents again, at his father. *I love you, Dad,* he wanted to call out. But it wasn't the time.

Anyway, the brothers had all they could've wanted. Their parents loved them. They were supportive and kind and their home was happy. The successes ahead for Jack and Shane were lined up like the palm trees along Albert Street here in Belize City.

Jack was sixteen, and Shane was fourteen. They attended the best school. Their father employed the best trainers for their baseball and football seasons. Yes, the two of them had all they needed for the best possible futures.

And they had each other. That most of all.

Down the beach Shane caught the football and shrugged, as if to say maybe they had longer than they thought. Their father was on another phone call and the storm wasn't getting worse. Shane flung the ball and Jack caught it again.

Rain was crossing over the water a ways out, staying out to sea, so there was no rush to get inside. Not until their parents insisted. Shane jogged closer and the two brothers sat on the sand and watched the storm.

"Could you live here?" Shane raked his fingers through his short dark hair. He turned his gaze to the ocean. "I mean, like get a house here and never leave?"

Jack considered that. "No." He chuckled. "Then it wouldn't be vacation."

"True." Shane looked over his shoulder at his parents. "Someone should tell Mom and Dad that."

"You still wanna do politics? Like them?" Jack grinned at his brother. "And don't tell me you'd be good at it. We already know that."

"Well." Shane's eyes lit up. "I *am* the outgoing brother. Like everyone says."

"Yeah, yeah." Jack elbowed him. "You can be whatever you want. I've heard it all."

"You, too." Shane flicked sand at Jack. "Don't pretend you can't do it all. Because you can. Star quarterback of Georgetown Prep." He changed his voice to sound like their father. "Presidents have that kind of résumé, my boy. *President Jack Ryder*."

Again Jack laughed. "You be president. I'll be a Navy SEAL."

"I'll be one with you." Shane stood and stretched his hands to the sky. He was tall and strong like Jack. "Best two Navy SEALs they ever had."

"Stick to politics, Brother. Navy SEALs have to swim." Jack flicked him the football and Shane jumped up and ran down the beach.

They had waited all their lives for this year. Shane would be a freshman at Georgetown Prep in the fall. Jack, a junior. The first of their two high school years together. Jack rose to his feet just in time to catch the ball.

Shane grinned at him. "You might have a little competition at quarterback, big brother."

"Bring it." Jack snagged the ball. He sure loved the kid. The two had been inseparable since the week their parents brought Shane home. But this annual trip to the beach was their favorite part of the year.

Usually they took a second flight further south to the longer stretches of beach on the peninsula. But their dad had business in town this week. So they were here.

Today was their third day and Jack only wished they had another week.

The storm looked like it was clearing, so the game of pass might have gone on all afternoon. But before Jack could wing the ball back to Shane, a woman down the beach began screaming and waving.

Jack jogged closer to his brother. The woman had drawn a small crowd now. A couple of big guys seemed to have run down from a bluff up above. Also a few families of anxious-looking tourists.

"What's happening?" Jack caught up to his brother and both of them jogged toward the woman.

"I don't know." Shane stopped and scanned the ocean. Panic seized his expression. "There!"

All at once they had their answer. Fifty yards out, flailing and grabbing at the surface of the choppy sea was what looked like a child.

"Help her, please!" the woman at the shoreline screamed. She ran into the water and back out again, then she covered her face and next she waved her arms. "Help!" She pointed out to sea. "I can't swim! Someone help her!"

Shane dropped the ball on the shore and ran for the water. Jack ran, too, but he shouted at his brother. "Stay here! I'll get her."

His brother stopped, his face a twist of hurt. "You need me."

"No, I don't! Stay here!" Jack took four running steps through the water and looked over his shoulder. *Good.* Shane was staying back in the ankle-deep water. Because the truth was, Shane really couldn't swim. Not like Jack.

His heart raced, but he felt better as he pulled at the rough surf. He would get the child and Shane would stay on the shore. Only one of them, that's all the kid needed.

A current just beneath the surface pulled at Jack's legs, but that didn't panic him. He was used to swimming through currents. He was on the summer surf team back home, training for the day when he really would be a Navy SEAL.

Swim with the current, he told himself. *Not against it.* He adjusted his position so the current would take him straight to the girl. The effort made his body feel heavy, but he kept on. Closer and closer until he could see the child's face.

The girl was maybe eight or nine, matted blond hair, tanned arms still clawing at the water. Her face was slipping under the surface and Jack doubled his intensity. She didn't have long, a minute, maybe less.

God, save her. The silent prayer filled Jack's mind.

Get me to her. Please. Before it's too late. And then, as he took two more strong strokes through the water, Jack saw something in the corner of his eye.

His brother, Shane.

Only Shane wasn't back at the shore where he was supposed to be. He was swimming out to Jack and the little girl. Halfway there, maybe, but he was struggling. Fear screamed from his younger brother's eyes.

"Shane!" Jack didn't have the energy to rise above the waves enough to be heard. "Shane, go back!"

Years later, Jack would rethink this single moment more than any in all his life. But no matter how he played it out, he wouldn't have changed a thing. He was ten yards from the little girl and if he didn't make it to her, if he didn't give his all to rescue her, she would die.

And so Jack pressed on. Shane would turn back. He had to turn back. His brother knew better. And if he needed help, their dad would get him. Dad knew how to swim. Jack locked his eyes on the child. *Faster,* he told himself. He grabbed at the water. Ten more strokes, eight . . . seven. A few more seconds and the little girl would be safe.

The same would be true for Shane. He had to be okay, had to be moving safely back to shore. Because Shane wasn't only his strapping little brother.

He was Jack's best friend in all the world.

Four more strokes and he reached her. The child should've looked terrified, but instead a strange peace filled her eyes. "Get on my back!"

Jack could swim for hours without getting tired, but this was different. Between the current and the child about to drown and Shane . . . Jack felt himself gasping for air. *Calm,* he told himself. The little girl was slipping under, so he lifted her out of the water and slid her on his back. Her pale blond hair clung to her face, and she didn't blink, didn't grab on to him.

Like she'd rather drown.

"Hey! Listen!" With a burst of strength he pulled her higher toward his shoulders. "Hold on!" *What about Shane?* Was he back on the beach? Had he turned around? Jack yelled so the child could hear him. "Don't let go!"

"O-o-o-k-kay." She was shivering. Definitely in shock. But she was clinging to him now.

The girl didn't weigh much, so Jack quickly turned around and began swimming to shore. The whole time— with every stroke—he searched the beach for Shane. *Come on, Brother. Where are you? God, where is he?*

Suddenly the girl began crying out. "Mama!" she screamed. "Come get me, Mama!"

Jack was working too hard to tell her everything was going to be okay. Her mother was waiting for her on the shore. But what about Shane?

"Daniel!" The girl was screaming again. "Don't leave without me!"

Poor kid. Jack could feel her shaking. Probably terrified. Another few seconds and she wouldn't have made it. He gritted his teeth and kept swimming. He could see his parents now and more people. The group of them formed a circle and they were looking at something on the sand.

He couldn't make it out. A sea turtle or was it the little girl's brother? A boy named Daniel? Another sweeping look across the beach and still he couldn't see Shane. His brother had to be there, standing in the circle. Looking at whatever was on the sand.

He might not have been a strong swimmer, but he could make his way back to shore. Of course he could.

Eight yards, six . . . four. And finally Jack could feel the ocean floor beneath his feet. Even then the girl didn't weigh anything. He took hold of her legs and she grabbed on to his shoulders as Jack walked through the water to the shore.

The girl's mother saw them and she screamed again. "Eliza! I'm here!"

"No." A faint cry came from the child. "No! Mama!"

"Your mama's coming." Jack was shivering now. Where was Shane? And what was everyone looking at on the shore?

Sirens screamed from just down the beach, an ambulance and fire truck coming their way. What was happening? He looked over his shoulder at the child. "We're almost to your mother."

"No! Mama, come get me!" She sounded more afraid now than she'd been out at sea. Like she was delirious. "Daniel, I'm here!"

The little girl was still in shock. That had to be it. Jack

was in ankle-deep water when he slid the girl into his arms and carried her up the sand to the woman. Later he would remember that something didn't add up. The woman looked more angry than fearful. And the two big guys standing just up the shore had machine guns.

Was the child an heiress from some European country? Were those her bodyguards? Whatever the situation, the little girl didn't want to go to her mother. Jack still cradled her in his arms and now he felt her go limp. "Here." He handed her to the woman. "She's fine."

But what about his brother? "Shane!" His yell sounded like a guttural cry. "Shane, where are you?"

Without waiting for the girl's mother to say anything, Jack ran up the beach to the spot where a dozen people were gathered. The ambulance was parked now and paramedics were running out with a stretcher. Running straight toward the circle of people on the sand.

A stretcher? Jack's heart began to pound. He felt like he was running through wet cement. *Faster,* he ordered himself. *Who's in that circle?* And then between the legs of his parents he saw that it was a boy. A teenage boy.

And he saw Shane's short dark hair and his rugged face. But his eyes were closed. Why was he sleeping? Here on the beach?

"Shane!" And suddenly everything slowed down. The roar of the angry ocean waves and the sirens from the fire truck and the paramedics yelling for everyone to clear the way, all of it faded until only one sound remained.

The sound of Jack's heartbeat.

He reached his brother and fell at his side. "Shane! Wake up!" He took his brother's hand and squeezed it and in a blink they weren't on the beach anymore.

Shane was running down the stairs ahead of him, Christmas morning ten years ago. And there parked beside the tree were a pair of bicycles. And Shane was saying, "That's all I ever wanted. This is the best Christmas ever!"

And it was summer, a dozen summers, and Shane was chasing him down Maya Beach and Jack was yelling back at him. "You'll never catch me, Shane. I'm too fast."

Shane laughed. "One day I will, Jack. I won't be little forever."

And then Shane wasn't little. He was a teenager and he was sitting beside his brother on the flight to Belize and he was staring out at the ocean and he was smiling. "I'm going to do something really special with my life, Jack," he was saying. "Just you watch."

Jack was nodding, because he already knew that. Shane was going to be President of the United States and the whole world would know his name. And Jack would be a Navy SEAL, but he'd have an office somewhere in the White House just so he could be close to his brother.

His best friend.

But then they were loading Shane onto a stretcher. "Keep the oxygen up," a paramedic shouted. "Don't stop!"

His dad and mom started running after the paramedics toward the ambulance and Jack jumped to his feet. Where were they taking him? *Breathe, Shane. Please, God, make him breathe. He's my best friend.*

Jack blinked and he was in the front of the ambulance with his mother. And she was weeping, her hands over her face. Jack put his arm around her but he couldn't catch his breath, couldn't talk or think or let himself imagine if—

No! Everything was going to be okay! Shane had made it back to the shore. Of course he was going to be okay. But then Jack realized something. His father's shirt and shorts had been drenched. Which could only mean . . . his dad had swum out and brought Shane back and now . . . now . . .

Jack closed his eyes and Shane was sitting beside him, football in his hands. *You might have a little competition at quarterback, big brother.*

And Jack was grinning because this was the third day of their vacation and they had forever till they had to go home again. A million hours of sun and sand and surf. And they were playing catch and the storm was moving on. They were still playing catch.

Please, God, let us still be playing catch.

But when Jack opened his eyes he wasn't on the beach, he was sitting in the front seat of the ambulance and his mother was still crying beside him and when he looked back, his father was still there next to Shane. And Shane still wasn't moving, no matter how hard the paramedics worked to make him breathe again.

The next two hours passed with Jack in the most horrible fog. He kept closing his eyes and finding himself in a place where yesterday lived. He didn't fully realize what had happened or why they were in a hospital until his father found him in the waiting room.

Shane had taken in too much water, his dad was saying. The paramedics did everything they could. They needed to take his body home and . . .

"No!" Jack tried to stand, but he couldn't make himself move. Instead he fell to the cold, dusty hospital floor and he could see the headlines. East Coast Teen Dies Saving Little Girl. And everyone would know his name. *Shane Ryder.* Not because he was President of the United States, but because his life had been cut short.

His best friend. His brother.

The ache in Jack was worse than anything in all his life. *Shane, where are you?* He couldn't see, couldn't believe it. Couldn't move. And one single thought pulled at Jack harder than the ocean current.

All of this was his fault. It had to be. He should've swum faster, rescued the little girl and then made it back to help Shane. There had to have been a way. But now Shane wasn't going to Georgetown Prep in the fall and Jack wasn't ever going to play catch with him on the beach again. His brother was gone.

And Jack would spend the rest of his life paying for it.

• • •

THE WATER WOULDN'T take her.

All she had wanted was to stay still, to slip down, down to the bottom of the ocean. So that God would take her to the edge of the ocean, where her mother and brother lived. But her arms hadn't listened to her heart. They kept drawing and pulling and grabbing at the water. And her lungs kept breathing.

Then she had seen something else.

Two boys swimming out to get her. And there on the shore, Aunt Betsy, waving at her, all wild-like. And the two Palace guards standing nearby with their guns. Like they might shoot her if she didn't get back to shore.

When the first boy reached her, Eliza tried to get away. *No,* she tried to shout. *I want my Mama. I want my brother. Daniel, I'm here!* But the boy had put her on his back and started swimming toward the beach.

Closer and closer and closer.

And with every passing second, as Aunt Betsy came into view, the truth became clearer. Her aunt was desperate to see Eliza saved. Not because she loved her. But because of the plans her father had for her. Big plans for some far-off day. Plans that involved drugs and men and money. At least that's what Eliza thought.

"No!" she screamed and the sound made her eyes fly open. *What was this?*

She sat straight up, her breaths coming hard and fast. *Where was she?* She wasn't in the ocean, she was in bed. Her bed. The sheets were silky satin and the bed coverings were fluffy white. Eliza put her hand to her chest and felt her heartbeat. Boom, boom, boom. Like a scary drum.

She ran her hands over her arms and her hair and it hit her. This wasn't the ocean and she wasn't on the boy's back. She wasn't drowning and her mother and brother were not here to help her.

Eliza was back in the Palace.

And the armed guards were just outside her door. She could see their shadows.

If she had fallen beneath the surface of the ocean, she would finally be with Mama and Daniel. Eating dinner with them on the other side of the sea. Instead she was here, in the room where her daddy kept her. The room that smelled like fine linen and perfume, across the house from the place where the other girls were sold to different men every night. She slid back down under the covers and snuggled her cheek into the pillow. No matter what she dreamed tonight, when she woke up she wouldn't be in heaven like she had hoped.

She'd be in hell.

CHAPTER THREE

*Fire consumed their young men, and their young
women had no wedding songs.*

—Psalm 78:63

Every once in a while, when the warm salty breeze
drifted up off the Caribbean Sea over shimmering sand,
when it brushed against Eliza's tired face as she sat alone
on the beach at the base of the familiar cliff, reading yet
another book from the Palace library, she would close the
cover and look up. And on her very best days in that moment she could still see the God of her childhood.

There at the far edge of the ocean. The way she had
a decade ago.

Eliza shaded her eyes, and stared out at the horizon,
searching for God. But He wasn't there. Not today. He
hadn't been for a long time. A sigh drifted up from her
frigid heart. Never mind. Nine days from now things
would get worse. Much worse. Her fear about what was
coming grew with every passing hour.

Because in nine days she would be forced to marry
Henry Thomas Ellington IV, a marriage Eliza had known

about nearly all her life. Henry Thomas was a dangerous young man, one her father had only recently identified as Eliza's future husband. The son of a friend of her father's. A man none of them had ever met.

But all that was about to change.

Henry Thomas was flying in from the States to meet her. "He wants to spend an evening with his bride," her father had told her this morning. "Before he signs off on the marriage."

The whole arrangement was sickening. Her forced marriage would join two drug and sex-trafficking dynasties— her father's and that of Henry Thomas's father. According to her dad, the senior Ellington was a lawyer who secretly ran a longtime trafficking ring that worked both Florida and southern Belize. By combining their illegal activities, the men believed they would make far more money and be nearly impossible to bring down.

Eliza understood the situation. She was merely a pawn in her father's dirty game of greed and power. She let her gaze drift twenty yards down the beach to a pair of men walking her way. Their laughter and cigar smoke carried in the wind, and Eliza stiffened. She'd seen them before. Eliza wasn't a little girl anymore. She knew the business her father was about at the Palace.

One of the men was a redhead, and the other, balding. Pasty white skin and champagne bellies. Trust fund parasites, casting shame on their fathers' old money. Or following in their footsteps. The men were members of a private yacht club with longtime privileges at the Palace.

One of them looked her way and stopped. He motioned to the others and all three gawked at her. Like lions sizing up a wounded gazelle. Eliza pulled her gauzy cover-up tight around her body and turned the other way.

She wasn't for sale. Not until next week, when Henry Thomas Ellington IV, came to visit.

"Hey, Princess, come for a swim!" It was the bald head. "The water's nice."

I'm not for sale, she wanted to shout at him. But then, the men already knew that. Everyone knew Eliza wasn't for sale. Not like the other sixteen girls at the Palace. Eliza refused to look up. If her father heard the men he'd turn his guards on them and they'd never be seen again. No one messed with Eliza. No one.

Not until the wedding on her twentieth birthday. The day she would leave the Palace in the arms of another evil man, a stranger she already hated.

The other girls would leave the Palace on their twentieth birthdays, too, the days when her father would set them free. The promise was part of the deal. Her father and his team would keep the girls till they turned twenty. Then they were free to go. Her father would give each of them a year's wages, a passport, and a suitcase of clothes. And that would be that.

"Come on, Eliza. You know you want to swim with us." The bald man was yelling at her now. Scratchy voice, thick guttural laugh. The same laugh that had echoed through the Palace the last three nights, just outside the door of one of the teenage girls.

No. She squeezed her eyes shut. *Make it stop. Please.* Eliza glanced up the hillside. The two armed bodyguards took a step forward. Customers or not, no one had the right to bother Eliza when she was on the beach.

Not while she still belonged to Anders McMillan.

Eventually the men gave up. They lit another round of cigars, and headed back down the beach. What was the point of harassing her, they probably figured. Eliza really wasn't for sale. Tonight, no doubt, they would be at the Palace in one of the other girls' rooms.

And Eliza would be forced to fall asleep knowing what was happening down the hall. But not for long. The wedding would be a grand affair and then Eliza would leave this place forever. Her next home was bound to be just as dark and dangerous. But at least she'd be away from her evil father.

A fresh breeze cleared the cigar smoke. Eliza breathed deep and wondered. Where would she live? In Florida with the rest of the Ellington family? Or would all of them move here? Like everything else about her life, she had no say in her future. Not like the other Palace girls.

She remembered one of them—Alexa. The girl had been a true and dear friend to Eliza. When they were twelve and ten, Alexa had thought Anders McMillan a good man. The one who kept the strange men from hurting them too badly.

"The customers are terrible," Alexa had told Eliza back then. "But your father cares about us. He buys us fine clothes and sweets whenever we want them." Her expression had grown fearful. "The world is dangerous, Eliza. Your father protects us."

"He does?" All Eliza had been able to think was that she wanted her mama and brother.

Alexa had been adamant. "Yes. Anders watches out for us girls."

Eliza had been so young, so innocent. "What does that mean? He takes care of you?"

"Hmm." The question had seemed to stump Alexa. "I think he gets mad at those men." She shrugged. "All I know is Anders takes care of it. We need him. That's what the oldest girls say."

Eventually, though, Alexa had become one of the older girls. She wasn't supposed to tell Eliza, but she had, anyway, and the story haunted Eliza still. Alexa had told her that on her fourteenth birthday, Eliza's father had pushed her into a dark-lit room. Not her usual bedroom. "The mattress smelled like stinky men and strong bleach," Alexa said. "Then one of the guards stepped into the room."

Eliza didn't like to think about the details. But what had remained of her friend's childhood had clearly died that day. Before the guard had left her, before housemaids came to tend to her battered body, her father had come back into the room and told her one thing. "You work for me now, Alexa. You keep the younger girls happy and you won't go through this again."

The wounds from that day would never heal. Not for Alexa or Eliza.

After that, Eliza better understood the sick truth about the Palace. The older girls were part of the operation, and in that sense, Eliza was no different. Like Alexa, Eliza would spend a few hours every month in the village. The armed guards would be at her back, never more than a few feet away.

When the guards saw some unsuspecting poor little girl, all by herself, it was Eliza's or Alexa's job to approach her. "Come with me," Eliza would say. "You'll have the best clothes and the best food! Even your own bedroom!"

And the lonely young girls would come.

Same with the teen girls flown in from other countries, property of Anders McMillan. Eliza and Alexa were often chosen to go with the guards to the airport. So that from the new girl's first few minutes in Belize, she would feel comfortable. At home.

I am a wretched, evil woman, Eliza told herself now. God should've already struck her down and sent her to Hades. There were sixteen girls younger than her currently living at the Palace, sixteen children whose precious souls had been ripped out one by one. And one way or another Eliza had helped coerce each of them into a life of slavery.

Every single one.

She comforted them and reassured them. She helped pick out pretty clothes for them and she combed their hair. And every hour of every day she lied to them. "You're safe here. No one will hurt you." Eliza would pat their shoulders and hug them when they cried. "Everything is going to be just fine."

All the while she told herself she was actually helping the girls. Otherwise they'd be afraid. *At least I'm on their side*, she would convince herself. But the truth always ate at her. She wasn't their friend. She was their tormentor, making it impossible for them to know up from down, right from wrong.

By helping them feel at home in the Palace, Eliza did her part to keep the girls locked in a prison of slavery as their childhoods were destroyed. The same way hers had been—even if the men never touched her. Eliza was part of the girls' terrible reality until they joined the older girls and finally understood the full truth about their captivity.

Eliza shuddered. If hell had rooms of torment and torture in direct relation to a person's dark life, Eliza expected hers to be the worst.

Two summers ago, a week before dear Alexa turned twenty, she had told Eliza everything she was going to do once she was out of the Palace. Once she was free.

"All that money!" Alexa had been like a new person, her eyes full of anticipation and life. "A year's wages? That's a fortune, Eliza." Her friend's brown eyes had sparkled. "And I know just what I'm going to do."

Eliza couldn't imagine. "What?"

Alexa had taken hold of Eliza's hands. "I'm moving to Colombia! I'll rent an apartment in the heart of a big city. Bogota, maybe. So I never have to see the beach again as long as I live." She grinned big. "And you can come visit me after . . ." Her voice fell off because Alexa knew the truth.

"If my husband lets me." Eliza had blinked back tears. Because whatever man her father would choose for her, he would keep her under lock and key. He would never let her travel alone.

But Eliza had been happy for her friend anyway. "Colombia will be wonderful!" Being even a mile from this place seemed too good to be true. Eliza had searched her friend's eyes. And for the first time, Eliza felt something warm and thrilling, strange and unfamiliar. A sensation as foreign as freedom itself.

The feeling was hope.

Because if Alexa was getting out on her twentieth birthday, then maybe Eliza's future husband would be kind to her. Maybe he wouldn't keep her locked in a room. She could at least hope for happier days ahead.

In the days that had followed, Alexa's excitement grew until it seemed woven into her very soul. Never mind the work she had that week. All the girl could talk about was turning twenty. And sure enough, on Alexa's birthday she ran and found Eliza. Alexa had never looked happier. Her words were practically a song. "I came to say goodbye."

Eliza stood and the two hugged. "He's really letting you go?"

"He is." She stood a little taller and smiled. Then she

pulled an envelope from the waistband of her short skirt. "Ten thousand U.S. dollars. Can you believe it?"

Eliza couldn't. Especially knowing her father. Alexa's release from the Palace seemed too good to be true, but the cash was there in her waistband, tucked inside a white envelope.

"How are you getting out?" The dots hadn't quite connected for Eliza. "Is my father taking you?"

"No, silly." Alexa giggled, one of the few times Eliza had heard her friend laugh. "The guards are taking me to the airport. They asked me where I wanted to go."

"Hmm." Eliza had questions, but she didn't ask them. No sense ruining Alexa's big day. "Okay, then." Eliza hugged her once more. "I'll find you. After I'm married. However long it takes."

"Yes! You can come and stay with me for a few days. The Palace will be long behind us."

Someone had called for Alexa from the main floor, and her grin faded. "I'll miss you."

"I'll see you again. I know I will." Eliza was lying. But it wasn't the time to say so. "I'll be fine."

Her friend nodded. "Bye, Eliza."

"Bye."

Then Alexa waved and disappeared out the door. It was the last time Eliza ever saw her friend. Last time she ever would.

Eliza stopped the memory there. She stood, dropped her beach cover-up on her towel, and walked toward the water. She cherished these few hours each day, time to sit on the beach, to swim and let the darkness of the night—the sounds and certainty of what was happening down the hall—wash off in the waves.

She pushed through the foamy surf and into the clear sea beyond. Her tan legs cut through the water and the swells lapped at her thighs. She had asked for a one-piece swimsuit this summer, but the guards had only laughed at her.

"A beautiful princess like you, Eliza?" her father had said. "This is your world, and you will wear only the best. In the water and out."

Once she was out a little farther, Eliza dove beneath the waves. There was no undertow today. Nothing but the satiny feel of the salt water against her skin. On days like this, when Eliza swam in the ocean, she liked to picture Alexa living in that apartment in Colombia. Right in the middle of the city. But Eliza had her doubts. The morning after Alexa left the Palace, Eliza had heard something that still made her sick. In the early hours of sunlight, Eliza had left her room in search of a drink of water. A team of housemaids were supposed to cater to the girls' needs, but that morning none of them answered Eliza's call. And the guards weren't at her door like usual.

As Eliza rounded the corner to the wet bar on her floor, she heard Anders talking with one of his goons down the stairs. Eliza froze and listened.

Anders asked, "Was the money still on her?"

The guard grunted. Eliza couldn't make out his words, but whatever he must've said or shown Anders, the Palace prince was quiet. After a few seconds he chuckled. "Good. She won't need cash where she is now." He paused. "You're sure you took care of her?"

"Yes, boss. She's gone."

Chills had run down Eliza's arms and legs and without making a sound she had tiptoed back to her room. Her heart had pounded so loud, she wondered if her father would come find her and beat her. Just for looking scared.

The way he had threatened to do more times than she could count.

So she had done what she often did when she was afraid. Eliza slid back under the covers, pulled the silk sheets and comforters up to her chin and squeezed her eyes shut.

What had happened to Alexa? Had the guards taken her to some remote spot and . . . ?

Eliza couldn't finish the thought. Not then or now.

A few more strokes through the water and Eliza reached her favorite part of the ocean. Beyond the rough waves but still close enough to see people on the shore. She treaded water as easily as she breathed. She'd been doing it long enough.

Her eyes searched the sandy beach. Aunt Betsy hadn't been around for two weeks. She could've been dead, for all Eliza knew. Not that it would matter. Her aunt had been an alcoholic for years, drunk morning to night. Eliza had a feeling her father had long since stopped paying the woman for her services. Eliza didn't need her mean aunt watching over her. Not when she had the guards.

Eliza remembered the last time she talked to her aunt. The woman was painfully thin now, her skin bunched and wrinkled from the sunshine and gin. "Where will you live, Eliza?" Her aunt tried to smile. "When you marry Mr. Ellington?"

It had taken Eliza a moment to realize why her aunt was asking. "The money . . . is that it? You know about the money?" Her father had promised her the same thing he'd promised all the girls on their twentieth birthdays. Ten thousand dollars. But she was to use it to purchase clothes and jewelry. So she could look the part of the princess.

Her aunt raised her eyebrows. "I've given my life for you, Eliza. A cut of that money is due me, don't you think?" The woman rocked back on her feet. "Plus . . . you'll need . . . someone to help you manage it."

Eliza didn't have to think about her response. "My father paid you for years. You've made enough money off me."

Aunt Betsy gasped. "I have no idea what you could possibly mean." Her hand flew to her chest. Resentment flashed in her eyes. "All you've ever been is ungrateful."

Ungrateful? If Eliza had it her way, her aunt would be arrested and thrown into prison for helping her father traffic girls at the Palace. But there had been no point explaining that to the old drunk woman.

Eliza tipped her head back into the water, and lifted her gaze to the cliff where the guards waited. They were talking, distracted by something down the beach. What if she swam a mile down the shore and climbed out over the rocks? Maybe she could simply walk away? She looked through the sea at her designer swimsuit. She wouldn't get far without her cover-up and some cash. The guards always told her if she stepped out of line . . . if she got swept away in a current or created any cause for attention, her father would turn on her. Eliza didn't want to know what that meant.

Because of her father, Eliza had always believed she had no choice. The other girls thought that, too. Her father controlled Belize City. People parted the crowd ahead of Anders and locals groveled for his attention. "Prince Anders!" they would call out. Like they actually believed he was a prince. Anders McMillan, royalty.

Even though they knew he dealt drugs and kept girls at the Palace.

The saddest thing was that not one person in the village ever tried to rescue Eliza or the other girls. Because the people didn't only seem impressed by her father. They feared him. Because Anders McMillan always found a way to escape the law. To avoid being busted, when he first started out her father had changed the name on the front of the big white house every year or so. It had been a bridal shop, and then a hotel. A school and later a salon. A massage parlor. And now it was simply the Palace. No one called the police about Anders. As if dealing drugs and selling girls to tourists was perfectly normal.

Maybe, after she was married, she could find a way to escape the younger Henry Thomas. She could run away in the dark of night and catch a plane to Colombia. Alexa might still be alive, and if she was, Eliza would find her and they would be roommates like they had dreamed of being. It could still happen.

And if she couldn't find Alexa, then Eliza would move to the South of France or somewhere in Sweden. An unassuming place, cold and clean. But one thing was certain. If Eliza could escape her forced marriage, if she couldn't reunite with her friend, then she would live alone all the days of her life. She would never fall in love, never give herself willingly to a man as long as she drew breath. Her life would be hers and hers alone. And she would certainly never have a baby.

Not in a world that cared so little for children.

If she could escape her groom, she would get a job waiting tables, so she could make enough money to survive. And she would spend the rest of her life reveling in the one thing she desperately wanted. The thing she hadn't had since her mama brought her and Daniel to Belize City.

Freedom.

Her swimming time was over. Eliza lifted her eyes to the blue sky. Whatever happened to the teenage boy?

The one who had rescued her? Couldn't he tell she didn't want to be dragged from the ocean that day? The water was her sanctuary. *Beneath* the water would've been even better.

Eliza wiped the water from her eyes. She could see the guards on the hillside, getting restless, watching her, adjusting their heavy black rifles. "I'm coming," she whispered. She made her way onto the shore and pulled her wet blond hair into a knot at the back of her head.

The future of her father's dynasty depended on her obedience.

Eliza slipped into her cover-up, and climbed the path built into the edge of the mountain. Halfway up on a narrow plateau she met the guards, and without saying a word, they fell in behind her and followed her to the biggest of the Palace bedrooms.

Top dollar deserved top accommodations. That's what her father always told her. And even though she'd never been with a man, her time was coming. Nine days from now.

Once Eliza was inside her room, when the door was shut, she thought of Alexa again. What if her father did have her killed and what if he'd gotten his money back? What if Henry Thomas was even meaner than her father? If that was the case, Eliza was ready.

She opened the top drawer of her armoire and sifted through her silk underclothes. Wrapped in a camisole at the bottom was a butcher knife. One she'd stolen from the kitchen late at night a week ago.

When she got married and left this place, the knife would be tucked into her suitcase, next to the cash her father was going to give her. If Henry Thomas tried to harm her or sell her . . . if his guards did anything to her, she would kill them.

Then she'd be on the next flight out of Belize.

CHAPTER FOUR

At least there is hope for a tree: If it is cut down, it will sprout again, and its new shoots will not fail.

—Job 14:7

Jack Ryder didn't care if he died.

That was why he was the best special agent in the San Antonio FBI. Jack took chances where other agents were careful. He was bold where the rest shrank back. He lived for the mission. At twenty-six, his superiors all told him the same thing.

They'd never had an agent like him.

Jack was a chameleon. He could grow out his beard and get intel on a Middle Eastern weapons cache. Cut his hair and shave and work undercover drug busts at a high school. Wear tennis shoes and ripped-up jeans and fit in on any college campus.

Since his twenty-third birthday, Jack had been working for the FBI, and in the past few years he'd moved to undercover missions, one after another. Oliver had told him that agents who joined the bureau younger than age

41

twenty-five rarely lasted, and that typically an agent had to be at least thirty to succeed at undercover work.

At every point, Jack was the exception.

Lately his missions were focused on international drug and sex-trafficking rings that also did business in the United States. The missions were getting more dangerous. That was okay with Jack. If there was a God, He had intended Jack for this job alone.

He gripped the wheel of his black Ford Explorer and stared at the road. To get to the FBI office in San Antonio, Jack had to drive past a cemetery. He made it a practice not to look. Better to keep his attention on the living, the ones who needed rescuing.

Cemeteries made him feel. And according to his personal rules, feelings were a sign of weakness, a waste of constructive time and energy, forbidden. Period.

It was Thursday, the first of July, and his meeting was on the fourth floor, where the most sensitive missions came together. Jack wore dark pants and a black belt, the white button-down shirt and navy tie and jacket—a size up to conceal his pistol.

FBI standard fare when Jack wasn't on a mission.

Martha Lou Henderson sat at the desk by the elevator. She'd worked there a hundred years at least, and trustworthy didn't begin to describe her. The woman didn't blink as Jack swept his badge beneath the sensor. Only when the light flashed blue did she smile. "Morning, Jack."

"You're still not sure it's me."

"Nope." She grinned. "And I feel that way about your boss. And his boss." She pressed four buttons on the control panel and the elevator door opened. "Have a good day, Jack."

"You, too, Martha Lou." He chuckled as he got on the elevator.

Everyone had to be kept accountable. Agents had turned against the FBI in the past, succumbing to the lure of drug money, bribes and the promise of power. Accountability was necessary even for those who, like Jack, would give their lives for the job, agents who embodied the FBI motto—Fidelity, Bravery, Integrity.

Jack passed through two additional security clearances before entering the meeting room. The walls on the fourth floor were solid glass and always clean. The view of San Antonio's Hill Country never got old. He looked around and smiled. Never mind that he was early, his boss was already there, talking with two of the bureau's other top undercover agents.

Jack took a seat at a desk in the front row and spread his legs in front of him. He had topped out at six-three, tall enough to play college football if he'd wanted to.

But after Shane died, football lost its allure. Like life itself.

Until Oliver Layton found him.

Oliver was bald and black, and before his days with the FBI he had set records at Ole Miss as a star running back. He spent the first two hours of every day in the gym and he looked like he could still outrun any defense. Oliver's mind was even faster than his feet and back in the day he had been best friends with Jack's father.

For two decades Oliver had run a division of the Transnational Organized Crime program from this office. Oliver's agents worked with governments and police forces from other countries, and with every branch and office of the U.S. military and law enforcement. Whereas police forces typically focused on taking down a criminal, the TOC unit took down criminal empires. Oliver saw to it. Every mission was secret, and each was critically important to the man.

Jack's respect for him knew no limits.

"This one will be dangerous." Oliver folded his arms and stared down the three men as the meeting began. He said the same thing before handing out every mission. The work they did was always dangerous. But something about Oliver's tone told Jack this one was worse.

"We've talked about Anders McMillan before." Oliver's expression hardened. "Drug lord, a trafficking demon doing business in Belize. In the past decade, he has run a blatant sex slave factory under the guise of eight different fake business names. Always with young teenage girls." He shook his head. "Sickening." He paused. "Anders has gotten a little sloppy this past year. Now he calls his place the Palace. Parades around thinking he's some kind of Belizean prince."

Anders McMillan. The name was immediately familiar to Jack. So was the country. "We've talked about him before. We never had evidence."

"Exactly." Oliver paced a few feet and looked at one of the senior operatives seated next to Jack. "Tell them what you found, Matthew."

Silver haired and sly as a fox, Matthew Pendergast opened a folder in front of him. "McMillan is still very careful. He advertises his girls a dozen different ways and changes his means of interacting with customers every few months."

Jack knew that much. The entire FBI knew. Until recently, Anders McMillan had used online shopping sites to traffic girls. The public might think that a $15,000 bed was a typo. With McMillan it wasn't. And once the sale was made the customer wouldn't get a bed. He'd get membership into the seediest of high-roller clubs.

Pendergast looked at his notes. "Lately he's pushed sales through the Blue Breeze Yacht Club, north of Belize City. He owns it. The place is a haven for wealthy playboys and customers of the Palace."

Blue Breeze Yacht Club. Jack pulled a notepad from his backpack and jotted it down. "Is that new?" He looked from Matthew to Oliver. "There are several yacht clubs on the shores of Belize. I haven't heard of that one."

"Exactly." Oliver nodded to Matthew. "Fill us in."

"This club is definitely new. And it's not a club as much as it's a front for trafficking. McMillan is relying on previous customers and beach-going regulars. Millionaire retirees who spend their days on the water."

"And their nights at the Palace." TJ Simpson tapped his pencil on the table. He was ebony black with the body of a Navy SEAL. If TJ was on the mission, it was big. He shook his head. "Scum."

"Right." Oliver took a deep breath. "We have a chance to connect with an insider this time around. Which is why we need to move now."

Jack felt his adrenaline kick in. Working missions for the FBI would never get old. "An informant?"

"Not yet." Oliver looked him in the eye. "This is where you come in, Jack."

Jack didn't blink, didn't say a word.

"McMillan has a daughter at the Palace. She's about to be forcibly married to the son of the boss of a massive trafficking ring that operates out of Florida but has lately been doing work in south Belize. At least that's what McMillan thinks." Oliver pulled three oversized photos from his folder. "This is McMillan's daughter. Her name is Eliza Ann Lawrence. Apparently Anders gave the girl an alias so no one outside the Palace would know he was her father. Unless the connection worked in McMillan's favor." He handed the pictures to Jack. "She's nineteen. She'll be twenty in a few days."

Anger turned Jack's stomach. *Nineteen?* "He's been trafficking his own daughter?"

"No." Oliver nodded at Pendergast and TJ. "From what we know, she's never been touched. Her dad's been saving her for the highest bidder. Pen . . . why don't you fill us in?"

Pendergast—Pen to the team at the bureau—thumbed through the pages on his desk. "Like many governments and royalty, for the past decade Anders McMillan always intended to use his daughter to join his kingdom with another. TJ and I have lots of data on this."

Jack listened intently as TJ explained the situation. McMillan had feelers out, trying to connect with a trafficking ring willing to agree to his terms. But none had jumped. So Pen and TJ had seized the moment and reached out to him on behalf of a major drug and sex ring out of Florida. A ring run by Henry Thomas Ellington III. The man had been a customer at the Palace a handful of times over the past five years, and was on friendly terms with McMillan.

"We faked a series of phone calls pretending to be Ellington the Third or his people." TJ paused. "The truth is, Ellington's organization is laying low right now. Rumors are that Ellington the Third is sick. End-stage cirrhosis. Either way, the Ellington family knows they're being watched, so they've temporarily stopped all illegal activity."

"Here's where it gets good." Oliver narrowed his eyes. "Pen?"

"Right." Pen checked his notes. "We've made contact with Ellington the Third's son. Henry Thomas Ellington the Fourth."

"Okay." Jack crossed his arms.

"The son has recently pulled away from his family. Doesn't want anything to do with his dad's dark empire." Pen paused. "We worked with the bureau in Florida and they had already connected with the young man. He's willing to testify against his family once protections can be set up for him."

Jack leaned forward. "How does that play into this mission?"

"Henry Thomas the Fourth has given us permission to assume his identity for the raid. Obviously without his ailing father's knowledge." He paused. "In other words, Jack, the mission kicks off with you flying to Belize and playing the role of the groom."

"McMillan will be convinced you're the real deal. Ellington the Fourth." TJ glanced at his partner. "Our contact with McMillan has been flawless, acting as Ellington the Third and his team, and arranging a marriage between his daughter and Ellington's son."

Pen crossed his arms. "McMillan has called for an in-person . . . trial, of sorts. He wants to meet Ellington the Fourth, show him the girl. Give him a few nights with her." He hesitated. "The girl is beautiful. McMillan wants half a million dollars up front if the marriage is agreed upon. And of course, a new joint operation between the trafficking rings, one that would make both families richer and more powerful."

The situation felt dicey, acting out the role of a groom in a power play that involved two crime families, lots of money, and no doubt even more danger. Jack took the pictures and studied them. The first showed a tanned girl with long pale blond hair. She was sitting on a rocky outcropping at the base of a cliff, her feet in the sand. The next was a close-up of the girl's face.

No wonder her father thought he could sell Eliza Ann into a forced marriage. She was easily one of the most beautiful girls Jack had ever seen. The final picture showed the young woman sitting on a small stretch of sand along a breathtaking and familiar Belizean beach.

Despite the sunny sky, the girl's blue eyes were colder than ice.

Never mind that her heart was still beating. It was obvious that the horrors she had lived alongside at the Palace had killed her long ago. Jack studied her. The anger and callousness in her eyes made her look older than her nineteen years.

Jack focused on what his boss was saying.

"Eliza and her father may have come from one of several Mennonite communities in central Belize. Or they may have come from the United States or Canada. We're not sure. The girl is sometimes cared for by a woman named Betsy Norman. Aunt Betsy to Eliza. The woman claims she's Eliza's aunt. We aren't sure about that. Surveillance tells us she's in on the trafficking, so we plan to take her during the raid, also."

"Yes." TJ nodded. "Anders showed up in Belize City roughly a dozen years ago. We have recon on him since then—though never enough to arrest him and dismantle his ring."

"Before that," Pen shrugged, "we have no idea where he was, what he did for a living."

Oliver crossed his arms. "We assume McMillan is a false name, since we have no record of him before his time in Belize City."

Oliver paced across the room and stared out the window. "You'll make a stop at a Mennonite village called Lower Barton Creek. There's a historian there who might know something. Ike is our best hope to verify whether McMillan and his daughter came from a Belizean Mennonite village."

"Right." Pen nodded. "Ike Armstrong made a report eleven years ago about the disappearance of his granddaughter—Susan James—and the woman's two young children. We haven't found a connection between them and McMillan. But it's worth looking into."

Jack set his notebook down. "If Eliza knows she's about to be forced into a marriage, why would she talk to me? Why would she trust anyone?"

"There's more to the story." Pen handed Jack a sheet of paper. It was a wanted poster with McMillan's face. The first charge listed was murder. Three counts. "Last week we learned about McMillan's other dirty secret. What happens to the Palace girls when they age out."

Oliver hesitated. "On a girl's twentieth birthday McMillan gives her an envelope of cash and a fake passport. Some fancy clothes, that sort of thing. Then he sends her off with a couple of his henchmen."

Jack shifted in his seat. The pieces were coming together. "The girls never make it off the compound, is that it?" He leaned forward.

"Exactly. At least that's what our research suggests." Oliver sighed. "At twenty, the girls know enough to take McMillan down. We believe just after their twentieth birthdays, he pretends to give them a send-off. Then he has them killed."

Jack clenched his jaw. "There has to be a special place in hell."

"I'm sure." TJ stood and paced to the window. After a few seconds he turned and looked at the others. "We have details about at least one case. We're working with the Belizean police, and one of our contacts at the department says a Palace girl went missing a few years ago—a friend of Eliza's named Alexa. Not long after, a tourist found the remains of a Palace girl. Beautiful brunette. Shot in the back. Her suitcase full of designer clothes was buried a few feet away."

Oliver shook his head. "Here's the point. If Eliza learns that Alexa was, indeed, killed by McMillan, by her very own father and his men, then we believe she might work with us. To save the other Palace girls."

Jack waited. The finer details of his assignment were coming.

"What you'll do, Jack, is head to Belize Monday morning. Like we said, you'll visit the Mennonite community first. Acting like a long-lost Mennonite grandson, you'll speak with Ike Armstrong, the community's historian. Two Mennonite girls have gone missing over the last decade. We believe one or both of them wound up at the Palace."

"Terrible." Jack jotted down the name. *Ike Armstrong.*

"Ask Ike about his missing family. Rumor is they drowned, but see what he knows. And see if he's heard of Anders McMillan."

"Got it." Jack looked at Oliver again. "Ask him whether Eliza and her father were Mennonites at some point, is that it?"

"Exactly. Like we said, we can't find any information on McMillan's past." Oliver returned to his folder and thumbed through it. "As if he landed on planet Earth a dozen years ago."

TJ turned to Jack. "Finding out about McMillan's past is key. No telling what he's covering up."

Jack nodded. "Makes sense."

"Then you'll switch gears and clothes and head to the beach." Oliver's voice fell. "You'll visit the Blue Breeze Yacht Club and connect with one of McMillan's guards. Once they believe you're the groom, they'll roll out the red carpet. You'll agree to the cash transfer—the half a million Anders wants—then you'll have access to Eliza."

Of all the undercover work Jack had ever done, trafficking was the toughest. Pretending to be a customer—even as a way of saving the lives of enslaved girls—was almost more than he could take. But this was different. Even worse in some ways. He had to pretend he was buying Eliza for life. That he was sleeping with her two nights in a row to see if she was worth marrying—strictly for business purposes.

Jack felt his determination rise. If that's what it took to rescue Eliza and the other girls at the Palace, he was ready.

Oliver opened a folder. "The guard will make arrangements for you to visit the Palace that night, and there you'll be given access to Eliza's bedroom." The matter clearly disgusted Oliver, too. But every step of the mission was calculated and necessary. "During your time with her you'll keep things completely platonic, of course. And you'll reveal the truth to Eliza. Tell her that her father killed Alexa and that others will be killed, too." He paused. "Then give her one more incentive."

"This is important." Pendergast pulled another paper from his folder and handed it to Jack. "Technically, Eliza is an accomplice. She's helped lure young girls to the Palace for several years now. We assume this has been against her will, but either way she's complicit. She's looking at a lengthy sentence if she's convicted."

Jack understood. The girl's options were limited. Allow other girls to be killed by her father, spend a chunk of time behind bars . . . or cooperate with the FBI.

"Provided she agrees to work with you, she's our insider." Oliver turned to Jack. "Minutes before the raid, she'll have to round up the girls and help them leave the compound safely. Because of the scope of the operation, we will have the Army and Navy working with us that night. We'll go over everything later today and tomorrow. At the completion of the raid, you and the other agents, and all seventeen girls, will be brought back here to San Antonio."

A few questions remained. "Who are the informants on the ground?" Jack looked from Matthew to TJ and finally to Oliver. "How trustworthy are they?"

Matthew lowered his voice, as if this part were more sensitive than the rest. "Belize City has a new chief of police. Manny Averes. He's been working with us for three months now, one of the good guys for sure. A few of his team are on the take from the Blue Breeze Yacht Club, and Chief Averes knows it. He plays along and because of that he has good information."

"We trust him." Oliver gave a firm nod. "And of course we have two operatives from the San Salvador office who have been monitoring the situation in Belize for several months. Even still, we don't know the layout of the Palace, where the armed guards sit and how best to rescue the girls without incident." He paused. "We think Eliza can help us with that, too."

Eliza Ann Lawrence. Jack added the girl's name to his notes. "How close is Eliza with her father? If she's helping him with his operation, why should we put faith in her?"

"That's the risk." TJ returned to his seat and looked to Jack. "You'll have to think fast, Ryder. Read the girl. If she's working with her dad, she might lie to you. Trick you. It'll take all your instincts on this one."

"Be very aware, Jack." Pendergast stood and sauntered

to the spot near Oliver. "Watch her hands and fingers. Her expression. Look for subtle cracks that indicate whether what she's telling you might be a lie."

"And be careful, man." TJ looked concerned. "Be so careful."

"The agents are right." Oliver set his folder down on the podium at the front of the room. "Eliza is either a victim or a mastermind, Jack. You'll have to figure that out."

Victim or not, Jack was suspicious of any girl who would help lure children into the Palace. Especially after she, herself, had seen the heartbreak and brokenness of the girls being trafficked by her father.

"Got it." Jack took the papers on his desk and looked them over. "When do we start with the details?"

"Ten minutes from now. In the computer lab down the hall. Every moment counts at this point." Oliver picked up a satchel from the podium and handed it to Jack. "Here's your flight itinerary, identification papers, Belizean money, falsified bank routing information, addresses, a cell phone, and the contact information you'll need for the Blue Breeze Yacht Club."

Oliver looked at TJ and Pen. "The two of you will lead the raid."

"Yes, sir." TJ collected his things.

Matthew did the same. "We'll be ready."

Jack felt the weight of the satchel in his hands. Just a few days to memorize his newest identity. This was standard. Jack was a quick study. It was one reason he was top of the list of agents sent out on TOC secret missions.

Oliver once said Jack assumed identities as if he didn't have one of his own.

The man didn't know how true the statement was.

When the other agents were out of the room, Oliver looked at Jack. "Belize."

The word hung in the air like the blade of a guillotine. Jack broke the silence. "It's not a problem."

Oliver knew the history, knew everything about Jack. It was why he had chosen Jack as an agent in the first place. Straight out of Navy SEAL training.

"You're my top pick. But be honest, Jack. I can have another agent on this in a minute." He sounded like Jack's father now. "I need to know."

"I'm fine." Jack nodded. "It's just another beach. Another operation." Tears stung his eyes but only for a few seconds. "I want the mission."

"Okay." Oliver looked satisfied. "See you in ten."

"Yes, sir." Jack pushed thoughts of Belize from his mind. He grabbed the satchel and headed down the hall.

After learning and relearning hundreds of details that would make up the Belizean operation, Jack finally left the building. By six o'clock he was back at his Magnolia Heights apartment on Broadway near San Antonio's famous River Walk. The bureau moved Jack around the city every six months or so, in case a criminal from a previous case figured out where he lived.

A few years ago an undercover agent was killed in

New York City by a guy dressed as a doorman. He couldn't be too careful.

Jack liked this particular apartment. He had a balcony overlooking the stream of people strolling along the famous stretch of shops and restaurants. Jack was one guy in one apartment on a street of apartment buildings. The place made him feel invisible.

Exactly how he liked it.

He took the satchel to the balcony and sat at the round metal table. Inside the package, on top of the pile, was his identification. Henry Thomas Ellington IV. A name Anders McMillan would trust.

Next in the stack of paperwork were several pages on the *real* man behind the set-up. Henry Thomas Ellington III had been an occasional customer at the Palace. McMillan and the senior Ellington had compared notes on their criminal empires. Then there was the airfare confirmation. First-class round trip to Belize City. He would take a cab to a local car rental agency. Going out of the way made it easier to stay under the radar. Like with every mission, he would have to trust a dozen people with his life. Any one of them could ruin the mission and put him in an early grave.

Whatever. Jack looked at the airline information again.

Belize.

Ten years ago he and his brother and their parents had flown first class, too. Jack stared at the distant clouds.

A storm was inching closer. He closed his eyes and he could still hear Shane calling to him from down the beach. *You might have a little competition at quarterback, big brother.* He was so young. Just fourteen.

Why didn't you stay on the shore, Shane? I told you to stay on the shore.

Jack opened his eyes. No, Belize wasn't going to be a problem. The country owed him one. *This one's for you, little brother.* Jack breathed deep. If only he believed in God the way he had back then. Back when his biggest problem was figuring out whether he was going to be a Navy SEAL or a politician like his father.

That endless summer all those years ago.

In the rare moments when he did still think God was possible, Jack could only ask the obvious question. Why? Why did Shane follow him into the water and how come Jack hadn't been able to swim fast enough to save them both? The little girl and Shane. His best friend. If God were real, He had to have the answers. But Jack never asked. If God was there, if He was real, then He didn't listen to Jack Ryder. Otherwise Shane would've lived.

The truth about God was that simple.

Jack stared at the sky again. The purpose he had felt that day—the way it felt to save the little girl—was all that mattered now. It drove him and compelled him to notch one successful mission after another. He lived for it. The feeling he would have at the end of the week when he returned home from Belize, sixteen trafficking victims and Eliza Ann McMillan free from the Palace forever.

The face of the little blond girl came to mind, the one Jack had saved instead of saving Shane. Some tourist, no doubt. Probably from Europe. Sweden, maybe. No big deal to her family, Jack guessed. The rescue was probably something her mother brought up every now and then at family parties. Like a favorite story.

Remember the time when . . .

Did the girl's family even realize that Jack's brother had died that day? Jack was never sure. But something had struck him about the girl's mother. Something that had always rubbed him the wrong way and made him question what kind of person she must've been. Even now.

Jack distinctly remembered the look in the mother's eyes. More anger than fear, a fact that still didn't make sense. The woman had made eye contact with Jack as he brought the child up the beach and as he handed her over, just before he turned and ran to Shane. But something had been missing from the exchange. It was still missing.

Her mother had never said thank you.

CHAPTER FIVE

*Streams of tears flow from my eyes because my
people are destroyed.*

—Lamentations 3:48

At eighty-six years old, Ike Armstrong knew everyone in the hillside Mennonite community of Lower Barton Creek, seventy miles west of Belize City. Most of them thought he was losing his mind, that he wasn't as sharp as he had once been and that the stories he told were more fables than fact.

Nothing could be further from the truth.

Sure, Ike talked slower than he had in his prime and he didn't always remember what he had eaten for breakfast. But he could tell you the history of the Mennonite settlements in Belize without missing a name or a date. He had been the historian of Lower Barton Creek since its founding.

Children of the settlement considered history nothing more than a list of facts. Ike knew better. For five decades, he had been not only keeper of the facts . . . but keeper of the stories. The heart of life here in Belize.

Passing on the more detailed village history was up to him, and to that end, he was sharper than anyone in the settlement.

The Belize City police chief knew that Ike had more information about Lower Barton than anyone. It was why the chief had dropped in on Ike yesterday, and why the man had arranged for the young FBI agent to come by today.

Ike was forbidden to tell anyone the truth about the agent. So he made up a reason for the young man's impending visit. "My great-grandson from the States is coming," he had told the elders of the village yesterday after the police chief stopped in. "Chief just wanted to let me know." Ike had smiled. "You remember my son, Ezekiel, who moved to the States in 1983. It's his grandson. Luke."

"That's nice." The elders had smiled and nodded and tipped their hats. "Should be a good time, Ike." Visits like that happened now and then. Mennonite family members coming to Belize from the United States or Canada. No one took much notice.

Which was why no one suspected the truth about today's visit.

Good thing, Ike thought. He wasn't sure what the FBI agent would want with him, but the conversation would be secretive, that much he'd been told. Secretive and serious. Ike lifted his face to the sky. He was willing to help. Whatever it took to aid officials in cleaning up the crime that had plagued Belize City in recent years. Today kill-

ings happened at an alarming rate, especially in and
around the capital city. Robberies and home invasions
were symptoms of a bigger problem—the international
drug cartel that used Belize as a gateway to Mexico.

The increasing crime in Belize was personal to Ike.
His granddaughter, Susan James, and her children—
Lizzie and Daniel—had disappeared more than a decade
ago. Just after Susan's husband, Paul David James, left his
family in the dead of night. No telling what Paul David
was into or why he left. Villagers had their suspicions.
Another woman, maybe. Gambling trouble. Whatever
happened to Paul David, Ike was almost positive Susan
and the children had been victims of a crime.

Ike sighed. Maybe the FBI agent had a lead on their
disappearance. Ike would do anything to help with that.
He gripped the arms of his rocking chair and stared at
the road that wound its way into Lower Barton. These
days, he spent most of his time here on the front porch
of his thatched-roof home. Rocking back and forth, con-
templating the history of the village.

Praying about the future.

He set the chair in motion again. Yes, the disappearance of his family was the darkest time in Ike's life. He
remembered how upset Susan was, and how after her
husband left, she and the children stayed indoors most of
the time. No one in the village knew what to say or do.
Mennonite men didn't leave their families. They worked
hard and helped each other and found a way to stick it
out. Ike didn't know another man who had left his fam-

ily the way Paul David had. Everyone expected the man to come back.

Instead no one ever saw him or his family again.

Sometime after their disappearance, word returned to Lower Barton that Susan and her children had drowned. A tourist had seen the trio head for the water at a Belizean Beach just south of the city. Right before Ike's family disappeared.

The conclusion had been sad and simple. Susan and the children had drowned. No telling about Paul David. *Terrible thing*, people of the village would say when the topic of Paul David, Susan, Lizzie and Daniel came up. Everyone but Ike agreed about what must have happened. Paul David must have run off with another woman, and his family was probably swept away in one of those awful undercurrents. The ones that plagued the eastern coast of Belize when a hurricane was moving through the Caribbean Sea—as it had been the day the three disappeared.

Ike had a different theory, and he was fairly sure that's why the FBI agent was coming to Lower Barton Creek today. Not to talk to the elders and leaders of the community, but to a tired old man rocking on his front porch.

Because Ike was the keeper of the stories.

In his hands was one of two letters he had written after getting news about his family's supposed drowning. The first detailed his guess about what had really happened to Susan and her children. That somehow they had been killed, maybe even killed by Paul David. The

second letter was to tell his granddaughter and her children the goodbye he never got to say.

Ike opened the first letter and stared at the words
meticulously printed across the top. With great care, he
had written *Concerning my Granddaughter, Susan James.*

For the third time that morning, Ike read his letter.
Even slower this time, in case there was something he'd
missed, something that could still be added. A detail that
might help the FBI agent.

To whom it may concern,

*In the month before my granddaughter, Susan
James, and her children went missing, her husband,
Paul David James, left in the middle of the night without warning. A few weeks later, Lower Barton Creek
was visited by a strange woman who presented herself
as Paul David's American sister. Aunt Agnes Potter, she
called herself. The woman came to the village to give
Susan a message: Paul David had started a job in
Belize City and he wanted Susan and the children to
come visit.*

*Agnes Potter had red hair and heavy makeup. She
was almost giddy, as if she'd known Susan and the
children all her life. But Susan had never met the
woman. Agnes worked hard to convince Susan to take
the trip to Belize City.*

*That's strange, right? Why did it matter so much to
Agnes Potter?*

That wasn't all. From the moment she met my

great-granddaughter, Lizzie James, Aunt Agnes never let
her out of her sight. It wasn't normal. The way she looked
at my little great-granddaughter made my skin crawl.

Ike lowered the letter and looked to a far-off spot
above a cluster of towering mahogany trees. He
should've taken charge, sent the woman on her way.
Maybe asked her to prove her connection to Paul David.
Because something had been off about her.

Instead, Ike had hung back. Sizing up Agnes Potter
and letting his suspicions grow.

That afternoon, when Lizzie ran off to join the other
children, Agnes had followed.

"Lizzie," the woman had called out. Agnes never
stopped smiling, but her eyes were flat. "Come here,
Lizzie! I have something for you."

Of course sweet little Lizzie had no reason to doubt
Agnes Potter's sincerity. The child had skipped closer and
when the strange woman pulled a blond porcelain doll
from her bag, Lizzie's eyes had lit up. Belize didn't have
dolls like that one.

"Really?" Lizzie's beautiful light blue eyes shone in
the sunlight. "For me?"

"Yes." Agnes put her hands on the child's shoulders.
"For the prettiest girl in Lower Barton."

Throughout the meal, Ike had watched Agnes from
his spot at the end of the table. The woman sat next to
Susan and across from Lizzie and Daniel. Before long
Susan was spilling her heart to the stranger.

"I miss Paul David, even though he left us," Susan told the woman. "I keep thinking he'll come home."

"That's just it." The pitch in Agnes's voice raised and she talked faster. Like she was nervous. "He would come to you if he could. But he can't because of his new job. He can't leave Belize City." She glanced at Lizzie. "He wants you to come to him."

Ike tried to be polite as Agnes Potter's visit came to a close, but every time his eyes met the woman's, a chill ran down his arms. There was a meanness in her. Ike had seen it. Like she was onto his doubts, and for a fraction of a moment he had seen past the occasional flash of friendliness in her eyes to something else.

The darkest of evil.

Before she left, Agnes worked even harder to convince Susan and the children about visiting Belize City. "Paul David is sorry, Susan," the woman told Ike's granddaughter. "He really wants to see you and the children."

By the time Agnes drove off, Susan had promised to come. Sometime the next week.

Ike took a deep breath as the memory faded. He should've said something, should've probed into the woman's story. He would never forgive himself for not acting on his doubts that day. Once more he lifted the letter and found his place.

When Agnes Potter left that day, I noticed two things.
First, she didn't look me in the eye. And second, she
didn't pay a bit of attention to little Daniel. Only Lizzie.

I wrote down my observations, because they matter.
Susan never should've gone to see Paul David. Never
should have listened to Agnes Potter.

Ike blinked back tears.

In my heart, I want to hope Susan and the children
are alive, even after all these years. I do not believe my
family members drowned. But I am concerned some-
thing more sinister happened to them. And I believe it
happened at the hands of Agnes Potter.
Possibly even Paul David James.

Sincerely,
Ike Armstrong
Historian—Lower Barton Creek, Belize

Ike never wept about this, not anymore. But once in
a while—times like this—he could feel tears push against
the walls of his heart. If Susan and Lizzie and Daniel
really were dead, then the FBI agent needed to find
Agnes Potter and Paul David James.

The only two people who knew the truth.

. . .

JACK'S FACIAL HAIR wasn't a true Mennonite beard,
but it would do. For this first part of the mission, Jack
was Luke Armstrong. Great-grandson of Ike Armstrong
of Lower Barton Creek, Belize.

The additional ID kit had been at the bottom of the

satchel. Jack was glad for the second fake name. Never mind that Oliver and the FBI brass trusted the old man at Lower Barton Creek. They couldn't risk a connection between Jack's visit to the village this morning and the work he had in the week ahead of him.

As he moved through customs, Jack wore a black and red plaid shirt and black chino pants. A Mennonite man in the line ahead of him looked back and nodded. Jack returned the greeting. Mennonites stuck together.

Jack passed the test.

The wait at baggage wasn't long. Jack grabbed his worn suitcase and caught a cab to a local car rental outfit. Ten minutes later he was driving a Jeep due east to Lower Barton Creek.

Ike Armstrong was just where Jack expected to find him. Sitting in his rocking chair on the front porch of his small house. Ike knew Jack was an agent, but not much beyond that. A few people from the settlement waved as he parked in front of Ike's house.

"Hello, there!" Jack smiled and returned the gesture. Then he met Ike with a firm handshake, the way a young man would greet the great-grandfather he'd never known. Jack took the rocking chair opposite Ike, as if a relaxing chat was the only reason he'd come.

Everything Jack had been told about Ike Armstrong looked to be true. The man was old, but his eyes were sharp. His senses seemed keen. Ike spoke first. "I'm not sure why you came here. But I want to help."

A smile tugged at Jack's lips, like the two were talking about long-forgotten family members. The villagers would've been shocked to know the truth. "We're taking down a sex- and drug-trafficking ring just south of Belize City." Jack looked to the distant jungle.

"Sex trafficking?" The man knit his brow together. "A prostitution ring."

"Yes. But these are teenage girls. Kept like prisoners. Slaves, really." Jack hated talking about it. "Most of the victims are very young."

Ike shook his head. His face turned several shades paler. "How could such a thing even happen?"

"Money." The answer was simple and sickening at the same time. Jack worked to keep his happy face. "It's a problem all over the world."

Ike stared at his hands for a long time and then took a sharp breath. "And people doubt there's a devil."

This is an ordinary family visit, Jack told himself. *Act the part.* He grinned at Ike. "Can you tell me anything about a missing little girl from a Mennonite village? About a decade ago? She'd be nineteen now."

For a few seconds the man only narrowed his eyes. Then he reached for the envelope on the table beside him. "Two letters inside. One about my family's disappearance. One, more personal, a letter for them . . . if you find them."

Jack understood the weight of it, of all it meant to the old man.

"My great-granddaughter went missing...around that time. Eleven years ago." Ike shook his head. "But she'd be twenty-three now, I believe."

"I know about that. Chief Averes shared the report from back then. Have you heard the name Anders McMillan?"

"McMillan?" Ike thought for a few seconds, but his answer was quick, decisive. "No. Should I have?"

"He runs the drug ring." Jack set his rocker in motion, his eyes on Ike. If they could figure out McMillan's past, they could figure out Eliza's. Which could lead to more witnesses and more convictions. "Any other blond girls who went missing from the Belizean Mennonite colonies?"

"Yes." Ike sighed. "Years ago a girl disappeared from Spanish Lookout, a colony northwest of here." He swallowed. "You think the missing girl, she might be trapped in this...trafficking?"

"We do." Jack explained that Chief Averes had an old report on file. "He told me you thought an American woman might have been involved in the disappearance of your family members. Is that right?"

"Yes." Ike bit his lip. "Agnes Potter. She claimed to be the children's aunt." Ike looked straight at Jack. "That woman couldn't take her eyes off Lizzie. My little granddaughter was so young."

Jack had read the report on Ike's missing family members. The case was closed, no foul play suspected. Jack had seen the police file from the day the family disappeared. Nothing had jumped out at him. But since Ike was the area historian, the bureau hoped he might know something about Eliza Lawrence and her father—Anders McMillan.

The old man blinked. "You . . . you think my Lizzie could be at this . . . Palace place?"

Twenty-three was too old. Which meant—with her blond hair and blue eyes—Eliza could've been the missing girl from Spanish Lookout, north of Lower Barton Creek . . . or maybe not. Maybe she was from the States. But if Ike's great-granddaughter didn't drown in the ocean with her family, and if she had been forced into slavery at the Palace, she was probably dead by now—*aged out* like Eliza's friend Alexa.

"Ike." Jack sighed. "I don't think your Lizzie is there." He didn't want to go into details. Not when the man had longed for his missing family members for so many years. "But your information just might help us form a case against McMillan. Connecting him to one or more missing girls."

Ike nodded. He looked off and tears built in his eyes. "My poor great-grandbabies." He brushed his hand over his face and seemed to force a smile. "There's a picture of my family in here. How they looked eleven years ago." He rifled through the envelope.

Suddenly Jack had a thought. "You don't think . . . maybe Paul David changed his name to Anders McMillan? I've seen photos of Anders. He's thin, tall and clean shaven with thick red hair. Very intelligent. He's kept from getting caught all these years."

Ike shook his head. "Paul David was a furniture maker. Sturdy man. Not much at conversation or finances. That's not him. But take this. It's a copy. I can't part with the original." Ike handed the image to Jack. "In case you see anything . . . hear anything."

The photo wasn't great quality, but it showed a family of four. Susan had been a brunette with a pretty face and Paul David was a heavy man with dark blond hair and a full beard. He looked nothing like McMillan. Jack sighed. It was worth a try. He looked at the towheaded children and his eyes landed on the image of Lizzie. Something stopped him.

The girl looked familiar. Or maybe she just looked like every other Mennonite child.

Ike handed Jack the envelope and he pulled the letters from inside and quickly read them. A pair of village men walked by and nodded at Ike and then Jack. "Morning," one of them said.

"Morning." Jack and Ike returned the greeting.

Jack looked at the letters again. He wasn't sure where the information fit in, but it was something. If he could connect Anders to the disappearance of the Spanish Lookout girl he could build a better case for conviction. The trip here had been worth the drive.

"Before you go." Ike stood and motioned for Jack to follow him. Inside on an end table was a small worn leather portfolio. "Here. Take it." Ike handed it to Jack. "It has things Susan saved over the years. Schoolwork and precious drawings by Lizzie and her brother. Lizzie's favorite miniature fuzzy teddy bear." He blinked back tears. "Some of the fur is worn off. Lizzie loved it so."

"I can see that." Jack touched the small bear. *Poor old man*, he thought. *Saving these all this time.*

"Inside, you'll also find other photos and letters Susan wrote to the children." Again Ike's eyes welled up. "I'd love to show you."

Jack had to get going. "I'll look through it later."

"Okay." Ike nodded. "If you ever find them, my family, give them this. Please."

"I will, Ike." Jack took the portfolio and ran his hand along the top. "I'll keep it with me."

They returned to the front porch and the two hugged. "I'm sorry." Jack looked deep into the old man's eyes. "About your family."

"Thank you." Ike pursed his lips and his eyes grew steely. "I'll be praying for you."

Jack hesitated at that. "I appreciate it." He nodded once more and then climbed in his rental car. Halfway to Belize City, Jack stopped at a gas station and changed clothes in the bathroom. He shaved in the stall and when he walked out he was no longer Luke Armstrong.

He was a finely dressed Henry Thomas Ellington IV.

By then another operative on the ground—someone dressed in a red plaid shirt and chinos was driving the Jeep back to the rental agency. In its place, out front of the gas station, a new-model Porsche was waiting, keys in the glove box. The operative had moved Jack's things into the backseat. Jack slipped on his Ray-Bans and climbed behind the wheel.

Two things hounded him as he continued on to Belize City. The heartbroken lined face of Ike Armstrong. And the intensity of the man's conviction. Old Ike really thought Agnes Potter and Paul David James had something to do with the disappearance of his family. And he truly believed the three might somehow still be alive. With every mile, Jack's belief in the man grew until he had a hunch about Ike Armstrong.

A hunch that just maybe the man was right.

CHAPTER SIX

The Lord detests those whose hearts are perverse.
—Proverbs 11:20

Noon was showtime at the Palace, and Eliza hated it. If a customer didn't already have a girl picked out, he could show up midday and choose his entertainment in person. The girls would take their places in the living room, the younger teens lined up on the two sofas, older girls in the chairs.

Eliza sat at the head of the room. No one ever bought Eliza, but today was different. Today she would meet her groom. Eliza held her breath for half a minute. If she didn't think the guards would catch her, she would've run away from this place years ago. The problem was the things her captors threatened if ever she went against her father. Things that were vile and unthinkable.

And they did not include death.

Death would be easy. Eliza had often longed for death—in the sea currents or on land, the method didn't matter. Death would mean she wouldn't have to spend her days waiting to be married off. She wouldn't live another night in the Palace, hearing the muffled cries of the girls down the hall.

But death had eluded her for the past ten years.

At this point Eliza had no choice but to sit in her velvet chair, untainted captive that she was. But she didn't have to smile. No one asked that of her. That job belonged to the younger girls.

Five minutes before noon, two housemaids entered the room—the way they did every day at this time. They moved among the girls, fixing hair and applying blush to the cheeks of the youngest. The older girls did their own makeup. Better than letting anyone touch them before nightfall, they had told Eliza.

The housemaids were older and indifferent. This was their living. When the customers arrived, they went home. Clocked out like this was some sort of twisted hotel. As if sex slavery was just one more aspect of the tourism industry in Belize. When the clock chimed noon, the women left. Lunch break. No big deal. No efforts to save the imprisoned girls.

Eliza exhaled. If the housemaids felt bad for their part in perpetuating Anders's trafficking ring, they didn't show it.

A minute later the doors opened, as predictable as the ocean waves. This part of the horror belonged to her father alone. Showtime, he called it. And every day Eliza had to be here to reassure the girls, to watch over them. To make them feel safe.

When she was little, Eliza had actually looked forward to this hour each day. Seeing the other girls, talking with them. They were like big sisters to her back then. Her father would enter the room and walk down the line of girls. Then he would stop and pat her head. Like she was the most special. His princess.

Eliza studied the girls on the two sofas. That was how *they* felt, now. They looked up to her and the older teens. Eliza could see it in their eyes. Whatever unspeakable things had been done to them the night before, all seemed well now.

The older girls would keep them safe.

After the beating when she turned fourteen, Alexa had told Eliza that her eyes had been opened to the demon her father was. Now when he smiled, chills ran down Eliza's spine and it took everything in her not to run.

"There you are, darlings." Her father waltzed into the room. He dressed in flamboyant costumes and strange suits. Like he'd lost his mind—which of course he had. Today's ridiculous costume was blue flouncy pants and an old English button-up blouse, high ruffled collar and all. His pointy leather shoes clicked on the tiled floor.

He looked more like a court jester than the prince he believed himself to be.

The younger girls sat straighter on the two sofas. They liked Anders McMillan, same as Eliza had when she was younger. Eliza could see that in their eyes, too. *Run*, she wanted to scream at them. Before the awakening happened. *Come with me! Let's get out of here.* Eliza closed her eyes and tried to breathe again. She couldn't help the girls now. It was her fault they were here.

First in the room with Anders was the redhead Eliza had seen on the beach a few days ago. He followed Anders down the row of dolled-up teens. "Maybe someone younger tonight." He looked over his shoulder and winked at Eliza. "Since I can't have the princess."

Eliza's father's eyes turned dark. He stopped and gave the redheaded man a shove. "That's my daughter. Don't look at her!" Another shove and the man stepped back. He was trembling. At the door, two guards moved closer, waiting for Eliza's father's command. Instead her father glared at the customer. "Do you hear me?"

"Yes." The redhead didn't dare glance at Eliza again. He made his choice from the younger teen girls and one of the guards escorted him out of the room.

One at a time the men filed in and chose their entertainment for the night. The men left, the evening housemaids took the girls back to their rooms and only Eliza and her father remained. She started to leave, but he held up his hand. "Not yet." He motioned to the guard still at the door. "Now. Bring him in now."

What was this? So soon? Eliza felt her heart rate quicken. Was her groom here to meet her already? She wanted to jump out the window and run as far and fast from here as she could.

Before Eliza could ask, another man entered the

room. He was tall and striking. Dark hair and a clean-shaven face. Not a day over thirty, if Eliza had to guess. This was her groom, Eliza had no doubt. *How did such a young guy lose his soul?* she wondered. *Or were all rich people wretched?*

"Eliza." Her father walked to her. "This is Henry Thomas Ellington, the Fourth." He motioned for the man to join them. "This is your groom."

Her father took gentle hold of her arm, like he was a doting, kindhearted parent. "Henry Thomas, this is Eliza Ann Lawrence."

"Hello." Henry Thomas held out his hand. He wore a sharp white dress shirt and a pale blue tie. An Italian suit that rivaled anything Eliza had seen at the Palace.

She gritted her teeth, but she didn't hesitate. "Hello." This was nonnegotiable. She curtsied and lifted her hand to his. He took it and kissed it. The motion repulsed her. How dare he come here to claim her, like she was a commodity?

"Eliza . . . I'll see you tonight." If Henry Thomas was trying to be charming it fell flat.

"Yes." Eliza nodded. This was a business deal, nothing more. She held her breath again until Henry Thomas left.

When he was gone, her father paced to the door and back. "You will have two nights with Henry Thomas. Consider it your honeymoon." He faced her. "After that, Mr. Ellington will sign papers committing to this marriage." His smile faded. "Be kind to him, Eliza. I've been planning this since you were nine years old." He touched her cheek.

Eliza wanted to scream at him. "I know that."

"Watch your sarcasm." He snarled. "I've given you everything, Eliza. All your life."

She looked away. What sort of monster would use his own daughter? For a business deal? *Sickening*, Eliza thought. And once more she remembered her dream of escaping. When Henry Thomas left her room tonight, she could escape the Palace and run to the police. She would tell them everything she knew, and if Henry Thomas or her father killed her, so be it. Because how could she marry Henry Thomas knowing that it would mean even more drug trafficking, even more girls captured and enslaved?

With almost imperceptible shifts of his eyes, her father surveyed her. "Don't let me down, Eliza." He turned and left the room.

Eliza wondered if she would throw up on the cold floor. Her knees shook and her head hurt. What would Henry Thomas expect of her tonight? She thought of her father. He must've seen the hatred in her eyes. Nausea consumed her. She would gladly push her father off a cliff and watch him hit the rocks below. But even that wouldn't be what he deserved. Nothing would.

Not until he wound up in hell.

One of the housemaids entered. "Miss, you need to

get down to the beach. Your father wants you to get your sun. Then you need to prepare for tonight."

Eliza glanced back at the window. She could leave. She could cross to the window, and jump and . . .

She turned to the housemaid. "I . . . I don't want to prepare."

"Your father insists."

Eliza squeezed her eyes shut. The girls had told her what would happen later. After her time at the beach. There would be bathing and essential oils, primping and makeup. Her father was right. In all ways that mattered, her honeymoon would begin tonight. A honeymoon for the most macabre wedding—a ceremony set to take place at the end of the week. If she lived up to Henry Thomas's standard.

The events were out of order—like everything about her life.

Eliza went to her room and dressed in her bathing suit and cover-up. Her groom would arrive at the Palace at eight o'clock. Just as the sun went down. Because the most horrible deeds were always done at night, where light couldn't touch them. Couldn't expose them. Eliza had read that in one of her books.

And where was God in all of this?

Most of the older girls didn't believe in God. Or they were angry at Him. *All of this is His fault,* they would say if the subject came up. Eliza didn't agree. God may have forgotten her, but He existed because that's what her mama taught her long ago. The devil was real. Tonight would prove that.

So there had to be a God.

But right now nighttime was still a long way off. The next few hours were the only part of the day when Eliza felt human. The beach was her time alone.

Which meant for the next few hours Eliza could breathe and remember her mama's face and little Daniel's voice. She could read. Something she did often. Strangely, the Palace had a library, and Eliza visited it as often as she could. Books let her live in a different world, if only until she read the last page. Anything good in her life happened at the shore. And it was where—if she were lucky—today she might even see God.

Out beyond the waves, there at the back edge of the ocean.

• • •

SOMETHING WAS OFF.

Anders McMillan knew it and for that reason, once Eliza was out of the house he had a meeting with four of his men. He gathered them in the boardroom on the first floor. They sat, but he paced.

The men knew better than to break the silence. This was Anders's meeting. After three minutes, he stopped and faced them. "What did you think of the men today, the customers?"

This wasn't the first time Anders had asked them this. His operation here at the Palace was risky. If they got sloppy, the feds from the States or even the Belizean police would shut him down. They would have done it by now if they could have. A long time ago.

None of his team made eye contact with him. As if they weren't sure what to say.

Anders slammed his fist on the table. "Talk to me! What did you think of today's customers?"

"Only a few of them were new." His lead guy looked around. "Right? Maybe six of the men?"

"Seven." Another of the men nodded. "I took notes."

"Okay." Anders rolled his eyes. He needed a Xanax. Or a whiskey. Something to take the edge off. "So there were seven. I'm not asking for a ledger, here." Maybe he needed a new team. He lowered his voice and stared at the men, one at a time. "I'm asking for your *opinion*. Did you sense anything? Suspect anyone?"

Asia, his biggest and most violent man, raised his hand. "The young guy, light blue tie." Asia was six-foot-five, a former heavyweight fighter. He had the scars to prove it. The man squinted. "I didn't like him."

"He's Eliza's groom." Now they were getting somewhere. Anders straightened and took a deep breath. "Me, either." He began pacing again. "Too young. Too . . . I don't know, too off."

"It wasn't his age." The first guy shook his head. "We get young guys from the yacht club. The sons of the owners. It wasn't that."

Anders thought about smacking the man for disagreeing with Asia. But the guy had a point. Anders looked out the window. "I talked to Henry Thomas's father last week. He told me his son was young. Which made sense, because Eliza is young." He faced his men again. "So what is it? Why didn't you like him?"

"It was his looks." Asia crossed his arms. "He doesn't look like his father. I remember Henry Thomas the Third."

"I think he *does* look like his father." Another of the men dared a comment. "I . . . thought that from the beginning."

Anders could feel his anger rising. "Asia is right."

"I don't need a reason." Asia crossed his arms. "I didn't like him."

That's the way Asia worked. On instincts, same as Anders. Asia was one reason the Palace was still in business. The big man picked up on threats before they played out.

Anders was finished here. He pointed to Asia. "*You* guard Eliza's door tonight. Make sure the honeymoon is legit." He hesitated. "If he's who he says he is, there won't be an issue. If not, you know what to do."

Asia nodded, and Anders dismissed his men.

He paced along the window again. He knew much about Henry Thomas Ellington III. The two had even shared a meal a few years ago. So the man's son shouldn't be a problem. But what if this Henry Thomas wasn't really the son at all? What if he was part of a sting? Anders gripped the window frame. He would go through his records and place a call to his old friend. Make sure everything was as it should be.

Then he remembered something, and it made him relax a little. The guard who dared speak up was right. The senior Ellington had always been a striking man. A man who turned heads. Ellington the Fourth was the same way. The resemblance was there not only in looks, but in the air the younger man held. The way he drew attention when he had walked into the Palace earlier. Anders exhaled. Everything would be fine. Of course the younger Ellington was who he said he was.

After all, like father, like son.

CHAPTER SEVEN

*Defend the weak and the fatherless; uphold the
cause of the poor and the oppressed. Rescue the
weak and the needy; deliver them from the hand of
the wicked.*

—Psalm 82:3–4

Four operatives had flown into Belize City on separate flights over the last two days. Jack had their itineraries memorized. Like with the waiting Porsche, his every move had been calculated by the entire team, choreographed with the precision of a brain surgery.

Anders McMillan's gang would expect him to spend a few hours at the water. He had made contact with Eliza, so now he could go about his vacation day. It was his honeymoon, after all. Jack had passed his first test. At least he thought so.

The FBI had been careful.

Anders knew Henry Thomas Ellington III well enough to feel safe with his son. Henry the Fourth would need no further background check. Of course, Anders had no idea that Henry the Third was laying low. Or that the man's real son had given the FBI permission to use his identity for the sting.

Which was why the actual Henry No. 4 was one more person the FBI had to trust.

The Blue Breeze Yacht Club sat at the north side of this nearly hidden sandy shoreline. Jack had gone there first after his brief time at the Palace. Not because he had a yacht in port on this trip. Stopping by the Blue Breeze was to legitimize Jack's visit. Nothing more.

Just another young millionaire with time on his hands and admission to his daddy's club—and the Palace. A chosen millionaire, set to marry Anders McMillan's beautiful daughter. To anyone paying attention, a short visit to the club made perfect sense.

The FBI was betting Jack's life on it.

Jack chugged back a couple sparkling waters and lime. "My old man drinks like a fish," Jack had told the bartender earlier. He could feel feigned arrogance seeping through every pore of his body. "I promised him I'd be different. So, I don't drink." He patted his abs. His six-pack was visible through his T-shirt. "Too many carbs."

There was truth to this story. Henry Thomas Ellington III had been to the club years back and he had, in fact, drunk too much. Now he was dying from his choices. Also, his son really was a health fanatic.

Playing the part of a millionaire playboy with a planned visit later that night to the Palace took all of Jack's acting ability. He loathed everything about this part of his job. When he wasn't talking to the other club members, he was talking to himself. *You're saving young girls, Jack. Keep your head. Keep smiling.*

He stayed at the club for an hour, chatting with a handful of members. Long enough to validate his story. He was Henry Thomas Ellington IV, and he was about to marry Eliza. About to join two of the most powerful crime families in the Western Hemisphere.

When he'd put in his time, Jack walked back to his Porsche and climbed inside. He checked his phone. Nothing from Oliver. No change of plans from the other operatives in town. He glanced at the time. He needed to get to the beach. If possible, the goal was to make contact with Eliza. But only if a meeting seemed natural. A quick stop at his hotel and he was ready for the water.

Jack parked the car at the beach lot, and walked down a narrow path toward the water. Most of the city had no sandy shoreline. Just a steel railing and a rock border. Typically tourists drove or flew the extra nearly two hundred miles south to the Placencia Peninsula, home of some of the prettiest beaches in the world. Jack and his family had vacationed there every year except the one time when . . .

He didn't finish the thought.

This stretch of sand just outside Belize City was only a few hundred yards long and hard to find off the main road. Tourists usually considered it a private beach. Just a small parking lot and a grove of palm trees that opened up to the beach, all of it nestled at the base of a mountain plateau a few hundred feet up from the sand.

The place where the Palace stood.

Members from the Blue Breeze were the main beachgoers here. Oh, and Anders McMillan's captives. Especially Eliza. Intelligence from other operatives had told Jack that Eliza came here at the same time every day. Her armed guards walked her halfway down the mountainside and waited there. She would walk the rest of the steep path by herself and for two or three hours she could sit in the sun and read or swim in the warm, clear water.

But Henry Thomas Ellington IV wouldn't have known any of that.

So Jack had to act totally unaware of Eliza. He didn't look around as he reached the clearing. Memorized instructions played in his head. *Walk straight to the water. Casually turn left and count out fifty yards. If she's not there, she's twenty yards up the sand in the shade of the palm trees. Whatever you do, don't look around. Her guards will be watching.*

Jack wore Tommy Bahama khaki shorts and a dark blue tank top. He worked out two hours a day and it showed. His body was part of the job. He carried a backpack over one shoulder, a beach chair over the other, and an oversized towel. *Focus, Jack. Don't look for Eliza. Keep your eyes straight ahead.*

He was definitely being watched. Jack could feel the eyes on him.

As soon as he reached the water and turned he spotted her. Ten yards down the beach, sitting in a low-slung chair reading; her pale hair was pulled back in a loose ponytail. Feet in the gentle surf. Jack slowed as he approached her.

Their eyes met and Eliza took off her sunglasses and stared at him. "My groom."

Jack hated this. "I was. I . . . um . . ." He looked up the beach a ways and back at her. *Play the part,* he told himself. "I didn't think I'd see you till tonight."

"You?" She sneered at him. "You won't *see* me. It's not a date." Hatred filled her tone. "You and your family . . . you *bought* me. It's a business deal. Tonight you collect your purchase." Her eyes were steel cold. "There's a difference."

Wow. Jack fought every instinct to apologize, to tell Eliza the truth that he would never buy a person. But this was the job, and if the mission was successful, it would save her life and the lives of every teen still being trafficked by Anders McMillan.

There was nothing Jack could say. He shook his head and stared out to sea for a beat. Then he started to walk past her.

"Wait." Anger rang in her voice. "Why?" She looked him up and down. "Why would you agree to an arranged marriage? Don't you have a choice?"

Jack felt his muscles tense. He didn't dare look up the hillside to the place where her guards stood. Eliza had a point, but Jack was ready. "Relationships are messy." He shrugged and cocked his head. *Keep the attitude,* he told himself. *She'll expect an attitude.* "I'm not looking for love, Eliza." He worked to keep a stone face. "I'm looking for obedience."

For a few seconds she only stared at him, her contempt a physical presence. Then she gripped the arms of her chair and set her eyes on the horizon. "We'll see about that."

Again Jack said nothing. He set his things down and crossed his arms. "The deal isn't set yet, Eliza. Remember that."

Her blond hair blew in the breeze and a pair of seagulls flew past. It took her a minute, but finally she looked at him again. This time there was a sense of fear about her. Even with her sunglasses on, Jack could see it. She pulled her cover-up more tightly around her body. "I'm sorry. Please . . . leave me alone. Until tonight."

Jack had no idea what to say next. He was her groom, not a customer. He steadied himself. "I'm sorry, too. For bothering you."

As he walked a hundred yards down the beach and set up his chair, as he stripped down to his bathing suit, walked through the surf and dove into the salty smooth water, he could only hope he had passed yet another in a series of tests. Should he have been meaner, more angry? Sarcastic? He had no room for error.

He swam for half an hour and then returned to his chair. By then Eliza was gone, back up the hill with the guards, back to her bedroom at the Palace to get ready. Jack looked at the spot where she had been. Did she know she was a victim? That it was sinful and illegal and vile for her father to keep her in a place where he sold girls for other men's pleasure? Or was she Anders's accomplice, with no qualms about what she did?

Jack returned to his Porsche and drove to the Great House Inn on Cork Street in the northern part of the city. The same hotel where he and his parents and brother had stayed during that terrible summer. Same room. He could practically see his brother and his parents in the lobby and hallways and stairwells. He could hear their laughter.

The soap and sheets and towels smelled as familiar as the memories.

His suitcase—with Ike's leather satchel—was already in his room, the place where he would stay until the mission Thursday night. When he would either helicopter out of here with every girl from the Palace.

Or die trying.

The hot shower and handmade coconut soap was exactly what he needed. He let the hot water run over his face and hair and body. *I don't know if You're there, God.* He closed his eyes and rinsed out the shampoo. *But if You are, I could use Your help tonight.*

If Anders's henchmen had a suspicion that Jack was only going to talk to Eliza tonight, or that he wasn't Ellington the Fourth, they'd kill him and dump his body in the canal. And that would be that. He stepped out of the shower and toweled off. There were a dozen reasons why God probably wasn't real. Jack didn't want to rehash them. But nights like this, he figured it didn't hurt to ask.

Just in case.

He dressed in white pants and a short-sleeve white button-up shirt. Fine leather loafers. No socks. Wedding attire. He still had time to kill so Jack grabbed a sandwich from the lobby and ate it on the deck outside his room. The spot faced the ocean, the place where he'd last seen his brother alive.

His family had always loved Belize. Of all the rooms, this one had the best view. He could remember sitting on this very deck with Shane, watching the puffy white clouds pass over the water. Each a unique shape. *That one's an elephant*, Jack had said the night before the tragedy. *And a tiger over there*, Shane had chimed in.

Jack closed his eyes. He pictured Eliza again. Of course she hated what her father was doing, selling her into marriage. The fact that she'd told him—a stranger—made the truth clear. She was desperate, and she'd be thankful to get out. Jack stood and filled his lungs with the warm sea air. It was time to go. Eliza was going to be free soon.

Tonight was only the first step to making that happen.

• • •

IN TRAINING, JACK had learned the art of disassociation. A way of taking his feelings and turning them to facts. Facts kept you alive in undercover agent work. Feelings killed. So as he parked his Porsche at the beach lot and walked a different path to a staircase that led to the Palace, Jack refused to feel for the beautiful, broken girl he would spend the next hour with.

This was a mission. Every step was a checklist item. A week from now he could celebrate the rescue, ache for the girls inside the mansion. But right now he needed to move and act and talk with precision.

At the other side of the parking lot, a woman sat on a rock. Dressed in a bohemian floral kimono, secret agent Terri Gunther, thirty-three, appeared to be meditating. A beach hippie focused on a palm tree. But Terri had a wicked aim and beneath her oversized beach garment was a Remington 270 with the best scope on earth.

Once Jack was out of sight, Terri would take his backpack from the Porsche and return to her rock. Then she would slip into the grove of trees and train her scope on Eliza's window until Jack returned.

If something went wrong, Terri would be the first to know.

Jack wasn't sure if the guards could see him, but he figured yes. There were a dozen other cars in the parking lot, sickos already here for their purchases. Like a man walking into a black-tie gala, Jack took the steps slowly. Cocksure. Ready.

At the top of the stairs he bent to tie his shoe. At the same time he dropped a cell phone and a loaded Glock in the grass. Once more he went over his escape plan. If Eliza didn't cooperate. If she screamed and tried to alert the armed guard outside her bedroom door, then Jack had a sedative-filled syringe in a plastic case in his shoe. He would keep it in his waistband once he was alone with her.

If he had no choice, he would stick her leg with the drug. It was fast-acting and would wear off in twenty minutes. Enough time for him to make his escape. If that happened, when she stopped moving, he would slip out her bedroom window, climb down, and sprint for the cell phone and gun at the top of the stairs.

A single button on the phone would signal every operative on the ground that there was a problem. By then Terri would've activated two agents parked on the main road, one of whom would drive into the lot. Terri and Jack would jump inside their car and an hour later— dressed as a monk—Jack would be on a plane headed for Miami. Oliver had overseen the details, so Jack wasn't worried.

Should he need to escape, every minute was orchestrated.

But that wasn't going to happen. Not tonight. With clear understanding of the facts he made his way to the massive front doors of the Palace. One of Anders's housemaids answered and pointed him to a room off the foyer. The same room where—earlier in the day—Jack had been introduced to Eliza.

He didn't have to wait long. A massive man carrying an assault rifle entered, and without saying a word he escorted Jack two floors up a spiral staircase. Jack felt his heart rate quicken. *Were the guards always like this? So intense?* Jack stayed cool. *He's on to me. How could he be on to me?*

Never mind, Jack was ready. He memorized every

detail of the walk up. Windows and hallways and the number of rooms each floor seemed to have. Guards at the end of each hallway. When they raided this place in three days, he would need to know where the exits were, and how best to handle the guards.

The burly man led Jack down the hallway on the third floor to a door trimmed in gold. Much nicer than the other doors that lined the hall. *Don't think about what's happening behind those doors,* he told himself. *Just get in the room and make the pitch.*

Jack's escort opened the door. "The walls are thick. You have an hour."

And like that, Jack was inside Eliza's soundproof room. Alone with her.

CHAPTER EIGHT

*For this is what the Sovereign Lord says: I myself
will search for my sheep and look after them. As a
shepherd looks after his scattered flock when he is
with them, so will I look after my sheep. I will
rescue them from all the places where they were
scattered on a day of clouds and darkness.*

—Ezekiel 34:11–12

No matter how indifferent or angry Eliza wanted to
appear, she couldn't get around the truth. She was scared
to death.

When Henry Thomas entered the room, Eliza rose
from her enormous satin-covered bed. She stood and
pulled her robe around her shivering body. Her father's
voice echoed in her head. *Be kind to him, Eliza. I've been
planning this since you were nine years old.*

The guard outside the door had given her a different
kind of warning.

"Don't disappoint your father, Eliza." That's all he
had to say. Something like hatred dripped from every
word.

Eliza's hair was a mass of pale curls, and her makeup made her look like a model in a bridal magazine. She wore a floor-length pink silk robe and she moved to the other side of the room, where she sat on a high-backed swivel princess chair. Henry Thomas closed the door behind him.

Their eyes met, but only for a few seconds before Eliza looked away. In days she'd be married to this man. But she couldn't stand the thought of being in the same room with him. Let alone . . . She felt sick to her stomach.

Earlier on the beach, he had tried to be cavalier. But Henry Thomas didn't have the eyes of a demon. After eleven years at the Palace, watching men come and go to the other girls' rooms, Eliza knew the difference.

It was time. She stood, and as she did, her robe opened just enough to show Henry Thomas a flash of leg and her four-inch high heels. *Don't disappoint your father . . . don't disappoint—* If there was any way out she would take it. Instead she blinked twice and said the only thing she could say. "This . . . is my first time."

Henry Thomas didn't take his eyes off hers. He slipped out of his shoes and shirt, then he slowly crossed the room and put his hands on her shoulders. His fingers were like velvet. "Eliza." He searched her eyes. "I'm not Henry Thomas."

"Okay." She forced a laugh, her robe still tight around her. Underneath it she wore a backless silk gown. But no man had ever seen her in such skimpy clothing. She would put off the inevitable as long as she could. *Be kind to him* . . . Eliza dropped her robe and leaned away from him at the same time. *What did he mean, he wasn't Henry Thomas?* "You want me to call you something else? Mr. Ellington, maybe?"

"Eliza, no." His expression changed. "Don't scream." He still had his hands on her shoulders. "I'm a special agent with the FBI. We're about to conduct a raid on the Palace and close it down. We need your help."

"What? . . . No!" Eliza shook her head. "Never!" Her heart pounded so hard she thought it would break out of her chest. How could this happen?

She was days from being married, days from leaving the Palace and finding a way to escape. And now this . . . this man had chosen *her* to help him take down her father? They would all die. She tried to jerk away from him, but he wouldn't let her go.

"Stop." His grip on her tightened. "Let me explain."

"Get away from me!" She knew how to take care of this stranger. She tilted her head back. "Asia! Hel—"

But before she could scream, the man spun her around and pressed her bare back tight against his chest. He covered her mouth with one hand and contained her with the other. "Eliza . . . I'm telling you the truth. My name is Luke and I work for the FBI. Your father is a very dangerous man. He killed your friend Alexa and he'll kill you, too, if you go against him. You have to believe me."

Fear grabbed at Eliza's throat and she felt the fight leave her. So her father had arranged for Alexa's murder.

Of course. And this man knew all about it. Which meant . . . he must be telling the truth.

"You've assisted your father in trafficking the younger girls." The man's voice was clear, decisive. "You'll spend years behind bars, Eliza. Or you'll be killed by him. Once he doesn't need you for his power play."

Suddenly Eliza believed him. This Luke person was telling the truth. She nodded and he removed his hand from her mouth. She spit the taste of him from her lips. She faced him. "What if . . . what if I just run away?"

"Why haven't you run away before this?"

The man had done his research. Eliza still detested him, the way she detested all men. But she had to know about her friend. "You . . . you're sure? About Alexa?"

A hint of compassion shone in the man's eyes. "Police found her body a week after she left. Your father got his money back and made room for the next victim." He gritted his teeth. "He covered his tracks. He always does."

She could still call Asia. Still prevent the raid from happening. "Why do you need me?"

"We need a witness, Eliza. Someone who heard or saw something regarding Alexa." He hesitated. "And of course you know about all of it. The drugs and trafficking. You're the best witness we could hope to have."

She was that. Eliza had heard the conversation with Anders's men and she'd never told anyone. Deep down hadn't she known what had happened to Alexa? Wasn't that why she had a knife hidden in her drawer?

The knife! Eliza could kill this man and be a hero to her father. Anyone claiming to be an FBI agent . . . anyone lying was an enemy of Anders McMillan. She stepped back. "I . . . I have information." She turned to her dresser and looked over her shoulder. "Come look."

Luke followed her and in a rush of motion Eliza grabbed the knife from the drawer, turned and raised it toward Luke. She was about to plunge it into the man's bare chest when he grabbed her wrist. With practiced ease he took the knife from her and tossed it across the room. "I already told you, Eliza," he hissed at her. "You'll be killed, you'll go to prison, or you'll work with me."

She would've done anything not to work with this man. Four days and she would've been married and out of this place. Until she could find a time to escape her groom. But none of that had been real. Now they'd probably all wind up killed. Then she remembered how her dream had changed, and how she no longer wanted to live by herself in some cold European city. Rather she imagined telling the authorities about the terrible things that were happening at the Palace.

But if this Luke was telling the truth, then she needed to hear him out. Now. She remembered Asia standing just outside her door. "The guard. He can check on us at any time. If . . . if he thinks you're not really my groom, he'll shoot you."

"Get in bed." Luke unbuttoned his pants and took them off.

Eliza started to pull off her nightgown but Luke held up his hand. "Don't." He shook his head. "Pull down the straps. But leave it on."

"Okay." The urgency in Luke's voice terrified Eliza. Clearly he knew the danger he was in. And if he was in danger, then the moment she agreed to help him, she would be in danger, too. She slipped under the heavy down comforter and between the cool sheets.

Luke kept his briefs on, then he climbed into bed with her. "Slide closer to me. Lay on your side."

Why did this have to happen to her? Eliza exhaled hard and did as he told her. She kept her voice to a whisper. "If that door opens, Asia has to believe we're celebrating our honeymoon. You understand, right?"

Luke clenched his jaw. "He'll believe."

A shiver ran down Eliza's arms. "Talk to me, Luke. What do I need to know?"

"I'll be back tomorrow. I'll have my second night with you and during that hour, I'll tell you the details."

"How . . . how many people are in on this?"

"Not enough." Luke didn't touch her. But his hand was inches from her waist—probably in case Asia walked in. "Many of the Belizean police are working with your father. You probably know that."

"I hate him." Eliza closed her eyes for a few seconds before looking at Luke again. She hadn't known. "Police officers never visit the Palace. That makes sense now."

"Exactly." Luke kept glancing at the door. "But we

have people on our side, too. And we've got FBI operatives on the ground. The raid is happening Thursday night."

Thursday night. The day before she turned twenty. The day before she was supposed to walk out of this place. She stared at him. "I heard a conversation. About Alexa."

"Good." Luke sighed. "We were hoping."

She still hated this. Hated him. But for now she needed to find a way to survive. "What do I have to do?"

"You have to agree to help us." Luke searched her eyes. "No tricks here, Eliza. You'll only get yourself killed sooner. Once your father knows you spent an hour with an undercover agent, you'll be taken out."

Eliza believed him. She didn't like it, but she had the sense that everything this man told her was the truth. Anger burned inside her. Given her options, she had no choice. "I'll help."

For the next ten minutes, Luke told her the plan. How he would scope out the place when he returned tomorrow night. "I need you to prepare the younger girls. Make sure they trust you."

"They do." It was the reason Eliza often hated herself. Because the girls at the Palace trusted her. "What do I tell them?"

"Before the first clients Thursday night, you'll convince the guards to let the girls spend time with you. All of them. Whatever you have to tell your father and his men, just make it happen."

Eliza had done that before. Thinking about it made her feel sick. The times when she had brought the girls into the boardroom or her own room, and talked them into being good girls for the customers. "I . . . I can do that."

"That'll be at seven thirty. At seven thirty-five we'll enter through every door on the property and the guards will be . . . neutralized. I'll work with another agent to get you and the girls out and onto a bus and then to a bluff half a mile down the beach. Once we're there, a helicopter will pick us up."

A helicopter? The plan sounded crazy. How could it ever work? She started to shiver again. "What if . . . what if it doesn't show up?"

"It will." There were no cracks in Luke's confidence. "There won't be time to—"

Eliza heard the sound of the doorknob turning. At the same instant, Luke rolled on top of her, his mouth on hers. Their bodies intertwined. Eliza had never done this before, but his kiss was warm and marked by a passion that took her breath. It lasted only a few seconds while Asia watched.

Then—as if he had only just noticed someone else was in the room, Luke jerked his head up. "Hey, man . . . what's this?" Luke shot Asia an angry look. "You're dishonoring my bride."

The guard stared at the two of them. Jack was still on top of her, moving in a way that would convince the bodyguard. The giant man chuckled. "Your time's almost

up." He leered at them again, and finally stepped back
into the hallway and shut the door.

Instantly Jack was off her, and laying on his side
again. "I'm sorry." His eyes were void of every emotion
but one—frustration. "He had to believe us."

"Yeah. I think he did." She wondered if he could hear
her heartbeat.

If this FBI agent was tempted . . . if he was feeling
anything physical for her, he didn't show it. Instead, he
studied her face. "You're a victim, here. Do you know
that? Just because your father never trafficked you,
doesn't mean you're not a victim. You are."

They were both whispering now. Eliza forced herself
not to think about his kiss. "You told me I was a criminal.
I could serve time."

"You could. But what you did . . . grooming those
girls . . . you had to do that." His eyes saw straight
through her. "We know all about your father. The goal is
to set you free, get you help so you can have a new life."
He paused. "You and all the girls here."

"What if . . ." Angry tears filled Eliza's eyes. She didn't
know how to feel. In this room she had always been
spared interaction with men. But not this one. Not Luke.
"What if I don't want to do this."

"I don't blame you. All you've known is captivity."
For the first time she heard sympathy in Luke's voice.
"But you will help me. That's what you said, right?"

Eliza closed her eyes so the tears wouldn't come. She
was going to get killed. She could already feel the bullet

ripping through her body. Or maybe...just maybe... She dabbed her fingertips beneath her eyes and looked at Luke. "I hate this. But yes. I'll help you."

For the next ten minutes, with the two of them lying beneath the sheets facing each other, Luke told her additional details about the raid. He promised there would be more information tomorrow. "Missions are always evolving." His body was inches from hers, but he spoke to her like they were sitting in a business meeting. "We have to keep the plan fluid until the final hour."

Eliza looked away. What was she feeling? For the first time since she was brought here, she'd kissed a man. A man who treated her with respect. A man nothing like the other men who visited the Palace. She had no choice but to go along with his plan. Never mind about the kiss or how it felt to be in his arms. If this plan worked, Eliza was sure of one thing. Once she was free, she would never lie in bed with a man again.

Not ever.

CHAPTER NINE

Blessed are those who have regard for the weak; the
Lord delivers them in times of trouble.

—Psalm 41:1

The mission was on. Eliza had agreed to help, which
was the only good thing that had happened last night.

Jack brought his coffee out onto the balcony of his
hotel room and looked at the afternoon sky. No clouds
today. Just a vast endless blue. He took a sip and shook
his head. He had expected Eliza's bodyguard might burst
in midhour. Agent's intuition, he called it. That knowing
sense.

There were lines an agent wouldn't cross when it
came to breaking up a trafficking ring. Jack wouldn't let
a woman touch him inappropriately, and he wouldn't
make a physical advance on her. Not unless his or her life
was in danger. And even in that case, the instructions
were to keep things platonic.

As much and as long as possible.

If Jack hadn't kissed her, he'd be dead. That much
was certain. Jack was tall, but the guard had a few inches

on him, easy. Between the man's size and his assault rifle, Jack wouldn't have had a chance. Still he hated what he'd had to do.

And tonight would be Round Two. Earlier Jack had stopped by the Palace to speak with Anders. No need to take part in "showtime" as the sick man called it. Jack told him he wanted to see Eliza again. Same time. Basically, Eliza had passed the first test. The big bodyguard stared at him throughout his brief visit, but Anders seemed pleased.

"I'll have to call your father one of these days." Anders gave Jack a pat on the back. "Tell him we've been pleased to host you here at the Palace."

If he ever got out of agent work, Jack figured he could be an actor. He didn't blink or act out of sorts at all. He simply allowed an easy laugh. "Tell him he owes me a golf game."

"Yes." Anders winked at him. "Your old man can play a mean game of golf. I remember that."

Somehow Jack had gotten out of there and back to his hotel without having anyone trail him or shoot at him or run him off the road. The other operatives were all on high alert, and each of them knew about the guard bursting into Eliza's room last night.

His phone lit up and Jack recognized the number. Oliver Layton. This was the conversation Jack was waiting for. "What's the word?"

Oliver was expert at collecting recon and condensing

it into the most action-based response. "Elisa's guard last night was probably Asia. He's one of Anders's favorites, and he's suspicious of everyone."

His boss went on to explain that one of the police officers who used to work for Anders had turned over evidence. The man was now working with Police Chief Averes. "Our informant says that every few months Asia drops in during the girls' sessions. Usually when Anders has a doubt."

"That's what I thought." Jake leaned over his knees and looked out across the ocean.

"Apparently you convinced him." Oliver sounded wary. "You kissed the girl?"

"I did. For a few seconds, yes, sir." Jack wanted to be up front. "I had no choice."

"I know." Oliver exhaled. "That's why we put you on the job. Your actions are always above reproach."

"Thank you, sir." Jack wished he felt that way about the choice he had to make. "So . . . are we good for tonight?"

"Yes." Oliver sighed. "Turns out Henry the Third left a journal. Apparently his first visit to the Palace was with Alexa. Eliza's friend."

Jack felt like someone had kicked him in the gut. Poor Alexa, whoever she was, wherever she had been taken from. Her life had been a nightmare. And no wonder Eliza was angry. As the kept princess of the Palace, she had watched the girls suffer through their daily existence. Year after year. Of course Eliza hated men, and she would hate Jack, too. He ran his fingers through his hair. "Terrible."

"It is." Oliver paused. "One of our informants heard Anders talking about having a full house last night. He was at the Blue Breeze during work hours."

McMillan was vile. Jack stood and walked to the balcony railing. Of course the man would hide at the yacht club through the night. In case of a raid. Such a coward. Thursday night couldn't come fast enough. He would gladly shoot Anders in the face if it came to that.

Gladly.

"We have to talk about Anders." Oliver was all business. "If he's at the Blue Breeze Thursday night, we need a way to take him in. I'd prefer we don't do a concurrent raid on the yacht club, obviously."

"I agree." Jack could imagine a hundred ways that could go wrong. They needed to focus their efforts.

Oliver explained his idea. The police chief would close the Blue Breeze for a twenty-four-hour period for a health inspection. Those were required across the beach, and inspectors were permitted to make unplanned visits if they received a complaint.

"I like it." The phone call ended and Jack finished his coffee. Missions like this required him to keep up his workout routine. He was in the field too often to rely on a gym, so he spent the next hour using his body weight to work his biceps, traps, chest, core and quads.

He needed to head to the beach and swim again. If he didn't get his cardio in he couldn't think straight. A superior of his once taught him that a special agent was part man, part machine. And the machine needed to work every day to be strong enough for the field.

Jack had time, so after his workout and before driving to the beach, he sat on his balcony again. *Shane, we were just here. Feels like a week ago.* His brother was in heaven, Jack was sure about that. The kid loved the Lord. They both had back then, they were even baptized on the same day. Jack imagined Shane playing football in some blue field in paradise. He smiled. But then he had to admit something else. If heaven was real, God was real, too.

Because if God wasn't real, what did that say about heaven?

Jack couldn't let his mind go there. For now, he would ask for help again. He needed it. *If You're there, You know the situation I'm in. What I'm up against tonight. I won't ask You to protect me. But could You please protect those girls?*

Eliza especially. Jack was still angry with himself for what he had done when Asia opened the bedroom door. Not that he'd kissed her. He'd had no choice in that matter. But something else, something he'd wrestled with and berated himself for since he left the Palace last night.

The fact that he had enjoyed it.

. . .

JACK HAD BEEN in Eliza's room for two minutes, and already they were under the sheets again, barely dressed, inches from each other. Everything about the situation felt uncomfortable to Jack, but he had no choice. This was the only way he could explain the ever-evolving mission details to her without risking being found out.

"Okay . . ." Jack looked into her angry blue eyes. "Do you remember everything I told you last night?"

"Sure." Now that she didn't have to marry him, didn't have to please him, Eliza was angry. "You taking off your pants again, FBI man? I mean . . . you bought me. Or is that not part of the job?"

Jack understood her rage. It was a cover-up for her fear. She had lost control of her life long ago. If Jack was going to force himself on her, she was ready. What choice did she have? If that was part of the business deal she wouldn't fight. She was too afraid of her father and maybe too afraid of Jack, too.

The only way to speak into Eliza's victimized heart was to tell her the truth. As many times as he needed to tell it. "Eliza." He searched her eyes. "Pretending I want to marry you was an act. I told you that."

"I don't believe you." She looked so young, so afraid. "When you . . . kissed me." She raised her brow. "I think you liked it."

She was right about the kiss, and Jack hated the fact. He gritted his teeth and moved a bit further from her. *Fine.* If she was going to make this difficult he was up to the challenge. She was a teenager, a prisoner. Agent or not, he had no interest in anything but rescuing her.

"Eliza." He heard the conviction in his voice. "I'm not here for that."

"All men are here for that."

"Not all men." His mind was focused tonight. Nothing but the mission. He exhaled. "I'm an undercover FBI agent, Eliza. My name is Luke. I had to kiss you because we are raiding this place Thursday night. . . . I kissed you to save your life . . . and the lives of every girl here."

"You really mean it?"

Something changed in her eyes. *Finally*, he told himself. Maybe he was getting through to her. "You are worth more than this, Eliza."

"Don't say my name." She rolled onto her back and stared at the ceiling. "Don't tell me what I'm worth when you don't even know me."

"You're a child. Every child is worth more than they know."

That seemed to give her something to think about, as if maybe for the first time it occurred to her that Jack was right. She blinked a few times. "I'm nineteen. I'm not a child."

"Yes, you are." Jack studied her. *Poor girl. What sort of monster would keep his own daughter locked in a place like this? All while making her wait for a forced marriage?* Jack was careful with his words. "You were eight when your father kidnapped you. You haven't lived a normal day since then. You grew up watching your only friends be trafficked night after night. Nine years old." He paused. "Until you get help, you'll always be that little girl."

"The men never touched me." She didn't look at him. "I had it better than the other girls."

"That's not true." Jack studied her defiant face. "Not every victim of sex slavery is violated physically. Your mental abuse is as much a crime."

Eliza seemed to resonate with that last part. Or maybe she was tired of fighting him, tired of trying to make sense of him. Whatever the reason, she rolled onto her side and faced him again. "Tell me once more. What I need to know."

And Jack did.

Eliza's part of the plan had changed only slightly. The raid was going down at seven forty-five now. "You need to get all the girls to a single first-floor room by seven thirty." He searched her eyes. He needed her to pay attention. "Fifteen minutes early. Do you understand?"

"Yes." She clearly loathed him. For being a man, for giving her no choice but to work with him. For putting her life at risk. But here and now, she had to be on his side.

"The boardroom." Eliza's voice fell flat. "That's where the older girls coach the younger ones. I'll call for the session." Her eyes looked dead. "Anders loves when we teach the children."

Jack's stomach turned. He asked Eliza to explain in detail where the boardroom was located. Eliza didn't hesitate. This prison had been her home for far too long. "My job is to coach the girls on *kindness*." She practically spit the word.

The irony was sickening. Jack studied her eyes, in case she was lying about the details. "Okay, then." *Stick to the facts, Ryder.* "You're sure? Back of the house, first floor?"

"Yes!" She didn't answer at first. "Yes, *Luke.* I'm sure."

"Good." He ignored her attitude. "Once the girls are in the boardroom, slip a wedge under the door and open the window. I'll put the wedge in your top drawer when I leave tonight."

She was listening.

"Tell the girls to be very quiet because your friend is coming, and he's going to take them on an adventure." This had worked in other trafficking stings, and Jack believed it would work here. "Make it fun for them. If the older girls are unsure, give them a wink or a smile. So they want to go along for the younger girls. So nothing spoils their fun."

Doubt crept into Eliza's eyes. "What if they don't believe me?"

"They will." Jack hesitated. "I'll arrive at that exact minute. I'll help you."

Jack would be sure the girls made it out the window, across the yard, down the stairs and into a waiting school bus—which would be driven by Agent Terri.

"Who's Terri?" More uncertainty showed in Eliza's expression.

"She works with me. You'll like her." Jack checked the time on Eliza's nightstand. He had twenty more minutes. "Terri is kind and she'll keep you all safe."

"What do I do then, once we're in the bus?" Venom flared in Eliza's eyes. "How do I know you're an *under-*

cover agent? You're probably another evil ruler like my father, taking us to a new house. New customers. Instead of joining families, you're taking all of us and making your own business."

"No." Only time would help Eliza understand. "I'm not like that. And I'm not making this up."

Eliza closed her eyes for nearly a minute, as if she didn't want Jack to see her afraid for even that long. When she opened them, the anger was still there. Same with her fear. But once again she'd made up her mind to help him. This time, no turning back. Jack could tell.

"Okay. I'll do it." She spit the words. "But I don't trust you, *Luke.* I'll only do it because I hate my father. And because if I don't go along with his plans, he'll kill me anyway." She softened just a bit. "The way he killed Alexa."

"Yes." Jack ached for the girl. "You're right."

He had one more order of business. He explained that he wouldn't be by tomorrow—Wednesday night. But he would arrange with her father to see her again on Thursday. The night of the raid. That way it wouldn't surprise Anders's men when Jack pulled up in his Porsche at seven forty-four.

"I have just one way to communicate with you." Jack explained that he would be at the beach both Wednesday and Thursday around noon—the same time she would be there. "If I wear a navy swimsuit, the plan remains the same." He took his time. This part was crucial. "If something changes, I'll wear a yellow suit. I'll approach you like yesterday afternoon and I'll tell you what you need to know."

"What about the guards? They'll be watching."

"We're supposed to be getting married at the end of the week. They won't suspect anything."

"True. I get it." She looked away. "Navy suit, the plan's on. Yellow suit, something's changed."

"Exactly." Relief flooded Jack's veins. "Now tell me where the exits to this place are. Be specific. Which doors have guards, and how many guards. Everything you know."

She did as he asked and when his time with her was almost over, he dressed, messed up the sheets and blankets and tossed two pillows on the floor. Then he made eye contact with her once more. "Thursday night. Girls in the boardroom at seven thirty. Door stopped, window open. I'll see you minutes after that."

Again she said nothing. But this time she nodded.

And that was all the assurance Jack needed.

• • •

A BREEZE OFF the Caribbean washed over Eliza as she set up her chair the next day. She was reading C. S. Lewis's *The Lion, the Witch and the Wardrobe*, trying to decide whether the children should run for their lives, or if Aslan, the lion, really was good.

The way she was trying to decide about Luke.

She was immersed in Aslan's world, midway through Chapter Eight, when Luke strolled onto the beach. If he was a secret agent, then he must've studied the way rich boys strut the shoreline. But what if he really was just another Anders McMillan? With the girls he would take in tomorrow night's raid, he could triple his business. Trafficking the Palace girls on some other beach.

If he was actually in the business and not an FBI agent.

Eliza refused to think about the possibility. She couldn't fixate on her doubts. Luke was her only way out, whether she liked it or not. And since he hadn't taken her knife, she would have that. She wouldn't dream of running away from the Palace without some way to protect herself and the girls.

None of whom had any idea what was about to go down.

This morning at breakfast, Eliza had been tempted to pull Rosa aside and tell her everything. Rosa was fifteen, and she looked up to Eliza. Even though Eliza had helped the girl accept her place at the Palace.

A chill ran down her spine all the way to her legs. A chill the hot summer sunshine couldn't touch. Because if not for tomorrow's raid, in a few months two other girls would turn twenty. The younger girls would think the two were off to Europe. Or gone to find help for the girls still held captive.

Instead they would be dead like Alexa.

Eliza kept her gaze straight ahead, the open book still on her lap. In her peripheral vision she could see Luke walking closer. She turned and looked at him, but only for a few seconds. Then she rolled her eyes and lifted the book closer to her face. So she wouldn't have to talk to him. Or so the guards would think that. Marriage or not, they couldn't seem too friendly. Everyone at the Palace knew Eliza didn't want to be forced into the arrangement.

She tried to focus on the words of the story. Mr. Beaver was explaining that the White Witch was behind Mr. Tumnus's kidnapping, the way the witch was behind all kidnappings. And Mr. Beaver was telling the children about Aslan, the great King, the lion, and how he was the true royalty of Narnia. The White Witch was only counterfeit royalty.

She was imagining her father as the White Witch. And she was trying to absorb a thought that had lodged in her soul and stayed there. When the children wanted to know if Aslan the lion was safe, if he was tame, Mr. Beaver told them something Eliza could only hope was true of Luke.

He isn't safe, children. But he is good.

But even with the book to distract her, all Eliza could think about then or the next afternoon when she was reading on the beach and Luke returned, was the single most important thing that mattered. Perhaps in all her life.

Both times, Luke's bathing suit was navy blue.

CHAPTER TEN

The house of the wicked will be destroyed, but the tent of the upright will flourish.

—Proverbs 14:11

Anders's doubts about Henry Thomas Ellington IV had eased. Clearly, the young man had come to the beach to claim his bride and to seal their deal with a marriage that would last forever. The way their crime conglomerate would last forever.

Every day since he'd flown into Belize, Henry Thomas had visited the Blue Breeze and the beach just below the Palace. Even still, the guards had been instructed to keep careful watch on him. "He will have spent two nights with Eliza by the end of the week," Anders had told them. "I want to know if you see any real connection between the two."

And the guards had done their job. According to their report, Henry Thomas showed up at the beach yesterday, like usual, and as he walked to his favorite spot, north of the Palace steps, he took a long look at Eliza. As any man would do. But Eliza had only buried her pretty face in a book.

Like she wanted nothing to do with him. Which was exactly what Anders would've expected. Nothing unusual.

The other report had come from Asia, the first night Henry was in town. Unannounced, Asia had pushed the bedroom door open while Eliza was celebrating her "honeymoon." And what the burly guard saw was proof enough. Henry was happy with his wife. He would pay up and sign the deal.

Anders's long-term plan, the one he'd made more than a decade ago when he sent for his then wife and children, was finally coming to fruition. He had paid the guards to get rid of Susan and Daniel. He didn't need them. But Lizzie . . . Eliza . . . yes, Anders had always known he would make a fortune off her. Not by selling her to the Palace's nightly customers. But by grooming her and prepping her . . . saving her for such a time as this. Of course Eliza didn't like the setup. Which was why Anders didn't expect his daughter to enjoy Henry Thomas.

If there had been a connection, Anders would've been concerned.

Instead, every report back from the guards was good news for Anders. As long as the young millionaire wasn't somehow conniving secretly with Eliza, all was well. Because Anders had one very troubling problem with his daughter. All that reading had made her the most intelligent girl at the Palace. As a father, he was proud of the fact. But now—when he needed her unwavering obedience—her book smarts made him nervous.

A smart girl could work with the police. She could express doubts about what happened when Palace girls turned twenty. And as such she could find a way to bring down Anders's entire multimillion-dollar operation.

Even if that smart girl was his own daughter.

Anders sat on his white leather sofa in his private room on the fourth floor of the Palace. His view was the best in Belize—a thin stretch of white sand and the prettiest ocean water anywhere in the world.

He leaned back and sighed. If only little girls didn't grow up, if only they never left their teens.

But they did, and so he'd figured out a plan from the beginning. He treated the little girls like so many daughters. He bought them pretty dresses and bows for their hair and made them feel like princesses. So long as they did what they were told.

Anders believed the younger girls loved him. Much like a father. When the customers frightened them, the girls had Anders to turn to. He told them the same thing, year after year. "In the nighttime hours, if someone ever hurts you, come to me. I'll take care of them."

And—as children do—the young teen girls believed him.

Also the children looked up to the older girls, who

had no choice but to make the younger ones feel at home. One big happy family, that's how Anders saw it. Until the girls grew up.

When the girls became teenagers, Anders could watch their attitudes change. In the mornings, when he tried to comfort them or ask about their nights, they would turn away at his touch. They didn't look forward to seeing him.

Which was why the awakening was so important.

After the awakening, the teenage girls better knew their place. They would make the younger girls happy, please the customers, and never—not ever—cross Anders McMillan. Otherwise the next awakening would be worse.

The fear he instilled in them from their fourteenth birthdays usually lasted till the girls turned nineteen. Then, somehow, another switch seemed to flip. Fear turned to sarcasm and obedience became arrogance. At that point, the girls clearly hated their existence and were smart enough to plot their escape. Whether they were reading from the house library or not.

So Anders had figured out a way to deal with this, also. As soon as the attitude surfaced, the older teen girls were given an incentive. Work hard, help the younger girls, recruit new children and take good care of the clients. If they did everything right, when they turned twenty they would get an envelope of cash. Ten thousand dollars.

And they could go free.

Anders took a sip of his Tanqueray and tonic. Since his business opened, every one of his girls had been gullible enough to believe him. It hadn't occurred to any of them that Anders would never dream of letting his girls go. Not when they had enough information to send him to prison for life.

Not with his money in their pockets.

Freedom was an illusion for Palace girls. By the time they were twenty, they were beyond miserable. So Anders considered their death a gift, in some ways. The gift of putting them out of their misery.

In the beginning, he had tried holding on to the older girls—after all, they were good at what they did. Like Alexa, they brought top dollar. But the older girls kept trying to run away. He could drug them. But then they didn't work well. So Anders had gotten in the habit of setting the girls free in another way.

Permanently.

He took another sip of his drink. The ocean was particularly beautiful today. Quiet. Serene. Each of his girls had this same view from the Palace. Every day. They were well fed and dressed like royalty. Why would any of them ever want to leave? Anders couldn't understand it.

Beside him on the sofa, a quiet alarm buzzed on his cell phone. Fifteen minutes till showtime. More new men had sailed into the harbor today, a few of them first-timers. Anders smiled. Business was booming.

He shut the alarm off and then stared at the phone.

How was old Henry Thomas Ellington III doing, anyway? It had been far too long since the senior Henry had been to the Palace. Surely his son had told him about his beautiful bride, and that the deal between the families was definitely on. Anders almost would've expected a call or a text from the young man's father. Some sort of connection or celebratory moment.

Anders had time, so without giving the matter another thought, he found Henry the Third in his contacts and tapped the number.

A chat with the man would be good for his soul. Henry and Anders. Just a couple of like-minded businessmen whose collective business was about to multiply threefold. At least. The phone rang. Then it rang again. Another time, and another. Henry didn't always pick up right away.

But as the phone rang and rang, a strange feeling began to work its way through Anders's gut. In the recent past—when this deal was being worked out—Henry's voice mail would pick up. But by the seventh ring, Anders knew something was wrong. Henry wouldn't change his cell number.

Anders set his drink down. In a few clicks he was calling Henry's law firm. After a few seconds, a serious-sounding woman answered. "Ellington, Benson, and Farmer, how can I help you?"

He exhaled. *Everything was fine.* Henry must've just been out of service or lost his phone. Anders cleared his throat. "Henry Ellington the Third, please."

On the other end, the woman went silent. Anders

counted the seconds, and it wasn't until five had passed that she spoke. "I'm sorry . . . who is this?"

Anders thought fast. "Mark Lewis from Rhode Island. A friend of Henry's. He didn't answer his cell phone."

"Oh." The woman paused again. "I'm sorry, Mr. Lewis. I hate to have to tell you this. Mr. Ellington passed away two days ago."

The floor felt like it was falling away, like the room might cave in on top of him. "Oh, my." Anders had no choice but to recover. "That *is* terrible news. I should've reached out sooner."

"Yes. I'm so sorry."

Anders's mind raced. "What about Henry's son. Henry, the Fourth. I assume he'll be taking over for his father."

"Uh . . ." The woman sounded uncomfortable. "No, sir. Young Henry . . . he doesn't work here."

"I always thought he would follow in his father's footsteps. Like father . . . like son."

"No. I'm afraid not." Another pause. "Did you want to leave a message for one of the partners? In lieu of flowers, donations are being sent to Henry's favorite—"

Anders hung up.

He stood and bumped the table near the sofa, sending his drink crashing to the wood floor. The glass broke and Anders stared at the mess. Then slowly he lifted his eyes to the water. If Henry Thomas Ellington IV hadn't taken over his father's firm, then the two must've had a falling-out. In which case the son would've been cut off from his wealthy father. He certainly wouldn't be here, traipsing around Belize City, chumming it up at the Blue Breeze and about to marry Anders's only daughter.

His hands clenched and he narrowed his eyes. What had he just stumbled onto?

The young man was coming back tonight to see Eliza. But *Henry Thomas* would have a surprise waiting when he got here. Anders imagined the look on the man's handsome face when he realized later tonight that he'd been caught. The guards would have fun with him and then dump his body in the river.

With weights around it.

"Helen!" Anders yelled. Almost immediately one of the housemaids appeared at the door. Anders waved his hand at the mess on the floor. He wasn't in the mood for pleasantries. "Clean it up. Hurry."

Anders retreated to his private balcony. *Calm*, he told himself. *Breathe*. He had found out the truth before it was too late. Wherever the man had come from and whatever business he had here in Belize, he was about to learn a very important lesson.

Don't lie to Anders McMillan.

• • •

JACK COULDN'T SEE it, but the ship was there.

Five miles off the coast of Belize, the USS *Tripoli*, an amphibious assault vessel that had been quietly patrolling the Caribbean Sea, was now ready for action. The *Tripoli* could house up to a thousand sailors, depending on the mission. But it specialized in Army helicopter support, mainly for busting up significant drug cartels and international sex-trafficking rings.

Like the one Anders McMillan was running.

Afternoon sunshine streamed across the Belizean shoreline as Jack took his spot on his balcony. Just another day in paradise as far as Anders and his men would be concerned. They didn't expect anything. Jack felt sure of it. From his hotel balcony, he saw nothing out of the ordinary. Same way Anders's men wouldn't.

The raid was in three hours.

Like before every mission, Jack would take the day to think through the details, seeing the events play out in his mind until they were so clear he wasn't only going through the motions. He was living them.

Sunset tonight was at six thirty-one, and an hour after that the sky would be dark. Raids often took place on the darkest nights, and this would be no exception. Tomorrow was a new moon, so tonight just the faintest sliver of light would hang in the sky.

The USS *Tripoli* would begin their part of the mission at seven forty sharp. That's when a pilot and two gunners from the Army's 160th Special Operations Aviation Regiment would lift off in a Black Hawk helicopter and fly it to the spot just over the rooftop of the Palace. The 160th regiment was a famous group, also known as the Night Stalkers.

Some people thought the Night Stalkers team was a thing of fiction, showing up only in action movies. That wasn't true. These were the Army's most elite pilots, able to fly under the cover of night and carry out some of the military's most dangerous missions. The purpose of the Night Stalkers was to serve the nation's elite military units—even if it cost them their lives. One of the division's most famous raids was against Osama bin Laden. The regiment's motto was simply: Night Stalkers Don't Quit.

And they didn't.

Jack felt good about their participation in tonight's operation. Eight Navy SEALs would rappel from the Black Hawk to the roof of the building. Until given an all-clear signal, the Night Stalkers would remain hovering overhead with the two gunners ready to add support from the air. Just in case.

Eliza had told Jack what to expect at each of the doors on every floor. In addition, one of the agents on the ground had verified a few of the entries. Eliza still hated Jack, but she was telling the truth. She probably figured no point getting them all killed tonight. The raid was going down with or without her help, and she knew it.

Wrong information would only harm all of them.

A breeze blew over the balcony and settled Jack's soul. Over the last few days, every bit of intelligence had been passed on to Oliver, and the information disseminated to the Army and Navy. The plan tonight had been analyzed from every angle. And the risks were substantial.

Guards at each of the doors were armed with auto-

matic weapons. The second they heard a helicopter overhead or someone crashing through a door, bullets would
fly. Each of the SEALs would be wearing helmet and
body armor, along with night-vision goggles. They would
be packing the very best M4 rifles, .45 handguns, six-
inch Daniel Winkler fixed blades, M79 grenade launch-
ers and M67 grenades. And their weapons would be
fitted with the best silencers on the market.

They would also have bolt cutters, tourniquets, various tools, and breaching devices—small flat boxes they
could quickly fix to a door and ignite to gain entry into
just about any room. In case the girls got separated and
had to be rescued individually.

Each SEAL would also carry a camera—to collect
every bit of evidence along the way. This was a multi-
dimensional raid. First and most important it was a rescue. But beyond that tonight they would capture and
arrest Anders McMillan and every one of his men. Captured alive was the goal, but if they met with resistance,
it was a takedown. Period. The mission was justified in
every sense of the word.

Jack only wished they'd had enough evidence to do
this sooner.

Anders would be brought back to the States, where
he would face enough charges to put him away for a
couple hundred years. And while the Army, Navy and
FBI pulled off the raid at the Palace, a Belizean police
contingency led by Chief Manny Averes would appre-
hend Betsy Norman, an American expat who helped kid-

nap girls and bring them to the Palace. For much of
Eliza's life, Betsy had been assigned to her. Making sure
she got her sun and that no man ever took advantage of
her. Not until her father said so. From what surveillance
suggested, the FBI had enough evidence to lock the
woman away for good.

Jack wondered how many Betsy Normans there were
in the world. Evil people willing to traffic girls—all to
make a paycheck. He angled his face toward the sky. So
many details, and each of them would have to work perfectly for the mission to succeed. In order for all of them
to return home alive. He wished he could call Shane . . .
or his parents. Someone who cared whether he made it
back tonight.

But there was no one to call, and anyway, all Jack
cared about was the rescue.

Eliza had told him most of the girls were U.S. citi-
zens. She wasn't sure about herself. "I tried to block out
everything from my childhood," she had told him.
Whether that was true or not, Jack couldn't tell. He
didn't blame Eliza for not wanting to talk about her life.
Anything she said could get her killed—at least until
after the mission.

Once they rescued the girls they would take them
back to Texas. Agents in San Antonio would match them
with girls on various missing children databases. If all
went well, tonight the girls would sleep at a safe shelter
outside the city.

And in a few days some of them could even be home.

The rest would be in the custody of the social services system, which would work to find their families or next of kin. The few Canadian children would be flown back to their country in the next week or so. Others, with no families, would be placed in foster care.

None of them would ever have to work another night in their lives.

Jack stood and sauntered to the railing. Adrenaline already flowed through his veins. On the day of a raid, the waiting was the hardest part. He went over the plan again. While six of the SEALs secured the building, apprehending the guards at every entrance, two more would break into the fourth floor. Anders's private quarters. Those SEALs would kick through the windows and, they hoped, catch him by surprise. Then, like his men, he would be arrested or neutralized.

If the mission went according to plan, that part would take about five minutes.

At that time, once the guards were no longer a threat, a signal would be given alerting Jack that he and Agent Terri could approach the boardroom at the back of the house and rescue the girls. She wasn't the driver of the bus any longer. That was TJ. Terri would be with the girls. Oliver thought the young ones might trust a female agent, and Jack agreed.

TJ would drive the bus to a nearby bluff, while the SEALs would continue to sweep the rest of the Palace and take Anders and his apprehended men to the Palace's grassy yard.

Seconds after the bus pulled up at the bluff, an Army Chinook helicopter, manned by another four Night Stalkers, would land and the girls and agents would be helped inside. The Chinook would fly to Placencia Peninsula, forty minutes south. From there a private plane waiting at the Placencia Maya Airstrip would take the group to the San Antonio airport, and on to the FBI building.

So many details. Jack took a deep breath. He could see the raid, hear it. Feel it.

The sun reflected off the water and splashed diamonds across the clear blue sea. By tonight he'd be back in his own bed. And Anders and his men and Betsy Norman would be on a second Black Hawk helicopter headed for federal prison.

CHAPTER ELEVEN

Though the mountains be shaken and the hills be removed, yet my unfailing love for you will not be shaken.

—Isaiah 54:10

The raid was about to go down.

Eliza had gathered the girls and brought them to the boardroom. Two guards stood watch just outside the double doors. Inside, she was holding court the way she had far too many times. Tonight's lesson was on kindness. Of all things.

"Be kind to the customers, and they'll be kind to you," Eliza said. She detested herself for moments like this, times when she had coaxed the girls to stay submissive, to listen to her father and make him happy.

At least this is the last time I have to do this, she told herself.

Rosa raised her hand and shrugged. "That doesn't always work, Eliza. Last night . . ."

The sweet girl launched into a story, but Eliza couldn't listen, couldn't stomach the details. She had to focus on the mission. They had eight minutes. Suddenly Eliza remembered. She didn't have her knife. Whatever was coming, she had no way to defend herself.

Images flashed in her mind. *The Lion, the Witch and the Wardrobe.* Today on the beach she had finished Chapter Thirteen, the part where Edmund was about to be killed by the Witch, but Aslan rescued him. Only then did the Witch bring up an irrefutable point. Edmund had been a traitor and he deserved death.

Eliza blinked. Wasn't that her? The Edmund of the story? Acting as traitor to every single girl in the room?

Rosa's sad tale was winding down.

Six minutes. Eliza walked to the room's entrance and pretended to pick up something from the floor. Instead she slid the wedge under the door. The whole time she kept talking. "Kindness puts people at ease. And when people are at ease . . ."

She crossed the room and opened the window. "It's warm in here. We need some air."

"Eliza." Across the room she saw Rosa furrow her brow. "We aren't supposed to open the windows."

"I know." Eliza tried to remember what Jack told her. *Give them a wink or a smile. So they want to go along.* Already the girls were dressed for the evening, in every sort of silk nightgown and sheer robe. They wore heavy eye makeup and lipstick and hairstyles far too sophisticated for their ages. Together they looked like little lambs headed for the slaughter.

Not tonight, Eliza steadied herself. *Not ever again.*

Finally she was doing something good for the girls. Even if it killed her. In minutes they would leave this place and the girls would never serve another customer again. *Hurry, Luke. Hurry.*

A clock hung on the wall. *Good thing*, she thought. Because otherwise, Eliza wouldn't have known how much time she had.

In the distance she heard a loud rhythmic whirring. *Four minutes.* They would be the longest four minutes in Eliza's life. What was this feeling? Until Jack, Eliza had never felt fear. Sadness, disgust . . . anxiety over the plans her father had for her. But never fear. Not like this.

Suddenly there came the sound of breaking glass and men yelling, one floor up, maybe two.

The girls all looked to her, their eyes wide. "Eliza . . . what's happening?" one of the youngest teens cried out. "I'm scared."

"I'm not sure." Eliza swallowed hard. It was the last time she would lie to the girls. "But whatever it is . . . I'll keep you safe. I promise."

Two minutes. There were muffled explosions and popping sounds from upstairs. Eliza clapped her hands. "Tell you what, let's take an adventure into the yard!"

Terror flickered in Rosa's eyes. "No, Eliza." She took a few steps back. "We can never . . . ever go outside without Anders or the guards. You know that."

Sixty seconds. Eliza forced a laugh. "We'll tell the guards later! They won't care—just this once. I'll tell my father it was my idea!"

The noise on the floors above them went quiet. And then Luke and a woman appeared at the window. This time Luke wasn't dressed like one of the men from the Blue Breeze. He was in dark jeans and a dark blue polo shirt and he had a gun in his hand.

He was breathtaking. The most handsome man Eliza had ever seen.

But Luke didn't make eye contact with her. He acted like he'd never met her and in a single heartbeat the room was in chaos. Luke and Terri pushed the window open wider and turned to the girls. "Come on." Luke smiled at the girls the way an older brother might do. "We need to go. Now."

Eliza felt sick and elated all at once. It was happening. They were really getting out of here, but they had only seconds. That's what Luke had told her. Seconds or something awful might happen.

One of the younger girls started to scream and Eliza rushed to her. "Don't!" She used her most urgent voice. "I said I'd keep you safe. These are good people." Eliza couldn't breathe, couldn't exhale. "This is Luke and Terri. They're getting us out of here." Eliza shot a look to Rosa. "Help me. Please. We don't have much time."

Rosa and the other teens seemed to suddenly understand the desperate stakes. As if they'd practiced for this moment a dozen times, they immediately began working with Eliza and Luke and Terri to help the girls one at a time out the window and into the yard.

Next Terri climbed out to be with the younger ones

and finally it was just Luke and Eliza. She was almost out the window when she saw the door fly open. It was her father standing in the doorway, his face a twist of rage and hatred. Before Eliza could duck or scream, he aimed a rifle at her head.

This is it, she thought. But at the same time, Luke threw himself in front of the window, in front of Eliza, like a human shield, and as her father's bullet hit him, Luke fired back.

In an instant, her father was on the ground, blood spilling out around him.

Eliza only stared, her body shaking. She was alive. What had just happened? Luke grabbed her father's gun and ran back to the window. His shoulder was bleeding, but Eliza was watching her father, waiting for him to say something. Her father always had the last word. But not this time. The man who had terrorized her and held her captive since she was nine years old didn't get up.

Didn't move.

"Come on." Luke climbed out the window and started to hurry across the grass. As if he wasn't in pain and he hadn't just been shot by her father. He looked back at her. "Keep up, Eliza."

She ran as fast as she could. She had no choice. As they reached the stairs, gunfire came from the side of the house and bullets whizzed near them. She was going to die, they both were. But then different bullets rained down from the helicopter still overhead and someone on the ground cried out. After that the shooting stopped.

"Go, Eliza!" Luke ran behind her as she took the stairs.

She saw the children ahead of her, trying to run in their terrible gowns. *Get in the bus,* she silently screamed at them. *God, get us to the bus.* And then finally in a blur they were all on board. Luke took the seat next to the driver and as the vehicle started to move, Eliza stood and counted.

Sixteen girls. They had all made it out alive.

Eliza shook as she sat down. What about Luke? Blood was soaking his dark blue shirt. Was he badly hurt? Eliza couldn't worry about him. She looked out the window as the white wooden porch of the Palace disappeared from sight.

Her father was dead.

The gunfight had taken only seconds, but now here they were and her father wasn't going to hurt any girl, ever again. The bus drove onto a skinny road and then onto a grassy cliff, where it parked close to the edge. And suddenly something occurred to Eliza.

Since she was first brought here, this was the only time she'd been off the Palace property without a gun at her back. She stood and motioned to the girls. "Come on." The young teens hurried from their seats, scrambling down the aisle.

Rosa put her hand on Eliza's shoulder as she rushed past. "Thank you."

Eliza nodded. They were the best words she'd heard in eleven years.

Even before she stepped out of the bus, a helicopter was landing, the largest one Eliza had ever seen. Two men in helmets and full military gear jumped out and began lifting the girls inside. Then one of the soldiers saw Luke and he shouted to someone in the aircraft. "Help! He needs a medic!"

A different soldier from inside the helicopter helped Luke up and moved him toward the back. At the same time, Agent Terri and the others on Luke's team helped the girls into two rows of seats facing each other.

Eliza sat three spots from the rear, where a man was working on Luke's shoulder. Four of the girls were quietly crying, but most of them just looked shocked. *Poor girls,* Eliza thought. She'd never seen them cry. Crying wasn't allowed at the Palace.

The sound of the helicopter filled the air. One door was still open, but the men in uniform sat at the edge, their feet dangling out, guns aimed at the ground. Like they were ready to fight anyone who tried to hurt them.

Eliza closed her eyes. Her head was spinning, trying to get her mind around so many details. Her life at the Palace was over. Her father was dead. And she was overcome by the fear that had been her constant companion since she met Luke.

Heart-stopping, unbridled fear.

In all her years at the Palace, when darkness fell and Eliza was alone, when she knew what was happening to her friends down the hall, Eliza had never felt afraid. Sick and angry, yes. But she knew how to handle that, too. She would simply close her eyes. And in a single moment she would not be alone in her princess bedroom.

She would be in Lower Barton Creek with her mother and brother, Daniel. The sun would be shining through the dense jungle palms and she and Daniel would be playing with the other children. And Mama's voice would sing across the open fields, the way it had called to her every afternoon when she was little. "Lizzie James, dinner! Bring your brother!"

"Yes, Mama!" And Lizzie would look at her mother standing in the distance, long brown hair blowing over her shoulders, those light blue eyes like Lizzie's. And she would grab hold of Daniel's hand. "Let's go! Chicken pie for dinner. Your favorite."

Or was it rice pudding?

The memory had faded and changed over time, like someone had taken an eraser to the lines. But when she put herself there, back in one of those beautiful Lower Barton days, Eliza could forget what was happening all around her. What the other girls were going through.

Eliza wasn't afraid, because if one of the guards killed her, she would go to be with Mama and Daniel. Even now she could hear her mother.

Of all God's gifts, her mama was saying, *you two are my favorites.*

But she couldn't find those memories now. Not with fear grabbing at her throat and making it hard to breathe. What was going to happen to her? Would they put her in jail for her part? Where would she live?

Eliza opened her eyes and looked at Luke. The man in the uniform was still tending to him, working a roll of heavy gauze under his arm and over his shoulder. "How's the pain?" the man was asking.

"It's fine." Luke shot a quick look at Eliza. First time since he showed up at the window. "It doesn't hurt."

Guilt rose inside her. She had been venomous toward Luke, because she detested him. The way he demanded her participation in the raid . . . and the fact that he had used her for information, the way her father had used her to grow his business. Even so, Luke was different. He didn't look at her and the other girls the way customers at the Palace always looked at them.

Her fear receded some. Whatever happened next, Luke had been honest with her. They were being rescued. She leaned back against the hard cushion, and as she did she became aware of her elaborate long white dress. Her father had insisted she wear white all week. She crossed her arms. What had seemed normal at the Palace was suddenly shameful, grotesque.

How come she hadn't tried to leave sooner? Tried to rescue the girls at the house? So what if the guards had killed her? Heaven held her mother and brother, both of them waiting for her.

The sound of the chopper blades grew louder and it felt like the craft was picking up speed. Were Anders's men following them? Would the evil guards always be there? Just around the corner . . . hiding in the shadows?

"Did you get them all?" The uniformed man was talking to Luke.

Eliza opened her eyes again and watched the two.

"Yes." Luke winced. No matter what he'd said earlier, he must have been in terrible pain. The white bandaging was growing red with his blood. "Seventeen."

Seventeen? Eliza squinted at Luke. Was that how he saw her? Just one of the girls at the Palace? She had been his partner, his confidante. The one who had helped him pull off this mission. She wasn't like the other girls—her father had seen to that. But now . . . now it was like they'd never spoken at all.

She looked down the two rows of girls, all facing each other. None of them were talking, and even those crying had settled down. Their lives hadn't been their own for so long. They had no idea where they were going or what would become of them, so they merely sat there, knee to knee, shoulder to shoulder.

Their faces blank.

Rosa was in the spot across from Eliza. She slid her bare foot over and tapped Eliza's. "Hey."

Eliza looked at her.

"Where are we going?" She talked loud enough to be heard over the helicopter. But not loud enough for anyone else to hear. "How come you didn't tell me about this?"

"I almost did." A sigh slipped through Eliza's lips, but the sound of it was lost in the noise. She stared at Luke. "He wouldn't let me."

Shock made its way across Rosa's expression. "So you worked this out with *him*? And now . . . now what?"

Eliza shook her head. "All I know is we're out of the Palace. We're headed to Texas."

Tears filled Rosa's eyes. "Texas?" She pressed the back of her hand to one eye, then the other. "I'm from Texas. I was . . . in foster care there. Before . . ."

Eliza had heard the other girls talk about foster care. Several had come from that system in the States. But if this was truly a rescue, Eliza hoped more for the girls than a return to the same lifestyle. Who would help them and where would they spend tonight and tomorrow?

Her head felt heavy. Too many questions.

Eventually the chopper began lowering to the ground. When it landed, the girls were helped out of the aircraft, across a runway and up a flight of stairs into a waiting airplane. Again Luke made sure each of them boarded safely. And again he didn't look at her. "Hurry," he told them. "Watch your step, but hurry."

Sirens sounded in the distance, and Eliza shuddered. Her father had people all over Belize. Some of his men were bound to be in pursuit.

Eliza entered the plane last. Inside were leather sofas and chairs, more like a living room than what she would've expected. She sat next to a window and looked out. She had never flown before. Not on a helicopter, not in an airplane. But the girls had told her that the men who came to see them sometimes talked about Placencia and Seine Bight and Maya Beach, here on this peninsula.

Belize's beautiful beaches. They told her about the great Belize Barrier Reef and the sixteen miles of sugar white sand that stretched north to south here.

"We'll both go there one day," Rosa had told her a month ago.

"Yes. That would be lovely." Eliza had wanted to hug the girl. She had no idea. "One day."

And it would've been lovely if she could've come here with Rosa. Or by herself . . . with the money her father had promised her. Often, when she was on the small beach in front of the Palace, she wondered what Seine Bight was like. How it would feel to walk for miles and miles in the silky white sand, to look out at the ocean without a gun trained on her back.

One of the youngest girls sat beside her, and ten minutes into the flight to Texas, she started to cry again. Not out loud. Just big tears making their way down her face. Her name was Maggie Mae, and she had soft dark curls and a freckled face. The girl was one of the ones Eliza had helped lure to the Palace.

"Maggie. It's okay." Eliza turned in her seat. "We'll be safe tonight."

"I . . . I was safe at the Palace." The child's tears came harder. "I want to go back."

Eliza gritted her teeth. Of all the diabolical ways her father and his men had treated the girls, brainwashing was one of the worst. She could hear the things he said to the girls before their fourteenth birthdays. *You'll be safe as long as you're here. No one will take care of you like*

I will. Don't ever leave, little ones. The world outside our gates is very, very dangerous.

"Maggie." Eliza looked into the child's eyes. "Honey, you don't want to go back."

Behind her she heard the voice of one of the soldiers. "We need to get you to a hospital once we land."

Eliza looked to the rear of the plane. Luke's arm was propped up on a pillow now, his eyes closed.

"You'll probably need some blood, Jack. The wrap's slowing it, but you're still bleeding."

"*Jack?*" Eliza whispered. She blinked a few times. *Jack!* So he had lied to her about his name. Again. Her anger toward him built once more. Of course he hadn't been completely honest with her. He was a man, and all men lied. They lied and they used girls.

Even *Jack.*

Eliza turned her attention back to Maggie. "Everything's going to be okay, sweetie." But how could she know that? Men weren't the only ones who lied. How many lies had she told these girls? *I want it to be true,* she thought. *Please let it be true. Let everything be okay.* She pulled the girl close. "No one will ever hurt you again, Maggie."

"Eliza . . . do you really think so?" Maggie sniffed a few times and lifted her blue eyes. "No one's going to hurt us?"

"No one." Eliza nodded. Then she closed her eyes. They had to be okay. Because these children needed a real life once they landed in Texas.

And suddenly Eliza felt a new and strange idea rise within her. Not an idea but an emotion. It felt like anger, but it was more than that. A desire for revenge and justice. She was the reason most of these girls had been at the Palace. Now she was going to do something to make things right. She would work to help these sixteen girls find new lives and she would somehow find her own, too.

Never mind what *Jack* believed. Eliza wasn't a child. She was old enough to make a difference, old enough to help these girls and others trapped in sex trafficking. Because there had to be others, and if she had been wily enough to help lure girls toward slavery, then she would be wise enough to draw them away.

The idea grew and took shape and as they landed in San Antonio, it became a fierce determination. She would become a police officer or . . . what was it Jack did? FBI work? Yes, that's what she would do. She would go undercover and she would spend her life putting people like her father behind bars forever. Rescuing girls like Maggie Mae and Rosa.

Making up for the past with every waking hour.

As long as she lived.

CHAPTER TWELVE

"For I know the plans I have for you," declares the
Lord, *"plans to prosper you and not to harm you,
plans to give you hope and a future."*
—Jeremiah 29:11

J ack spent two days in the hospital. A surgeon removed
Anders's bullet from his shoulder and put him on IV
antibiotics for the infection that had started. The bullet
had missed his major muscles and tendons, so he would
have full use of his shoulder.

Which was the only way he could continue working
as a special agent. Aiming a gun required the use of both
arms.

Now he checked the wound in the bathroom mirror.
The incision was smaller than he'd expected, just a red
and pink indentation to show that he'd ever been back
to Belize, ever encountered Anders McMillan.

Nothing compared to the price he'd paid last time he
visited the country.

Today was his first day back at the office, and Jack
could think of just one person. Eliza Lawrence. The vic-

tim recovery plan for the sixteen minor girls was going better than expected. Oliver had given Jack the update. After they spent a few nights in a safe home, social services had taken over. Four of the girls had already been reunited with their families. Mothers and fathers who had still been hoping their little girls would be found.

Jack smiled. He could only imagine those reunions.

Of course, the state would follow up to make sure the girls got medical assistance and psychological care. Counseling would be part of their lives, maybe forever. The other twelve girls had been placed in foster care—at a new group home. Oliver had apparently met the two sets of parents running the place.

"As bad as life has been for these girls, today they finally got a break." Oliver had sounded emotional. "The house parents are kind people, people of faith. They quit their jobs as counselors, bought a parcel of land and built a massive group home. All so they could help children coming out of trafficking."

The news was more than Jack could've hoped for. Maybe God was listening, after all. According to the commanders in charge of the Night Stalker unit and the Navy SEALs, the mission couldn't have gone better. None of the Night Stalkers or SEALs were injured in the raid.

The outcome wasn't so good for Anders's men. Three of them had died in the battle, along with Anders. *Good riddance*, Jack thought. Another six of the man's guards had been apprehended and brought back to Los Angeles, where more of these cases were heard, and where the guards would be held behind bars without bail until their trial.

Betsy Norman was arrested without incident. She was currently booked on enough charges to lock her up forever.

Jack drew a deep breath. *Can't ask for more than that.*

His arm was still in a sling. So he dressed with his other hand and an hour later he was sitting in Oliver Layton's office, the first time Jack had seen his boss since he returned from Belize.

"I talked to Terri." Oliver leaned back and studied him. "The bullet in your shoulder. You saved our informant's life. Eliza Lawrence."

This was exactly what Jack wanted to talk about. "Where is she?"

"Yes, that. I'm not happy about it." A shadow fell over Oliver's face. "We're struggling."

That's what Jack figured. "Terri told me she was sent to a residential placement center."

"We tried that." Oliver hesitated. "The place was full. She's an adult, so she can't stay with the other girls. The services we have for children don't apply to her."

Frustration filled Jack's veins. "That's wrong, sir." He could picture Eliza's blue eyes. "So what if she's twenty. She might as well be fifteen. She's never known anything but the Palace. We can't just turn her out on the streets."

"I agree." Oliver stood and faced the window behind

his desk. "Since 2000 we've tried to find the exact right way to help victims of trafficking. But our programs are all very specific."

Jack knew only too well. As a victim of trafficking—which she was, even though she was never technically sold—if Eliza wanted citizenship, no problem. If she applied for a small business loan, she'd get preference. But how was she supposed to live in the meantime? Jack clutched the arms of the chair. "Where is she now, sir?"

"She's not a Texas resident, Jack. That excludes her from a number of services. The ones she's eligible for are full." He paused. "And honestly, she'd face the same thing in any state." Oliver turned to Jack again. He paused longer than usual. "She's in a homeless shelter. I gave her food vouchers and a bag of clothes from the Goodwill. I had nothing else, Jack."

"What about hotels?"

"We're out of vouchers. I put a social worker on the case. If one opens up, Eliza will be the first to get it."

Jack was on his feet. "Are you kidding me?" His voice was louder than he intended. He stared at Oliver, then he dropped back to his chair again. Even now he couldn't be rude. None of this was Oliver's fault. But he was seething. "A homeless shelter, sir? Really?"

"I was lucky to get her that." Oliver sorted through a folder on his desk. "There's a facility for domestic violence victims that might have a spot in a month or so."

"What?" Jack couldn't believe this. Eliza was at a homeless shelter, alone in San Antonio? "You said she can't be with the other girls." His mind began to spin. The floor felt unsteady. Eliza would feel tricked for sure. Lying on a mattress on the shelter floor, no doubt surrounded by some of the scariest people in the city? "Let's get an exception."

"That won't work." Oliver shook his head. "The new group home is licensed only for minors. She would be considered a liability to the younger girls."

A liability? Jack was ready to blow up. "Sir, I'm requesting this day to figure out housing for the girl. She helped me. That's the least I can do."

Oliver hesitated, but only for a minute. "Yes." He sighed. "The system is far from perfect, Jack. You know that." He handed over the girl's folder. "If you can find her something, it'll be the best news since the raid."

· · ·

JACK'S FIRST STOP was the group home where the twelve girls were staying. Stan and Melinda Largo met with him in the front room. The two were born in Nigeria and moved to the United States to attend medical school.

They listened while Jack talked about Eliza, how she needed a place to live while she got on her feet, found work and an apartment.

"Please. You have to help her." *God . . . if You're there, please.* "She's at a downtown shelter. She needs you."

Melinda looked like she was about to cry.

Despite the kindness in his brown eyes, her husband

shook his head. "I'd love to help her, Jack. The younger girls talk about her all the time. Especially Rosa."

"I'm thinking, maybe just this once." Jack was ready to beg the couple. "Something temporary. We could get the state to make an exception."

"There are no exceptions, Jack." Stan frowned. "The law is in place to protect children."

Again Jack's mind raced. "What about . . . hiring her? She could be a housekeeper, help do the dishes and laundry. Help the children with their homework. She's extremely bright."

Melinda's eyes lit up. "Does she have a criminal record?"

"No." Charges wouldn't be pressed against Eliza because she had helped the FBI with the raid. It was the first ray of hope. Jack grabbed the possibility. "Eliza's new here, but I can get her fingerprinted and cleared, all her paperwork finished by tomorrow. So you could hire her."

Stan put his arm around his wife. "You might be onto something here." He stood and poured a glass of water. Then he handed it to Jack. "So you're sure? She's safe around the other girls?"

Clearly Stan and Melinda knew the earmarks of a trafficked victim. Sometimes those who were abused went on to abuse others. But that wasn't the case with Eliza. Jack had spent enough time with her to tell. At least he hoped so. "She's safe. We'll have an evaluation done later today."

"Okay, then." Stan nodded. "We will watch her. Just in case."

Now Jack had to find Eliza. Before she took off or gave up. Too often, when the system failed them, trafficked victims wound up returning to slavery. At least that way they would have food and a place to sleep. Because it was the only life they had ever known.

Jack pulled up at the downtown San Antonio shelter just before one o'clock. He tried to walk straight back to the living quarters, but the man at the front desk rose from his seat. "This is a private place, buddy." The man was in his forties, and he looked ready to fight. "You gotta get approved before you walk back."

"FBI." Jack flashed his badge and stopped short. "I'm looking for Eliza Lawrence. She came here about a week ago."

The guy squinted at him. "Let me see that badge."

Time was slipping away. Jack pulled his badge out once more. He raised his voice. "Give me her room number."

"Someone gave her a voucher." The guy crossed his arms. "A hotel voucher."

"Who?" Panic grabbed at Jack. Eliza could be anywhere in the city. "A social worker?"

"Yeah, that's it." The man shrugged, still gruff. "Holiday Inn, I think. Or maybe the Courtyard. One of those. If I remember right."

Jack took off. His heart raced in time with his feet. He drove to the Holiday Inn first, but the young woman at the desk didn't find Eliza's name in her records. "Sometimes people give different names when they use vouchers." She frowned.

He was halfway to the car when he spotted her. She was crossing the street, headed back to the hotel. She wore a baggy pair of jeans and a sweatshirt, despite the sweltering Texas heat.

"Eliza!" He jogged toward her. "Wait!"

She stopped and looked his way. But when she saw it was him, she turned and hurried for the front door.

"Please, Eliza." This time Jack raised his voice. In case she couldn't hear him. "I have to talk to you."

"Why?" She stopped short and glared at him. "So you can lie to me again?"

"I never lied to you." Jack reached her, but he kept his distance. He didn't want her to feel threatened.

"You did." She moved to a patch of grass, away from the door.

Jack followed her. He lowered his voice. "Please . . . Eliza. I told you I was FBI. I told you we were going to raid the Palace, and I said I needed your help."

The anger in her eyes was fire.

"Tell me the lie." Jack tried to be patient.

"You told me you were Luke." Eliza stepped back. "But on the plane . . . on the plane the other agent called you Jack."

He relaxed a little. "That wasn't a lie. It was part of the job. I go by a lot of names."

"And what about *Jack?*" Her anger faded. But in its

place came an ocean of hurt and distrust. "Is that part of the job?"

"No. Jack is my name." Giving her that information couldn't hurt him now. "For real." She clutched her paper bag and tilted her head back. Her eyes caught the sunlight. Prettiest blue eyes Jack had ever seen. "I want to help you."

"Why? The mission's over." She looked at the Holiday Inn sign. "I'm free now. Right, Jack?"

Her sarcasm wasn't lost on him. "Just hear me out. Please."

For a long time Eliza only stared at him. Then without saying a word, she led him through the iron gate to the hotel's outdoor pool, and to a table in the corner of the patio. She took one chair and he sat opposite her.

"Talk, Jack. You have five minutes."

Maybe this wouldn't work. Jack leaned forward on the table and looked straight into her eyes. "We don't want you here at this hotel. Or at some homeless shelter." He exhaled. "You deserve better than that, Eliza."

For a long time she only looked at him. Then she opened the bag and took out three tacos. "Vouchers." She didn't make eye contact. Slowly, meticulously she ate one of the tacos. Then another.

Jack looked out at the pool. Agents around the world risked their lives to break up trafficking rings. But only to treat the victims like this? Three tacos? Was that her dinner? Had she eaten anything else today?

"At least at the Palace they fed us." She was still

chewing. "We had a bed every night of the year." She finally turned her eyes to him. "But I'm rescued now, right, Jack? Except . . . where do I go when I run out of vouchers?"

She was right. Jack laced his fingers together behind his head and stared at her. "The FBI wants to help you. We'll get you your citizenship and identification, some cash. Something to start a new life."

"What if I don't *want* to be a U.S. citizen?" She sounded less harsh. More matter of fact. "My home is in Belize. Doesn't that mean anything to you people?"

"Eliza, your father has men all over Belize. Your life would be in danger every minute, every day."

"I'm used to that." Her words were quick and sharp. "I don't care if I die. Death would be a reward."

He felt the same way, but he couldn't tell her that. She was just twenty. Intelligent, beautiful, and despite her horrific past she had her whole life ahead of her. "You don't want to die. Your life is just beginning."

"You're wrong." For the first time since he'd known her, she didn't sound furious or jaded. She tilted her head to the sky again. "I thought I would arrive here and become a police officer. Work to save girls like the ones at the Palace." She paused. "But who was I kidding? I have no family. Nowhere to go, no way to make a living. No friends." She hesitated. "Yes. Death would be a gift."

The poor girl. He looked down at a spot on the table. "What happened to your mother?"

"I don't feel like talking about it." She sighed. "Do you understand, Jack? Why I'd rather die?"

"Yes." He clenched his jaw. "I feel the same way sometimes."

"You?" Her comeback was quick. "Hotshot secret agent. Gorgeous face and body." She laughed, but it didn't touch her eyes. "You have life by the tail, Jack. Why in the world would *you* feel that way?"

No chance he was telling her his life story now. He remained quiet.

Eventually she looked off. "I almost died. Did you know that?" She didn't wait for him to speak. "I was nine years old and there was a hurricane in the Caribbean. The undertow was the worst I could remember."

Jack winced. So young. "You went to the beach every day even then, when you were little?"

"Yes." Her expression grew stone-cold. "My father insisted. I'd been at the Palace for a year by then. I was only nine years old." She opened her last taco and set it on her napkin. After a few seconds she wrapped it up and tossed it in the paper bag. Her eyes found his again. "That day something grabbed me . . . like a monster. I actually looked down expecting to see an octopus or a sea creature. But it was the current." Her eyes never softened. "My aunt was on the shore, like always back then."

Jack tried to picture the scene.

"I could barely keep my head above water, but for some reason I screamed. And my scream got the attention of my aunt. And a couple of teenage boys on the beach."

A couple of . . . Jack felt the color drain from his face. "That was . . . eleven years ago?"

"Yes." She looked off again. "Two white boys—tourists probably. I had never seen them before, not on my father's beach. I never saw them again. How could they know I didn't want to live, didn't want them to save me? I told myself to let go, fall beneath the surface and sink. But my legs kept kicking, kept fighting."

What? Jack reminded himself to breathe. *It wasn't possible.* She was rescued as a nine-year-old? On the beach in front of the Palace? *Was she the same . . . ?* Jack's heart pounded so loud he was sure she could hear it. Was she . . . was Eliza the child he had rescued from the beach that day? He could see her still, the little girl, panicked, mouth open.

Matted blond hair and . . . and blue eyes.

Jack needed a minute to process this, but he didn't have it. He had to stay with the story, let her talk. He couldn't let on about what he was feeling. All that mattered here and now was gaining her trust.

Clearly, her story wasn't finished. Eliza looked off. "Something happened to one of the boys, because people were working on him . . . there on the sand." She shook her head. "By then I was with my aunt again. She took me back to the Palace. And she beat me for half an hour for straying so far out to sea."

"What?" Anger rose in his heart. "That wasn't your fault."

"My aunt worked for my father. If she let something happen to me he would've killed her." She turned her eyes to him again. "The beating was a warning."

Jack felt dizzy. Of course the woman on the shore that day had been Betsy Norman. That explained why she had seemed angry instead of afraid. Why she never looked at Jack. Never thanked him.

She had only been worried about losing her job.

A sick feeling wrapped itself around Jack's gut. Of all the girls in all the world, how could the one he rescued have been Eliza? He tried to steady his heart, stuff his reaction.

Lost in the story, Eliza didn't notice. She lifted her face to the sky again. "If I had died that day, I would have woken up in heaven. With the rest of my family." She met his eyes again. "Instead I woke up in hell." She turned to him, hate dripping from every word. "With my father and his men."

Jack had no idea what to say. He had lost his own brother in that rescue. And here the girl hadn't even wanted to be saved. If only they'd known she was a victim back then. Held against her will in a house of torture. If they had known, Jack and his family would've called the authorities and had the place shut down that very day.

Even with Shane lying dead at the hospital.

He drew a slow breath. "I'm sorry."

"Yes, well..." Eliza crumpled up her paper bag. "Here I am. Rescued again." She looked back at him. "But I still wish I had drowned that day."

Jack was just barely able to concentrate. She was the same girl! She really was. He pushed the truth from his mind. He couldn't tell her now, couldn't break the fragile trust between them. "Maybe you won't wish that. Once I tell you the news."

And then Jack explained about the housekeeping job at the home where the other girls lived. "You would make ten dollars an hour and help with homework. But you would have your own room. You'd be free to come and go." Something Eliza had never known.

She didn't say anything, but his words had hit their mark. She was thankful, he could tell. Because he watched her eyes fill with tears. The same blue eyes as the little girl he had rescued not once, but twice. From a place Jack would remember as long as he lived, the last place he had ever seen his brother, Shane.

A distant shore in the heart of Belize.

CHAPTER THIRTEEN

*Many are the plans in a person's heart, but it is the
Lord's purpose that prevails.*

—Proverbs 19:21

To Eliza, Jack Ryder served just one purpose. He was
her way out.

Already he had secured her a place to live and work.
In her new home, she could finally treat the Palace girls
the way they deserved to be treated. With kindness and
respect. With honesty. And now that she had a place to
live, with every passing hour, Eliza became more convinced that she didn't want to work at the group home.

She really did want to work with the FBI. Eliminate
traffickers from the streets and get them behind bars, as
many as possible. And rescue girls like herself and the
sixteen from the Palace.

Until now, Eliza hadn't had access to the Internet.
But the group home had a computer for schoolwork.
She had asked Stan and Melinda for an hour of Internet
time, and they had agreed.

"The system is protected from inappropriate content," Melinda told her. The woman was kind, but she didn't quite trust Eliza. Not yet, anyway. "We'll have a record of whatever you search."

"That's fine." Eliza wanted to learn just one thing: how the FBI informant program worked. She told Melinda as much, and over the next few days, Eliza found all she needed to know.

It was Monday, July 19, more than a week since her birthday, and Jack was on his way to pick her up at the house. He was taking her to the field office, where his boss, Oliver Layton, already knew what she wanted to talk about.

She was ready for the meeting. Last week Melinda took Eliza to get her hair trimmed and layered. Then, yesterday after church, the woman took Eliza shopping. "If you want to work for the FBI, you'll need the right clothes," Melinda had said.

Eliza left with a pair of slim black dress pants, low-healed black booties, and a navy blue blouse. Professional, but pretty. When she tried the outfit on, Eliza had looked in the mirror and gasped. She had never seen herself like this. Like an actual person. She had spent the last eleven years in nightgowns and bathing suits.

Now she was ready and waiting outside when Jack pulled up.

She could tell he thought she was pretty. Never mind that he had treated her like a child during the rescue. Eliza could tell when a man found her attractive. He got out of the car and opened her door. "Hi." He stepped back. Like he wanted to work to keep his distance. "You look nice."

"This is a big meeting." She didn't smile. But she tried not to sound angry, either. Hope was beginning to grow in Eliza's soul, hope that gave her a reason to look forward to tomorrow. And if there was one person who could turn her life around at this point it was Jack Ryder. She knew his full name now. And she didn't have to like him.

But she could at least be civil.

• • •

IN ALL HIS days with the bureau, Oliver Layton had never had a situation like this. Breaking up international drug cartels and disbanding trafficking rings was what he did for a living. He orchestrated and masterminded raids, and he hired the best agents in the business to pull them off.

Yes, there were times—like in this recent mission in Belize—where an agent would need to infiltrate in order to find a victim to work with. Often, the threat of charges against that victim was very real. Dropping those charges was a way of persuading the victim to turn on her captor and help the bureau.

But now, Eliza Lawrence had some unshakable idea of wanting to work for the FBI. Help out on secret raids and operations. Something that—to Oliver's understanding— had never been done before in San Antonio. Not this soon after a rescue, anyway.

Eliza and Jack entered the office just before ten that

morning. The moment he saw the two of them together, Oliver knew. Jack had feelings for the girl. Oliver could see it in the way Jack held the door for her and walked protectively at her side.

His observation wasn't something he could put into words, not in front of Eliza. But Oliver made a mental note. He would talk to Jack about this later. Never mind that Eliza wasn't trafficked, she was still a victim. She'd been trapped in a lifestyle that would scar her forever. There could be absolutely no romantic connection between Jack and the girl.

Not if she worked for the department, and not if she didn't.

The three of them sat in an interview room lined with windows. Oliver took the lead. "Eliza, I'm sorry. I hate to waste your time, but there is no way I can hire you. You don't have experience or training . . . you're too young, and honestly, as a victim, you will need a great deal of counseling."

Eliza's determination was as evident as her beauty. She sat straight in her chair, unmoving, and waited until Oliver was finished. Then she leveled her gaze straight at him. "Sir . . . I want you to charge me with the crime of sex trafficking."

Oliver saw Jack shift in the chair beside her. Like he was uncomfortable with this, but not surprised. If Jack had filled the young woman's head with these ideas, then he would need to be reprimanded. Eliza needed help, not to be thrown into the field.

"We aren't charging you." Oliver glanced at Jack, then back at Eliza. "That should've been made clear to you."

"It was." Eliza didn't look away. "But what I did . . . luring those girls to the Palace. It was wrong and I want you to charge me."

Suddenly Oliver knew where this was going. "What's your reason, Eliza?"

"Press charges against me so that I can work them off." She slid to the edge of her chair, her eyes blazing with intensity. "I want to be a CI . . . a confidential informant." She hesitated. "Unless you send me on the most difficult missions, which is what I'd prefer. Then I'd like to be an HLCI. High-level confidential informant."

This was Jack's doing, Oliver was sure. He looked at the young agent. "Did you put her up to this?"

"No, sir." Jack didn't blink. "She did the research. She figured it out herself."

Jack had never lied to him. Oliver took a deep breath and faced Eliza. "You need counseling, young woman. You've been trapped in a crime ring for more than a decade."

"And I survived." She lifted her chin. "I don't want to fold laundry and clean the kitchen at a group home, sir. No one can spot trafficking activity like I can. Try me."

Again Oliver looked at Jack, but his favorite agent only shrugged.

Oliver stood and paced the length of the room. What Eliza was offering was interesting. Just last week the brass had held a meeting about international sex-trafficking rings, and how they were elusive in areas like the Bahamas and Columbia and other South American and Caribbean countries. Eliza was right. Having her on the job could be a tremendous asset to the bureau.

He turned to her. "What about counseling?"

"I'll get it. Sooner the better." Her confidence was breathtaking. "So I can start making a difference for other girls. Like Alexa and Rosa and Maggie." She paused. "This very minute there are girls being trafficked all around the world. If you'd had someone like me five years ago, the Palace might have been shut down sooner. Before Alexa turned twenty."

Oliver stared at the floor for a few seconds and then back at Eliza. Could the girl really be ready to work as an informant? He would want a psychological evaluation performed and intensive counseling before she set foot on a mission.

But Eliza had his attention.

The conversation continued for another hour, and whatever questions Oliver had, Eliza had answers. In the end she convinced him. Jack was right, the girl had done her homework. Oliver agreed to talk to his superiors about the timing, and by the next day she had passed her second psychological evaluation and the task of making Eliza an informant was under way.

From the top down, everyone agreed that Eliza Lawrence would make the best HLCI the department had worked with in years. The paperwork had to be meticulous. The charges were detailed against Eliza, same with her willingness to work off her crime for the FBI. She agreed to stay within the confines of the law and to be honest at every turn.

Oliver even worked out financial compensation for a three-year obligation, which Eliza gladly agreed to. Oliver was assigned as her case agent.

Every detail had to adhere to the Attorney General's CI guidelines, and when the papers were finally ready, Jack brought Eliza into the office to sign them. Five agents including Terri, who had taken part in the rescue in Belize, were there to witness the signing.

The whole time Eliza was in the room, Oliver watched Jack. He had been right the first time, he was sure about it. Jack had feelings for the young woman. The truth was there in the gentle way he looked at her, the softness in his eyes. Not the way other men on the street probably looked at Eliza.

Jack looked like a man in love.

Eliza didn't seem to notice. She signed the papers and then she turned to Oliver. "Thank you, sir." She glanced around the room. If anything she avoided looking at Jack. Her eyes met Oliver's again. "You won't regret this, sir."

And with little other fanfare, Eliza Lawrence was no longer a former captive in a trafficking organization trying to find a room at the Holiday Inn. She was Masey Benson, paid HLCI with the FBI.

When the meeting was over, Oliver approached their

newest informant. "For the time being, I'd like to see you work in the office." He hesitated. "You could sit at a computer and do virtual surveillance of a dozen places where we have concerns."

"Virtual?" Eliza shook her head. "No, sir. I don't want to be in an office. A camera can't pick up the subtle details." She hesitated. "Otherwise you would have closed down the Palace before now."

She had a point. But putting her in the field made him nervous. "Your next counseling appointment is tomorrow. On the first floor in this building." He thought for a minute. "Let's talk after that."

The Transnational Organized Crime unit had called in a psychiatrist who specialized in victim work. Eliza wasn't the typical victim. She, herself, had never been trafficked. But she grew up with girls who were, and between that and her father's threats she was absolutely in need of help. The doctor would meet with her for the next four weeks, every day. At that point—even though counseling would continue indefinitely, Oliver would talk to the counselor.

If Eliza wasn't ready, they would find out soon enough.

Eliza was slated to spend the next few hours in the research room, where she would learn more about being an informant. Data and details she couldn't find on the web. Terri would be her guide for the process. The two left the office.

Only Oliver and Jack remained. Oliver faced his agent. "I need to speak with you."

"Sir?" Jack didn't look guilty. Maybe he didn't know the signals he was giving off when it came to Eliza.

"In my office."

"Yes, sir."

Oliver led the way, and they sat across from each other. He took his time, looking long at Jack, analyzing him. "Talk to me about the girl."

Jack hesitated. "The girl?" He leaned forward. "Eliza?"

"Yes." Oliver raised his eyebrows. "You know who I mean."

A blank look came over Jack's face. "What about her, sir?"

Oliver didn't want to waste his time or Jack's. "I need to know." He took a slow breath. "Are you in love with her?"

From the moment his words were out, Oliver could tell two things. First, he was right. And second, Jack wasn't going to admit it because he didn't yet see the truth himself.

"Sir . . ." Despite his tanned face, the young agent's cheeks grew ruddy. "Definitely not." His tone was more shocked than defensive. Then gradually his expression changed. "However, sir . . . there is more to the situation."

"I'm listening."

And then Jack told him a story that seemed straight out of the movies, like something no one could dream of making up. Eliza was the little girl Jack had rescued? The summer his brother drowned in Belize?

Oliver felt his forehead grow damp. This definitely complicated things. "Are you sure?"

"Yes, sir. She even knew about my brother being hurt, laying on the beach." He paused. "She didn't mention that he had died. I don't think she knows what happened."

"So that's it." Oliver studied Jack. "You saved her as a child, and now . . . you have feelings for her."

"No." He gave a few slow shakes of his head. "No, sir, I don't. Nothing more than when we first returned from the mission. I want her to succeed. I want her to make a difference." Jack crossed his arms. "I want her to have a reason to live."

Oliver considered that for a long moment. Then he nodded. Maybe that was it. Maybe Jack wasn't in love with the girl. Either way, his agent needed the reminder. "You do understand, Jack, that agents cannot have any romantic dealings with informants."

"Yes, sir. Of course." Jack knit his brows together. "I would think you'd know me better."

"Well . . . it's a rule worth repeating." Oliver softened his tone. "You never know. The two of you might work together at some point. The lines need to be clear-cut."

"Always, sir." Jack looked stone sure. "You don't have to tell me again."

. . .

AS IT TURNED out, Oliver *did* have to tell Jack again. Jack and Eliza, both. Because four weeks later the brass decided they could use Eliza for a surveillance trip to Nassau, Bahamas. And Jack was the perfect operative to go with her. He was closest to her age, and he was the agent she knew and trusted most.

By then Oliver and his superiors had talked with Eliza's counselor at length. The woman had found no reason to keep Eliza from the field. "Being on mission is her reason to exist," the therapist told them. "She is singly focused. Not afraid or anxious. No nightmares. Very different than victims who have actually been trafficked."

The psychiatrist went on to say that outward expressions of trauma might come later. "Jack knows her best. I approve of the two of them working together. If she starts to show signs of a breakdown or repressed anxiety, he'll see it. And he can get her back here the same day."

Details of the mission came together quickly.

A group of six high-level traffickers had been working in Nassau for the past three months, recruiting girls and customers at a record rate. But there was a problem. The FBI's data on the group was incomplete. Sending a team in to raid the operation would be a mistake at this point.

The bureau needed additional surveillance. Someone to trail the men when they went into town and watch the way they talked to solitary young girls. No one in the FBI would be as adept at recognizing that as Eliza.

Jack and Eliza would train together for two weeks, studying photos of the stretch of beach where the criminal operation was most likely taking place. They would rehearse surveillance scenarios and practice what to do if things went wrong.

The trip would be less dangerous than most. A good starting point for the two, since the higher-ups had decided the pair might work together again someday. This first time out together they would fly to Nassau, pretending to be a newly married couple. They would stay on Paradise Island at the Reef, a part of the Atlantis Resort.

A corner Topaz suite would be their home base, a deluxe accommodation with two separate bedrooms, two separate locked entrances behind a single locked front door. From there they would daily venture over the arched white bridge a few miles into Nassau, to the strip of fish markets and tourist stands.

Before Eliza had agreed to the mission, Oliver and his superior first met with her to ask if she felt comfortable pretending to be married. "You and Jack will have to hold hands." Oliver studied the young woman. "You must act like you're in love with him. Otherwise the mission cannot work."

Eliza hadn't blinked. "That's fine."

Oliver's boss chimed in. "There will be no kissing—unless it's needed for yours or Jack's safety. And of course you will stay in your separate rooms." He paused. "Whenever you're in public, you'll play the part. When you're in private quarters you'll keep to your own rooms."

"Sir"—Eliza's answer had been chilling—"I've been

acting all my life. Talking girls into coming to the Palace."
Her eyes had held a certainty even greater than before. "I
am not interested in romance or love or sex. Pretending
will be easy . . . especially with Agent Ryder."

And with that, Oliver had the assurance he needed.
He didn't have to worry about Jack and Eliza falling in
love. Hardly. She wasn't a risk when it came to romantic
dealings with his star undercover agent. Or any agent at
the bureau. Terri had questioned the girl extensively in
the days after her rescue. The fact was, Eliza had just one
set of feelings for men.

She hated them.

CHAPTER FOURTEEN

How long must I wrestle with my thoughts and day
after day have sorrow in my heart?

—Psalm 13:2

The one truth Jack could not admit to anyone, not even himself, was the thing Oliver Layton had so easily seen. He was falling for Eliza.

Jack didn't want to care about the girl. He had made up his mind years ago never to fall in love. He would never marry and he wouldn't have children. Rather, he would spend his days and months and years working for the bureau, putting his life in danger.

Again and again and again.

And if he died doing it, that was fine. This was the only life worth living.

But now, for the first time since he'd been sworn in, Jack cared about whether he came home at the end of the day. Because he wanted one more chance to see Eliza, to talk to her. To be near her. His feelings confused him and taunted him and mocked him when he tried to sleep at night.

It wasn't that he cared for her the way an ordinary man might care for an ordinary woman. This wasn't romance or love or butterflies. It was that one unbelievable truth, the single detail Jack couldn't get past.

The fact that Eliza was the little girl he had saved.

Lately, Jack relived that single moment over and over, so that once again he was pushing through the current, swimming to the little girl. He had almost reached her when he could hear shouting from the beach behind him. And he was looking over his shoulder and seeing Shane, swimming toward him.

He'll get back to shore, Jack would tell himself again. *Someone will swim out to help.* The little girl needed him. *Who else is going to save her?* And every time he replayed the moment, Jack chose the little girl. Every single time.

Her life . . . or his brother's.

Jack had always wondered if rescuing the child had even mattered. Had she gone home from vacation and forgotten the ordeal ever took place? But now he knew the truth. So yes, he had feelings for her. Of course he did. He could still remember her clinging to his shoulders as he swam her to shore. Still feel her nearly dead body cradled against his chest as he ran up the beach. He handed her over and he could still see the way she lay limp in the woman's arms.

Because of the constant memories, he found himself thinking about God in a way he hadn't in years. Someone who had lost all that he had lost might not believe in God. Unless it was to believe God had singled him out for pain.

But now, Jack wasn't sure. That blond little girl was back in his life, about to take a mission with him to the Bahamas. How could it not feel like some master plan that God had orchestrated?

Jack had his bag packed. A bureau black SUV looking very much like an Uber would pick him up in half an hour. Eliza was staying at a Marriott near the airport booked under her assumed name, so there would be no doubt about who she was—and who she wasn't. From this morning on, she was not Eliza. He couldn't call her that or think of her that way.

She was Masey. And he was Luke.

He looked around the room and spotted his father's old leather Bible at the top of his bookcase. Of all things. Jack hadn't read a Bible since before Shane died. He crossed the room and pulled it from its place. This was the Bible his dad would read aloud on Sunday evenings before the family readied for another week. Jack turned to his father's favorite chapter. The man knew it by heart. Jack did, too. But right now he wanted to read the words for himself. The way he hadn't in so many years.

The passage was from Psalm 23.

He started at the beginning and read the words silently.

The Lord is my Shepherd; I shall not want.
He makes me lie down in green pastures.
He leads me beside still waters.
He restores my soul.
He guides me in paths of righteousness for His name's
    sake.
Even though I walk through the valley of the shadow of
    death, I will fear no evil.
For You are with me; Your rod and Your staff, they
    comfort me.
You prepare a table before me in the presence of my
    enemies.
You anoint my head with oil; my cup overflows.
Surely, goodness and love will follow me all the days of
    my life,
and I will dwell in the house of the Lord forever.

Jack ran his thumb over the thin, worn page. "I miss you, Dad." He whispered the words. "More than you know."

Whether God was real or not, whether He was for him or against him, Jack needed help on this mission. Not because it was overtly dangerous. It wasn't. Not compared with the raid in Belize.

But because of Eliza. If he couldn't keep his heart from caring about her now, before the mission, how was he going to stay indifferent once they were overseas? Especially now that he knew the truth about her? A truth he didn't dare tell her. He couldn't risk her reaction, not at this point. With a mission just ahead of them.

Also, they'd had one bad interaction a few days ago. Oliver had brought them together in a meeting room and asked if either of them had doubts. For any reason.

Jack turned to Eliza. "I'm a little concerned about your age, Eliza. You've never dated or . . ." He didn't state the obvious. "Are you sure you want to do this? Play a married woman?"

Eliza's eyes had burned in response. "I grew up in a brothel. I think I can handle being married to *you*."

"I was just trying to think of—"

"Jack." Oliver shook his head. "She'll be fine."

In hindsight, Jack never should have asked her about any of it. But he still thought it was a valid point. In the end Oliver convinced him it was a nonissue. Eliza wouldn't have to do more than stay at Jack's side and hold his hand.

"Her counselor thinks she's ready," Oliver told him the other day. "She's received training. I think she can handle it."

The incident created an even greater divide between him and Eliza. He was surprised she hadn't asked to work with a different agent. He understood now that she had probably been embarrassed by Jack's concerns. Now she wouldn't look at him, like she hated him. Jack understood. Even before the conversation with Oliver, Eliza hadn't liked him, not even a little. She tolerated him, nothing more. She was using him to get what she wanted—the chance to put away traffickers.

It was the same thing Jack wanted. Nothing more.

Yesterday in their final briefing together, Jack had waited until they were the last people in the room. Then he had looked into her eyes. "I don't doubt you can do this. But are you sure you want to? Pretend we're married?"

"Yes." She looked away and gathered her various folders. "With you . . . pretending will be easy. Right, *Luke*?"

So she was upset with him for several things. Including, no doubt, the fact that he was a guy. He longed to know more about her, about her childhood and her family, about where she had grown up and whether she remembered anyone from her past. Had she ever been to Lower Barton Creek or Spanish Lookout like Lizzie James—the great-granddaughter of Ike Armstrong? Those questions would have to wait until she lowered her guard some.

If she ever did.

No, somehow he had to keep it all to himself. His questions, his feelings—and the knowledge about that terrible summer. All while pretending to be Eliza Lawrence's husband on an island with beaches as beautiful as any in the world. Any other time, Jack wouldn't have blinked. Wouldn't have doubted for a moment that he could pull this off. He was a machine.

Undercover operations with a female agent were nothing new for him. He'd worked in tandem on covert missions in years past. Just never in a situation like this, with a girl he was trying not to fall for. The SUV pulled up in front of the hotel and Eliza walked out and toward the vehicle.

She looked gorgeous, every bit the happy bride ready for her honeymoon. They both wore wedding rings. Terri had taken her shopping again, this time for designer clothes and new sunglasses. As Eliza climbed into the SUV, as she took the seat beside him in the second row, Jack sensed something different about her. It only took a few minutes to figure it out.

Eliza wasn't a victim anymore.

She wasn't trapped in a situation where she had no choice about her days, no way to leave her father's captivity. Working as an informant was her choosing. It was how she wanted to spend her days, and the victory she clearly felt must have been palpable. He knew all that before she even said a word.

The driver was an agent, so they didn't need to pretend yet. Jack shifted so he could see her better. "You look the part."

"Thank you." She adjusted her sunglasses and stared out her side window. "Is the weather in the Bahamas warm like Belize?"

It was going to be a long four days if she wouldn't look at him. But Jack had to trust her. She had told Oliver she could pretend better than anyone. Time would tell.

"Yes." He pulled his own sunglasses from his backpack and slipped them on. "Summer in the Bahamas is hot and humid. The water has more jellyfish in mid-August. We'll have to be careful."

"In every possible way." She sighed and looked straight ahead past the driver. "If they're selling girls the way the bureau suspects, we'll identify the traffickers. I'll know." She finally looked at him. "I want to rescue a hundred children for each one I convinced to go to the Palace. Even that won't be enough."

Her knowledge and passion to see justice done made Eliza the most skilled informant Jack had worked with. He looked away. The faint scent of Eliza's perfume filled the car. The question wasn't whether Eliza could pull off the operation ahead.

But whether he could.

• • •

THEIR FLIGHT DEPARTED out of Dallas–Fort Worth International Airport, four hours from San Antonio. But it was worth the drive. That way they would take a nonstop into Nassau, arriving just before six o'clock.

Fewer chances to make a mistake.

Jack would've paid a million dollars to know what Eliza was thinking during the drive, but she stayed quiet. Mostly staring out her window. Maybe she didn't hate him. Maybe her attitude was the hatred she had for the people who bought and sold kids. Or maybe she was focused on the mission. The seriousness of it. The danger.

Again, he had many questions for her, but already he

had asked the only one that mattered when it came to the mission. And he was still paying the price for that.

From the moment they stepped out of the SUV and gathered their bags, Jack felt a shift in Eliza. She walked shoulder to shoulder with him, looking up at him with an adoration Jack had never seen before. She was quite the actor.

When they reached the check-in line, she worked her fingers up into his hair and kissed his cheek. "I can't believe we're married."

Jack took a moment to catch his breath. "Yeah." He slipped his arm around her shoulders. "Me, either."

The act never stopped for Eliza. They sat side by side at the gate and she slid her fingers between his. Then she settled back into her seat, as if holding hands with him was something she did as easily as breathing. When she pulled away to sip her coffee, she would look at her left hand, admiring the ring. Then she'd smile at him again.

Young and beautiful and in love.

No one in the world would have doubted her.

An armed federal agent in street clothes was on the plane, just in case. Jack never knew who might be following him. He had a thousand enemies, at least. Eliza took the window and Jack, the middle seat. The aisle seat was empty—purchased by the bureau.

For much of the flight Eliza looked out the window, like she'd done in the SUV. *What is she thinking?* Jack wondered. *What's in her heart?* Or did her heart ever get a voice in that pretty tortured head of hers?

Every ten minutes or so, she'd turn to him and kiss his cheek or lean her head on his shoulder. *This is just a mission, it's pretend*, Jack told himself. Only for him it could never be completely an act, no matter what he'd told Oliver. Because this was the girl he had saved. And now God had brought them back together again as only He could do. Unless the whole thing was one big coincidence.

Before they landed in Nassau, Eliza turned to him. "I never wanted a big wedding."

"Yeah . . . me, neither." He searched her face. She was taking this a bit far. No one in the Bahamas trafficking business could hear them, after all. Even if one of their dirty gang was on the plane, they wouldn't require this conversation for Jack and Eliza to be convincing.

"But what a wedding, right?" Her eyes sparkled.

Fine. If she wanted to go all in, he would play along. He looked deep into her eyes. "Almost as beautiful as you."

"Mmm. Thanks." She framed his cheek with her fingers. Even the tone of her voice was different. Lighter, less serious. "I'll remember it forever."

They were still talking like that when the pilot announced they were about to land. Then Eliza did the thing he least expected. She tenderly took his face in her hands and kissed him on the lips. Not a seductive kiss, but a loving one. Slow and easy, like she'd done this a thousand times.

Her eyes looked straight through him and she smiled. One of the only smiles Jack had ever seen from her. "I love being married to you, Luke."

If they hadn't been in public, Jack would've slid to the empty aisle seat. They weren't supposed to kiss like this, that was part of the deal. Affection, admiration, starry eyes—all good. But the mission was not to include anything more. Not unless absolutely necessary.

There was the hint of victory in Eliza's eyes. As if she wanted him to know she could handle the mission. Despite her lack of experience when it came to relationships. She kissed him once more, her lips on his, and then she turned to the window.

What was he supposed to do? He couldn't pull away or act uninterested. In case one of the traffickers actually was on the plane. That wasn't likely, but still. Jack closed his eyes and leaned back. Her kiss stayed with him. It captured his breath and undid his mind so that even five minutes later the feeling was all he could think about.

Everything in him wanted nothing more than to take her in his arms and kiss *her*. The way she had kissed him. But that would never work. He was the experienced agent, the one who knew the rules and the price he'd pay if he broke them.

The sooner he could tell her that, the better.

She didn't try to kiss him as they made their way of the plane and through customs, or as they picked up their bags and hired a van outside the airport to take

them to Atlantis. She gushed about the flight and re-marked about the pale blue water and white sand. As if she'd never been to the beach.

But she didn't kiss him. Didn't do more than hold his hand.

"This is going to be the best week." She leaned her head on his shoulder again as they drove up and over the bridge to Paradise Island, home of Atlantis. "I love you, Luke."

"Love you, too." He smiled at her, then glanced at the rearview mirror. Locals involved in trafficking sometimes worked as drivers to cover up their illegal activity. So un-less the two of them were behind doors in their hotel suite, they had to play their parts. Jack kissed Eliza's forehead.

Jack had said those words before in situations like this. But there was something different about saying them this time. Something that made his knees tremble. *Stop*, he told himself. *This is a mission. You're a machine, Jack Ryder. Don't let her get to you.* She was pouring it on, goading him, challenging him. Trying to prove she was up for the mission. That's what this was.

He took a long breath and felt himself relax. The things she'd said, they were just words, nothing more. She didn't love him. This was a job. And she was playing a part.

They checked in at the front desk of the Reef, the nicest of the seven hotels that made up Atlantis. Any doubt about Eliza's intentions dissolved when they got

to their suite. Often these suites were rented by different parties altogether. They were that private.

Eliza's smile faded as soon as the bellman closed the main door behind him. She pointed to the separate room on the right. "I'll take that one." She grabbed her bag, unlocked the door and slipped into the room without looking back.

Jack watched her go. This was the last mission he would do with Eliza Lawrence. If she hated him, if she enjoyed mocking him, then she could work with someone else. And he would do his very best to put her out of his mind forever.

If only he could forget the way she had kissed him.

CHAPTER FIFTEEN

*Listen! My beloved! Look! Here he comes, leaping
across the mountains, bounding over the hills.*
                                   —Song of Solomon 2:8

The wall around Eliza's heart had stood firmly in place
since her first day at the Palace, the day she found out
that her mother and Daniel were dead. It was a barrier
made of solid brick and razor wire, that no one would
ever breach. But today the fortress she'd built to protect
herself was beginning to crumble, one chunk of cement
after another.

All because of Jack Ryder.

Jack was different. He was the first man she'd ever
known who didn't want her body. He was also the first
man she had ever kissed, though he didn't want that, either. That much was obvious on the plane. He didn't
think she was capable of being an informant, pretending to be married and in love. Yet, for some reason, he
treated her with kindness. Not the way she'd seen men
treat the other girls at the Palace. Which created a
situation Eliza wasn't familiar with. Rather than hating

Jack Ryder for not believing in her, she found herself falling for him, needing him.

The way she'd treated Jack earlier hadn't felt like acting at all.

Jack was waiting for her when she left her room later that day. The two of them needed to walk the grounds, give off the appearance of a normal couple on their honeymoon. After how she'd broken the rules and kissed him, Eliza expected Jack would barely speak to her.

Instead, he held out his hand. "I'll carry your things." He smiled at her. "If you want."

"That's okay." Eliza clutched her oversized leather bag to her body. She'd never had a purse and now this one held a cell phone, bottled water, and a small makeup bag, along with a scarf and perfume.

No one would carry it but her.

Jack looked tanned and muscled, dressed in the same short-sleeve button-up shirt and khaki shorts he'd worn in Belize. The sun was still low in the sky out the window at the end of the hall, and Eliza glanced at Jack. He wasn't wearing sunglasses, but Eliza was. She planned to keep them on.

One more attempt at keeping the walls from falling apart.

Eliza allowed an exaggerated sigh. As if she were bored and not distracted by his cologne. "Tell me the plan again."

"Okay." If Jack was frustrated by her cool attitude, he didn't show it. "We'll walk from here to Marina Village on the other side of the island, get dinner, then walk back." He reached for her hand. "Like any other newly-weds."

Eliza said nothing. Before she could push the elevator button, Jack suddenly stopped walking. She had no choice but to do the same.

"Hold on. I need to talk to you." Jack faced her and took her other hand. He kept his voice low. "Don't kiss me again."

The directive stung. Eliza released her hands from his and told him what she wished were true. "You liked it."

"No." He looked as serious as she'd ever seen him. "That was part of the deal, Eliza. Unless it's absolutely necessary, we don't kiss. This is a mission . . . not a vacation."

She wanted to come back with something smart. What was he going to do, send her home? "Let me guess, Luke." She stood a bit straighter and kept her cool. "At least you can't accuse me of being inept."

"Eliza." His eyes pierced hers, even through her sunglasses. "You said you were ready to come to Nassau. Which means we do the operation by the rules."

There it was again. His doubts about her ability to do this. "I had to prove myself."

He didn't blink. "Prove yourself . . . by following the rules."

There. Her walls were intact again. He clearly didn't care about her. She shot a mean look at him. "I get it."

She turned and pushed the elevator button. *Why did I say that?* She didn't want anything from Jack Ryder. Not friendship, not admiration—least of all love.

In the elevator he took her hand again. When another couple joined them halfway to the lobby, he whispered near her face, "You look beautiful tonight. If I haven't told you yet."

Don't believe it, she told herself. *This is a job. Nothing more.* She gave him a plastic grin. "Aren't you sweet."

They strolled through the Reef lobby, outside and up the stairs to the Cove, the property adjacent to the building where they were staying. Eliza had thought the Palace was nice. It was nothing compared to the opulence and grandeur of Atlantis.

The outdoor walkway meandered under stunning massive chandeliers. Jazz played along the pathway from speakers hidden in tropical landscaping, and water spilled from ornate fixtures. They took another turn and after ten minutes walking in silence they were inside the Royal Tower.

He moved a little closer to her side. His smile was brighter than she'd seen it. "Rumor is Michael Jackson used to rent out the entire top floor here."

"Really." She took off her sunglasses and slipped them into her purse. Her smile was in place, but only on the outside. "Interesting." What was she feeling? Like she hated him and never wanted to see him again? Or that all she wanted in all her life was for him to kiss her? To find her attractive, for real?

They were about to enter the casino when an enormous guard stepped in front of them. He looked like Asia from the Palace. "Hey! You have to be twenty-one to be here."

"I . . . I'm sorry." She pressed in close to Jack. What was the darkness circling around the man's head? Or were those spots in her eyes?

"She's twenty-three." Jack stepped up. "Let us by."

Again the man scowled and Eliza couldn't look at him. The darkness around him was as terrifying as it was familiar. Finally the man turned and walked off.

Eliza could feel her body shaking. "C-can we go another way?"

"Of course." Jack put his arm around her and led her away from the casino and out a side door. When they were a few feet down the path, he stopped and faced her. "I'm sorry. I have no idea why he would—"

"I do." She was trembling harder now. "He's . . . in the business. I could . . . feel it." They were alone on this dimly lit part of the resort path. She leaned her forehead on his chest. "Did you see it?"

"See what?" Jack stroked her hair and held her. Like he really cared.

"The black spots. Little black clouds." She lifted her eyes to his. "They were all around that man."

Jack only searched her eyes. Finally he shook his head. "No. But I believe you."

And the walls around her heart began to crumble again. No one was watching them, no tourists or workers or guards to give them a reason to keep up the façade. But still he held her. Her heart was still pounding. "He knew, too. That's why he stopped us."

"Knew what?" Jack took a step back and brought his hand to her face. "Your age, you mean?"

"No." She felt filthy, like damaged goods. "That I used to . . . that I lived at a place where girls were trafficked and that I helped lure them into the Palace and that . . . that I'm a . . ." She hung her head.

"A victim?" Jack's tone was tender in a way Eliza hadn't heard it before. "That's why you still need counseling, Eliza. So you can believe what all the rest of us believe." He cupped her face in his hands. "That you're a victim. In a different way from the other girls, but a victim all the same. Nothing about your last eleven years was ever your fault."

Eliza nodded and after a few seconds they started walking again. Jack kept his arm around her and she stared through the palm trees to the starry sky above. Why was he so nice to her? No matter what he said about her being a victim, it wasn't true. She had been good at her job. Even against her will, she had no trouble convincing other girls to come to the Palace. She was a terrible person.

And what was this vulnerable feeling she had around him? Whatever it was, she didn't like it.

At Marina Village, they walked past a dozen ostentatious yachts, boats with helicopter landing pads and open dining rooms where staff served their wealthy guests.

The very sight of the yachts made Eliza sick to her stomach. The Palace customers all came off yachts.

They kept walking. Maybe she was wrong. Maybe it was too soon to be on a mission. She drew a deep breath and kept her eyes forward. No, she wasn't wrong. This was where she needed to be. She remembered Rosa and Alexa. *Forget about the yachts and the man at the casino,* she told herself. *I'm more than ready.*

If she didn't help Jack identify the bad guys and at-risk children on this island, who would?

They ate at Carmine's, and since it was too much work to keep up the role, Eliza relaxed a little. "Where are you from, Jack?"

"The East Coast. Maryland." He held her look for a moment. "What about you?"

All she'd told the FBI—or Jack for that matter—was that she had been a Mennonite. She didn't want to say more than that. What if the bureau found their way to Lower Barton Creek? She didn't want to connect the safe world of her young childhood with this one.

Eliza took her time. "There are Mennonite communities in the United States." She held the crystal water goblet in her hand and took a sip. "Did you know that?" She'd never eaten at a restaurant like this, but she didn't want to tell him that.

"Yes." Jack didn't look surprised. He reached across the table and took her hand. "I've been there. Pennsylvania and Ohio. Nice people."

"They are." Eliza pictured her mama and Daniel, her

great-grandpa Ike. The grassy fields of Lower Barton Creek. "Very nice." She blinked to keep her tears from coming. "What about your parents? Tell me about them."

No one could hear what they were saying. The clinks of glasses and the sound of silverware and conversation around them were too loud. Jack only smiled. "It's a long story."

"I have time." It was true. Their meal hadn't even arrived yet.

"It isn't pretty." Jack's eyes softened.

"Neither is mine." This hardly felt like make-believe. Their fingers together made her feel safe. Her smile felt different now. More real. "Tell me."

"Okay." He released her hand and sat straighter. "I had one brother. Two years younger than me." He paused. "Shane died when I was sixteen."

Eliza felt a strange ache for the man across from her. "I'm sorry."

"For a few years, my parents grieved in silence. They were there at my football and baseball games. They spent more time with me than before, but they were never the same." He paused. "They were in the Middle East a few years later, visiting U.S. troops, when their vehicle hit a roadside bomb." He looked at his water glass. "The Army told me they never knew what hit them."

Eliza had no idea what to say. "They were . . . military?"

"Diplomats." Jack's smile was heavy now. "I was a senior in high school."

The meal came and they made small talk again. But

on the walk back to the Reef, Eliza stopped and turned to him. "I really am sorry. About your family."

"Thanks." A breeze made its way across the path and Jack brushed a loose strand of hair from her face. "I've been alone for a long time."

Again, she wanted to kiss him, not to prove herself. But because she'd never felt like this. She kept her feelings to herself. "Is that why you became an undercover agent?"

"Sort of." A couple was walking up behind them, and Jack kissed Eliza's forehead. They started moving again, slower this time. "I was going to be a Navy SEAL. Oliver found me after I graduated from the Naval Academy. He was my father's best friend, when the two were younger."

The pieces of his story were coming together. "You joining the FBI, that was Oliver's idea?"

Jack was quiet for a long moment. Like there were pieces of his story he didn't want to share. At least not yet. "Someone at the Navy knew that Oliver and my dad were friends. Oliver got word that I might not survive SEAL training."

"Why?" That didn't seem possible. Eliza couldn't imagine a soldier stronger than Jack.

"I pushed too hard. Didn't care if I lived or not." Jack shrugged. "Oliver believed that attitude would be better put to use with the FBI."

Eliza kept walking. They had more in common than she'd thought, this FBI agent and her. As they passed the casino, Jack put his arm around her again. Once, when two guards were walking their way, he stopped and pulled her into his arms. Again he kissed her forehead. "I love you, Masey. It's only been a few days, but I love being married to you."

Masey. This was for the sake of the men. In case they were in on the trafficking ring. She leaned her face against his chest. "Me, too."

Love was a word she'd heard every day of her life. The customers loved the girls at the Palace. Her father loved her. The men from the yacht club loved how she looked. She was the princess, so they loved her more than all the other girls.

But here, even when he was only pretending, the way Jack had said the word made her feel something she'd never felt before. She closed her eyes and she could only think one thing: the way it would feel to have him say those words and actually mean them.

• • •

THE NEXT MORNING it was time to work. Eliza couldn't wait.

Dressed in shorts and colorful tank tops, she and Jack took a ride over the bridge into Nassau. They walked past the fish fry markets and tourist shops and park benches on West Bay Street. Jack was a head taller than her, but their bodies fit together perfectly. Like they'd known and loved each other for years.

Ahead of them was the busiest and most visible stretch of sand in Nassau. Everything about the bustling area felt familiar.

Eliza spotted trouble almost immediately. Two men in white dress shirts and black pants stood near a swing set, talking to a young girl. The child was maybe twelve or thirteen and she was dressed in rags. Her parents didn't seem to be anywhere nearby.

Eliza stiffened. "There." She smiled at Jack. *Nothing but happiness,* she told herself. *Keep smiling.* Their lives were on the line here. "By the swings."

Jack slowed and led her to a nearby bench. The seat had a perfect view of the playground. "Tell me what you see."

"They're about to capture the girl on the swings." Ten feet away from the men, two older teenage girls stood together, nervous, unsure. "And those girls are already being trafficked." She laughed, like she was saying something funny. Anything to keep up the act. "Watch them. They're waiting for a signal from the men."

He pulled her close and kissed her cheek this time. Both of them looked straight ahead, like they were trying to see the beach past the swings. Sure enough, the men suddenly backed away from the younger girl, leaving her alone. And in their place, the older girls stepped up, suddenly all giggles and grins.

"That young girl has maybe five minutes." Eliza had seen this played out too many times to count. Times when she was the one convincing an unsuspecting child that all her dreams were about to come true—if only she would follow Eliza back to the Palace.

No! Eliza's heart raced. *No, not here. Not now.* There was still time to save this one. She stood and pulled Jack to his feet. Then without waiting for him, she half ran, half skipped to the swing set. Like she was a child herself. "Hey, girls!"

The two older teens looked at her and then at the child. They moved closer to the girl. Eliza could only imagine what terrible things would happen to the teens if the little girl got away. Things Alexa and Rosa had told her about.

"Honey!" Jack was at her side. "Want me to push you?" He grinned at the older girls. "It's our honeymoon."

The teens weren't smiling. Instead they glanced over their shoulders at the men waiting near the trees. They shifted and took a few more steps toward the swing set. Eliza had seen the look in their eyes before. They weren't going to stand by and let Eliza ruin this for them.

She leaned her head back and kicked her feet to the sky. "Swings . . . right by the beach!"

Jack gave her a light push. "Anything for you, baby."

From the shadows, the two men started to approach. *Not today, you monsters.* Eliza clenched her teeth and jumped off the swing, all while maintaining her smile. She hurried to the younger girl and crouched down in front of the child's swing. "Want some ice cream? I saw your mama over there." Eliza stood and pointed down the beach a ways. "Come on, sweetie. I'll race you."

The child looked confused. But at the mention of ice cream she was off her swing and running beside Eliza. Jack took the rear, jogging just behind them. Eliza had never felt more safe.

"Hey!"

From the corner of her eye, Eliza saw one of the men start chasing them. But then the other grabbed his partner's arm. The second man scowled and shook his head, as if to say they'd get the next one.

But they won't take this one. Eliza reached for the girl's hand. "What's your name?"

"Bella." She looked up, clearly concerned.

"I'm Masey." Eliza stopped for a moment and bent down to eye level with the girl. "Everything's going to be okay."

They took Bella to the nearest ice cream stand and bought her a vanilla cone. Then Eliza put her hands on her knees and dropped to the young teen's level again. "Where is your mama, little one?"

The girl only blinked and ate her ice cream. After a few seconds she shrugged. "I don't have a mama."

Jack put his arm around Eliza and joined the conversation. "We're going to get you help. Where do you live?"

The girl was Hispanic. No telling how she got stranded in the Bahamas. "Down there." She pointed to a street that headed inland.

Eliza couldn't believe it. Wherever the child lived, her guardians didn't care if she roamed the street. It took all her energy not to look furious. Whatever the girl's prior situation, it was going to change today.

The men were probably still watching. Eliza took Bella's hand again and faced Jack. "We have to get her out of here."

"I know." Jack nuzzled his face alongside Eliza's. His voice was little more than a whisper. "Follow me."

Jack hailed a cab and he and Eliza and Bella stepped inside. Only then did Eliza allow herself to breathe. She glanced over her shoulder at the children's play area. The two men and teenage girls were gone.

Even now they couldn't be too careful. The driver could be connected with the trafficking ring. Jack had his arm around Eliza, who was sitting in the middle, with Bella on the other side. "Well, Bella, it's time for you to go home." Jack grinned. "But let's get something to eat first."

Jack instructed the driver to take them to Solomon's Fresh Market, not far from the bridge to Atlantis. Jack made the event sound fun. "I've been there before. They have the best cookies."

"Okay." Bella didn't say anything to give them away. Almost as if she knew she could trust them.

As soon as they were out of the car, Jack took hold of Eliza's hand, and she took hold of Bella's. They had talked about this, how if they were able to rescue children in danger they would bring them here. A local informant worked at the Logos Christian bookstore, a few doors down from Solomon's.

With the right knock, their door would open any
time during the next few days. Right now that wasn't
necessary, since these were business hours. The three
stepped inside the bookshop. There the clerk must've
recognized Jack. She was a young woman in her early
twenties, a Bahamian native who was working with several honest police officers—all of them aware of the like-
lihood of the trafficking ring in their midst.

When the raid went down in this city, it would be in
part because this woman had helped make it happen.
Brave and determined to save children, even if she died
for the cause.

Eliza wanted to be just like her.

"I'm looking for an old Michael W. Smith album."
Jack smiled at the young woman. "Vinyl."

"Ah, yes. Vinyl." There didn't seem to be other customers in the place, but they wouldn't take a chance.
"We keep the vinyls back here."

She led them to a room at the rear of the store, and
from there Jack called his police contact in Nassau. The
conversation played on speakerphone, just loud enough
for Eliza to hear. The Bahamian woman took Bella into
an adjacent office so she wouldn't hear what was happening.

The police officer confirmed that Bella lived in a
troubled group home. Children had been taken from the
house in recent months, with no sign of their where-
abouts. Public officials were trying to get the home
closed.

The man said he was dispatching an unmarked car to the rear of the store. "There is a couple from my church." The officer sounded hopeful. "Bella will stay there. We can make a case for the girl to be handed over to this couple permanently."

Eliza leaned against the wall in the back room. Her heart rate slowly returned to normal. She had done it! She had saved one child from trafficking! They had showed up just in time, and risked their cover to take her away from the predators.

Nothing had ever felt this good in all her life, not since her days in Lower Barton Creek.

Jack turned to her. Then he took her in his arms. For a long time he just held her, his hand on the back of her head, their hearts beating in time. Eliza had never known this feeling, the way it felt to be protected and cared for. She closed her eyes. Maybe love felt like this. And then something else occurred to her. There wasn't a single person watching them. Which could only mean one thing.

Here, in this moment, Jack wasn't acting.

CHAPTER SIXTEEN

My heart pounds, my strength fails me; even the
light has gone from my eyes.

—Psalm 38:10

Jack got the news from an informant still on the ground
in Belize. Ike Armstrong, the historian from Lower Barton Creek, had died in his sleep. He hadn't been reunited
with his family, after all. The news hit hard. Jack made
himself a morning coffee and took it out on his deck. The
Topaz had a bigger balcony than any other suite at the
Reef. He angled the chaise lounge toward the water.

Poor Ike. He had been so sure he'd meet his family
again one day, that somehow they'd be found and come
home. That they'd all be together in time.

Jack downed a swig of his coffee and stared out at
the sea. Maybe Ike and his family really were in the same
place now. The place where Jack's brother and parents
lived . . . if God were real. He pulled one knee up and remembered the rescue yesterday.

When Oliver first brought up the idea of pairing him
with Eliza, Jack obviously had his doubts. Not that he

didn't want to spend four days walking the Bahamian beaches with her. But he had wondered if she'd really bring an advantage to the surveillance efforts.

Jack shouldn't have second-guessed her.

Eliza had an innate ability to spot traffickers, victims and children about to be captured. She couldn't just see it, she could sense it. But there was a problem. In her fervor, she had almost blown their cover. Jack pictured the events again. If he hadn't run up with his story about Eliza loving the swings, the men might've taken her at gunpoint.

Of course they were armed. The handle of one of their guns was visible the entire time. Eliza had seen it, too, but she hadn't cared. She only wanted to save the young girl. *She's like me,* Jack thought. But Eliza would need to be more careful, and he would have to make sure nothing happened to her.

He remembered again the moment in the back room of the bookstore. The victory was so tangible, so important, he could do nothing but take her in his arms. Yes, they'd gotten comfortable in the last two days, playing with ease the role of a married couple.

Until they returned to the room. At that point she'd pulled back, instantly cooler, which was exactly what she was supposed to do. Still, for those few minutes in that quiet bookstore back room, the two of them had shared something real. Very real.

Jack took another drink of his coffee. *She's an informant,* he told himself. *Don't think about her.* But he couldn't help himself. And he could never let her see the truth—that he was falling for her. She really was a victim, after all. Anything beyond friendship was forbidden.

And what about him? He had joined the FBI because he never wanted love, never wanted a family. God had taken the three people he loved most, so there was no reason to ever love again. Better to be an island. Fight hard, rescue people, put away bad guys, and stay on mission. Until one day a bullet pierced not just his shoulder . . . but his heart. His head.

Deep breath, he told himself. *What about Eliza, God? She doesn't even know what love is.* A part of him wanted to show her, to stop pretending and let her know how much he cared for her, the child he had rescued that long-ago day. He could tell her about that life-altering event and how he was the one who had saved her. They could at least be friends, then.

The possibility dissolved. None of it could happen. They had more work today, and in a few sunsets they'd be back in San Antonio. Where he'd be thankful that he'd stuck to the job, and that he hadn't let himself really fall for her.

Thankful that moments like the one in the back of the bookstore were few and far between.

• • •

THE ACTION ON the beach was about to pick up, that's what Eliza had told him. Jack spread a blanket down on the sand and the two sat side by side, leaning back on their hands, shoulders touching. It was only ten in the morning, but they wanted to be here early. So they wouldn't miss a thing.

So no other child was taken into captivity before Jack and Eliza had the chance to help.

There were only a few couples on the beach. Eliza wore a straw sunhat and a white lace cover-up over her bathing suit. He wore the navy swim trunks he'd worn in Belize and no shirt. The only way traffickers would believe he was a tourist on his honeymoon and not an agent.

Jack breathed in the sweet salty air. He wrapped his little finger around hers. "I got sad news today." She was an informant now. She might as well know something of his work. Especially when it came to Belize.

"You did?" Eliza leaned her shoulder into his. "One of the agents?"

"No." He breathed in the scent of her hair, her suntan lotion. *It's a job, Jack. Put her out of your mind.* "On the day I met you, earlier that morning, I went to a Mennonite village called Lower Barton Creek."

"You did?" She sat straight up and faced him. "Why didn't you tell me?"

"It wasn't about you." He sat up and faced her. "I met with the town's old historian. A man who I hoped would give me information about the disappearance of a different little Mennonite girl."

"Oh." She was wearing her sunglasses again, but he could still see her confusion. "I hope he helped you."

"He did. But I just got word . . . he passed away." Jack slid closer to her and eased her back against his chest. They both faced the water, and their conversation was easy. Gone was the snappy tone she'd used when they first landed in Nassau. "He told me that an American woman showed up one day with gifts and promises to host his granddaughter and her children at their beach house."

Again Eliza sat up. This time she got up on her knees and faced him. "What . . . was the man's name?"

"Ike. Ike Armstrong."

Eliza gasped and she was suddenly on her feet. "Walk with me. Please."

Jack had no idea what nerve he'd struck, but he did as she asked. He grabbed his backpack, his go-bag if something went terribly wrong during their time here today. With his free hand, he took hold of hers. "Eliza." There was no one in earshot, so he used her real name. "What is it?"

She wanted to run, he could feel it in the way she gripped his hand. But she kept her pace even with his. When they were a long way down the beach, she stopped and faced him. Like a lover unable to keep her eyes from his, she framed his face with her hands. She was shaking. "Jack . . . Ike Armstrong . . . he's my great-grandfather."

Jack took a few seconds, but then he shook his head. "No . . . no, he told me his great-granddaughter's name. He was very worried about her." He searched her face. "The girl's name was—"

"Lizzie." Eliza moved into his arms and brought her face alongside his. "Lizzie James, Jack. That's me." She lowered her hands and eased her arms around his bare waist. Then she pressed her face to his chest and did something that absolutely wasn't an act, something Jack had never expected with Eliza. She started to cry.

"I should've told you I was from Lower Barton Creek. I was trying . . . trying to keep my two worlds separate. It was the part of my past I wanted to keep to myself." She closed her eyes for a moment before looking at him again. "And now . . . now my great-grandfather is gone."

Her crying was too soft for anyone to notice but him. Still, he could feel her tears spilling onto his skin. Jack didn't care if someone was watching them or not. He ran his hand along her hair and then wrapped his arms around her.

This can't be happening! Eliza was Lizzie James? That meant that the woman Ike had talked about—Agnes Potter—was probably Betsy Norman. He felt sick. How come he hadn't connected those dots sooner?

And why hadn't he pushed her about where she'd been from? She had told him she couldn't remember, but of course she could. And of course the girl was from Lower Barton Creek. The whole thing made sense now.

"Eliza, I'm sorry." He moved back a few inches and faced her. "I didn't know you were from Lower . . . How come I didn't see it?"

"You mean . . . you knew his great-granddaughter was

Lizzie James?" Tears still streamed down her face. "You met with my great-grandfather?"

Jack felt terrible. "He was a very . . . very kind man, Eliza." He brought her hand to his lips and kissed it. Even though the last thing on his mind was the role he was supposed to be playing.

Eliza shaded her eyes. "What did he say . . . about me?"

"He believed you were still alive. You and your mother and brother." Again Jack could see the sincerity in the old man's face. "He told me your age. I think he was off several years." Disappointment washed over Jack. "We figured out his great-granddaughter would've been in her early twenties. And there were no girls that age at the Palace."

Eliza closed her eyes. When she opened them, it was clear she didn't blame him for not realizing earlier who she was. "What did he tell you?"

"How this strange American woman named Agnes Potter came to the village and how he thought the woman was trouble. I had no idea the woman was Betsy Norman." He hurt for Eliza. "When your mother and brother and you didn't come home, your great-grandfather told me that word came back to the village that all of you had drowned." Jack pulled her close again. "Your great-grandfather knew I was doing a raid on the Palace. It was beyond him, that something so wicked had made its way to Belize."

"My great-papa." She looked up, her eyes brimming

with fresh tears. "He was the nicest man. He loved me . . . so much."

Anyone watching them would merely think they were anxious to get back to the hotel. No one would've guessed they were having the most important conversation in Eliza's life. Jack felt a sting in his own eyes. "So . . . Agnes Potter changed her name to Betsy Norman?"

"I guess." Eliza sniffed. "I never knew her as anything other than Aunt Betsy." She eased back and searched his face. "You're saying Betsy returned to Lower Barton Creek and told my great-papa that I'd drowned with my mother and brother?"

"Yes." Jack brushed his fingers against her cheek. Her skin was softer than air. "There were police photos of three sets of footprints headed to the shore. And none coming out. Your father's men must have set that up, swimming down the beach before exiting the water. And making it look like three people drowned. You, your mother, and your brother."

Eliza shook her head. She studied him. "They told me there were *two* sets that day. So obviously their whole story was a lie." Anger began to set in her features.

"Careful." He kissed the top of her head. "By now, we're being watched." The longer they stayed on the beach, lost in each other, the more the traffickers would believe their act.

Eliza worked to find her smile again. "What if my mother and brother are still alive?"

It was the exact question Jack had asked himself a

dozen times since meeting with Ike Armstrong. Not because he had thought Eliza was related to the man. But
because he hoped to get an operative to Little Belize—
another local Mennonite community to the north—to
see if maybe the man was right.

But that was the last thing he could tell Eliza now.
"The department knows about Ike's concerns." Jack
shook his head. "We have no reason to believe your family is still alive, Eliza. I'm sorry."

Over the next few seconds, Jack could feel something in Eliza change. She grew more stiff and less sad.
She took off her sunglasses and dried her eyes. Like she
had sand in them from the breeze off the water.

Then she turned to him and took his hand. "Let's go
save some children."

The work that day was more helpful to the upcoming raid than anything they'd seen or done so far. They
bought snow cones and sat on the bench near the playground. A few times, Eliza took to the swings again. Just
so her story would hold true.

And in the next several hours Eliza identified four
men working the beach. She would nod toward the
north. "Those two by the yellow car. They're the experienced ones. The men on the beach are new. They have to
bring in girls or the guy in charge will get rid of them."

She didn't have to spell out what that meant. Jack
knew far too well how dangerous these sorts of operations were—even for the bad guys. When the men
climbed in their car, Eliza ran with Jack to a waiting cab.

All the while she laughed and looked back at him, her snow cone dripping, long blond hair blowing in the wind. Once they were in the car, she took a chance he might not have taken.

"See that yellow car." She practically giggled the words. "We know those guys! We met them a few years ago when we visited." She leaned forward and smiled at the driver. "Could you follow them? Please?"

Jack didn't lose his smile. "Yes, it'd be great to see them again."

If the driver knew the men in the other car, he'd know Jack and Eliza were lying. He might even text the men and turn them in. At the end of the ride, the men might have an ambush waiting for Jack and Eliza.

Jack didn't care. Eliza was right to do this. The bureau had no idea where the ring was operating from. They suspected that the group was transient because the men and children seemed to move every few days. But now he had a feeling they were following the men to headquarters. A more stable location. And if the FBI had that, a raid would be imminent.

The driver did a U-turn and weaved through traffic until he was a few cars behind the yellow one. Jack held his breath. They had to do this. Taking risks was necessary in an operation like this. Risks brought down trafficking rings. Without taking chances, there would be no victory to celebrate later.

So why did everything seem different this time? Instead of nerves of steel, all Jack could feel was his arm around Eliza in the backseat of the car. The touch of her skin beneath his fingers. Twice he had risked his life to save hers. And now . . . now they were both rushing into danger. What if they never returned to Atlantis?

Stop, he told himself. *Get the job done, Jack.* He leaned forward, allowing space between him and Eliza for the first time in hours. There. Now he could think. "I thought they lived up this way."

"Exactly." Eliza played along. She sounded excited. "I can't believe we spotted them."

Down one narrow street and then another, the yellow car led the way.

"I can't keep up." Their driver scowled in the rearview mirror. "Last thing I need is a ticket."

"Right. Don't break the law." Jack was glad the traffickers were speeding. Otherwise the cabbie would be right on their tail. And that would almost certainly give them away. Jack felt for his gun in his waistband.

He hoped he wouldn't need it.

A few blocks up, Jack saw the yellow car pull into the driveway of a two-story white brick home. "You know what." He leaned up and patted their driver on his shoulder. "Wrong guys."

"Really?" Eliza sounded disappointed. "They looked so familiar."

"Nope." Jack leaned back. "The guys we know live by the big church. Remember?"

"Aww. That's right." Eliza sighed. "I guess you can take us back to the beach."

"Back to Atlantis, actually." Jack put his arm around Eliza and drew her close. "I've had enough sun today." He winked at her.

"Me, too." She turned to him and looked at him for a long moment. Then she took his face and did the thing she was never supposed to do. She kissed him . . . on the lips. Slow and sensual, until he put his hand on her shoulder and pulled back. He kept his tone playful. "Honey. Not here!"

Now if the man driving the cab actually did work for the goons on the beach, he couldn't possibly think Jack and Eliza were anything other than typical honeymooning tourists. Jack didn't say another word until they were behind the main door to their suite at the Reef.

"I asked you." He dropped his backpack and searched her eyes. "Please . . . don't kiss me like that."

"We're supposed to be married." She sounded hurt. She set her bag down and moved closer to him. "I felt unsafe. So I kissed you."

Jack had known the rigors of mission work in a hundred different ways. But never had he worked so hard as in this single moment not to take her in his arms and tell her how he really felt. He gathered his determination. "It's my job to decide what's safe . . . and what's unsafe." He worked to control his breathing. Then he stepped back and held up one hand. "Eliza . . . please . . . don't do that again. That's all I'm asking."

"Fine." She turned and used her key to enter her room. The door shut with a loud thud.

Jack grabbed his backpack, opened his door and stepped inside. He didn't exhale until he heard the latch close behind him. Almost. He dropped to the sofa. He had almost kissed her. No one would've seen. No one would ever know.

Thank You, he thought. *Keep me from doing something stupid, God. Please.* The next hour was his, before he had to see her again. Jack stood and walked out onto the balcony. How had he gotten into this situation? Why had he agreed to do a mission with Eliza? His attraction had been there from the first time he saw her.

Jack gripped the rail with both hands. It took a minute for him to catch his breath. *God, I need Your help. If she kisses me again . . .*

He didn't finish the silent prayer. God—if He was listening—had to know the trouble Jack was in. He and Eliza still had twenty-four hours together on Paradise Island. If Jack could survive without breaking down, without giving in and kissing her every chance he had, it would be a miracle. And he had to survive, because this was his job and lives were at stake. He didn't dare break orders. But one thing was certain. When he got back to San Antonio he would have a talk with Oliver Layton.

Because he could never, ever take a mission like this with Eliza again.

CHAPTER SEVENTEEN

May all who want to take my life be put to shame
and confusion; may all who desire my ruin be
turned back in disgrace.

—Psalm 40:14

They were back in San Antonio, and Eliza still hadn't forgiven Jack for the way he'd treated her. Yes, he had been kind. He had listened to her and comforted her and shared his past with her.

But he had also rejected her. Not just as a woman but as an informant. Insisting he alone could decide when they should and shouldn't kiss. She had tried kissing him again when they visited the underground Dig Aquarium and when they bodysurfed on the public beach. If ever there was a place where a newly married couple would kiss, it would be in the shallow breakers of a Caribbean shoreline.

The kiss in the waves had been the only time Jack didn't fight her, the single incident where he didn't step back or push her away. Instead he had drawn her into his arms and returned the kiss. And for the single sweetest moment in Eliza's life she allowed herself to believe Jack Ryder really loved her.

And that he wanted her the way she wanted him.

But even then he had pulled away before she did. His eyes told her all she needed to know. That he was attracted to her, and that her advances were hitting their mark. But maybe she was wrong. Maybe he didn't find her appealing—because of her past, no doubt. Her life at the Palace. Because the ocean kiss had only seemed to make Jack more removed. She could still remember how without saying a word or looking at her again, he had shaken the water from his hair and made his way back up the beach.

When they had returned to their suite, she called him out on it. "You kissed me back out there. I felt it. But now you're acting like you barely know me."

Jack's expression was all business. "I wanted to keep us both alive. Everyone could see us." He stared at her. "What choice did I have?"

After that, Eliza hadn't tried again. His rejection made her angry. And so she had played the part, but she had played it with hurt and anger in her veins. And when he'd dropped her off at the group home last night, she hadn't said goodbye.

Now they were having their debriefing with Oliver Layton along with several other agents and senior officials. Never mind how she felt about Jack. They had done great work in Nassau. They had rescued a child and they knew how many men were working the beach.

They had photos of the teenage girls who were clearly in charge of luring girls into the operation. And they knew where the kingpin of the trafficking ring lived.

At the end of the meeting, Oliver went over their collective notes and nodded. "Amazing work. We'll get a few operatives on the ground and set up the raid." When the other agents had left the room, Oliver looked at Eliza and then Jack. "How would the two of you feel about taking another honeymoon, to San Pedro Sula? The Honduras police need our help with a ring."

Eliza was about to tell the man no. She couldn't possibly do another mission with Jack Ryder. But before she could speak, Jack cleared his throat. "I'm sorry, sir. I don't think that's a good idea." He glanced at her and then back at their boss. "I recommend she get more counseling before she goes out in the field again."

"Excuse me." Eliza was on her feet. "I don't need more counseling." She glared at Jack. "And *I* was going to recommend that I work with another agent." Her tone couldn't have been more biting. "Mr. Ryder and I are not . . . compatible." She felt the meanness in her smile. "I guess I'm not that good at pretending, after all."

Oliver looked from Jack to Eliza and back again. The man could clearly see there was more to the story. But if Oliver was aware of the issues, he didn't say anything. Instead, he picked up his files and formed them into a neat stack. Then he faced Eliza. "Where would you like to work?"

"Sports rings." She lifted her chin. No undercover

agent was going to make her feel like trash. "Put me in the roughest school you have. Where girls are most likely to be dragged into trafficking." She didn't have to ask if such a role would be more dangerous.

Of course it would be.

Eliza didn't care. "You can mic me and put me right in the path of the worst of them." She snarled at Jack. "Then you can see what I'm worth to the bureau."

Oliver nodded. "Okay. I'll talk with the team and see if that's a possibility." He motioned to the door. "Eliza, if you could give me and Jack a minute alone."

She hesitated, but she had no choice. *Fine.* She walked out the door and shut it hard behind her. Her throat was dry, so she walked to the office break room and grabbed a water. She didn't need surveillance equipment to know what was being said about her right now. Jack would explain how Eliza had a crush on him, always trying to kiss him. And how she was too immature and lovestruck to work as an informant—at least with him.

He would look like an FBI expert, and she . . . she would look like a fool.

She returned and waited down the hall from the office door. By the time Jack came out, Eliza couldn't look at him or talk to him. He must've felt the same way because he walked by without saying a word.

How could she ever have had feelings for him? He was cold and callous without a hint of genuine compassion. His kindness had been nothing more than an act. She met with Oliver Layton then, but only for a few minutes. Just long enough for him to promise he would try to get her undercover at a high school, one where sex traffickers often lured girls to work hotels during major sporting events.

Back at the group home, Eliza forced herself not to think about him. She would never work with Jack Ryder again, no matter what. Every gentle word or tender moment had been another of his lies. For the job, he would tell her if she gave him the chance. But where did that leave her? Didn't he care about her feelings?

Two days later Oliver worked out the details so she could, indeed, go undercover at one of the toughest high schools in San Antonio. The bureau had decided Eliza's lack of high school experience wasn't a problem. The kids she'd be hanging with didn't have much classroom experience, either.

Eliza couldn't have been happier.

If she needed training, she would do it. Whatever it took to get out in the field and help catch parasites like her father. The man who had stolen her childhood and nearly sold her into marriage. Her father had taken her childhood and her heart. Emotionally, she was damaged goods, and she always would be. Because her father had taken something else.

He had stolen her ability to ever be attractive to a guy like Jack Ryder.

• • •

THE TRAINING WAS more intense than Eliza had expected. She had never attended a high school, let alone one in the roughest part of a city like San Antonio. Terri and a team of agents worked with her, teaching her how to talk and dress and walk like someone from the east side of the city. This wasn't a typical high school undercover job, something local police would operate. This was connected to national trafficking rings that preyed on high school girls in certain areas in conjunction with sporting events.

Especially pro sporting events.

"It'll be hard enough, getting them to believe a messed-up white girl just happened to wind up at their school." Camille was black, one of the most intelligent and street-savvy agents in the bureau. "You gotta rat your hair and walk with an attitude. Don't smile. Wear heavy makeup. You'll talk different and sit different, cocky bad to the core. So they don't only believe you. They respect you."

On the inside, Eliza was already that girl. For years she'd seen that behavior modeled by the older girls at the Palace. But she didn't say that to Camille.

Instead Eliza worked at being even more what the bureau wanted. All day, every day she worked. And on the weekends in her bedroom at the group home she read about high school behavior and successful informants—books Camille had given her. She trained and studied morning to night, stopping to eat and sleep only when she absolutely had no choice.

One Sunday afternoon, Rosa found her in the living room looking over her class schedule, memorizing it. "This work you're doing . . . is it dangerous?" The girl looked worried.

Eliza smiled at her. "Not really."

"Good." Rosa sighed. "You're my best friend, Eliza. I don't want anything to happen to you."

Eliza looked at her for a long moment. "You get why I'm doing this, right?"

"Why?" Rosa was younger, but not that much.

"For you. For all the girls." She smiled at her young friend. "I'd give my life tomorrow if it meant putting men like my father behind bars."

Fear shone in Rosa's eyes. "But . . . you said—"

"Yes." She kept her tone light. "I'll be fine. I'm just saying, even if my new work becomes dangerous, I won't stop." Her voice wasn't much more than a whisper. She didn't want Stan and Melinda to worry about her. "I'd give my life to save girls like you."

"Okay." And in that moment a different look filled Rosa's face. The look of pride. "Maybe one day, I'll do that, too."

"Yeah, well." Eliza patted Rosa's shoulder. "For now worry about algebra. I want you girls to be the smartest in your classes."

Later Eliza thought about that. She wanted to be the smartest in her classroom, too. And in the coming weeks, that meant pretending to be a complete failure. She knew her part well by now. Transferred from a Dallas school. Living with her cousin's family. A record of drug convictions and petty theft and truancy.

Getting good grades wouldn't impress anyone at her new school. The exact opposite.

. . .

ELIZA'S TRAINING CONTINUED with basic martial arts. A street-smart girl would know what to do if some high school punk made a pass at her. "The guy needs to be on the ground before he can say his name," Camille told her.

Then Camille showed her.

After three days of practice, Eliza had no doubt she could take care of herself in a rough high school setting. She would get in with the worst of the tough kids and join them on their trips to the abandoned shopping mall across the street. Apparently the principal looked the other way, even when the bad students left halfway through the day.

"Too much crime and drug use going on to make a difference," Camille said. "Most educators would work around the clock to help kids. Not this one. For him, it's too much work to care."

In this case, that was a plus for Eliza. She didn't want to be busted by the principal. She wanted the feds to bust up the trafficking and drug sales happening at the mall across the street. Because it was there in that abandoned mall, Camille told her, that predators often preyed on girls from Northeast San Antonio High. The FBI suspected one or two of the senior girls were acting as go-betweens, convincing other girls to hang out across the street, and getting a financial reward if those girls fell into being trafficked.

"I'm impressed." Camille crossed her arms and smiled when Eliza demonstrated her best takedown of one of the male agents. "You're going to be great out there, Lawrence."

Eliza liked Camille's spunk. She wasn't sure of the agent's story, but she had a feeling the woman had overcome big obstacles in her past. Something that had driven her to one of the toughest jobs on earth.

Camille taught her in the classroom, too. The typical system of sex slavery was different from the one at the Palace. Eliza learned new information every hour. Of the twenty-five million people being trafficked around the world, twenty percent were trapped in a sex-slave ring. But not all of those lived in a mansion like Eliza had.

Many of the victims worked for traffickers during the day. The men would lure young girls—sometimes boys—into the circle by promising them jewelry or cash. At first the victims felt like they were on top of the world. Many of them had been neglected or overlooked by their parents, so the new attention from a predator was a rush.

But as soon as the girls turned a single trick, as soon as they realized they weren't going to keep any of the money, the abusers would flip things on them. Camille had talked with one of the girls who had turned herself in and made the bureau aware of the ring happening at East San Antonio.

"You know what she told me?" Camille's eyes were clear and sharp.

Eliza shook her head. She had no idea.

"She told me her mom was a single parent. Worked three jobs to keep food on the table and pay rent. A good mom, true to the core." Camille paused. "But as soon as that girl worked one time for the jerk, her trafficker swore if she didn't keep working he'd kill the girl's mother. So even though the girl went home to her mom every night, the woman never knew what was happening to her daughter during the daytime. Because the girl believed her abuser. She was scared to death. If she didn't work, she'd lose her mom."

Eliza knew what that felt like. She stared out the window of the bureau office. So much pain in the world. The darkness would've been too much if she hadn't already lived through it, herself. Watching her friends be forced into slavery night after night after night. She could hardly wait to mix in with the kids at East San Antonio High and identify the parasites preying on them.

Finally it was her last day of training. For the whole two weeks, Eliza hadn't seen Jack. He was working with the Dallas office, preparing for the raid in the Bahamas. Now that Eliza and Jack weren't working together, he was going to take part in the raid about to go down in Nassau. Pretending to be a customer this time. One of the most harrowing jobs an agent could have, according to Camille.

In some ways Eliza felt guilty about how she'd treated Jack. He had been doing his job, after all. His disinterest and rejection, the way he had only pretended to kiss her, all of it was exactly the way he was supposed to act. She should've grasped that, should've talked herself out of feeling rejected. If she could've tolerated his indifference, the way he had only acted like he cared for her, then they'd be headed for Honduras this week.

Instead they were taking part in separate, very dangerous missions.

Eliza didn't dwell on the fact. She didn't want to work with Jack, anyway. He should've known she was new to this whole undercover thing. Of course she would struggle with understanding the difference between the job and real life.

But there were moments when all she wanted was to be back on Paradise Island, walking the silky white sand, hand in hand with Jack Ryder. Times when she was at the group home and she would slip out back and sit on the family swing. Out there, under the stars, she would remember her time with Jack in the Bahamas very differently.

The touch of his hands on her skin, the way she felt safe and whole in his arms. And even the look in his eyes when they kissed. Especially the last time, in the surf off the beach on Bay Street. If only Jack really was attracted to her. But he wasn't. Otherwise he would've told her—

behind closed doors—that he had feelings for her and that he was only pushing her away because his job wouldn't let him fall in love with an informant.

But he never said that because it wasn't true. His lack of feelings for her was as clear as the Caribbean Sea.

At the end of the two weeks, Eliza was at the FBI building, sure Jack was still in Dallas and that he would leave for Nassau from there. Which was why she felt her breath catch that afternoon when he walked past her desk in the room where she was working. Jack met with Oliver for half an hour, and then he came back to her. She was still going over names of high school teachers and photos of students she needed to connect with.

"Hey." He waited a few feet from her. "Am I interrupting?"

She wanted to be mean, reject him the way he had rejected her. But she couldn't take her eyes off him. The sound of his voice was the best thing she'd heard since he'd gone to Dallas. She slid back from the desk. "I'm surprised you want to be seen with me."

"Eliza . . ." He stopped himself. Like there was more he wanted to say. Instead he asked her about training and the work she had ahead of her that Monday. "You have to be careful. The traffickers who work across the street from that school will be armed."

"Yes." She stood and walked toward him. But she stopped short. Well short. "They told me that, Jack. Camille's good. She taught me everything I need to know."

He bit his lip. "You've never been on the streets."

"I've been in worse." Did he care what happened to her? Was that what this was? She felt her expression soften. "I'll be fine."

Jack nodded. "Okay." He hesitated. "I leave in the morning."

"That's what I heard."

"Hey . . . so I've been doing a lot of thinking, Eliza." He looked uncomfortable. As if he were crossing lines just by sharing this much. "I'd like to talk with you. Tonight maybe? At the River Walk."

Eliza couldn't have been more surprised if he had told her he'd quit the bureau. She had no idea what he could possibly want to talk about, but she wanted to know. "All right." She kept her walls up. This was probably only him wanting to apologize. For how he had rejected her in Nassau.

He agreed to pick her up at six o'clock and bring her back by ten. He slid his hands in his pockets. "I can't be out late."

"Me, either." She wouldn't let him make the rules for her. She was perfectly capable of setting the parameters. "I'd rather be back by nine."

"Nine it is." He almost smiled at her. Or at least it looked that way. Instead he kept a straight face and nodded. "See you at six."

And Eliza could think about only one thing.

What in the world would she wear?

CHAPTER EIGHTEEN

Do not forget to show hospitality to strangers, for by
so doing some people have shown hospitality to
angels without knowing it.

—Hebrews 13:2

Jack had decided to tell her the truth—he had feelings for her. There was no way around the fact. Still, there could be nothing between them as long as she was an HLCI, as long as she was being paid to do mission work for the FBI and as long as he was an agent.

But she had to know how he felt. So he could explain himself.

She was angry with him, and God had made it clear why. God had made a lot of things clear. Which was one more thing he wanted to talk to Eliza about.

On the way to pick her up that evening, Jack thought about the events of the past two weeks. He and six other agents had stayed at a luxury condo in the pristine Lakeside Tower on Lake Grapevine, a quick drive from the Dallas FBI office. The place was owned by a friend of the bureau, a man who currently lived overseas.

Training took twelve hours a day, three days a week in the condo's spacious dining room. The other days, agents could do what they wanted. Golf or see the city or make time by themselves. Jack preferred the latter. His favorite spot had been the Northshore Trail, not far from the condo. Whenever he had a spare moment, Jack took to the trail. He had brought his hiking pants and a pair of Shimano trail boots. Work relationships were often built on the golf courses in and near Dallas.

But Jack had wanted to work on a different relationship.

His relationship with Jesus.

The first week at the condo, Jack spent every free hour hiking the trail. It wound twenty-two miles along the northern shore of Lake Grapevine, up hills and through thick brush with frequent views of the expansive stretch of dark blue water. Both cyclists and hikers used the trail, but the terrain wasn't for beginners.

At the start of the second week, Jack rented a mountain bike. He had ridden often in his days at the Naval Academy, the more challenging the course, the better. The lake trail was one of the most difficult Jack had ridden, and he attacked it each time, flying along the edges of cliffs and powering up steep hills with no care for his safety.

That Thursday Jack left the condo early and rode the bike to the trailhead. He had planned to cover the whole thing, push through the narrow, tougher areas the way he needed to work through the roadblocks in his life.

One mile had led to another and another, and Jack didn't stop for anything. He forced the bike down craggy sections of rock and along cliffs that seemed barely wide enough to hold a bike and rider. In some ways, the trail reminded him of the Cliffs of Moher, which he'd walked once on a mission in Ireland.

The faster Jack rode that day, the more he became lost in a world all his own. Like he wasn't really in Texas at all. At first he couldn't ride fast enough to escape the problems plaguing him. Then, one at a time, the questions began to catch up. Questions were good things, his dad had always told him.

Because the answers wouldn't be far behind.

Why didn't he care if he lived? Was that how his family would've wanted him to treat life? And how about love? Did he really want to spend his days alone? What about Eliza? Who was going to care for her? Love her? And of course the greatest question of all—was God real and if so, why had He taken Jack's family?

The questions ran on repeat in his mind. The harder he pushed himself—the more he asked of the bike and his lungs—the louder the questions grew until suddenly he turned a corner on the trail and came to a clearing.

Easily the prettiest spot on Lake Grapevine.

His sides heaved. Jack walked the bike up the grassy hill till he reached the top. There he laid the bike down and he sat on a flat rock, and all at once he saw his whole life play out before him. The Christmas mornings and summers in Belize, the conversations around the dinner table and the way his busy parents had spent more time with him after Shane died.

Like he was watching an actual movie, Jack could see every detail.

And then he heard the voice. A voice he hadn't heard since he was a boy.

Jack, I have loved you with an everlasting love. I still love you.

So clear and crisp were the words, Jack stood and jerked his head one way, then the other. He put his hand on his waistband, ready to draw his gun. But there was no one else on the hilltop. The trail was quiet today. Jack had only seen a few hikers the entire morning.

He dropped slowly to the rock again. "God . . . is that You?"

A warm wind came up off the water and washed over him. *I know the plans I have for you, Jack. Plans to give you a hope and a future . . . and not to harm you.*

Agents didn't cry. That was a rule Jack had set for himself when he began working for the FBI. He wouldn't let himself linger in sadness over losing Shane or his parents. And so his heart and mind and soul had become a computer. A machine capable of great heroism and unmatched courage and physical strength.

But along the way he had trained himself not to feel sadness.

Until that moment on the hill.

Tears welled in his eyes. "You love me?" Jack spoke the words into the wind. "You took my family!"

There was no answer, no voice in the breeze. But a story came to Jack, one his mother used to tell him and Shane when they were little. Before they went to school each morning.

"A boy makes his plans," she would say, a hand on each of their small shoulders. "But God ordains his steps."

At first Jack hadn't understood why his mother had quoted that Bible verse. But in time the words made sense. The people of God ought not write their to-do lists with indelible ink, but rather with the faintest pencil. Because in the end, God would have the final say about a person's story.

"This world is not our home," their father had told Jack after they buried Shane. "God decides the number of our days. The miracle is in having had Shane at all. Every day of his life was a gift, a blessing from God."

And there were other reminders. His mother would tell him that he was the clay and God the potter. "He will make of your days what He wants. So long as you keep loving, Jack. Love God. Love people. Don't ever stop loving."

Her words had filled his heart on that lonely hilltop, and he closed his eyes. *Love God. Love people.* Jack was very good at his job. But he had long since stopped doing either of those things. He hadn't loved God and he certainly hadn't loved people. Not when they could be gone in a single undertow or the instant detonation of a roadside bomb.

There on that flat rock overlooking Lake Grapevine,

everything his parents had ever told him, everything he'd ever read in the Bible, all of it landed on him again, with crystal clarity. And he understood something he hadn't before.

While he had used his life with the FBI for good work, he had missed out on really living.

Tears stung his eyes. "Good plans . . . even now, Lord? I'm supposed to believe that?"

And then the strangest thing had happened. As if out of thin air, a man had appeared on the trail below. He stopped when he saw Jack and then he made his way up to the top. The guy was young, black and athletic with pale brown eyes that had seemed the very definition of peace.

"Hey," the guy said. "Can I join you?"

Jack felt himself tense up. He squinted at the man, every instinct on high alert. Had he been trailing Jack? Was he part of a drug ring sent to kill Jack in the isolation of the trail? Jack had his gun, but suddenly as he studied the man he knew the answer. Knew it deep inside him. He wasn't going to need his weapon. The guy clearly didn't want a fight. And if he was out to get him, Jack would know soon enough. He hesitated before answering the man. He nodded. "Sure."

The guy was maybe in his mid-twenties, same as Jack. He brushed a pile of old leaves from a flat rock a few feet away and sat down. Then he looked directly at Jack. "I'm Beck." He paused. "You've been running hard, Jack."

A chill ran down Jack's body. He was wrong about the guy. He must've been trailing him, watching him. Probably a hired assassin sent from one of the traffickers Jack had taken down. He started to stand, started to reach for his gun.

But before Jack could say or do anything, Beck smiled. "I won't hurt you, Jack. I bring you good news."

Jack looked around again. How did the guy know his name? Was he being punked by the other Dallas agents? Or had he hit his head and now he was dreaming? He blinked a few times and stared at the man. "Beck?"

"Yes." He bent down and picked up a handful of loose dirt. "God is the potter. We're the clay." He turned to Jack again. "Your mother used to say that."

"How . . . how do you know that?" Jack's mouth had felt dry. He wasn't sure whether to run or fall to his knees.

"See, Jack." The strange man let the dirt sift through his fingers back to the ground. "Even though we're only clay, God loves us." He turned his otherworldly eyes to Jack. "He loves *you*." A soft chuckle came from the guy. "And yes, God is real. But then . . . you already knew that."

For the next half hour Beck had sat there, talking about what it meant to live and love. To put off all fear of loss, and embrace life. "By the way." Beck leaned over his knees and stared at Jack. "Shane and your parents . . . they're good." His smile faded. "But they want more for you. We all do."

"My family is dead."

Beck shook his head. "No." He looked out over the lake and his eyes lifted to the blue sky above. "They trusted in Jesus." Once more he turned to Jack. "They don't live here. But they're more alive than ever before."

Jack had wondered if he might pass out from the strangeness of the situation. *Who was this guy and why was he saying these things?* How could he have known not only Jack's name, but Shane's . . . and the fact that his family was long gone.

A minute of silence had passed between them. Then Beck stood and faced Jack. "Live life to the fullest, Jack. Jesus died so you could do that." Beck's kindness pierced straight through him. "Have you been living that way?"

Jack's answer wasn't needed. Obviously Beck already knew the truth. Jack looked at the water. "I made a lot of bad choices. After my parents died." It was true. Jack was a good guy by the world's standards. But he had moved from one girl to another.

Getting girls had been as easy as getting grades. No telling how many he had hurt along the way. Nothing had mattered to Jack back then. Right up until he met Oliver Layton. Shame filled Jack's voice as he explained that to Beck.

But the man only nodded. "All people sin. Everyone falls short." He waited a beat. "Even you. That's why you need a Savior, Jack. It's never too late, no matter what. Not for anyone."

Why had Jack never understood that before? He had

figured his chance with God—if there was a God—was behind him. His bad choices and reckless living had sealed the deal. But Beck was right, of course. There was still time to turn things around.

Jack hadn't been sure what to say.

After a few seconds, Beck reached out his hand and the two shook. As their fingers touched, another chill ran down Jack's spine. Beck lowered his voice, as if this was the most important part. "God is always a whisper away." He smiled. "Let go of the past, Jack. Love God. Love people . . . love again."

There they were. The same words his mother had always told him. *Love God. Love people.*

Tears filled Jack's eyes, and there, with the stranger standing before him, Jack did something he had never done in front of anyone. Not since Shane died. He covered his face with his hands and he began to weep. He missed them so much, his family. Training himself to feel nothing, care about nothing but the mission ahead of him, had also denied him this.

The chance to grieve.

"God . . ." He still had his hands over his face. "I'm sorry. I . . . I need You." He wanted to love again, he really did. And maybe now . . . maybe in light of this conversation, he and Eliza could . . . maybe they could . . .

He didn't let himself go there.

Jack wanted to thank Beck, whoever he was and however he knew so much, so he lowered his hands. He wanted to explain to the guy that this moment had answered questions he'd had for ten years. But when he blinked his eyes open . . . the man was gone.

"Beck!" He called the guy's name out loud, loud enough so that he'd hear him. But there wasn't a rustle or sound, no snapping twigs or footsteps on the distant trail to indicate which way Beck had walked off.

The man had vanished.

Jack looked at the flat rock beside him, the one where Beck had been sitting. The dirt and leaves were there again, and there were no signs of the brush marks Beck had made when he dusted off the surface.

A dizzy feeling came over Jack, and he covered his face again. What had happened? How could the guy just disappear? And how had he known Jack's name and his story, the situation with his family?

But his efforts at making sense of the moment lasted only a few seconds. Then he dropped his hands again and stared out at the water. Another memory came to him. His mother explaining to him about God's messengers, beings sent to take part in a rescue or a mission, heavenly soldiers with a word from the Lord.

One Christmas she had told him, "Angels are real. Not just in the story of the birth of Jesus. But today. For you and me and your father. For all people."

An angel? Was Beck a soldier sent from heaven? he had wondered. *Sent to talk to him here on this hillside?* The longer Jack thought about the possibility, the more he was sure. Beck was definitely an angel. He had to be. And the words Jack had heard when he first reached the top of the hill were true.

God did love him. He always had.

Earth was . . . well, it was just earth. Eternity lay on the other side. Each day in a person's life this side of heaven was a gift. Nothing more. No guarantees about tomorrow. And in that knowledge God wanted one thing from him.

Jack had seen it all clearly in that moment. His Father in heaven wanted him to let go of the past and look to the future. *Love God, love people.* And God had brought a girl into his life who was just like him. She didn't care if she lived or died. She didn't love God and didn't love people.

Eliza Lawrence. Lizzie James.

In all the world, Jack was the only person who understood her, who knew what it was like to lose everything and hate the world. Hate life itself—all at the same time. What it felt like to care only about the mission.

Back at the hotel, Jack spent the next hour reading his Bible, Psalm 23 and then Hebrews Chapter Two and all of First John. The words filled Jack's soul and gradually they changed him. God had loved Jack first, and because of that He wanted Jack to love people.

Especially Eliza.

Not romantically, no matter how attracted he was to her. Because of the job. But with the love of God, so that Eliza would understand her worth. So he could tell her about how much God cared about her . . . and about the new life He offered for her. For him, too. And so she could see herself the way God saw her—as a child whole and set free and fully loved by God.

Defined by love, not victimhood. By grace, not the grievous things she'd been forced to do in bringing other girls to the Palace. God's love was a love Eliza desperately needed. The way Jack himself needed it.

The memory of that day in Dallas faded and Jack gripped the steering wheel. *Don't get ahead of yourself,* he told himself. *She won't be expecting this. Take your time.* As he drove down her street, he forced himself to relax. He had no idea how he was going to tell her all of this, but he had to try. Tomorrow they would face great dangers.

After tonight, he might not have another chance.

• • •

THEY PARKED IN the first spot Jack could find. He wasn't sure it was smart, heading out like this so soon before a mission. But he had no choice. He wanted to see her before they parted ways, especially with the missions that lay ahead for them both.

"I've only heard about this place." Eliza wore a sleeveless white pantsuit. She looked so beautiful, he could hardly breathe.

"The River Walk is what San Antonio is known for." He wanted so bad to take her hand. But this wasn't work, and he wouldn't cross that line. It wasn't right. "I have a surprise for you."

"A surprise?" She sounded cautious, hopeful.

Jack tried to imagine who Lizzie James would've been if she'd had the chance to grow up in Lower Barton Creek. Under the watchful, loving eyes of Ike Armstrong. He pushed the thought from his mind.

Friday nights at the River Walk were always crowded and tonight was no exception. Once in a while Jack came here to people-watch. Tonight he was doing something he'd only seen other people do. He was taking Eliza on a dinner cruise.

She was different tonight, somehow. Softer. Kinder. More comfortable in her own skin. Maybe the two weeks away from him and her continued counseling had helped her relax a little. Not that any amount of counseling could ever undo the trauma of her life. But it could at least teach her to cope.

And to believe she had purpose beyond what her evil father had planned for her.

As they reached the boat dock, Jack saw two middle-aged guys running toward them. They weren't targeting Jack and Eliza but they were aggressive all the same. Jack put his arm around her slim shoulders and moved her out of the path of the men. He turned to her. "Sorry. They would've run right over you."

"Thanks." She took a quick breath. "I'm not used to being around so many people."

"Here." Jack took her hand. *This isn't crossing lines*, he told himself. He was only helping her navigate the walkway. He grinned at her. "Where we're going, there won't be crowds."

He led her down a few stairs to a ticket booth and minutes later he was helping her onto a pink flat-bottomed boat. Jack walked with her to a spot near the back. The name "Luke" was on the Reserved sign.

"Really?" Eliza's happiness was genuine. "For me?" As if she were any other twenty-year-old. Like she hadn't spent half her life in captivity.

She wore a white and yellow ribbon in her hair, and as she took her seat, her smile remained. "I've never done anything like this."

That was true. Growing up captive in the Palace, Eliza hadn't taken part in most normal activities. But Jack didn't mention that. "It looks like Venice. In Italy." He glanced behind them and ahead. "Don't you think?"

A soft laugh came from her. "I've read about Venice. But . . . I haven't been there."

"Yeah, I guess not." They had so little in common in some ways. And so much, all at the same time. "Well, now you know a little of what Venice looks like."

Sitting across from her, Jack could almost believe this was their first date. Almost.

When the cruise was under way and they were me-andering down the narrow river, Jack took a deep breath. There was no easy way to begin. "Eliza . . . I'm sorry." He kept his hands on his knees beneath the table. So he wouldn't be tempted to take hold of hers again. The last thing he wanted was to confuse her . . . or himself. "I brought you here so I could apologize."

"You didn't do anything wrong." Her anger was gone. That was the difference. The change only made her more beautiful.

"Yes, I did. I wasn't honest with you." He leaned closer. This conversation was for just the two of them. "You thought I didn't like pretending to be your husband, is that right?"

"Yes." She looked down for a moment. "That was obvious."

"Okay . . . so that's why I'm sorry. Because that wasn't it at all." He ran his fingers through his hair. There was no easy way to get to the point. "Eliza . . . you won't believe this." He chuckled. "I think I met an angel." He shook his head. "Anyway, I've been talking to God. For real. I really believe He wanted me to meet with you."

"You talked to God?" She narrowed her eyes. "You said you weren't sure you even believed. Because of . . . what happened."

"Right. That was before. But these last few weeks I realized . . . whenever I needed Him, I was still praying. Still asking for His help." He paused. "So I asked Him again and this guy . . . this stranger showed up. I can tell you more later, but when he left, I asked God about you."

"Me?" She looked to the deepest part of him. "Why?"

"Because I'd hurt you. I knew it." Jack had to make

her understand. He chose his words with great care. "But now I know *why* I hurt you."

This time she didn't respond, but her eyes never left his.

Nothing could've stopped him from taking her hands now, not with what he was about to tell her. He reached out and gently eased his fingers between hers. Friends could do this, right? If not, they could sort out the confusion later. For now there was only the river, the San Antonio September sky, and the two of them.

He ran his thumbs over her soft hands. "Eliza, it wasn't that I didn't like pretending to be your husband." He let himself get lost in her eyes. "It was that I couldn't make myself pretend *not* to be."

Doubt and disbelief seemed to come over her in a rush. She pulled her hands free and sat back in her seat. "What . . . what are you saying?"

"I'm saying . . . I *couldn't* kiss you. Because . . . I was falling for you."

Her expression changed with every breath. Trust and belief. Joy and delight, gratitude and hope. In an instant, his words had set her free from her darkest fear. That he could never see her as worth pursuing . . . because of what she viewed as her criminal past.

There was still much to tell her, and even now this could only be a friendship. Because of the important work they both had to do. But it would be a friendship deeper than either of them had known. A love with God at the center. But before he could put his thoughts into words, Eliza did something that told Jack everything would be okay. Even though they could not possibly be romantically involved, and even though they would never kiss again, at least she didn't hate him anymore. She forgave him.

Jack knew. Because in that next moment she took his hands in hers.

And this time, neither of them let go.

CHAPTER NINETEEN

As surely as the Lord lives and as you live, I will
not leave you.

—2 Kings 2:2

Eliza was dreaming. That was the only way to explain
what was happening. Had Jack Ryder really just said he
was falling for her? And that's why he hadn't wanted to
kiss her? She fought to keep her reaction measured.

I still don't want love, she told herself. *I don't want to*
date him.

But at least now she understood what had happened
in the Bahamas. Jack wanted her, he was attracted to her.
Nothing that he'd done while they were in Nassau had
been a rejection. And even though she still worked to
keep her walls up, they were falling apart with every
passing moment. Because Jack was different. He wasn't
like any man she'd ever imagined knowing. Right now all
she wanted was to sit in this moment. Live in it. In case
this time with him really was only a dream.

Eventually their dinner arrived. Eliza wanted to
freeze time so she could hear what Jack meant about

God telling him to meet with her. And so she could hear about this angel. If that's what it was. When they were done eating, she folded her hands in her lap. "Thank you. For telling me about the Bahamas." She didn't look down this time. "I thought it was because of . . . the Palace."

"I know. I get that now." Jack shook his head. "That's behind you, Eliza. Another lifetime ago." His blue eyes darkened. "Besides . . . I have my past, too."

Whatever he was referring to, his yesterdays certainly would have paled in comparison with hers. But Eliza let the subject go. "So . . . we can be friends. Is that what you're saying?"

"It is." Sincerity shone in his expression. "I need to learn to care again. God made that clear last week, too."

"And He told you to care about *me*?" She couldn't believe it. This was what he'd wanted to tell her? It was the last thing she'd expected.

"Yes." He slid his hands across the table again. "Is it okay? If we hold hands?" He paused. "We have to be careful."

"We will be." She did a slight shrug. "Friends hold hands."

"Exactly." His eyes never left hers. "Eliza . . . I've been alone since my parents died. I haven't let my heart connect. Not with anyone."

One of the walls fell. "Me, either." She moved her hands toward his. *Until now*, she wanted to say. But she didn't want to give him the wrong impression. She could use a friend in this new life of hers. Nothing more. Even so, when their fingers were connected she felt the most wonderful sensation.

Like she could actually breathe. For the first time since her days in Lower Barton Creek.

. . .

THEY WERE WALKING back to the car when it happened.

Jack had gone to the restroom and left her at a well-lit table along the river walkway. Eliza had learned long ago how to keep guys from looking at her. Don't make eye contact. Looking into the eyes of a man could sometimes make him think he had the right to approach.

So Eliza kept her attention on the river, on the next boat making its way down the water. But then out of nowhere, she heard someone yell. She turned and saw a man sitting at a table directly across the path. He looked right at her.

"Hey, beautiful!" He was tall with dark hair and a tank top. Three guys sat with him.

Again Eliza looked away.

The man must've been drunk. Because his tone grew angry and he cussed at her. "Don't disrespect me!" He was on his feet, and one of his friends tried to grab his hand. But the guy was undaunted.

If he touched her she'd flip him to the ground. Like Camille had taught her to do back at the FBI office. But what if he was a trafficker? What if he wanted to kidnap her? Fear seized her as she looked toward the pavilion. If Jack didn't come now, she would run. But if she ran, how would she meet up with him again? Then she remembered. She had a cell phone, and she knew Jack's number.

She stood, but even as she did, the man stormed across the pathway toward her.

Come on, Jack. Eliza glanced toward the restrooms. She was deciding which way to run when suddenly the guy was on her. He grabbed her by the shoulders and started to pull her toward his sweaty body. Eliza wrapped her right foot around his ankle and tried to drop the guy to the ground.

But he was too big, too strong.

"Stop—" She started to scream, but before the sound was out of her mouth someone grabbed the guy. Eliza spun around and there was Jack.

He took rough hold of the tall man's shoulder and then drove his fist straight into the guy's face. The attacker reeled back and dropped to his knees. At the same time his friends ran up.

"Sorry, man," one of them said to Jack. "Too much beer. He won't bug you again."

Jack was still staring at the guy on the ground. Like he wanted to kill him. He said nothing to the other three. Just shot the drunk man one final, menacing look and then turned to her. "Are you okay?" He fixed her hair and put his arm around her shoulders. "I'm sorry, Eliza. That . . . that never should've happened."

"I tried to trip him." Her teeth were chattering. "He . . . he was stronger."

"You're stronger than you think, Eliza. You just need practice."

"I thought . . . he would kidnap me."

"No." Jack searched her eyes. "No one will ever do that to you." He studied her. "Come on." He led her through the crowd. "I have somewhere I want to take you. Is that all right?"

"Yes." She didn't hesitate. It was nearly nine already, but Eliza didn't care. Tomorrow they'd be separated for months. Maybe forever. Right now she didn't want to be anywhere in the world but with Jack Ryder.

He drove her to the bureau building. "This won't take long."

"Are you allowed to be here? After hours?" The place looked dark. Only a few windows had lights behind them.

"Twenty-four-seven." He winked at her. "FBI agents have flexible hours."

He parked and hurried around the car to hold her door. Eliza hesitated because who was this guy? Treating her like a *real* princess? She'd read about guys like him in books, but she never dreamed they really existed.

Especially for a girl like her.

Jack entered a code on a panel near the elevator, and they rode up to the top floor. Eliza felt her heart beating hard against her chest as Jack walked with her to a small room marked STORAGE. "I know." He looked at her as he worked the key in the door. "Now you think I'm crazy."

"True." She laughed and waited. "Long before this."

Finally he made his way inside and after a few seconds he came out holding a flat leather bag, weathered and worn. The old bag looked somehow familiar. Jack pointed up. "Have you been to the rooftop?"

"Here at the bureau?" She had no idea what he was up to. "This building has a rooftop?"

"Let's find out."

She laughed. "Lead the way."

Jack took her hand and when they were back in the elevator he pushed the R button. "Rooftop." He grinned at her. "That's . . . the R."

"There's always something new to learn around here." Eliza studied him. The curve of his face and the strength in his arms. In the morning he would be on a flight to Nassau. Eliza had heard Camille say it was going to be the most dangerous raid of the year.

But right now Jack looked more like a college kid than a daring undercover agent.

The elevator doors opened again and they stepped out into a lush garden. Trees and bushes, a meandering pathway. All on the top of the FBI building. "It's beautiful. I had no idea."

"An oasis in the Hill Country of Texas." Jack led her down the path to a covered swing with a view of the city. "You . . . said you like to swing."

She laughed again. "See? We're already friends." She

took the spot on one side of the swing. "Look how well you know me."

"So true." He sat beside her and held the worn bag on his lap. It wasn't any bigger than a briefcase. The air between them grew more serious, and after a long moment he turned and handed it to her. "This is yours."

"Mine?" She took the bag. No wonder it looked familiar. "How . . . where would you find something that belonged to me?"

"From your great-grandfather." Jack set the swing in motion. Slow and easy. "Before I left that day, he went back into the house and brought out this. He wanted to go through the items one at a time. The things inside, they were precious to him. He asked me to give them to you." He paused. "In case by some miracle I ever found Lizzie James alive."

Eliza took the bag and then slowly she hugged it close. She remembered the feel of it. Her great-papa had loved her so much. She lifted her eyes to Jack's again. "And here we are."

"Right." Jack shifted so he could see her better. "Here we are."

She wasn't sure she wanted to look through the contents now. But Jack was waiting, watching her. So she opened the soft container and one at a time, she removed the items. Her very best handwriting samples and a page of math work. A drawing of Eliza and her family with her name scribbled at the bottom.

Lizzie James.

Next was her drawing of their house, and finally a picture she'd colored of the ocean. Eliza stared at it for a long time. "I always loved the water."

"You could see God there." Jack rested his arm on the back of the swing. "I remember."

"Yes." She pulled out an old teddy bear. The one she had loved as a little girl. She held it to her face for a long moment. She could still smell her home in its fur. Finally she set the bag down and closed her eyes. "I saw Him . . . there at the far edge of the sea." After a moment she opened her eyes and slid the items back into the bag. "My mother loved my drawings."

He was looking at her the way he had looked at her in the Bahamas, when he thought people might be paying attention. Only no one was watching now. This feeling, the electricity between them was something he must have felt, too. Because he lightly brushed his fingers against her bare shoulder.

And then almost at the same time he folded his arms. He studied her for a long while. "Can I tell you about the angel?"

"Yes." She exhaled. He was right to change the subject. If they were going to be friends, they couldn't linger in times like this. "By angel . . . you mean a real angel? With wings?"

"No." He smiled. "His name was Beck. He looked like a person. Like a police officer, maybe. Or an athlete. He showed up out of nowhere when I was taking a break on a trail near a lake."

Then he told her how he'd been flying down the trail on the rented mountain bike, asking God question after question. "About life and my family." He hesitated. "About you."

She wanted desperately to know what he had asked God about her. But that could wait. "Is that when you took the break?"

"Yes. I sat on this hill overlooking the water and all these stories kept coming back. Things my parents had taught me from the Bible."

The words hit hard. She had been raised in the same type of family. A mother who told Daniel and her stories from the Bible.

Jack continued, about how suddenly Beck had shown up. "He knew my name." Jack moved the swing forward again. "Then he told me something no one could know. He said my family was doing good."

"Your family?" She felt a chill run down her arms. "Did Beck maybe have you confused with someone else?"

"No." Jack looked out at the night sky. "He knew my name, Eliza. And he knew my parents and my brother. He knew they didn't live here. But he told me they were more alive now than ever. Because they had trusted Jesus."

The words filled Eliza's heart. *More alive than ever?* Was that how her mama and Daniel were? Running and playing and working in a city beyond the sky? Counting the days until she might join them? Was that where she'd be now if she hadn't been rescued from the ocean that day?

Jack brought the angel story to life, every detail. Beck had told him that his family wanted more for him. Same with God. And that's why he had come to talk with Jack. "And at the end he told me God was only a whisper away, and to forget the past." Jack turned to her. "He told me God wanted me to love again. Then he disappeared."

She didn't move, didn't speak.

"Eliza. I think he meant you." He took her hand once more, and his eyes stayed on hers. "I have no one else to love . . . no one to care about . . . except you."

And she had no one to love but him. But she didn't say as much. This wasn't the time, alone here on the rooftop, with him so close that all she wanted was for him to kiss her. He had moved nearer in the telling of the story. She didn't trust herself another minute longer, so she eased her hand free and stood. "It's beautiful up here."

"It is." He joined her, taking the spot beside her. But he didn't touch her, didn't take her hand. "Where you're going . . . East San Antonio High. It's dangerous, Eliza."

"I know." She faced him. The moonlight in his eyes was something she would remember forever. "You, too."

"I always know I might not come back. With every mission." He didn't look away. "And that was always okay. Because I had no one waiting for me. Back here."

She could feel his arms around her even though he was a foot away. She searched his eyes. "And now?"

"I don't know what tomorrow will bring. Or the next year or the year after that." He held out his hands to her. "I only know I want to come home. I want to see you again."

How could she do anything but take his hands? And as she did he closed the gap between them and eased her into his arms. "Be careful," he whispered near the side of her face. "Please, Eliza."

"I will." She pressed her cheek against his. The heat of his body made her tremble. "You, too."

He took a step back, but it was like pulling steel from a magnet. The connection between them remained. "I . . . I asked Jesus to forgive me." He took a slow breath. "I'll never know who Beck was or why he found me in that exact moment. But I do know something for sure."

"You know God is real." She could see it in his eyes. "That's it, right?"

"Yes." His expression changed. Like he was imploring her. "You know it too, right, Eliza?"

The answer had come to her gradually in the past hour. She nodded. "I do. Otherwise we wouldn't be standing here."

Jack pulled her into another hug and swayed with her for a minute or two. Finally he took hold of both her hands and exhaled. "Being friends is a tricky thing."

She was glad for the cover of night. So he wouldn't see the blush in her cheeks. "I can't come back here after tomorrow. Oliver said I'll have to use the Dallas office. It's close to where I'll be working."

"I know." He put his hand alongside her face and brushed her hair back with his thumb. "It'll be a while before I see you again."

If only he would kiss her. Friends could kiss, right? She put the thought out of her mind. That wasn't the kind of friendship either of them could have. It wasn't allowed. No matter how they felt here, now.

A long breath came from Jack. He was clearly struggling, too. The physical temptation was real for him, she understood that now. Like he had told her over dinner. But with all they were feeling, Jack said something she could never have expected.

"Eliza . . . can I pray for you?"

Her tears came without warning. Not since her mother had disappeared in the ocean had anyone ever prayed for her. Not until this moment. She couldn't speak, couldn't look at him. Instead she closed her eyes and nodded.

"Father, the two of us, we're alone in the world." Jack held her hands a little more tightly. "But at least now we have You. And we have each other." His hesitation told her he was struggling with his emotions. "Please, God. Keep Eliza safe. If Beck was an angel . . . then put Your angels around us both." He pulled her close once more, his breath in her hair. "Until we can be together again. In Jesus's name, amen."

Any other man Eliza had ever known in the past decade would have taken advantage of her on a night like this. Not Jack Ryder. And as they rode the elevator back to ground level and as he took her home and held her door and hugged her goodbye, Eliza was struck by the most beautiful thought.

For the first time in her life, she had seen God somewhere other than the ocean.

CHAPTER TWENTY

. . . Because they cried out to Him during the battle.
He answered their prayers, because they trusted
in Him.

—1 Chronicles 5:20

The mission was different this time. Jack felt like he saw danger around every corner, guns aimed in his direction and people looking at him longer than necessary. Like everyone could tell he was an agent and not a client.

Or maybe not. Maybe the only thing different was Jack. Because he wasn't the same person now. After his talk on the rooftop with Eliza, for the first time in his life with the FBI he wanted something more than a successful mission.

He wanted to live.

There had been no word from Eliza, but that wasn't a surprise. She had a new phone, a new name, new identity. Crystal Caldwell. Bad girl up from Dallas. That's what they had decided for her cover. Her laptop and phone. Her iPad. All of it was set up to match her new persona. She could email him through the bureau's server, but not until she felt established in her new environment—which he hoped would be any day.

For now, the last thing she could do was reach out to Jack Ryder, FBI agent.

It was Day Three in the Nassau operation, and Jack and the other operatives were about to make their various moves. Jack played the part of a wealthy college kid, hanging out at the beach. He wasn't clean shaven like when he was here with Eliza, and he wore a flat white straw hat. So none of the bad guys from before would recognize him.

At first, Oliver had wanted to send someone else on this mission. Just in case Jack was spotted as being the same guy who'd been there with Eliza. But Jack was the only agent on the operation who had seen the men the first time around. He knew their patterns and their cars and their home base. He would recognize the men and the teenage girls they used to recruit the younger girls. No, the mission was Jack's to finish, and he wasn't afraid to do so.

He just wanted to come home when it was completed.

The raid was set to begin at three-eleven that afternoon. It was an intentional number. One of the trafficked girls had been murdered recently, and her body had washed up on shore not far from the fish fry strip. Her birthday was March 11.

Jack watched the time on his phone. The men had approached him a few times, testing him, making vague offers. Three days in and Jack had their trust. At three ten he stood and stretched. His go bag was in a vehicle with the agents who would take him to a private airstrip when the raid was over. Fifteen minutes from now, if all went well. Part of the reason the traffickers would trust him was because he didn't have a backpack or beach bag.

Just a Smith & Wesson in his waistband.

He sauntered to the area near the playground where he'd talked with the traffickers yesterday. *This is for you, Eliza. Help me, God. Let's get these guys off the street.* He leaned against a palm tree and waited. But not for long.

After a few seconds a guy walked up. One of the two who had tried to take the little girl when Jack was here with Eliza. "You looking for something?" The man didn't make eye contact. He kept his gaze on pivot, watching, worried.

"Just a little fun." That was the code phrase. The men had told him yesterday that they had ways to entertain tourists. If he was interested, he needed only to say the words. And now he had.

The man nodded and lit a cigarette. "Come on." He nodded for Jack to follow him. There was no further conversation, but a hundred yards down Bay Street Jack saw the yellow car. This goon's buddy was in the driver's seat, no doubt.

After a minute the car pulled up. The trafficker slid into the passenger seat and Jack took the backseat. From this point to the house, he was on his own. If they figured out his real identity, they would take him to some remote spot and kill him. No one would ever find his body.

Jack worked to keep his cool. "Hey . . . you got a smoke?"

"No." The driver snapped at him. Then he laughed—a sickening laugh. "I got something better."

Locking these two up was going to be one of the highlights of Jack's career. He clenched his jaw and stared out the window. The driver seemed to be going a different way than before, and Jack felt his heart skip a beat. Was this it? Would the agents on the ground know where they were taking him?

They drove another ten minutes and pulled up at a dilapidated ranch house surrounded by a chain-link fence and weeds three feet high. This definitely wasn't the right house. Swagger was critical. "This don't look like any kind of fun to me."

"Shut up." The man in the passenger seat glared at Jack over his shoulder. "We got a pickup."

The driver looked back, too. "Two hundred dollars. Cash."

"Forget it." Jack lowered his head and stared out the window at the house. "Not till I see what I'm buying."

For the longest moment in Jack's life the two just looked at him, studied him. Then the driver said something to his buddy, and that guy got out of the car. Jack guessed he was picking up cocaine. All the better. None of their recon had ever proved that the men were dealing drugs, too. But the more charges the better.

So this gang would never again see the light of day.

It felt like an hour, but after a few minutes the passenger seat goon returned and climbed inside. He carried a large grocery bag. It looked heavy. He shot Jack another look. "You ain't seen nothin'. Got it?"

Jack held both hands up. "Hey . . . you're the one making a sale, buddy. If you're not selling, take me back to the beach."

They were the right words. Because both men turned their attention to the road and after another few minutes they pulled up at the white brick house Jack had seen when he was with Eliza. The one that looked like a mansion. At least in this part of Nassau.

Every move, every word, it all mattered now. Jack climbed out and slid his hands into his shorts pockets. "This looks better."

The driver walked straight up to him, inches from Jack's face. "Pay me."

It was a test. No one would pay now, when there was no proof of a girl waiting on the other side of the front door. Jack laughed. He looked one way and then the other. "What is this, a sting?" He took a step toward the man. "Take me inside or take me back to the beach. I see what I buy. That's the way it works."

Without turning around, Jack could hear a car on the street behind this one. Two cars maybe. Agents getting ready for the raid. He shifted. "Look, forget it."

Again the wary man relaxed. They were about the same height, but the other guy looked like an NFL lineman, muscles on muscles and skeleton tattoos on every inch of his body. He wasn't the gang leader, though. That coward was inside and he usually didn't leave the place until well after midnight. Scurrying around in the dark like a cockroach. When no one was looking.

Jack followed the lineman to the front door. The smaller man from the passenger seat had already gone inside with his bag of drugs. Again, this could be an ambush. Jack was armed, but it wouldn't do him any good until he had backup.

Four against one was a death trap.

Help me, God . . . I need You. Jack stepped inside behind the big guy and his eyes tried to adjust. The house was dimly lit by candles and incense burning in the foyer and on tables down a long hallway. *Sickening,* he thought. According to surveillance, ten young teenage girls rotated in and out of these rooms.

From down the hall, a door opened and the smaller guy poked his head out. Then he pulled from inside the room one of the teenage girls Jack and Eliza had seen on the beach. She looked drugged, her legs unsteady, her face and eyes caked with thick makeup. Her short black silk gown barely covered anything.

"Here," the man yelled. "A little fun."

He pulled the girl back into the room. Jack's training had taught him how to slow his heart rate in situations like this. Steady breathing, focus on objects not people. But again this time was different.

By now two agents and the Bahamian police would

be in the backyard, surrounding the dwelling. One of them would be on the roof of the detached garage, a rifle scope trained on the guy trying to get his money.

"You saw what you're getting." The man crossed his arms, legs spread. He was looking angrier by the second. "Two hundred dollars."

Jack pulled his wallet from his pocket, his hands cool and steady. *Get me out of here, God. Rescue me from this.* He peeled ten twenties from the billfold and handed them to the man. At the same time windows broke in every direction.

"Police!" The cry rang from all four corners of the house.

"What the . . . ?" Jack was supposed to run out, the way a would-be customer might do if a raid went down.

Instead, the big guy shoved Jack against the wall and before he could do anything about it, the man had a gun at his temple. "Everyone freeze." He spit at Jack's face. "Or your pretty informant's a dead guy."

So he did know. This was the worst possible situation. The agents creeping their way closer didn't dare do anything to get Jack killed. He closed his eyes. *This is my hour, God. Help me, please. Right now.*

The smaller guy bolted out of one of the rooms down the hall, gun raised. But before he could pull the trigger, the lineman turned and fired a single bullet through the man's forehead.

"That's for ratting on me." The big guy watched his buddy fall to the floor, facefirst. Then the shooter pushed his face against Jack's. "Open your eyes, pig. I want my face to be the last you see."

Jack kept his eyes closed. He wasn't about to do what the man said. His next breath would be his last, he was certain. *Watch over Eliza, Lord. She needs You.*

A single gunshot rang out and the lineman fell to the floor.

Nothing made sense. Jack had been in a fatal trap, no way out. So how did his captor . . .

"Go!" It was a Bahamian police officer in uniform. "Out the front door."

Jack hesitated only a moment. Something about the man was familiar, but then, that was impossible. He ran outside as gunfire broke out in the building. The shooting lasted only ten seconds or so and then agents and police officers began streaming through the front door.

A little while after, two agents including Camille walked the girls from the bedrooms onto the front lawn. They'd killed a total of three traffickers and arrested another two. None of the agents or officers were harmed.

All because of that one cop. Jack needed to catch a plane back to Texas, but he wanted to find the guy first. Jack had no idea how the man had breached the building, but his aim and shot had been perfect, taking out the lineman before the guy could pull his trigger.

Half a second off and Jack would be dead.

He walked through the small crowd gathered on the lawn and then around to the back of the house. But he couldn't find the man. He asked a few Bahamian police, but none of them seemed familiar with him. "None of our officers were in the house when the shot was fired," the captain told Jack.

That's when it hit him who the officer looked like. Of course.

The man had looked like Beck.

. . .

JACK WAITED TILL he was in the plane before taking out his laptop. Maybe this would be the day he'd have a first email from Eliza. If she had found a secure location, and if she felt safe, she could log in and tell him everything he was dying to know.

Eliza would also use the server to talk to her superiors, let them know if anything unusual was happening or if she needed a quick rescue. The brass watched everything that came and went through the server, but Jack didn't care.

He had talked to Oliver about his friendship with Eliza, and how it was definitely not anything more. "She needs someone who cares about her," Jack had explained before he left.

Oliver had hesitated. After all, he was the first to notice Jack's feeling for the Belizean girl. But in the end his boss agreed. "Everything you write to her will be read by a dozen people. Just so you know."

Jack had nodded. "I have nothing to hide, sir."

So it was that now Jack opened a blank email and began to write.

Dear Eliza,

I'm alive. The mission was successful, but I won't lie. It got a little dicey at the end. I don't want to think about what could've happened, but at the last moment a Bahamian police officer saved my life. He looked a lot like Beck.

Remember him? The guy I told you about.

Jack wasn't about to talk angels here, where everyone could read about it. The brass would think he'd lost his mind. And maybe he had. Maybe the whole story with Beck had only been his imagination. God's way of getting his attention. It didn't matter. Eliza would know what he meant. He started typing again.

Anyway, I'm fine and the operation is behind us. The girls were rescued—all of them. Camille was with us, and she saw to that. Be safe out there.

Until next time,
Jack

There was so much more he wanted to say. But that would do for now. He sent the email and then saw another one land in his inbox. From the agent on the ground in Belize. The subject line read only "Answers."

Jack opened it and read through the letter as quickly as he could.

Jack, I want to let you know I made a careful sweep through the Mennonite communities in Belize. The bureau agreed with you that your informant Ike Armstrong in Lower Barton Creek might've been onto something. We had hoped to find Eliza Lawrence's mother and brother, because they would make great witnesses in our growing case against Betsy Norman.

Unfortunately, the woman and her son are not living in Belize. Not in one of the Mennonite communities, anyway. We're going to wrap up this part of our investigation. Just wanted you to know.

CJ

No! Jack's heart sank as he closed the laptop. He hadn't told Eliza that he'd asked for a search of the small Mennonite communities. The places where Ike Armstrong believed his granddaughter and her children might be living—if they were alive. Deep in Jack's soul, he'd had a hunch about Eliza's mother and brother. A hunch that Ike Armstrong had somehow been right.

After years working the job, Jack's hunches were usually spot-on. Or at least close. But not this time, not if they were closing that part of the investigation. If Eliza's family members weren't in one of the Mennonite villages in Belize then only one conclusion remained.

They had drowned on the Belizean beach the day

before Eliza was taken captive by her father and Betsy Norman.

Hunch or not, this time Jack had been wrong.

• • •

SIX MONTHS HAD passed and still Eliza couldn't stop thinking about Jack. All they had was email, and even that didn't happen often. Sometimes at night she would remember the Bahamas and the River Walk and the rooftop. The things he had said to her.

So she wouldn't forget his voice.

Eliza had gone to East San Antonio High School for three months before the traffickers made their move on her. She had stood up to them, and in the most terrifying moment of her life, they had grabbed her and dragged her toward a waiting car.

Let me live, God, she had prayed silently. They were words she never thought she'd say. And suddenly, like something from a movie, agents converged on them, guns drawn.

"I knew you was undercover," the bad guy said as agents whisked her to a waiting bureau car. A sports sex-trafficking ring that had been in business for two years was now broken up and its leaders jailed because of her work.

Next Eliza was moved to Dallas. There she worked a high school for just three weeks before leading agents to a national drug and trafficking ring operating out of a seedy restaurant.

These past two months, she'd been in Fort Worth, not far from Dallas, but far enough. Spring break was next week, so this was her chance to bring down a slavery ring. The trafficking was centered at a gas station–convenience store.

It had taken Eliza one day to know that the cigarettes and lottery cards were only a cover. In the warehouse behind the gas station, five men and a woman ran an escort service. Only in this setup, the escorting happened in a series of makeshift bedrooms at the back of the windowless building.

The traffickers wanted Eliza. If anyone knew the signs, she did. But they had taken their time. She'd walk across the street with a group of girls and she'd linger near the back door of the convenience store. The one that led to the warehouse.

Every time, the guys would see her and flirt with her. But their crude remarks never led to a proposition. Until this afternoon.

Eliza had ditched last period and walked to the gas station with Veronica, a girl who was definitely working for the ring. The girl had even come home with her last weekend. "You never talk about your parents," Veronica had challenged her. "They must be awful."

"Just my mom. And she is . . . she's drunk all the time." Eliza had shrugged. "Come on over. My mom keeps vodka under the sink."

And so Veronica had come. The whole time Eliza had figured the girl was only checking out her story.

Eliza was living in a squalid apartment with a retired
agent, a woman pretending to be Eliza's drunk mother.
When they had walked through the door that day, the
older woman was sprawled out on the sofa, looking
drunk—just like Eliza had said. But when they checked
under the sink all that was there was an empty liquor
bottle. Also part of the plan. Informants didn't drink.
And Eliza had never touched the stuff.

Now Veronica seemed distant as they entered the gas
station. She nodded to the refrigerator case. "I'm getting
a beer."

"Get me one," Eliza said. She had the strangest feeling, like the girl was no longer her friend. "Make it two."

Something was wrong. Eliza moved down the dusty
snack aisle toward the back of the room, closer to the
door the traffickers used. Why hadn't anyone proposi-
tioned her? Maybe they had enough girls, or maybe they
were onto her. Veronica made her nervous. Especially
today.

She pulled out her cell phone and hit the emergency
code. Three digits that would alert nearby agents to the
possibility she was in trouble. She had barely sent the
signal when a door opened and a thin guy with a beard
stepped out. "What's it like?"

Eliza looked over her shoulder, then she sneered at
him. "You can't be talking to me."

"Actually, I am." He grabbed her arm and pulled her
inside, behind the closed door. She hadn't even had time
to scream.

On the other side was a dark storeroom. She and the guy seemed to be the only two people there. "I said"—he jerked her arm—"What's it like?"

Don't let him see you're afraid, she told herself. "I don't even know you."

"No." He sneered at her. "But you will." He shook her again. "What's it like . . . working undercover?"

"Look. I don't work under covers," she hissed at him. Then she raised one suggestive eyebrow. "Not without getting paid."

"We'll see about that." He jerked her toward the back of the space and out a thin doorway. There was maybe ten feet of asphalt between that building and the warehouse where the trafficking happened. If he got her that far, she had no idea what would happen.

Or whether she'd see the light of day again.

They were two steps from the larger building when three unmarked cars and two police vehicles squealed around the corner. Six guns were aimed at the man before he could reach for his own.

Camille was one of the agents, and she helped Eliza to a waiting car. Eliza had seen the girls at the Palace get roughed up by men—sometimes in the hallways of the mansion when they didn't know she was looking. But no one had ever touched her before this. She ran her hand over her arm. Already bruises were forming.

"Are you all right?"

"Yes." She looked out the window. All she wanted

was to live long enough to be in Jack Ryder's embrace again. To see him one more time.

Then she remembered something. She'd been told by her case agent that if ever her life had been in danger, if she was afraid and not sure she could do another mission as an HLCI, she could break her cover and make a single phone call. At that time the agent with her would allow a one-time use of a bureau phone. Something that couldn't be traced back to Eliza.

She felt the tears on her cheeks. Her breathing was still not back to normal.

This was that time.

"Please, Camille." Her teeth chattered. "Please . . . can I make a call?"

"Of course." Camille looked concerned. "I'm sorry. About what happened." She checked her phone. "They did the raid. If that helps you feel better. They're still making arrests and rescuing children."

Eliza nodded. She was glad.

"Who would you like to call, Eliza?"

This was what she had signed up to do and she would do it again. But right now there was only one person she wanted to talk to. She stilled her trembling long enough to answer the question.

"Jack Ryder."

CHAPTER TWENTY-ONE

*For God so loved the world that He gave His one
and only Son, that whoever believes in Him shall
not perish but have eternal life.*

—John 3:16

There were days when Eliza seemed more like a dream
to Jack, like a figment of his imagination, or a vision he
couldn't quite figure out. Not like someone real at all.
But today, after twenty months, Jack was in the back of a
black SUV two hours from finally seeing her.

And that felt better than real.

Eliza lived in Houston now, where she'd just finished
an assignment in the city's most crime-ridden neighbor-
hood. Jack leaned back and closed his eyes. The FBI
loved Eliza Lawrence. She was becoming a legend, not
just in Texas but all the way up to headquarters in Washington, D.C.

As informants went, Eliza had it all. She was nearly
twenty-two now, but she looked young enough to pass
for a junior in high school. And she was incredibly intel-

ligent. She had an uncanny sense about traffickers and danger. So far she had helped take down eight trafficking rings and one drug cartel, all while looking like the picture of innocence. But her work had come at a cost.

She'd been nearly killed three times, and once she had been bound and gagged, stuffed in the trunk of a trafficker's car. Each time God had saved her. Jack was sure now. He hadn't doubted that since his time at Lake Grapevine.

And his missions had been just as dangerous.

They were meeting up today for one reason only. For the next four days they were set to do another mission as a married couple—this time in Cancún.

At first, Eliza hadn't wanted to do this operation. She wanted to see him, she had written in her email. She looked forward to finding someplace in the world where they could spend a few days catching up. Something to fill in the miles and months of distance between the letters they had exchanged.

But she wasn't sure she could pretend to be his wife.

It was only after their last email exchange that Jack had felt her attitude toward the mission change. She mentioned that maybe it had been long enough to not let feelings get in the way. *I really only see you as a friend, Jack.* Those were her words.

Like always, Oliver had been in on that communication. So had Eliza's case agent.

Oliver had talked with Jack just a few days ago, making sure there was no reason to call off the trip. "I want her to have time with you. I think she needs it." He leveled his gaze. "She's a machine. Just like you, Jack."

"I know." Jack was proud of her. But he worried about her, too. "So the mission . . . it's also time for her to have a break. Is that it?"

"It's soft surveillance. No contact needed. We want information about buildings and points of entry." Oliver hesitated. "But to answer your question, no."

"No?" Jack was confused.

"She has one more year on her contract. You need her on this one." Oliver stood and walked around his desk. "Also . . . we have possible information on her family."

Jack hesitated. "Eliza's mother and brother?"

Oliver took a folder from his desk and handed it to Jack. "Here. You can read about it. There's a slight chance they could be in Lancaster County, Pennsylvania." Oliver went on to explain that a Belizean police officer had gotten a tip from someone in Little Belize. A woman and her young son had come to the village around the time of the disappearance. But not long after, the two had left with a few other families and started a new outpost deeper into the mountains.

"What makes them think the mother and son might be in Pennsylvania?"

"That's where the other two families wound up." Oliver hesitated. "The thing is, Susan James and her son should've gone back to Lower Barton Creek. Back to Ike Armstrong. Which is why I'm doubtful about the tip."

Jack wasn't going to tell Eliza. He wouldn't dare get her hopes up. Not unless her family was actually found. Until then, every sign pointed to Eliza's mother and brother being dead.

At least the trip to Cancún was on. Jack remembered Eliza's email again. *I really only see you as a friend, Jack.* The words still made him sad. If she had been honest in her email, then whatever feelings she'd had for him were gone.

Jack would have to be okay with that. She was his friend—his only friend—and he was hers. From the moment he'd heard about the chance to work with her again, he had been counting down the days.

Two hours later the SUV pulled up in front of her hotel, where Eliza was waiting in the lobby.

Jack stepped out to help with her bag, but instead he couldn't do anything but look at her. It took about two seconds to wonder if maybe everything she'd written in her email had only been a cover.

So that the next four days would be theirs alone.

She looked younger, if that were possible. Maybe after pretending for so long to be a seventeen-year-old. Or maybe it was God's Spirit inside her. Either way, she left him unable to move or breathe. "Eliza." That's all he could say. Just her name.

And without another word between them, she was in his arms. "You're really here." She clung to him, pressing her cheek to his chest. "I thought I'd never see you again."

Jack wished he could freeze time. With her, he didn't want the sun to set, didn't want four days to come and go with cavalier indifference.

They were still undercover, still working a honeymoon mission, so this was appropriate behavior. But he wasn't acting. She stepped back and kissed his cheek. Slowly. "I missed you every day, Jack."

"Me, too." And once more he had doubts about the operation. How was he supposed to say goodbye to her again? After spending time with her at a beach resort, talking with her and holding her hand? Pretending she was his wife?

Jack tried not to think about that. He would figure it out. They had work to do, and since this was a job, he couldn't allow himself to feel more than friendship for her. *You're a machine, Ryder. Be a machine.* That was his order from Oliver. Even if it took every bit of concentration and willpower he had.

Otherwise, even a less dangerous mission, like this, could get them killed.

. . .

THEY HAD THEIR hotel keys and they were walking down the hall of the eighteenth floor to the end suite. The setup was similar to the one in the Bahamas. A single door leading to a pair of separate doors. Other honeymooners might rent the full suite simply for privacy. But the situation here was the same as before. Eliza had her room and Jack had his.

They spent an hour apart and then headed for the beach.

Surveillance from a few weeks ago on this part of the beach told Jack the operatives in a local trafficking ring were probably somewhere on the shore. Maybe working at the hotel, or serving piña coladas to the tourists.

He wore a hundred-dollar black T-shirt and white shorts. She looked stunning in a breezy blue strapless dress. Her pale blond hair was longer now, spilling halfway down her back. He took her hand and tried not to stare.

How am I supposed to do this, God? I should never have taken this mission.

With every step at her side, Jack realized how much trouble he was in. The idea of being Eliza Lawrence's friend was dying faster than daylight. Taking this mission was the worst decision of his career.

Jack looked at her again. Or was it the best?

When they were a few yards down the beach, he turned and took her other hand, too. There weren't words to describe the way he was drawn to her. "I can't believe you're here." No one could hear their conversation, not when they were so close to the surf.

"Where did you think I'd be?" She smiled, teasing him. "This is our honeymoon."

If only it were true. Jack eased her into his arms and held her body against his. The surf washed over their feet and he wanted to stay like that forever.

You have a job to do, Ryder. He stepped away from

her and they kept walking. But a hundred yards down the beach he stopped again. He couldn't help himself. Again he took her in his arms and this time he searched her eyes. "Can we sit on your balcony, Eliza? I've wanted to be with you every day since we said goodbye."

"Yes." She lay her head against his chest. "I'd like that very much."

A pair of men were walking their way, paying special attention to Eliza. As if they somehow knew she was an informant. One of the men said something to the other, and they slowed their pace.

Without giving his actions a second thought, Jack took her face in his hands. "Don't look at them, Eliza." Then, with a barely constrained passion, slow and tender he kissed her. The way he'd wanted to kiss her since that time in the waves in Nassau. Jack had no idea if the men were informants or spies or part of a ring.

Protocol said to kiss her in this situation. So no one would doubt they were a married couple. She kissed him next, and the hunger was there for both of them. Whatever happened after this mission, one thing was certain. The kiss had proven it. They weren't acting.

And Eliza Lawrence could never be just his friend.

• • •

THE FBI DIDN'T forbid Jack to cross the threshold into Eliza's room. But the decision had to be mutually agreed upon. And they could only meet in a gathering room or on a balcony. Never in the bedroom.

That wouldn't be a problem. Jack had no intention of doing anything that would compromise Eliza. Not with her past, and not with the way he was better understanding God's will for his life. Not with his commitment to the FBI. No, he would cherish her, that alone. Friend or more. God had told him to love her, and on this trip he would show her the meaning of the word.

They sat on her balcony in two chairs, side by side, their arms touching. For a long time they said nothing. Eliza spoke first. "I've been reading the Bible."

"You have?" Jack had no idea. "Why didn't you tell me?"

"I feel funny. Sharing my feelings in an email half the bureau will read." She raised one shoulder. "It's weird, right?"

He considered that for a moment. His emails had been just as shallow as hers. "It is." He sighed. "I hate that it's been our only way of communicating."

"Me, too." She tilted her face to the sun. "But since I couldn't call you whenever I wanted, I bought a used Bible at a secondhand store." She smiled at him. "I can't stop reading it."

He'd been doing the same. "I'm loving the Psalms. David was always in danger."

"Mmm. Just like us." There was an easiness about their conversation, like they'd never been apart at all. "There's something I want to do while I'm here. If you could help me."

"What is it?" He found his best Jimmy Stewart voice.

"You want me to lasso the moon for you, Eliza. Huh, is that what you want?"

"What?" She laughed out loud. "You sound just like him."

"Sure. Okay." Jack grinned as he studied her eyes, her face. "You wrote that you'd seen the movie, so . . . I'll have to believe you." Her quiet laughter was better than anything he had ever heard. Because the sound meant she was healing. Even while working one dangerous operation after another, she was moving on from her past.

Her eyes sparkled as she pointed at him. "You don't think I saw it."

"No, no." He loved playing with her like this. Everything between them had always been so serious. He chuckled. "Just making sure not everything in those emails was a lie."

"It wasn't!" She was still laughing. "We turned on the TV over Christmas break and there it was. *It's a Wonderful Life.* I asked if you'd heard of it." Her joy faded a little. "Because . . . I never watched an hour of TV . . . back when . . ."

A sinking feeling hit him. Of course she had been telling the truth. Where would she have seen a Christmas classic before? "Eliza . . ." *Don't let her close off, God. Please.* "I was just teasing." He uttered a quiet chuckle, trying to salvage the moment. "Sometimes it felt like you were just filling space with what you wrote."

Her smile remained. "I know." She tilted her head.

Her beauty took his breath. "But I would never really lie to you." She grew more serious. "Except once."

"Okay. You don't have to tell me about that." This wasn't the time to ask her. She would tell him when she wanted to . . . if she wanted to. He stared at the distant water for a few minutes. "So . . . what is it you want to do while you're here?"

She didn't hesitate. "I want you to baptize me." A light filled her eyes and their eyes met. "In the ocean."

Again his heart soared. God had heard his prayers. During the dangerous missions and months apart, her faith had changed her. "Baptizing you . . ." His soul was almost too full for him to speak. "That would be an honor, Eliza."

"Thank you." She turned to him. "Were you baptized?"

"I was. At our family's church when I was twelve." He could picture the moment. Shane and him choosing to get baptized that day. "My brother and I had been studying what the Bible teaches about baptism." He smiled at the memory. "Finally we couldn't wait another week."

She nodded. "That's how I feel. I want to bury my old life . . . in the waters of the sea. Leave it behind me for good." She breathed in, her face toward the sky. "When I come up out of that water, everything will be new."

"Yes." He blinked back tears. He hadn't dreamed they

would have this conversation their first day together. "When do you want to do it?"

Her smile gave him the answer even before she did. "Now."

. . .

THE SUN HUNG just above the horizon as they reached the water. They held hands and faced the waves, their feet in the gentle surf. Jack pictured Eliza's life, the loneliness and loss.

"If I could go back and take you from that place . . . give you the life you deserved, Eliza . . ." He slipped his arm around her shoulders. "Nothing . . . nothing you ever saw or did at that place was your fault." He gently faced her. "You know that."

"Yes." The peace in her eyes was not of this world. "But I made choices I regret. If I had it to do again, I'd let the guards shoot me rather than talk a single girl into going to the Palace." She sighed. "I want to put everything about that time behind me." She slipped off her swimsuit cover-up and tossed it on the dry sand. Then she took a few steps into the shallow water. "Please?"

From his phone app, Jack had read the Scriptures about baptism on the elevator ride down to the lobby. He peeled off his T-shirt and set it on the shore. He was ready to do this. They walked out ten yards or so, where the water was waist deep. It was only May, so the sea was chilly.

Eliza didn't seem to mind. She wasn't shivering or jittery. Her eyes met his. "Go ahead, Jack."

He nodded. "Throughout the book of Acts, when someone came to life-changing faith in Jesus, they got baptized. Jesus, Himself, was baptized by John—to show us the way." A hope that knew no limits filled him. "Eliza . . . do you want Jesus to be your Lord and Savior?"

"I do." A smile lit up her face.

Jack remembered how this was done. When he was growing up, baptisms happened regularly at his church.

He stood beside her and brought her hand to her face so she could hold her nose. "I baptize you in the name of the Father, the Son, and the Holy Spirit. For the forgiveness of your sins and for the gift of the Holy Spirit. Buried with Him in death"—Jack laid her backward under the water and then carefully lifted her out again—"raised with Him to new life, Eliza. Now and evermore."

Salt water streamed down her hair and brow, but nothing could dampen the joy on her face, the healing that filled her eyes. She laughed and raised her hands in the air. "Yes!" She looked to the sky again. "Yes, God!"

"Congratulations." He searched her eyes. Maybe this was only the beginning for the two of them. It was possible, right? They had made it this far. He put his hand alongside her face. "I've never . . . experienced anything like that."

Laughter spilled from her lips. "I feel it. I feel God

here." Then she turned to Jack and held him, like she might never let go. "I'm brand-new, Jack. Like when I was little."

When she was little . . .

Suddenly, in that very instant, Jack knew what he had to do. He could remember again her child-sized body, limp in his arms when she was just nine years old, the way it felt to rescue her from the waves and carry her to shore. Her arms around his neck like they were right now.

I need to tell her, God.

Yes, my son. Today is a new beginning.

Jack took a deep breath. As pinks and blues streaked across the Cancún sky, they gathered their things and walked up the beach. She dried off with one of the resort's blue-striped towels, but though the air was still warm, she was shivering. Jack found a sweatshirt in her bag, and gave it to her. "Here."

"Thanks." She pulled it over her head. "I think I'm just . . . amazed. In awe." Her damp hair hung down her back, but her face was dry now. "I can't believe it."

Jack had a feeling that was about to be a theme. Again, there could be traffickers watching them, but he wasn't worried. He and Eliza were more than convincing. They had long since moved past pretending. He took her into his arms and hugged her again. For a long time.

Finally he stepped back. "Eliza, what was the one thing?"

She was still smiling. "The one thing?"

"Yes." He searched her face. "You said you only lied about one thing in your emails. What was it?"

The look in her eyes changed and the attraction was back. He could see it in her sudden shyness. "You want me to tell you?"

Hidden facts and clandestine behavior were part of life for undercover agents and informants. But not with the two of them. Not anymore. "Yes." He looked all the way to her heart. "No more secrets between us."

"Okay." She stepped back, but she didn't look away. "When I told you I only saw you as a friend." She laced her fingers between his, still facing him, their faces inches apart. "That wasn't true, Jack. You could never be just a friend."

"No." He drew her closer still, and brushed his cheek against hers. "You'll never be only a friend to me, either."

"Really?" Tears filled her eyes. "You mean it?"

"Eliza . . ." Everything disappeared except her. "I love you. I'm in love with you."

There were no people on the beach, no strangers walking toward them or studying them, not that Jack could see. He could barely remember his name let alone the mission they were on. And in a way that he couldn't stop if he had all the strength in the world, he kissed her.

The fire between them was instant, and after a minute Jack moved a few feet away from her. Now was the time. He had to tell her the truth. No matter what she thought of him after today. Before he changed his mind.

He breathed in sharp. "There's something . . . something I have to tell you, too."

Concern flickered in her face. Like she couldn't imagine anything that might cause him to break the moment they'd been in.

He eased his fingers between hers once more. *Make her understand, please, God.* "You aren't going to believe this. Because . . . when I found out, I didn't believe it either."

She held more tightly to his hands and waited.

"When I met you at the Palace that day . . . it wasn't the first time."

Confusion filled her expression. "It was." She shook her head. "I'd . . . I'd never seen you before."

"You had." Jack hesitated. "Eliza, that day in the ocean . . . the teenage boy who rescued you." He fought to keep eye contact, to hold on to the connection with her. "That was me. My family and I . . . we went to that exact beach every summer. Including the summer of your rescue."

Even in the fading light, he could see the blood drain from her face. "No . . . that boy was younger than you and he was with his—" Eliza released his hands and moved a few feet away. Her body began to shake. "Your brother." She put her hand over her mouth and when she dropped it, she shook her head. "No, Jack. Not your brother!"

Then she turned and ran from him, along the shore away from the resort. As if by running she could put distance between the two of them, distance from something she hadn't known until now. The awful truth about her rescue. A rescue she had never wanted in the first place.

And the price Jack had paid to make it happen.

CHAPTER TWENTY-TWO

*Be strong and courageous. Do not be afraid or
terrified because of them, for the Lord your God
goes with you; he will never leave you nor
forsake you.*

—Deuteronomy 31:6

If she ran for the next week, she couldn't get far enough
from Jack. She didn't care that she couldn't breathe or
that night was falling. *Don't stop*, she told herself. *Keep
running.* All the way to the other end of the beach. Or the
other side of the world. However far and fast she could
go to get away from him.

It couldn't have been true. It wasn't possible. And
how come he hadn't told her sooner? She had no idea
he'd ever been to Belize before. Her mind raced faster
than her bare feet. Of all the people in all the world,
how could it be?

Jack Ryder had rescued her that day?

Finally when the resort was so far behind her she
couldn't see it, and when darkness spread across the shoreline ahead of her, Eliza stopped. She gasped for breath the

way she had as a child that day. *No! No, God, please. Not Jack. Not his brother.*

She couldn't take it, couldn't stand the thought that he was telling the truth. He had lost his brother because of her, and if he'd only turned back . . . if he'd gone after Shane instead of her . . . they would all be so much better off today.

Her tears came and she dropped to her knees. She fell forward and wept like she'd never done in all her life. It was her fault Jack had lost his brother. How could she face him now? And if it was true . . . why hadn't he told her?

Eliza could feel his presence even before he touched her. He didn't say a word, just knelt beside her and wrapped his arms around her. He waited until her crying eased, until her quiet sobs were all that remained. Then he whispered the words that would stay with her the rest of her life.

"I was supposed to save you that day, Eliza." He pressed her head gently against his chest. "We'll never . . . never understand God's plans. But . . ." He took hold of her shoulders. "You're here, Eliza. And I'm here."

She hung her head and fresh tears streamed down her face. "Your brother . . ."

"He's fine." Jack's eyes welled up. He could hear Beck's voice again. "My brother is completely whole . . . my parents are with him."

"No." She leaned into him and slid her arms around his neck. "I'm sorry . . . it was my fault. I swam out too far and . . . I didn't want to come back to the beach." She shook her head. "I didn't want you to rescue me."

He held her so close, like they were one person, not two. Until finally he helped her to her feet and pulled her into his arms. Minutes passed and the ocean air dried her cheeks. Still she stayed in his embrace. "How can I look at you, Jack?" She stared at the sea. "How? When I've cost you so much?"

His answer didn't come right away. He stroked her hair and her back and finally he stepped away enough so he could see her. "What if . . . I was supposed to save you? For this?"

In that same moment, the two men appeared again on the beach, walking toward them, looking at them. Without hesitating Jack's hands were on her face, in her hair, and in a single breathless instant he was kissing her.

And she was kissing him.

His kiss was warm and safe and everything she'd never dreamed. She had never wanted to know a man's love, she hadn't believed in such a thing. And yet here, with his lips on hers, and her heart in his hands, Eliza knew.

Jack loved her. He did.

And no matter how terrible their past, no matter how great the losses they'd both suffered, she didn't want to go a day without him. Not as long as she lived. Her tears came again and as the men walked past them, she searched his eyes. "It was really you? You saved me?"

"I did." His eyes were clear now. "You were so little. I thought . . . I thought you needed me."

Of course. How could he have known that she didn't want to wake up in the Palace the next day or that the awful woman on the shore wasn't her mother? She sniffed and closed her eyes for a long moment; when she opened them she noticed something. There was no regret or condemnation in Jack's eyes.

He had chosen to save her. And now . . . now it was up to her to accept the fact. To be thankful for it and believe that maybe Jack was right. Maybe he was supposed to save her. So that at the end of her nightmare he might rescue her again.

"Don't run from me, Eliza." He looked deep into her soul. "You're all I have on earth."

His words touched her and healed her from the very great grief of knowing the truth. "And you . . . I have no one but you, Jack."

And then, without either of them saying another word, they walked back to their hotel suite.

He kissed her forehead. Because neither of them could kiss here, the way they'd kissed down at the beach. Not with the fire between them. Jack touched her cheek. "Call me. If you need me."

They said good night and went to their separate rooms. Work would come tomorrow, and they would do the surveillance. But for now they had this day.

A day of honesty and heartbreak and new beginnings.

. . .

ELIZA SAT ON her balcony alone until after midnight, staring at the water, replaying the scene in her mind again and again. Her little legs being dragged under and Betsy screaming at her from the shore.

The Lord is my Shepherd; I shall not want . . .

And there were Jack and his family on vacation. Playing football on the beach. Eliza had seen them, like any wonderful family. Like the family she had lost. Laughing and running on the sand, all of time ahead of them. Jack and Shane, two best friends.

She could see it all, like it was happening for the first time. Jack spotting her, seeing that she was drowning and running across the beach toward her. And his brother chasing after him. Because not another soul on the beach had done anything about it. Not cruel Betsy or some other tourist. Not the armed guards on the hillside.

Only Jack and Shane.

Again and again she played the scene over until she had no more tears, until the image of that teenage Jack became the man. The one who had baptized her and run after her and held her in his strong, safe arms. The one she loved.

And finally, fully, her sadness lifted and she accepted the truth.

Jack was right. God hadn't made some colossal mistake when Eliza was rescued from the ocean that day. God had ordained Jack to save her. For the work she was

doing to bring down trafficking rings, for such a time as
this, and for the life she had yet to live. And for the man
she would love as long as she drew breath. The one who
had rescued her not once but twice, along a distant shore.

Jack Ryder.

. . .

THE SURVEILLANCE MISSION was more difficult than
either of them had expected, but Eliza wasn't worried.
God was with them. He had brought them to this point.
He wasn't going to abandon them now.

They walked hand in hand along a tourist street just
off the strip and after a few minutes Eliza recognized the
men. The same ones who had walked by them on the
beach. God had given her eyes to see, and she was thankful for the chance to use them.

"The men on the corner up ahead. They were on the
beach yesterday." She smiled at Jack, as if she hadn't a
care in the world. "That building behind them. I think
they're operating from there."

"Have I told you how beautiful you are, my love?"
Jack was playing the part. But he wasn't, all at the same
time. She could see that in his eyes. He pulled his phone
from his shorts pocket. "Let me take your picture. With
those trees in the background."

Of course, it wasn't the trees he wanted, but the men
on the corner. The building behind them. Eliza kicked up
one heel and smiled while Jack snapped the shot. "What
should we do now?" Eliza walked past the surly-looking

men and straight up to the door of the building. She tugged on it a few times.

Immediately one of the men turned around. "Get away from there!" He took a few sharp steps toward her, but Jack stepped in front of her.

"Back off." Jack was taller than the guy. Obviously stronger. "We're shopping, okay?"

The man retreated, but his scowl remained. "That's not a store."

Eliza pretended that was all she needed to hear. "Sorry." She tugged on Jack's hand. "Come on. Let's find some ice cream."

Jack didn't look away from the guy until they were a few feet down the sidewalk. The next shop on the strip read "Sweet Treats." Eliza was laughing again by the time they ducked inside.

"Go out the back door." Jack stayed behind her. In case the guy on the corner followed them. Then with an ease she'd learned these past two years, Eliza hurried past the ice cream counter, down a narrow hallway and out the back door.

When they were in the alley, they jogged by a few stores and walked through the back of a souvenir shop. The place was bigger than most, so the two were safe here. Eliza could feel it. She was breathing hard as they found their spot between two racks of discount T-shirts.

"Your instincts are uncanny." He had his arm around her again. "Which is another reason I love you, by the way." He lowered his voice. "The question is, where are the girls?"

Eliza believed she knew. "There was a hotel across the street from where that guy was standing." She took a bright pink T-shirt from the rack and held it up. "Let's get ice cream and sit on the bench just down the street. That'll tell us."

Ten minutes later they were eating chocolate chip ice cream cones, acting like they were the only two people in the world, but Eliza had a view of the hotel. Again she'd been right. Three teenage girls appeared near the front door wearing short skirts and high heels. A man in a Hawaiian print shirt approached and one of the girls disappeared with him behind the hotel doors.

"There it is. Plain as day," Jack said as they walked back to their hotel. No question they were being watched. He kept his tone and expression light. "But it took you, Eliza, to know where to look."

Yes, Eliza thought. Because in another lifetime the girl standing outside the hotel had been her friend, Alexa. Or Rosa. Girls she had been forced to bring to the Palace. Eliza could accept that now. The past was behind her . . . she was a new creation because of her faith.

Jack had read her a Bible verse this morning over breakfast on her balcony. Before work started. It was from Romans 8:28. *And we know that in all things God works for the good of those who love Him, who have been called according to His purpose.*

"See," he had told her as he closed his Bible app. "No

matter what it took to get here, today we will do good. We will fulfill His purpose in all this."

The verse filled Eliza with hope and peace.

Halfway back to their hotel she had to use the restroom. He stayed outside the door of the building. If someone tried to follow her or harm her, Jack would stop them. Eliza had no doubt. He had loved her in ways she didn't know existed. With his very life.

They filed separate reports late that afternoon and then strolled the resort grounds on their way to dinner. Tomorrow they would walk the street again, looking for other men, other traffickers. But already they had what they'd come for.

Now since they weren't looking for traffickers, they could focus on the best part of the job. Pretending they were honeymooners.

Something had been on her mind since she had woken up that morning. She didn't bring it up at breakfast, but maybe now was the time. She would have to talk in code. There was no such thing as being too careful, she'd learned that.

After dinner, the waiter brought coffee. Eliza looked at Jack, to the deepest parts of his heart. "I have one more year . . . at my current job."

"I've been thinking about that." He was telling the truth. She could see in his eyes that he was thinking the same thing. "I have one more year, too."

"Hmm." She nodded, but she felt dizzy. From the moment the mission began, she had dreaded the goodbye that was coming. Especially because there was no telling how long before they would see each other again. Or if they would. But now . . .

Jack smiled. "I'm thinking about a career change. Maybe moving to the South." His eyes said so much more. "I've always wanted to be a professor."

"Nice." Her smile came easily. Did he mean it? Was he really thinking of leaving the bureau?

"What about you?" He set his coffee down and reached both hands across the table. "You could do anything, you know."

"Yes." A thrill filled her senses. "Well . . . I might open a house. For girls . . . girls who have no one."

"I like it." He angled his head, clearly proud of her. "The world needs more places like that."

When dinner was over they found a spot on the sand and kicked off their shoes. They walked until everyone on the beach was too far away to hear them. Then he stopped and faced her. And before she knew what was happening, he dropped to one knee. Right there on the sandy shoreline.

"Eliza, I meant what I said earlier. I wasn't acting."

"Jack . . ." She put her free hand over her mouth. People would think they were playing around, or that this was an engagement trip and not a honeymoon. Eliza didn't care what they thought.

He pulled something from his pocket. "A ring will have to wait. But I found this while you were in the restroom. A jewelry table was set up right there on the sidewalk." He handed her the daintiest necklace. Etched into the tiny pendant were the words:

I will wait for you.

Her hand started to tremble. Was this really happening?

"Eliza." His eyes held hers. "It will be a year before we see each other again. But when we do ... whenever we're together next ..." He stood and took a step closer to her. "Will you marry me?"

Her heart felt like it would burst from her chest. She squeezed his hand, so she would know for sure she was really here. And that this moment was actually real. "Yes, Jack." She still had hold of the necklace as she placed her hands on either side of his face. "Yes, a million times yes."

"Good." He kissed her, a kiss that took her breath and made her long for next year. His smile started in his eyes and then filled his face. "I was hoping you'd say yes. Because the next time we're on a honeymoon ... I want to share a room."

"Yes!" She laughed and handed him the necklace. "Put it on me. Please, Jack. Because I'm never taking it off again."

She moved her hair to the side, and his fingers on her neck sent shivers down her spine. When the necklace was clasped, he turned her toward him. He chuckled. "I promise ... the ring will make up for it. One day."

"No ... I love it. I told you, I'll wear it every day until I see you again. However long it takes." She kissed him this time, and she was glad he was holding her. Otherwise she would've floated away.

His very presence made her feel alive. When he drew breath, she felt oxygen course through her veins. His laughter made her believe anything was possible. Except one thing. The thing she would have to do in twenty-four hours.

Tell him goodbye.

• • •

THEIR LAST PRIVATE moment was on her balcony the next day, five minutes before they had to leave for the airport. They were still employees of the FBI. Once they set foot on American soil, there could be no sign of romance, no relationship waiting in the wings.

So this was it.

He held her in his arms, and Eliza had never felt more safe. More loved. "Another year of missions." She lifted her face to his. "What if . . ."

"Shh." Jack kissed her forehead and then her lips. "Don't say it, Eliza. God has the number of our days."

Yes. That's what she needed to tell herself. She would have to remember that a month from now and three months and six. When she was in danger or his mission took a turn for the worse. God had brought them this far.

His plans were far better than anything she could imagine.

They kissed once more, longer this time. Jack traced her jaw with his thumb. "I love you with all my life,

Eliza. When I'm out fighting through a mission, I'll be fighting for you."

She nodded. "Me, too." She touched the pendant on her necklace. "You'll be with me always."

Once more they kissed, and then it was time to go. Through customs and airport security, on the flight back to Houston and as the SUV dropped her off at the same hotel where he'd found her four days ago, Eliza knew she wouldn't have to wait to hear Jack's voice. His words would be with her, wherever she went. Right there in her heart and hanging from her neck.

I'll wait for you.

And with everything in her, Eliza would do the same.

CHAPTER TWENTY-THREE

*The Lord is my Shepherd; I shall not want. He
makes me lie down in green pastures. He leads me
beside still waters, He restores my soul.*

—Psalm 23:1–3

Oliver was about to lose his best undercover agent,
but he wasn't upset about the fact. As summer gave way
to fall and the holidays faded into winter, Oliver had
watched the changes in Jack Ryder. And they didn't make
him want to reprimand the operative.

They made him smile.

As for Jack and Eliza's mission to Cancún, Oliver
had ulterior motives for requesting the two work together. His actual reason had to do with something Jack's
father had told Oliver the month before he and his wife
were killed.

His next meeting with Jack was in five minutes. A
meeting Jack had requested.

Oliver thought he knew what the young man wanted
to talk about. In the meantime, Oliver allowed himself
to go back to that dinner, the last time he was with Jack's

father. The man had been pensive over the meal. Missing his son, Shane, and longing for more time with Jack. Then the man had said something Oliver remembered still.

Something he wanted to share with Jack today.

There was a knock at his door, and as it opened, Jack entered. "Sir?"

"Come in, Jack." Oliver stood and the two shook hands. "Have a seat."

Jack did, but before he could say what was on his mind, Oliver took hold of the moment. "Did you know I had dinner with your father, a month before he died?"

It took Jack a moment. "No ... No, sir, I didn't. I knew ... you two were friends."

Oliver hadn't brought this up before, because he was afraid it would make Jack doubt his work with the FBI. And that would not have been good for Jack. Because when Oliver found the boy back at Navy SEAL training, his commander had told Oliver one thing.

"That one pushes beyond the limits." He had shaken his head. "I'm not sure he'll make it out alive."

Oliver agreed. And so with the consent of the Navy, Oliver had approached his friend's son knowing one thing for certain.

Jack Ryder needed the bureau. Needed the work as an FBI agent so he'd have a reason to keep going.

But now ... now, Oliver was fairly sure Jack had a different reason to live. Which was why he wanted to tell him this story. He leaned forward. "Your father and I, we talked a great deal that day." Oliver narrowed his eyes. "He said something I thought you should know."

The look in Jack's eyes was that of a much younger boy. Looking for any information he could get about the father he had lost. "What did he say?"

"He was missing Shane. Missing the times when your family was together." Oliver allowed a sad smile. "He said he wished he'd been more present. Thrown a ball with the two of you."

Jack worked the muscles in his jaw and he nodded. "My father . . . he was busy. But he was a good man."

"He was that." Oliver breathed in deep. "At the end of the meal, he told me he was worried about you, Jack."

"Me?"

"Yes." Oliver looked straight at the young man. "He didn't want you to work in politics or law or the military." Maybe Oliver should've said this sooner. But there was no time for doubt now. "Your dad wanted you to have a different life, Jack. He wanted you to marry and have children and be present in their lives. Coach their Little League teams and play with them on the beach." Oliver hesitated. "The way he wished he had done with you."

Jack stared out the window. His eyes glistened, but he didn't cry. Finally, when he had more control, he looked at Oliver again. "Thank you, sir. For telling me." He nodded. "I'll . . . keep that."

"Yes." Oliver studied his top agent for a moment. He

was going to miss him. "Now . . . what did you want to tell me, Jack?"

"Sir . . . My anniversary with the FBI is at the start of July." Again, Jack seemed to fight his emotions. "I wanted to tell you . . . I'll be leaving at that time." He was doing his best to hold it together. "I do want you to know . . . I have loved everything about this job, about working for you and the bureau, sir. I have loved it all."

"But . . . there is someone you love more." Oliver raised one eyebrow. "Is that it?"

The hint of a smile played on Jack's lips. "Maybe."

Oliver grinned at him. Jack didn't need to answer questions about Eliza. The two hadn't crossed any lines, and in fact their work together had been brilliant. "I'm going to miss you, Agent Ryder. You're one of the best. And you never . . . ever give up." He paused. "But I have to say . . . I think you're making the right choice."

"Thank you." Jack looked like the weight of the world was suddenly off his shoulders. "Let's just say . . . I'm going to make my father proud."

• • •

TEXAS WAS NO longer an option for Eliza, not with so many traffickers aware of her identity. So in August she had been sent to headquarters in D.C. Her new case agent there handled her assignments. Through the fall she worked at a school near the capital, and in November she became a junior at a troubled academy in Virginia.

Through it all, with every mission and tense moment, she thought of Jack. She wore the necklace backward, but she wore it every day. His words as close to her heart as they could possibly get.

January saw her in Maine and February in New Hampshire. With every school, she helped bring down another gang of traffickers and drug dealers until she was one of the most hated informants in FBI history. Even so she wanted to see her year out.

Her case agent sent her to New Mexico in March and to Oregon after that. Traffickers weren't organized enough to figure out where she was headed or who she was going to take down next.

Along the way, Eliza found another copy of *The Lion, the Witch and the Wardrobe*. She had lost hers during the raid at the Palace, and never had a chance to finish it. But in April, she made the time.

The story was everything Eliza had hoped it would be. And as she finished the school year in California she fancied herself much like Queen Lucy, the valiant. Brave enough to take on whatever task was asked of her, and certain that Aslan of Narnia was looking out for her.

Because once a king or queen of Narnia, always a king or queen of Narnia.

Between moments of danger, Eliza also read the Bible. She read how with God at her side, there was nothing man could do to her. Because man could only take her physical body, but never her soul. That would belong to God alone, forever.

The way her heart would belong to Jack.

She spent the last month of her service as an HLCI in the office, identifying traffickers from surveillance footage and helping decipher illegal solicitations. And then suddenly it was July 9, her twenty-third birthday, and her years of working for the FBI were over.

To celebrate, the bureau surprised Eliza with a ceremony. In the room were every case agent and teammate she had worked with except Jack. He was completing a mission in Honduras. One fraught with the very worst kind of danger.

Oliver had flown into Washington, D.C., to join the celebration. He handed over her final check. "Your record has been expunged of all charges. We will set you up wherever you'd like to go, Eliza. You'll have a new name, a new identity."

She had known that was coming, and she had the name picked out. Lizzie James. The name she had been given by her parents would be the one she would finish life with. She liked the sound of it. As if nothing bad had ever happened to her, and she was still that little girl headed to the beach with her mama and little Daniel.

When the ceremony was over and the other agents had said their goodbyes, Oliver approached. He handed her a satchel, the way her case agent had done before every mission. "Sir?" She had been told she wouldn't get her new paperwork for at least a week. "Is this . . . for me?"

"Open it." Oliver took a step back and smiled. Like a proud father, anxious to see her reaction to what was clearly her best birthday gift.

Eliza opened the leather cover and pulled out the contents. It was her new paperwork, a California driver's license with her new name—Lizzie James. Next was a birth certificate and a passport and finally a travel itinerary.

To Belize.

"What?" Eliza held her breath so she wouldn't gasp. "I can't . . . Sir? What is this?"

"Belize is safe for you, Eliza. You'll fly into Belize City and then to Placencia." He smiled. "Someone will be waiting for you." Emotion sounded in his voice. "Someone who will make a very fine professor one day."

Eliza wondered if she would drop to the floor from sheer joy. How could this be happening? She put the paperwork back in the satchel and hugged Oliver. "Thank you. I can't . . . I can't thank you enough, sir."

"Go . . ." He gave her one last smile. "Live your life, Lizzie. You deserve it."

And with that, Eliza gathered her things and left the FBI building for the last time. At six the next morning she was on a flight back home to Belize. Her country, the country of her childhood and her family. And she was headed to Placencia and the Belizean Great Barrier Reef and sixteen miles of sand that she'd never walked in all her life.

But that wasn't what kept her on the edge of her aisle seat. The reason was a small note she'd found at the bottom of the satchel. It was in Jack's handwriting and it said only two words.

Wear white.

CHAPTER TWENTY-FOUR

You have stolen my heart, my sister, my bride; you have stolen my heart with one glance of your eyes.
> —Song of Solomon 4:9

Their eyes met as soon as she stepped off the small plane, and Jack had to force himself not to run to her. How could a whole year have passed without Eliza near him, without her in his arms?

Jack had on white khaki pants and a white short-sleeve button-down. Five days ago he was nearly killed in Honduras, but that was behind him now. Somehow he had finished his last mission with breath in his lungs.

And now he was here. Ready to start the rest of his life.

There was a yellow line on the ground, one he couldn't cross. He watched her take her bag from the cart and then turn to him. She must've found his note because the look of her made his heart skip a beat.

Her white sundress fluttered in the breeze.

She also wore a wide-brimmed straw hat, as if she still had to be careful about who saw her and what danger that might put her in. There was no danger now, but the hat worked. It made her look like the true princess she was. Like royalty from a faraway land.

Then, in a way he would remember as long as he lived, she came to him. She didn't look around or seem aware of the other people deplaning. Her eyes were on his alone. And finally she was in his arms.

He removed her hat and dropped it to the ground. Then he kissed her like he'd wanted to since they'd said goodbye in Cancún. The years and danger and missions were behind them. From this day forward it would be him and Eliza. Nothing could tear him away from her.

She looked into his eyes. "Every day I missed you, Jack."

"You're so beautiful." And all he could think was that she was here, in his arms. He wasn't dreaming. Once more he kissed her. "Don't ever leave me again, Eliza. Promise."

She laughed, the sort of unguarded laugh he wanted to spend the rest of his life listening to. "I promise."

They collected her things and walked to his rented BMW, then he drove south down the peninsula. Jack had worked out a deal with the owner of a private resort. Four bungalows and a luxury suite all on the most beautiful strip of sand he'd ever seen. He pulled into the parking lot and cut the engine.

"I have a surprise for you."

"I see that." She stared out the window at the stretch

of shoreline ahead of her. "I've always wanted to walk this beach. Did you know that?"

"I did." He smiled. That wasn't the surprise. "We'll get your things later. Come on."

He opened her door and led her to a path lined with lit lanterns and Mason jars of white flowers. His heart pounded and his breathing was shallow. He'd worked on this surprise longer than she knew. He turned to her. "I love you, Eliza." He brushed a lock of hair from her cheek. "Lizzie James. I'll always love you."

"I love you, too." A bit of laughter lifted her lips. "What am I supposed to call you now?"

"Jonathan Ryder." He winked at her. "But you can call me Jack. It'll be my nickname. It's sort of grown on me."

"Me, too." She put her hand alongside his face. "The candles . . . the flowers? How did you do this?"

"I had help." He took her hand in his and they walked down the path and out onto the sand, where four people sat in white wooden folding chairs, two on each side of a white cloth runner. They faced the water and a white gazebo.

Jack smiled. Just like he had arranged.

"What . . . Jack, what is this?" She looked at him. "Who are they?"

He hugged her. "It's okay. Just some friends of mine."

They took off their shoes and walked barefoot in the sand.

Then from one side of the aisle, a woman stood. She

had long brown hair and the same face as Eliza's. A second later, the young man next to the woman also stood, and when he turned Eliza gasped.

She held on to Jack so she wouldn't fall to the ground. "Mama? Daniel?"

Jack felt his eyes well up. He waited until Eliza's mother reached her, then he stepped back. The love of his life had longed for this moment since she was a small child. He couldn't believe God was letting him watch it play out.

"Lizzie! My baby girl, you're alive!" Her mother wrapped Eliza in her arms and both of them held on to each other. The way the children of soldiers hold on when their parents return from war. "I can't believe it. After all this time. My precious girl."

"They told me . . . you drowned." Eliza clung to her mother and then turned to the young man. "Daniel. My brother." She took hold of him. "Is it really you?"

Jack watched from a few feet away. This was the greatest gift he could ever give her. And it had almost not happened.

Her brother put his arm around Eliza's shoulders. "Lizzie." Tears streamed down his face. "I've missed you every day. Father told us you had drowned, too." He held her close, like no time had passed. Then the three of them formed a circle and held each other for a long time.

Daniel stepped back first. "Jack found us. He sent an agent to Lancaster." He touched Eliza's face. "I never stopped believing you were really alive. You were out there somewhere, looking for us."

"Jack?" Eliza still had one arm around her mother and the other around her brother. "How did you...? When...?"

He could watch Eliza with her family for the rest of the afternoon, but he tried to find his voice. "It was your great-grandfather, Lizzie." He looked from her to her mother and brother. "He believed you were all alive. After talking with him, I couldn't let the idea go."

He could tell her later how he hadn't gotten word that her mother and brother were found until three days ago, when he returned home from Honduras. CJ, his undercover agent friend, was working a drug ring in eastern Pennsylvania when he got a tip on her family.

Jack hadn't been sure it was them until he flew there and met with the pair himself. He needed only one look at Susan James to know without a doubt. This was Eliza's mother. She looked like a carbon copy of Eliza, a little older, darker hair. But the same blue eyes, same smile.

And since then he had come to learn something else about the woman. She and Eliza had the same heart. Her brother was twenty-one, and Jack could see the resemblance in him, too. So he had flown her family here for the moment that was about to happen.

As they reached the aisle, an older man stood and took his place near the gazebo. He wore a suit and he nodded at Jack.

"That's the pastor," Jack whispered near her ear. "The woman is his wife."

"I can't believe this." Eliza looked like she could barely feel the sand beneath her feet.

Her mom hugged her again and stared at her. Like all she wanted was to stare at Eliza as long as she could. Finally she stepped back. Tears still shone on her face. "I have something for you." She walked to a bag behind the folding chairs and returned with a simple bouquet of white stars, a flower native to Belize. "I think you might need this."

"True." Jack kissed Eliza's cheek and then he left her and walked down the aisle. He took his place next to the pastor. Everything was moving in slow motion, like the dream he'd imagined every day since he last saw her.

Eliza took the flowers, and kissed her mother's cheek. The two held hands for a long moment and then Susan James went back to sit in the front row, across the aisle from the pastor's wife.

Jack couldn't stop smiling at the look on Eliza's face. His note asking her to wear white today had to have given away the fact that a wedding was coming. But this . . . Jack blinked back tears. This was greater than anything he could've imagined.

Daniel stood beside her and held out his arm. "May I walk you down the aisle, Lizzie?"

"Yes!" She stood on her tiptoes and kissed his cheek. "Yes, Daniel, you may walk me down the aisle." She was clearly trying not to cry, trying to soak in every moment. Jack could tell.

The aisle wasn't long or glamorous, but until his final breath Jack would remember the way Lizzie James looked walking toward him, clinging to the brother she thought she'd lost forever. Even then she had eyes for Jack alone. And he realized they were no longer on a private stretch of Belizean beach.

They were on holy ground.

. . .

THE SWEET SCENT of the flowers in her hand made her certain she wasn't dreaming. But nothing else about the moment seemed real. Her mother and brother were alive! And they were here, with her, beside her!

God had brought them back to her. And He'd brought her back to Jack. All in one beautiful day. She had no idea how he'd found a pastor here on the Placencia Peninsula, but that didn't matter. The man looked kind and he had a Bible in his hands.

She reached the end of the aisle, and Daniel put his hands on her shoulders. "I love you, Lizzie."

"I love you, Daniel." She hugged him for a long while, and then he sat down beside their mother.

Eliza looked at the woman. She hadn't changed. Her hair, her face. Just like the images Eliza had imagined every time she looked out at the ocean. Their eyes held for a long moment, and then Eliza turned to Jack.

"I'm Pastor Joseph." The man smiled. "Looks like we've got much to celebrate today."

You have no idea, she wanted to say. But she only nodded. Somewhere in heaven, she hoped Jack's parents and Shane had a front-row spot. Because if God could do this, He could do that, too.

The pastor continued. "I understand you two haven't seen each other for a year's time." He shook his head. "I'm sure you don't have vows prepared. But do you both intend to—"

Eliza raised her hand.

"Yes, Ms. James." Pastor Joseph looked confused.

"I have vows." She smiled at Jack and gave a small shrug of her shoulders. "I had all year to memorize them."

Jack chuckled. "Me, too."

The pastor nodded. He looked a little dazed. Surely he'd never done a wedding like this one. "Okay then. Lizzie . . . Jonathan. Marriage is a covenant between a man and a woman, a covenant ordained by God. Are you two prepared to enter into that covenant now?"

She met Jack's eyes. They both nodded and said, "Yes . . . we are."

"Very well." Pastor Joseph looked at Daniel. "Do you and your mother approve of this union?"

Eliza's brother reached for their mother's hand as he nodded. "We do."

"Lizzie, you may join your groom."

"Thank you." Eliza loved the old pastor. He seemed

determined to keep the sense of reverence and propriety even when the wedding wouldn't take more than five minutes. As if he could tell something very special was happening in his presence.

Never mind that she had only her sundress and bare feet. Eliza might as well have been wearing a gown fit for a queen. And this sandy spot of beach might as well have been a cathedral. She handed her bouquet to her mother and walked to the spot in front of Jack. He took her hands in his.

"Jonathan." The pastor nodded at Jack. "You may go first."

For a long time Jack only looked at her, like he was trying to memorize her face, her eyes, everything about this moment. "I, Jonathan Jack Ryder, I ask you, Lizzie James, to be my lawfully wedded wife. When all the world is falling down around us, I will hold you up. And when you can't see through to tomorrow, I will help you believe."

He searched her eyes. "I promise to stand by you and pray for you, love you and lead you to God. Again and again and again. And when life gets loud, I'll remind you that even in the beginning when it was you and me against the world, we were never alone. Because God ordained you for me . . . and me for you." He blinked back tears. "I love you with my very life, Lizzie."

She took her time before speaking. The beauty of his words, his feelings for her needed a moment all their own. Finally she drew a slow breath, her eyes never leaving his. "I, Lizzie Susan James, choose you, Jonathan Jack Ryder, to be my lawfully wedded husband. I will look to you when I can't find my way, and I will lift you up, if ever you forget the hero you are."

Tears tried to come, but Eliza refused them. *Steady me, God.* She was too happy to cry. "I will stand by you whatever life holds, and I will believe that every day together with you is not only a gift from God . . . but a miracle. I will feel your touch when I'm alone and remember your voice when I'm afraid."

She grinned at him. "I noticed something when we were working together. When you breathed in, I felt life." She paused. "And so it shall be forever and ever. Because you will always be a part of me. And I will always be a part of you. Undivided. Forever on this side of heaven . . . and that side." She squeezed his hands. "I love you with every heartbeat. I always will."

Pastor Joseph raised his brow. "I believe those might have been the most beautiful vows I have ever heard." He gave a single nod. "I will ask the questions, then." He looked at Jack. "Do you, Jonathan Ryder, take Lizzie Susan James, to be your wife, to have and to hold, to love and to cherish until death do you part?"

Jack looked to the center of her heart. "I do."

The pastor smiled. "And do you, Lizzie Susan James, take Jonathan Jack Ryder, to be your husband, to have and to hold, to love and to cherish until death do you part?"

"Yes!" She had never been so happy in all her life. "I do."

"Very well . . . will you two be exchanging rings?"

Eliza hadn't even remembered the rings.

"Yes." Jack grinned at her. "We have rings." He pulled them from his pants pocket and handed his to Lizzie.

"You bought rings?"

"The week after I said goodbye to you in Cancún." Tears glistened in his eyes, but his smile kept them from falling. "I've carried them with me ever since."

Her ring held a stunning center diamond, as pure and brilliant and bright as their future. It glistened in the Belizean sun with small diamonds on either side of the larger one. Jack slipped it onto her finger . . . and it fit her perfectly. Like the two of them.

Next she put a simple gold band on his ring finger. "Jack," she whispered, "the rings are beautiful." She leaned closer and put her hand to the necklace he had given her on the beach in Mexico. The one she had worn every day since. "You kept your promise. You waited for me."

"Every day, Lizzie. Every day." He looked like he'd forgotten anyone else was there.

A chuckle came from the pastor. "I have a feeling this one's going to last." He looked from Jack to Eliza and back again. "By the power of the government of Belize, it is my privilege to pronounce you husband and wife." He smiled. "Jonathan, you may kiss your bride."

Jack worked his hands into her hair. Then he drew her into his arms. His kiss took her breath and she felt like she might float away. Because this wasn't pretend. It wasn't a mission or an act or part of a job they had to do.

It was forever.

Jack stepped back and smiled at her. "I can't believe it."

"Me, either." Eliza kissed him this time, and a chorus of soft laughter came from the front row. She barely noticed. She was Jack's wife now, and truly nothing but death could ever separate them.

When it was over, when she had Jack on one side and her mother and brother on the other, Eliza realized she had no idea where they were going to live or what life looked like moving forward. But it didn't matter.

God had given her everything she ever needed. Right here.

In this single moment.

Seven Years Later

CHAPTER TWENTY-FIVE

*Surely, goodness and love will follow me all the
days of my life, and I will dwell in the house of the
Lord forever.*

—Psalm 23:6

Jack pulled out of the parking lot of the University of
North Carolina's Wilmington campus and turned left
toward the interstate. He was teaching five classes in
criminal justice this semester and school would be out
in two weeks.

But today was a celebration all its own.

He had already changed into his Little Sluggers
T-shirt and as he drove he grabbed his baseball cap from
the passenger seat. Today was Luke's first T-ball game
and Jack needed to be there early.

After all, he was the coach.

The field wasn't far, halfway between the school and
home. Jack's parents had left him a fortune—money he

never thought he'd want or need. But it had given him the chance to give Eliza a very special gift.

A house on a bluff, overlooking the beach. It was the view they woke up to every morning, wrapped in each other's arms. Jack smiled. He was more in love with Eliza every day. Like the honeymoon they'd taken in Belize had never really ended.

He pulled in to the ball field twenty minutes early, but he could see that his family was already there. Eliza and their two kids—Luke and Masey. Eliza's mother, and Daniel and his wife, along with their two little boys. Jack still couldn't believe they all lived here, five minutes from each other in Wilmington.

Daniel had become Jack's best friend—next to Eliza of course. The two couples got together at least once a week and they took all the kids to the beach every Sunday afternoon.

Jack smiled as he approached the group. Eliza and her mother sat next to each other. For the past five years, the two had worked together running six safe homes in major cities along the East Coast. Rosa and Maggie from the Palace volunteered at one of them.

Eliza had used her own money to buy the first one. Just like she had dreamed.

"Daddy!" His little boy came running up. "Guess what?"

"What, buddy?" Jack set the gear bag down on the bleachers and hugged his son.

"I found a frog today! Behind the tree out back!"

"A frog! I can't wait to see it." He tugged Luke's baseball cap. "Hey so . . . today's the big day!"

"I know! I'm gonna hit a home run!" Luke waved at Eliza in the stands a few feet away. "That's what Mommy said."

Little Masey skipped up, her long blond ponytail swishing side to side. She was six and Luke was five. "I told him he'll hit *two* home runs!" She hugged Luke. "Because he's my best friend."

Jack felt the presence of God as he set up the bases and the T, and as he welcomed the other Little Sluggers to the field. Because this was the life he had chosen, the one where he was teaching the next generation how to police well.

And where he came home to Eliza and their kids every night.

He had so much precious time with his family. Time to spend an afternoon celebrating with Eliza all the ways her safe houses were bringing life to the victims of trafficking. Time for the two of them to teach Masey's Sunday School class and time to read the Bible together as a family. Every single night.

Jack *knew* Eliza and Masey and Luke—really knew them—and he loved them with every breath, every heartbeat. He was present, the way his father had wanted him to be.

The game was about to begin, and from behind him Jack heard one of the other parents talking to Eliza. "So, Lizzie. How long have you lived in Wilmington?"

Jack smiled. His wife was a pro at conversations like this. A quick look over his shoulder and he saw Eliza engage. "Oh, forever!"

"Lucky." The woman was new to the area. Her son was one of Luke's friends on the team. "I love the sunrises on the shore. Nothing more beautiful."

"Yes." Jack's wife took her time. "I've always loved the water." She paused. "I see God there. At the far end of the ocean."

Jack's heart warmed. *Indeed, Lizzie. Indeed.* He grabbed his glove and a T-ball.

A lifetime ago he and Eliza had been alone in a world where neither of them wanted to live. But God had changed that. He had taken their broken pieces and made something beautiful of them. Because today . . . well, today he and Lizzie were the most alive people Jack knew, filled with hope and faith, laughter and joy. They wanted to live to be a hundred, at least. Side by side.

This is the life you wanted for me, Dad. I hope you know.

The game was about to begin, and as Jack took his place on the mound, as he waited for his son to hit the ball off the tee, he had a feeling Shane and his parents really were watching.

And that somewhere in the bleachers of heaven, his father wasn't only smiling.

He was giving him a standing ovation.

ACKNOWLEDGMENTS

This book took a hundred times more research and courage than any I've ever written. Along the way, many people helped make it possible. I simply cannot leave the beaches of Belize without giving thanks where it is so deeply deserved.

First, a special thanks to a retired FBI agent who specialized in human trafficking. The agent read this book with little turnaround time, and the notes and advice given to me took the story to another level. Thank you for your service with the bureau, and for your meticulous attention to detail with this book. You were the difference down the stretch.

Also to my amazing Simon & Schuster editor, Trish Todd, and my publishing team, including the keenly talented Libby McGuire, Suzanne Donahue, Lisa Sciambra, Isabel DaSilva, Paula Amendolara, Kristin Fassler and Dana Trocker, along with so many others! When I told you I had a book that was very different from one of my Baxter stories, you all hesitated. But you read my proposal and loved it! Thank you for believing I could write about undercover agents, surveillance and trafficking and still tell a story with heart.

Thanks also to former Simon & Schuster CEO Carolyn Reidy, who passed away during the writing of this book. Carolyn, I still miss you dearly. Your passing came far too soon, but I will do as you asked. I will keep writing the best possible book God places on my heart. To everyone at Simon & Schuster, you clearly desire to raise the bar at every turn. Thank you for that. It's an honor to work with you!

Also thanks to Rose Garden Creative, my design team—Kyle and Kelsey Kupecky—whose unmatched talent in the industry is recognized from Los Angeles to New York. Very simply you are the best in the business! My website, social media, video trailers and newsletter—along with so many other aspects of my virtual conferences and television pieces—are at the top of the business because of you two. Thank you for working your own dreams around mine. I love you and I thank God for you every single day.

A huge thanks to my sisters, Tricia and Susan, along with my mom, Anne. You give your whole hearts to helping me love my readers. Tricia, as my executive assistant for fifteen years; and Susan, as the president of my Facebook Official Online Book Club and Team KK. And, Mom, thank you for being Queen of the Readers. Anyone who has ever sent me an email and received a response from "Karen's mom" is blessed indeed. The three of you are making a tremendous impact in changing this world for the better. I love you and I thank God for you always!

Thanks also to my son Austin, for helping me navigate the difference between a Black Hawk and a Chinook helicopter along with a hundred other details in this book that had to be right. You knew just how to help me and just where to lead me in my weeks of research. It was a blast working with you!

Thanks to EJ for praying for me every day while I was writing this book, and to Tyler for doing more than his share of the work on our other projects while I camped out on *A Distant Shore*.

Also, thank you to my office assistant, Aurora Galvin. You create space for me to write! My storytelling wouldn't be possible without you.

I'm also grateful to my Team KK members, who step in at the final stage in writing a book. The galley pages come to me, and I send them to you, my most dedicated reader friends and family. My nieces Shannon Fairley, Melissa Viernes and Kristen Springer. Also Hope Burke, Donna Keene, Renette Steele, Zac Weikal and Sheila Holman. You are my volunteer test team! It always amazes me, the typos you catch at the final hour. Thank you for loving my work, and thanks for your availability to read my novels first and fast.

Also, my books only happen with the help of my family, especially my amazing husband, Donald. Honey, thank you for your spiritual wisdom and leadership in our home, and thanks for talking through books like this one from outline to editing. The countless ways you help me when I'm on deadline make all the difference. I love you!

And a special thanks to a man who has believed in my career for two decades, my amazing agent, Rick Christian. From the beginning, Rick, you've told me to dream big, set my sights high. Movies, TV series, world-wide reach. All of it for God and through Him. You imagined this, believed it and prayed for it alongside me and my family. You saw it happening and you still do! While I write, you work behind the scenes on film projects and my future books, the Baxter family TV series and details regarding every word I've ever written. You are brilliant and driven, compassionate and dedicated. I used to dream of having you as my agent. Now Tyler and I are the only authors who do. God is amazing. Thank you, Rick, and thank you for praying for me and my family. That most of all.

Finally, my greatest thanks to God Almighty, who is First and Last and all things in between. I write for You, through You and because of You. Thank you with my whole being.

Dear Reader Friend,

Some books are deeper than others, grittier. This book was one of those. I can remember sitting on my back porch and imagining a scenario where a child is rescued on some distant shore. Only the little girl never wanted to be rescued.

Because she was trapped in an existence we can't begin to imagine.

When I wrote *Truly, Madly, Deeply*—one of my recent books—I touched on the topic of trafficking. But the story only skimmed the surface. It never went beyond the doors and walls of places where children lose their lives and their innocence.

This book goes there. I did my best not to be terribly graphic, not to take you too intensely to places you would never want to go. But the truth is, the victims lost to trafficking don't want to be there, either. Maybe there's some way you can get involved in stopping this scourge. Check with your local law enforcement agencies and churches. They'll have ideas for you, if you're interested.

A Distant Shore is complex and unforgettable. A story just like this has certainly never happened, and for a while I wondered if it was too far-fetched to write about. But then the tale of Eliza and Jack became an allegory—like *The Lion, the Witch and the Wardrobe*. Because the great Aslan still roams about today, fighting on our behalf. On behalf of Jack and Eliza.

And so I had to write this book. I couldn't escape it.

I could read *A Distant Shore* again and again. The way God wove hope into the most hopeless story line I've ever written about. I hope you feel the same way.

There is one thing I pray you take away from *A Distant Shore*. No matter how broken your life, God is the giver of a new day, a second chance. He is the God of redemption and restoration. He can take your shattered pieces and make them into a beautiful creation. That's the point of the cross. You can find new life. You can rise again. I'm praying for you.

As you close the cover on this book, do me a favor. Think about who you can share this with. A friend or a sister. Your mother or a co-worker. The librarian at your local high school. Someone struggling to make sense of a loss or someone who needs to believe they can find life again. Maybe just a person who loves to read. Please . . . give this book away when you finish it.

Remember, a story dies if it is left on the shelf. So please pass this one on.

By now you may have heard about the TV series— *The Baxters*. This was something I only dreamed about back when God gave me those very special characters. The series has the material to go on for a very long time, so look for it. I know you'll love it like the rest of us do.

To find out more about *The Baxters* on TV or any of

my other books, television series or movies, visit my website, www.KarenKingsbury.com. There you can enter your email address to sign up for my free weekly newsletter. I make my big announcements in my newsletter first! These emails come straight to you and include free short pieces and devotions written by me, also news about my events. And always a little something to encourage you.

Like I said, the biggest news will be in my newsletter first, so sign up today!

At my website, you can also find out how to stay encouraged with me on social media or how to attend one of my Karen Kingsbury Virtual Conference events.

Finally, if you are seeking a faith like Jack and Eliza's, find a Bible-believing church and get connected. There is a reason you came across this book. God is always at work connecting, speaking, helping us see Him and hear Him. Maybe reading this book was that moment for you.

Until next time. Love you all!

READER GUIDE

A DISTANT SHORE

KAREN KINGSBURY

1 Jack's life changed in a single moment, the instant he saw Eliza drowning out in the ocean. Have you ever taken part in a sudden rescue? Or have you ever been rescued by a stranger? Talk about that time. How did it change you?

2 Sex trafficking can look a lot of different ways. It happens to children and adults, male and female. If

you ran the world, what would you do to solve this problem?

3 What advice would you give parents of children, so their sons and daughters wouldn't ever become victims? If you or someone you know has ever been trafficked, what are three things you would teach all children to protect them?

4 Eliza thought she saw God at the far edge of the ocean. Where do you most easily see or feel God's presence? Share about that.

5 With much loss comes much testing of one's faith. Talk about a loss you or someone you know has gone through. How did that event change or affect your faith?

6 Jack's parents were loving and kind, but they were too busy to spend time with their boys. Share about a season when you or someone you know let work take away from family time. What was the outcome?

7 Jack was one of the best undercover agents at the FBI because he wasn't afraid to die. But he also wasn't interested in truly living. Are you afraid of death? Why or why not?

8 Do you think the life you're living now is one where you are truly living? Why or why not? What

would you like to change about your life? Be specific.

9 Ike Armstrong never gave up hope that his family was still alive. His adamancy was one of the reasons Jack never gave up looking for Susan and Daniel James. What is something you've prayed a long time for? Talk about that situation.

10 The Army, Navy and FBI all worked together with local Belizean police to pull off the raid on the Palace. Which is your favorite branch of the military, or favorite division of law enforcement? If you have personal experience, share that.

11 When Eliza is rescued and taken to San Antonio, she finds herself with little food and no place to live. Many rescued victims return to their traffickers because they cannot make it on their own. How does this make you feel? What can be done about this?

12 Eliza is a victim because she was held against her will at the Palace. But she is also a fighter. How have you made good out of bad or troublesome situations in your life? What would you still like to do to find purpose in your past pain?

13 When Eliza realized she could help take down trafficking rings, she gave up everything to make that happen. How have you volunteered for a cause or

helped your community in some way? Did that change your perspective on life? Explain.

14 After losing first his brother, Shane, and then his parents, Jack was determined never to love again. What were some things that worked to change his mind?

15 Imagine how Jack felt when he realized that Eliza was the same girl he had rescued from the beach a decade ago. Talk about some great and mysterious coincidence or circumstance in your life or the life of someone you know. How did it affect you or them?

16 Eliza had never known love or kindness from a man. In what ways did Jack show her both of these? Share your favorite moments from the story.

17 With her hatred toward men, Eliza was certain she would never marry or fall in love. How did her feelings change? Why did they change?

18 Have you or someone you know ever been sure you weren't going to fall in love or like a specific person only to be wrong? Talk about that.

19 Jack quoted Romans 8:28 in one important conversation with Eliza. *And we know that in all things, God works for the good of those who love Him, who have been called according to His purpose.* How have you seen this truth play out in your life? Be specific.

20 God loves to surprise us. Were you surprised when Eliza's family was there at her wedding? Tell of a time when God surprised you.

21 *A Distant Shore* is about learning to live again, finding a second chance at life even when all hope seems lost. Tell of a time when you or someone you know found hope and faith to live again. How did that time inspire you?

YOU WERE SEEN MOVEMENT

His name was Henry, and I will remember him as long as I live.

Henry was our waiter at a fancy restaurant when I was on tour for one of my books. Toward the end of the meal something unusual happened. I started to cry. Slow tears, just trickling down my cheeks. My husband was with me and he looked concerned. "Karen, what's wrong?"

"Our waiter," I said. "He needs to know God loves him. But there's no time. We have to get to our event and he has six other tables to serve."

Henry was an incredibly attentive server. He smiled and got our order right and he worked hard to do it. Everywhere he went on the restaurant floor, he practically sprinted to get his job done. But when he was just off the floor, when he thought no one was looking, Henry's smile faded. He looked discouraged and hopeless. Beaten up.

That very day I began dreaming about the "You Were Seen" movement. Many of you are aware of this organization, but I'll summarize it. Very simply, you get a pack of You Were Seen cards and you hand them out. Where acceptable, tip—generously.

From my office in the past few months more than 250,000 You Were Seen cards have gone out. We partner with the Billy Graham Evangelistic Association's plan for salvation and other help links.

And so it is really happening! People like you are truly seeing those in their path each day. You are finding purpose by living your life on mission and not overlooking the delivery person and cashier, the banker and business contact, the server and barista, the police officer and teacher, the doctor and nurse. You are letting strangers see God's love in action. Why?

Because Christians should love better than anyone. We should be more generous. Kinder. More affirming. More patient. The Bible tells us to love God and love others. And to tell others the good news of the gospel— that we have a Father who is for us, not against us. He loves us so much that He made a way for us to get to heaven.

Hand out a pack of You Were Seen cards in the coming weeks and watch how every card given makes you feel a little better. Go to www.YouWereSeen.com to get your cards and start showing gratitude and generosity to everyone you meet.

Always when you leave a You Were Seen card, you will let a stranger know that their hard work was seen in that moment. They were noticed! What better way to spread love? The You Were Seen card will then direct people to the website—www.YouWereSeen.com. At the website, people will be encouraged and reminded that God sees them every day. Always. He knows what they are going through. Every day should be marked by a miraculous encounter.

www.YouWereSeen.com

ONE CHANCE FOUNDATION

The Kingsbury family is also passionate about seeing orphans all over the world brought home to their forever families. As a result, they created a charity called the One Chance Foundation.

This foundation was inspired by the memory of Karen's father, Ted C. Kingsbury. Ted always said, "Life is not a dress rehearsal. We have one chance to love, one chance to truly live!"

Karen often tells her reader friends, "You have one chance to write the story of your life!"™ Now, with Karen's One Chance Foundation, readers can join her in the belief that all of us have one chance to make a difference in the lives of orphans.

In the Bible, James 1:27 says people with pure and faultless religion are those who look after orphans and widows. If you are interested in giving to Karen's One Chance Foundation and having your dedication printed in one of Karen's upcoming novels, visit www.KarenKingsbury.com. Below are dedications from Karen's readers who have contributed to the One Chance Foundation:

One Chance Foundation for *A Distant Shore*

- To all of the NYPD, FDNY, PANY & the DSNY for your bravery on 9/11. We will never forget and will forever remember those lost that day. We heart NY forever! Love, Hope Burke & Kingston Painter
- Madeleine a gift from God chosen by Him to fill our home with laughter & love. Happy Birthday, Mommy
- Happy Birthday Grandmom! We love you! Love, Ken, MH, Blake, Parker, Janie, Avery, Hallie & Sullivan
- Dedicated to all who bear the unseen scars of sexual trauma . . . you are seen and loved! Sheila & Kurt Holman
- LMG, My love forever! LLG
- Lundee, Love you Forever, Joe
- In loving memory of my husband, William Rolfe, six months without you already. Love is forever, Janie
- For my Mom, Jackie Jones! Love, Emily
- Blessings to Kathy Conquest, a prayer warrior and my heart-to-heart partner of 19 years!! Love Jan Miller
- Blessings to Emmeline, Joe
- Happy 60th Mom, Julia Haverlock! Love, Your Family
- To My Mom, Irene. Love you! Terry
- To my wonderful mom who went halfway around the world for me—I love you like crazy cakes Mom. —Emma
- Riley Jaxon, We love you! Gramma Becky & Papa John

- Tandy & Pat—2gether 4ever
- To my mom, Barbara Matley, who taught me a love of books. Love you forever mom! Pamela Sheldon
- Susan, you helped me find my way to the Lord!—Kim
- John, our love story is my favorite. God, you & me, a cord of strength and love. Always & forever, D
- To my "grand" Emma Nelson & my son Cody— Bloomington IN—Happy Birthday! Love you forever! Dena Patrick
- Happy 50th Anniversary to my love!! ❤❤❤ 02/20/1971—Janell
- To all my family and friends! Love you! Tyler B.
- Mama, you are my hero and I love you! Teresa Lynn
- Jodee Lynn our true queen
- To My Heather, thank you for always being my rock. —Charles
- To my beloved husband.—Ellen Miller
- Sedi Graham
- Jordyn Grobleben, I am so proud of you! Love, Mom
- Great Mother, Pansy and terrific mate, Ken, Love, Elaine
- Pam Todd, My Best Friend & Book Buddy! —Pam Edmiston
- To everyone going through the covid19 pandemic. Mathew 11:28 "Come to me all you who are weary and burdened, and I will give you rest."—Judy Resley
- To the 3 most important women in my life; Jody Mathews, Jennifer Lawrence, and Abby Mathews! —Poppy

- To Michelle Wimmer, love me!
- To Liane Keaton—My Barnabus—Love you buddy!
  —Shawna
- I love you forever, Paul!—Rose
- Happy 60th B-day Mom! We love u! Love, S, C, J, B
- Happy 40th Christine! Love You! Yours Always,
  Bobby
- You are God's masterpiece. Ephesians 2:10 Love,
  Aunt Kieny & Uncle Chris
- A/C Carter D. Pittman
- Chief Amos Johnson District Fire Chief Dave Brown
- To our mom, Carol, your faith and unconditional love
  inspire us to be moms like you. We love you!
- Dennis Wayne Bloomfield
- To JBM, my husband & hero. Love Rachel
- AJS You are beautiful!—Lori
- Sherry McClellan, you are loved more than you know.
  —Calley
- We love you Grandma Foster! Love, Fawn and Billie
- Chelsea Donelson, a NICU nurse who battled cancer
  with courage and grace. 1990–2020 #TheChelseaWay
- Mom, I hope this gift is special. Love, Carolyn
- May God Bless you always! Love, Jane
- To my precious son Brandon, my life's joy.
- In memory of my mom, Ruth Rodriguez! Love, Mary
- In memory of Phyllis Ann! Love, Ronald Lewis
- To the living Christ who makes all things possible!
  Love, Elizabeth
- So blessed & thankful!—Bethany T

- My Prayer Warrior, My Mother. Marjory Grigsby!
  Love, Pamela
- Konnie & Steve Yoho God bless—Mark 9:36–37
  Love, KSD
- To my Mom and Dad who loved their nine children.
- In loving memory of my mom, Sue Lucky. Miss you!
  —Toni
- Levi, UR God's miracle!!! Love, Nana & Papa
- God Bless You!—Christina
- Dedicate my prayers 2 you!—Eddie
- To my dearest love Hannah!—Jarrett
- My beautiful Mama, IdaBeth & her joy of books!
  Love, Lynn
- Dedicated to my dad, Mack Harris. I lost him to cancer 7 years ago. Love, Sheree
- JoAnn Francis—THANKS!
- To My Mom for her love of Family and Books!
  —Linda
- Becky & Eric. My two greatest gifts of pure joy.
- Thank u, DePrimos for loving 3 children.
- We have the best Busha & Nana! Love Hudson & Huck
- Abigail ("Your Father's Joy") Katharine, you are an answer to prayer, Jeremiah 29:11, we love you!
- Morry, Thank you for showing me what love is!
  Miss u, Brenda
- Mom, Thanks for always believing in me! I love you so much! My Mom & My Friend! Love Jennifer Zwickl

- To Barbara Bankett, a beautiful Godly mother!
  Love, Tracy
- Jess W.—A library + long walks/great talks + Karen
  Kingsbury's amazing books = a friendship given by
  God.—Angela
- JA—Greg, gone too soon!
- To Rita—you were always her best birthday gift!
  —Lauren
- Kylie + Caroline—Be Still & Know. Love You, Momma
- Baukina Van Meekeren Miss your humour & hugs,
  Mom!

REAL-LIFE POLICE OFFICERS

Typically I use this section to recognize my top fans, the reader friends who follow me on social media and are first to open my newsletters each week. But this time I thought to highlight all the real-life Jack Ryder types, the ones who work long hours for little pay, sacrificing their lives to protect you and me.

I put out a call for readers to honor the police officers and first responders in their lives, and the outpouring was overwhelming. Not just in the number of readers who submitted the names of their family members and friends. But in what else they said in those heart-rending emails. "No one has wanted to honor my police officer wife in a very long time," one man wrote. "I am writing this with tears in my eyes." Many others wrote similar letters.

So . . . friends, take a minute and read this list.

I'd like to add to it several others. First, during the writing of this book, FBI agents Daniel Alfin and Laura Schwartzenberger were killed and three other agents were wounded in a raid on a Florida trafficker's house. I'd like to honor them. I'd also like to recognize the six police officers who worked against a ticking massive bomb to save the lives of hundreds of residents in downtown Nashville on Christmas Day, 2020. And finally, I recognize these officers: my cousin Eddie; my husband's cousins John and Charlie; Aaron, who has always been like a son to us; and our friends John and Charlie—all officers who devoted many, many years to serving their communities.

Friends, pray for the men and women honored here. Pray for the families of those whose watch ended far too soon. And the next time you see a police officer or first responder, buy them a coffee. Hand them a You Were Seen Card . . . or just thank them.

And may God bless and protect those who serve.

A.T. Lee—LEO—1 year

Aaron Bommersbach—LEO —5 years

Aaron Compton—LEO—20 years

Aaron Klauss, Dep.—LEO—4 years

Aaron Knoerzer—LEO

Abby Lewis—First Responder —3 months

Abigail Whitehill—First Responder —6 years

AC Harmon Martin Roberts— LEO —18 years

Adam Bickler—LEO—1 year

Adam Cash—LEO—9 years

Adam Farnsler—LEO—6 years

Adam Flanigan—First Responder —6 years

Adam Host, Sgt.—LEO

Adam Hounshell—First Responder—27 years

Adam Kardel, DS—LEO—7 years

Adam Yates—LEO—23 years

Adrian Kuschnereit—LEO—13 years

Adrianna Caraballo—LEO—1 year

Al Byrum—First Responder —38 years

Alan Blomquist—LEO—32 yesrs

Alane Larison—First Responder —35 years

Alex Farnsler—LEO—3 years

Alex Spears—LEO—2 years

Alexus Jones—LEO—15 years

Alfred Chambers—LEO —7 years

Allen Farley—LEO—37 years

Allen Hightower—First
Responder—24 years

Allen Pearson, Det.—LEO, 8
years—End of Watch 4/8/09

Amaury Quinones—LEO
—6 years

Amber Riedel—First Responder
—14 years

Amos Johnson—First Responder
—21 years

Andrea Warfel, Mstr. Cpl.—LEO
—15 years

Andrew Cox—First Responder
—6 years

Andrew Farnsler—LEO—5 years

Andrew Horton—LEO—15 years

Andrew J. Gillette, Cpl.—LEO,
10 years—End of Watch
2/25/20

Andrew Krnjeu—LEO—15 years

Andrew Lynn—LEO—2 years

Andrew M.—LEO—9.5 years

Andrew Morse—LEO, K9—20
years

Andrew Rollin Baughman—First
Responder—12 years

Andrew Voight—Volunteer
Firefighter—5 years

Andy Daigneau—First Responder
—28 years

Andy Erlandson—LEO—19 years

Angel De Anda—LEO—1 year

Angela Neufeld—First Responder
—16 years

Anita Winn—First Responder
—25 years

Anthony Callicutt—LEO
—10 years

Anthony Connell—First

Responder, 24 years—LEO,
23 years

Anthony Minnis—LEO—43 years

Anthony Petito—First Responder
—5 years

Anthony Pressnell—LEO
—32 years

Anthony Rodriguez—LEO
—18 years

Arlin Lee Jackson—First
Responder—17 years

Ashley Googe—First Responder
—9 years

Ashley N. Payne—First Responder

Ashlyn Mortell—First Responder
—19 years

Austin Blomquist—LEO—4 years

Austin Coallier—LEO—3 years

Austin S. Diekevers—LEO—4
years

Bailey C. Martin, Jr.—First
Responder—18 years

Barett Duren—LEO—8 years

Barry Bond—LEO—16 years

Becky Sargeant—LEO—25 years

Ben C.—LEO—5 years

Ben Farrell—LEO—4 years

Ben Neitzel—LEO—32 years

Ben Perkins—LEO—26 years

Benjamin Hinson—First
Responder—18 years

Benjamin Johnson—LEO—6 years

Benjamin McRary—LEO—1 year

Benjamin Spurgeon—LEO
—8.5 years

Benjamin Weaver—LEO—5 years

Benjamin West—LEO—11 years

Bill Brown—LEO—25 years

Bill Elfo, Sheriff—LEO—20+
years

Bill Hammack—LEO—34 years

Bill Hoedebeck—LEO—28 years

Bill Walker—LEO—20 years

Billy Banta—First Responder
—10 years

Billy Winn—First Responder
—24 years

Blaine Thomason—First
Responder—19 years

Blake Davis—LEO—1 year

Blake Escobar—LEO—2 years

Blake Gammill—LEO, 7 years—
End of Watch 2/24/05

Blake Riley—LEO—3 years

Bobby Hallman, ASD—LEO

Bobby Long—LEO—8 years

Bobby Moree—LEO—24 years

Brad Counce—LEO—24 years

Brad Gailey, DS—LEO—12 years

Brad Hart—First Responder
—25 years

Brandon Boykin—First Responder
—8 years

Brandon Deas—LEO

Brandon Flamm—LEO—9 years

Brandon Gray—First Responder
—16 years

Brandon Gueiss—LEO

Brandon Kuschnereit—LEO
—9 years

Brandon Thomasy, Cpl.—LEO
—5 years

Brandon Watson—LEO—1 year

Brant Halfin—LEO—3 years

Brendan Byrum—First Responder
—1 year

Brendan Warren—First Responder
—5 years

Brennan Gandy—LEO—5 years

Brent Ball—LEO, K9—6 years

Brent D. Smith, Cpl.—LEO
—16 years

Brent McConnell—First
Responder—14 years

Brent Moening, Lt.—LEO—13
years

Brent Phelps, Chf.—LEO—24
years

Brett Cockrum—First Responder
—3 years

Brett Ver Velde—LEO—27 years

Brett Watkins—LEO—4 years

Brian Barnett—LEO, Volunteer
Fire Fighter—14.5 years

Brian Barrick—LEO—16 years

Brian C. Young—LEO, 29
years—First Responder, 30
years

Brian D. O'Callaghan—LEO
—33 years

Brian David Shaw—LEO, 3
years—End of Watch 11-17-17

Brian Ferguson—LEO—15 years

Brian Goodson—LEO—17 years

Brian Haddix—LEO—14 years

Brian Larison—LEO—17 years

Brian Milton—First Responder
—17 years

Brian Moore—LEO—31 years

Brian Pelock, Sgt.—LEO—10
years

Brian VanVickle—LEO—13
years

Brian Warczakoski—LEO, First
Responder—18 years

Brian Zillmer—LEO—25 years

Bricesen Burton—LEO—2 years

Brion Delap—LEO—3 years

Brooke Tallent—First Responder
—1 year

Brooks N.—LEO—14 years

Brooks T. Goddard—LEO—2.5 years

Bruce A. Saller—LEO—25 years

Bruce Cantrell—LEO—33 years

Bruce D. Jackson—LEO—34 years

Bruce Morgan—LEO—12 years

Bryan (Dana) Hixson—LEO—24 years

Bryan Morris—LEO—11 years

Bryan Ortiz—LEO—10 years

Bryan Osborne—LEO—2 years

Bryan Vickers—LEO—8 years

Bryce Peterson—LEO—15 years

Bryon Scott Egelski—LEO, 5 years—End of Watch 7/11/94

Bryson W. McDaniel, Sgt.—LEO—8 years

Bubba Smith—LEO—6 months

C. J. Lee—LEO—19 years

C. K. Day—LEO—35 years

Caleb Johnson—LEO—5 years

Caleb Johnson—LEO—6 years

Caleb Ray—LEO—2 years

Cameron Chance—LEO—1.5 years

Cameron Moran—First Responder—2 years

Candace Duncan—LEO—7 years

Carl Donnelly—LEO—17 years

Carl Shrake—LEO—26 years

Carlos Canelos—First Responder—12 years

Carmen Galderisi Jr.—Volunteer First Responder

Carter Pittman, AC—First Responder—31 years

Casey F. Day—LEO—5+ years

Chad A. Richmond—LEO—14 years

Chad Enzor—First Responder—20 years

Chad Ginn, Det.—LEO—26 years

Chad Host, BATT CHF—First Responder

Chad Luis Meek—LEO—20 years

Chad Sloan, Sgt.—LEO—20 years

Chad Stapler—First Responder—18 years

Chad Stone—LEO, 18 years—Volunteer Firefighter, 14 years

Charles (Buddy) Sumner, Jr.—LEO—29 years

Charles (Charlie) Stanley Tull, Sr.—LEO—31 years

Charles (Chuck) E. Palmer—LEO—21 years

Charles (Chuck) Tull, Jr.—First Responder—15 years

Charles B. Arnold—LEO—25 years

Charles Daniel Carter, In Memory Of—First Responder—13 years

Charles Johnson—LEO—33 years

Charles Joseph Wright—LEO—17 years

Charles Romine—LEO—33 years

Charles Warner, Lt. Chief Spokesman—FPD—22 years

Chase Elizabeth Rusbridge—LEO—2 years

Chase Messer Sr., Sgt.—LEO—12 years

Chase Smith—LEO—8 years

Chong & Angela Wong—First Responders—10 years

Chris Aelvoet—First Responder —9 years

Chris Applebee—First Responder —7 years

Chris Byrum—First Responder —30 years

Chris Dixon—LEO—5 years

Chris Douglas—LEO—2 years

Chris Dye, Cpl.—LEO, 5 years— End of Watch 11/4/20

Chris Gibson—LEO—15 years

Chris Herring—First Responder —24 years

Chris Kelley—LEO—19 years

Chris Rowley—LEO—16 years

Chris Smith—LEO—28 years

Chris Smith—LEO—4 years

Chris Tautges Richter—First Responder—15 years

Chris Thompson—LEO—23 years

Chris Tull—First Responder —16 years

Chris Weertz—First Responder —22 years

Christi Paynter—LEO— 30 years

Christopher Bryan—LEO—20 years

Christopher Clair—LEO—7 years

Christopher Clark—First Responder—16 years

Christopher D. Cox—First Responder—9 years

Christopher D'Avanzon—LEO —5 years

Christopher Garcia—LEO—8 years

Christopher Hall, Sr.—LEO—7 years

Christopher Jackson—First Responder—14 years

Christopher M. Phillips—LEO —22 years

Christopher Murphy—LEO—7 years

Christopher Parmentier—LEO —15 years

Christopher Rozman, Cpt.—LEO —19 years

Christopher Ryan Morton— LEO—End of Watch 3/6/19

Christopher Spurgeon—LEO —6 years

Christopher Stadler, Det.—LEO —15 years

Claude E. Leslie, III—LEO —40 years

Clifford Harris, In Memory Of— First Responder—20 years

Clifford Morrison, DS—LEO —25 years

Clifford Weatherbee—First Responder—32 years

Cody Holte—LEO, 2 years—End of Watch 5/27/20

Colby Childress—LEO—2 years

Cole Butler—LEO—40 years

Cole Ferrell—LEO—3 years

Colin Millison—LEO—32 years

Collin Douglas—First Responder —5 years

Colton Lucas—First Responder —4 years

Connor Branderhorst—First Responder—4 years

Connor Michael Jones—First
Responder
Corey Kernell—LEO—26 years
Cori Hale—LEO—16 years
Cory Parker—LEO—3 years
Cory Parker—LEO, 13 years—
First Responder, 14 years
Cory Rupe, Sgt.—LEO—28
years
Craig G. Story—LEO, 7 years—
End of Watch 1/13/10
Craig Hamrick—First Responder
—35 years
Craig Harris, Sgt.—LEO—
Retired—28 years
Craig Hightower—LEO—31
years
Curtis Howard—First Responder
—21 years
Dakota Carter—First Responder
—1.5 years
Dale Needham—Volunteer First
Responder—39 years
Dale Ten Haken—LEO, 5
years—End of Watch 9/23/98
Dale Woods—LEO, First
Responder—30 years
Dalton Bagwell—LEO—17 years
Dan Lavoie—LEO—36 years
Dan Stone—LEO—10 years
Dan T. R. Uptegraff, In Memory
Of—LEO—15 years
Daniel Benner—LEO—14 years
Daniel Bingham—LEO—12
years
Daniel David Edenfield, Sgt.—
LEO, 26 years—End of Watch
1998
Daniel Geeting—LEO—3 years
Daniel Heckard—LEO—4 years

Daniel Morris—First Responder
—14 years
Daniel Ninedorf—LEO—4 years
Daniel Robert Hille—First
Responder—6 years
Daniel Smetters—LEO—15 years
Daniel Smith—LEO—9 years
Daniel Sweiger—LEO—24 years
Daniel Twist—LEO—5 years
Danny Arredondo—LEO
—32 years
Danny Ball, Cpt.—LEO—43 years
Danny Brosnan—LEO—2.5 years
Danny Champness—LEO—15
years
Danny Graham—LEO—23 years
Danny Moran—First Responder
—8 years
Darin Carter—LEO
Darren Keuhl—LEO—32 years
Darryl Bailey—LEO
Daryn Blake Jackson—First
Responder—4 years
Dave Lawrence—LEO—34 years
David Arnold, COP—LEO
—32 years
David Benjamin—First
Responder—28 years
David C. Knepp—LEO
—24.5 years
David Cook, DS—LEO
—19 years
David Cox—First Responder
—41 years
David Curtis—LEO, 3+ years—
End of Watch 6/29/10
David Hendry, Sgt.—LEO
—20 years
David Hodge—First Responder,
LEO—20 years

David Jackson, Sgt.—LEO
—11 years
David Johnson—LEO—20 years
David L. Williams—LEO
—18 years
David LeBaron—First Responder
—28 years
David Livingston—LEO
—20 years
David Markins—First Responder
—3 years
David Moody—LEO—11 years
David Munsey, Sgt.—LEO
—13 years
David R. Jackson—LEO—5 years
David Rose, Dep.—LEO—9 years
David Smith—LEO—22 years
David Stewart—LEO—35 years
David W. Henderson—LEO
—28 years
David Weatherspoon—First
Responder—42 years
David West—First Responder
—30 years
Dean Johnson—LEO—35 years
Dean O. White—LEO, First
Responder—15 years
Dean Vietmeier—LEO
—12 years
Debbie D. (Croft) Richmond—
LEO—23 years
Deborah Hope—First Responder
—18 years
Denis M. Snyder—LEO—30
years
Dennis Bennewitz—First
Responder—31 years
Dennis Newton—LEO—31 years
Dennis Parker—First Responder
—45 years

Dennis Schebig—LEO—32 years
Denny Jones—LEO—40 years
Derek Luke, Sgt.—LEO—23
years
Derek Riley—First Responder
—5 years
Derick Dodson—First Responder
—8 years
Derrick Ard—LEO—22 years
Derrick D. Parish—LEO—5 years
Derrick Learned—LEO—26 years
Derrick Pierce—LEO—2 years
Devon Lockett—First Responder
—6 years
Dick Cooper—LEO—26.5 years
Dillion Chaney—LEO—3 years
Dillon Cromley—LEO—17 years
Dima Karpenko—First Responder
Dominic Gradozzi, III—LEO
—2+ years
Don D. Taylor—LEO—23 years
Don Davis, Lt.—LEO—25 years
Don Forbes—First Responder
—50 years
Don Gates—First Responder
—16 years
Don Williams, Lt. Chaplain—
LEO—30 years
Donald Gates—First Responder
—17 years
Donald George—First Responder
—60 years
Donald L.—First Responder
—40 years
Donald L. Mays, Sr.—LEO
—40 years
Donald Swenson—LEO—25
years
Donathan R. Thomas, Jr.—First
Responder—24 years

Donnie Johnson—LEO—29 years
Donnie Lyle, Lt.—LEO
—24.5 years
Donnie McDaniel—LEO—2
years
Doug Conway—LEO—35 years
Doug DeBord, Lt.—LEO
—28 years
Doug Heimkreiter—LEO
—21 years
Doug McCullough—LEO
—34 years
Douglas Ames—LEO—20 years
Douglas Nagel Parkhurst—LEO
—30 years
Drake Hawkins—LEO—1 year
Drew B.—LEO—9 years
Drew Michael—LEO—10 years
Drew Neese—LEO—15 years
Duane Allen Benell, Sgt.—LEO
—30 years
Durwood Evans—First Responder
—40 years
Dustin A. Armentrout—LEO
—10 years
Dustin Roemeling—LEO
—12 years
Dylan Alexander—LEO—2 years
Dylan Blythe—LEO—6 years
Dylan Goodison—LEO—1 year
E. R. Mowry—LEO—31 years
Earl Blevins—First Responder
—25 years
Ed Butterworth—LEO—14 years
Ed Mcmahon—LEO
Eddie Grissom—LEO—5 years
Eddie Kasaba—LEO—17 years
Eduardo Morales—LEO
—5 years
Edward Lang—LEO—25 years

Edward Little, Jr.—LEO
—27 years
Edward Shepherd—LEO
—25 years
Elvin (Sonny) Brown—First
Responder—58 years
Emily Brantley—LEO—
4 years
Emily Burnette—First Responder
—4 years
Emily Smith—First Responder
—8 years
Eric Chisom—LEO, First
Responder—25 years
Eric E. Hoffman—First Responder
—36 years
Eric Finnvik—LEO—10 years
Eric Keech—LEO—15 years
Eric Olivier—First Responder
Eric Passarelli, COP—LEO
—26 years
Eric S.—First Responder
—6 years
Eric W. Roosa—LEO—9 years
Eric Zapata—First Responder
—10 years
Erik Raines—LEO—20 years
Erik Wilder—LEO—12 years
Erin McDowell—First Responder
—15 years
Ethan Brown—LEO—4 years
Ethan Conseen—LEO—5 years
Evan C. Brock—LEO—8 years
Evan Romine—LEO—6 years
Fawn McHenry—LEO
—18.5 years
Floyd Simpson—LEO—25 years
Frank Gamble—LEO—22 years
Frank Hernandez—LEO
—28 years

Frank Lopez—LEO—23 years

Frank M. Conoly, Lt.—LEO
—21 years

Fred Kliora—LEO—32 years

Fredrick Feazel, Sr.—LEO
—19 years

Garry Morning—LEO—22 years

Gary Bourgeois—First Responder
—23 years

Gary Eble—First Responder
—34 years

Gary J. Kornegay, Cpt., In
Memory Of—LEO—30 years

Gary L. Austin, In Memory Of—
LEO—30 years

Gary L. Schroyer—LEO
—25 years

Gary Michael, Jr.—LEO—End of
Watch 8/6/18

Gary Shavers, Lt.—LEO
—24 years

Gary Vickery Kent, Dep.—LEO
—24 years

Gene Roller—Volunteer First
Responder—17 years

George B. Swartwood, COP—
LEO—36 years

George Camp—LEO—31 years

George R. Farmer—LEO
—25 years

Gerald R. Smith—LEO—4 years

Gerald T. Carter, Sr.—LEO
—4 years

Gerardo Duran, Jr., Sgt.—LEO
—10 years

Glen Brower—LEO—28 years

Glenn & Ann Petty & sons—
Volunteer First Responders

Glenn Backstrom—LEO
—36 years

Gordon Hutchinson—RCMP
—16 years

Grafton Bowersox—LEO
—16 years

Grahm Dennis—LEO

Grant B. Jacobs—First Responder
—2 years

Grant Martin—LEO—5 years

Grant Thomas—LEO—11 years

Greg Bergland—LEO—8 years

Greg Johnston—First Responder
—25 years

Greg Koss—LEO—31 years

Greg Nichols, Sgt.—LEO
—33 years

Gregory Currin—LEO
—15 years

Gregory G. Turnell, Lt.—First
Responder—34 years

Gregory K. Smith—LEO
—31 years

Gregory S. Oselinsky, Lt.—LEO
—30 years

H. Nelson Croft, Jr.—LEO
—30 years

Hale Guyer—LEO—32 years

Haley R. Roddy—First
Responder—24 years

Harry E. Schroyer, Jr.—LEO
—36 years

Harry E. Schroyer, Sr.—LEO
—25 years

Harry N. Croft, Sr.—LEO
—34 years

Harry Pence—LEO—23 years

Helen Smith—First Responder
—4 years

Hunter Armstrong—First
Responder—5 years

Hunter Roller—LEO, 2 years—

Volunteer & First Responder,
5 years

Ian Bridge—LEO—5 years

Ian Dent—LEO—10+ years

Isaac Palmer, DS—LEO—3 years

Isaac Tanksley—First responder
—1 year

Isaac Warren—PSP, 1 year—
Army MP, 5 years

J. Tyler Snoddy, Sgt.—LEO
—9 years

J.C. Carroll—First Responder
—21 years

J.D. King, Jr.—LEO—46 years

J.R. Johnson—LEO—7 years

J.T. Osborne—First Responder
—10 years

Jack Richardson—LEO—30 years

Jack Schoder—LEO

Jackson Hall—LEO Academy

Jacob Halferty—First Responder
—5 years

Jacob Reichard—Trooper Pilot
SP—4 years

Jadon Miller—LEO—1 year

Jake Grubbs—LEO—3 years

Jake Medhurst—LEO—11 years

Jake Patterson—First Responder
—1 year

Jaleel Gatling—LEO—4 years

Jalone Walker—LEO—5 years

James B. (JB) Smith—LEO
—22 years

James Caudle—First Responder
—20+ years

James Edwards—LEO—31 years

James H. Dep.—LEO—20 years

James Harkins, Jr.—LEO—13 years

James Headrick—LEO—17 years

James Hilliard—LEO—33 years

James Hollowell—First
Responder—30 years

James Horn, Jr.—LEO—12 years

James Ingle—First Responder
—1 year

James J. Phillips, Sgt.—LEO &
K9 Officer Arees Phillips

James Jardine, Sgt.—LEO
—15 years

James Kyle Kirk—LEO
—27 years

James M.—LEO—10 years

James McCoy—LEO—30 years

James Michael Jones—First
Responder—Retired

James P. Van Horn—LEO
—5 years

James R. Bowman, III—First
Responder—48 years

James R. Evans—LEO—30 years

James Schier—First Responder
—32 years

James T. Woodward—LEO
—32 years

James Williams—LEO—18 years

James Willyard—LEO—20 years

Jamie Aistrop—LEO—9 years

Jared Durham—LEO—6 years

Jared Rowling—LEO—20 years

Jarid Taylor—LEO—End of
Watch 1/14/20

Jarrett Tilley—Volunteer First
Responder—2 years

Jason Catto—LEO—24 years

Jason Fogle—LEO—24 years

Jason Gray—LEO—17 years

Jason Hutchens—LEO—13 years

Jason Jost—LEO—28 years

Jason Keith—First Responder
—20 years

Jason Morrison, Maj.—LEO
—24 years
Jason Postma—LEO—15 years
Jason Schmitz—LEO—7 years
Jason Shaw—LEO—24 years
Jason Vanosdol—First Responder
—20 years
JD Holdman—LEO—32 years
Jeff Benkert—LEO—19 years
Jeff Bouma—LEO
Jeff Childers, Lt.—LEO—19 years
Jeff Crosby—LEO—32 years
Jeff Davis—LEO—18 years
Jeff Fiorita—LEO—30 years
Jeff Gilbert, Sgt.—LEO—25 years
Jeff Haley—First Responder
—33 years
Jeff Harrison—LEO—29 years
Jeff Martin—LEO
Jeff McIntosh, Lt.—LEO—31
years
Jeff Sewell, Cpt., In Memory
Of—LEO
Jeffrey Davenport—First
Responder—9 years
Jeffrey Kocab—LEO, 1+ years—
End of Watch 6/29/10
Jeffrey T. Hause, ST—LEO
—18 years
Jenna M. Van Horn—LEO
—4 years
Jennifer Alsip—First Responder
—3 years
Jennifer Porsche—Volunteer First
Responder—18 years
Jeremiah Eaton—LEO—16 years
Jeremiah J.—First Responder
—7 years
Jeremy Alderman—LEO
—15 years

Jeremy C.—First Responder
—29 years
Jeremy Helsel—First Responder
—10 years
Jeremy Wortz—LEO—27 years
Jerry L. Jimison—LEO—25 years
Jerry Lindsay, MAJ—LEO
—21 years
Jerry M. Rhodes—LEO
—47 years
Jerry Roberts—LEO—30 years
Jesse Jensen—First Responder
—4 years
Jessica DeLisle—First Responder
—2 years
Jessika Cave—LEO—3 years
Jim Barker, Lt.—LEO—33 years
Jim Couch—LEO—43 years
Jim Devlin—LEO—26 years
Jim Goetluck—LEO, First
Responder
Jim Knott—LEO—14 years
Jim Lueke—LEO—32 years
Jim Player—LEO—24 years
Jim Proctor, Sheriff—LEO
—8 years
Jim Rains—LEO—10 years
Jim Wilson—2020 Fire Chief
of the Year—First Responder,
41 years
Jimbo Russell, Cpt.—First
Responder—25 years
Jimmy McVey—LEO—20 years
Jimmy Sellers, Chf.—LEO
—27 years
Jimmy Spurling Chattanooga—
First Responder—25 years
Joe Abood—LEO—21 years
Joe Abruzzese—LEO—39 years
Joe Morris—LEO

Joe Mullet—First Responder

Joe Stroud—LEO—28 years

Joeann Chestnut—LEO—42 years

Joel J. Johnson, Sgt.—First
Responder—23 years

Joel Newsom—LEO—16 years

Joel R. Smith, Cpt.—First
Responder—14 years

John C.—LEO—18 years

John Chapman—LEO—37 years

John Cook—LEO—24 years

John Freiberger, Sgt.—LEO
—20 years

John Halferty—LEO—34 years

John Hampton—LEO—24 years

John Hill, Jr.—First Responder
—2 years

John Johnson—First Responder
—8 years

John Lafferty—LEO—23 years

John Matassa—LEO—25 years

John Neill—LEO—30 years

John Plumb, Sgt.—LEO—19 years

John Sellers, Sgt.—LEO—22 years

John T. Hause, Cpl.—LEO
—37 years

John T. Modglin—1 year

John Weiher—First Responder
—20 years

John West—LEO—44 years

John Wren—LEO—7 years

Johnathan Brown—First
Responder—2 years

Johnny Lawson ("Johnny Law"),
Dep.—LEO—14 years

Jon Alkema, Lt.—First Responder

Jon Geeting—LEO—32 years

Jon Goetluck—LEO—30 years

Jon Sears—First Responder
—8 years

Jonathan Aydelott—LEO
—17 years

Jonathan Bishop—First Responder
—6 years

Jonathan Body—LEO—1 year

Jonathan Boen—First Responder
—10 years

Jonathan C. Hoover—LEO
—27 years

Jonathan Evans—RCMP
—13 years

Jonathan Hontz—LEO—6 years

Jonathan Lendermon, DS—LEO

Jonathan Spohn—First
Responder—14 years

Jonathan Vasquez—LEO
—27 years

Jonathon Sizemore—LEO
—22 years

Jonathon Vanderwall—LEO
—4 months

Jordan Cramer—LEO—7 years

Jordan Dowling—LEO—8 years

Jordan Green—LEO

Joseph Ashmore—LEO—39 years

Joseph Dalton—LEO—34 years

Joseph Dupras—LEO—5 years

Joseph E. Orange, Sherriff—LEO
—30 years

Joseph Fitzpatrick—38 years

Joseph K. Urban, Jr.—LEO
—20 years

Joseph L. Miolla, Lt.—LEO
—21 years

Joseph M. Garcia—LEO—25
years

Joseph McNairy, Lt.—LEO
—29 years

Josh Buller—LEO—14 years

Josh Ellis—LEO—2 years

Josh Gates—LEO—10 years
Josh Harris—LEO—3 years
Joshua Bustin—LEO—6 years
Joshua F. Dula, Sgt.—LEO—5
years
Joshua Horton—LEO—4 years
Joshua Hutchison—First
Responder—11 years
Joshua Jones—LEO—10 years
Joshua Lucas—LEO—11 years
Joshua Maguire—First
Responder —4 years
Joshua McCord—LEO—4.5
years
Joshua Moore—LEO—14 years
Joshua Myers—LEO—10 years
Joshua Smith—LEO—3 years
Joshua T. Welch, Lt.—LEO
—23 years
Joshua Vannoy—Volunteer First
Responder—1 year
Joshua Wachob—Volunteer
Firefighter—20 years
Juan J. Gonzalez, Jr.—LEO
—4 years
Judy Bergthold—Search and
Rescue—1 year·
Judy Lawrence—LEO—
33 years
Julie Emory—LEO—2 years
Justin B.—LEO—18 years
Justin Barley—LEO—23 years
Justin Bowles, Cpl.—LEO—8
years
Justin Brown, Sgt.—LEO—18
years
Justin Ferguson—LEO
Justin Ivey—LEO—2 years
Justin Mortell—First Responder
—16 years

Justin Newcomb—LEO—14
years
Justin Shiflett—LEO—10 years
K. White, Sgt.—LEO—18 years
Karen Dukes—LEO—21 years
Karen Noffsinger, DS—LEO
—13 years
Karlee Philpott—First Responder
—2 years
Kassi Peak—LEO—4 years
Kathi Osborn—First Responder
—5 years
Kaye Wagner, Dep.—First
Responder—20 years
Kayla M. Consuegra—First
Responder—5 years
Keanan Austin, Sgt.—LEO, 3
years—First Responder, 15
years
Keith Asbill—First Responder
—4 years
Keith Seibert—LEO—22 years
Kelli Bishop—LEO—17 years
Kelli C.—First Responder—19
years
Kelly Johnson, Cpt.—First
Responder—25 years
Kelly McLean—LEO—30 years
Kelly McMillin—LEO—
17 years
Ken Arnold—LEO—19 years
Ken Nichols—LEO—21 years
Kendall Englund—LEO—15
years
Kenneth Baker—First Responder
—20 years
Kenneth Chapple—LEO—19
years
Kenneth Chapple, Jr.—LEO—4
years

Kenneth S. Cottrill—LEO—5 years

Kerri Hall, Sgt.—LEO—27 years

Kevin Aldridge—LEO—24 years

Kevin Burns—LEO—8 years

Kevin E. Orndorff—LEO—13 years

Kevin Elliott—LEO—3 years

Kevin Fisher—LEO—7 years

Kevin Kosten—LEO—25 years

Kevin Nummerdor—LEO—18 years

Kevin Quinn—LEO—26 years

Kevin Richmond—First Responder —25 years

Kevin Wilbanks—First Responder —19 years

Kim Hanson—LEO—21+ years

Kimberly Thompson—LEO —20 years

Kresten Green—LEO—10 years

Kris Delap, Sgt.—LEO—28 years

Kristi Boyce Smith—3 years

Kristian Hernandez—LEO—5 years

Kurt Brian Wyman—LEO, 3 years —End of Watch—6/7/11

Kyle Gallen—LEO—4 years

Kyle McCarty—LEO—10 years

L.J. White, Lt.—LEO—42 years

Lance Beatty—First Responder —16 years

Lance G.—LEO—14 years

Lance M. MacLaughlin—LEO —25 years

Lance Shields—LEO— 3 years

Lance Vines—LEO—25 years

Landon E. Weaver—LEO, 6/17/16—End of Watch 12/30/16

Larry A. Schroyer—LEO—27 years

Larry Amerson—LEO—42 years

Larry Eastridge—LEO, First Responder—25 years

Larry Thomas Walton—LEO— End of Watch 12/2/72

Lee Rohrbach, Jr.—LEO—11 years

Lee S. Gliddon, Sr., DS—LEO —10 years

Leo D. Blackwell—LEO—24 years

Leon Riley—LEO—8 years

Leona Keith—First Responder —5 years

Leonard Corral, Jr.—LEO—27 years

Lisa J. Zipp-Hoffman—First Responder—25 years

Lisa Lister—First Responder —4 years

Lonnie Flowers—Volunteer First Responder—10+ years

Lowell "Bud" Ulery—LEO —36 years

Lucas Bartley Dowell—LEO, 5 years—End of Watch 2/4/19

Luke Appell—LEO—1 year

Luke Humke—LEO—16 years

Lyle Smith—LEO—29 years

M. Poole, Cpt.—LEO—18 years

M.B. Truesdell—LEO

M.C. Dodson, Lt.—LEO—11 years

Mackenzie Roller—First Responder

Maddy Clinton, In Memory Of—

Vol. First Responder.
—35 years
Madison Haigh—LEO
—7+ months
Madison Ward—First Responder
—6 months
Marcella Weaver—LEO
Margaret Sutton Bateson—LEO
—20 years
Margery Gerbec, Sgt.—LEO
Mariah Johnson—LEO—4 years
Mariah Newton Johnson—LEO
—5 years
Marie Evans—First Responder
—30 years
Mark Bergthold—Search and
Rescue—2 years
Mark Considine—First
Responder—41 years
Mark Konynenbelt, Lt.—LEO
Mark L. Mitchell—LEO—27 years
Mark Moore—LEO—40 years
Mark Nickel—LEO—35 years
Mark Ruffin—LEO—15 years
Mark S. Lowery—First Responder
Mark Sanders—LEO—25 years
Mark Schumacher—LEO
—4 years
Mark Spears—First Responder
—25 years
Mark Swihart—First Responder
—38 years
Mark Todd—LEO—21 years
Marshal R. Floyd—LEO—20 years
Martin J. Stewart—LEO—27
years
Marty Clinton—Volunteer
Firefighter—25 years
Marty V. Donini—LEO
—42 years

Matt Fracker—LEO—12 years
Matt Horn, Cpt.—First
Responder—30 years
Matteo Lopez—LEO—1 year
Matthew "Mark" Chitwood—
LEO—25 years
Matthew Dunn—LEO—20 years
Matthew Elias Gatti—LEO,
1 year—End of Watch 5/6/19
Matthew Gorman—LEO
—11 years
Matthew Hinson—First
Responder—21 years
Matthew Hoggatt—LEO
—19 years
Matthew J. Croft—LEO—23 years
Matthew Licht—First Responder
—5 years
Matthew Lytle—LEO—2.5 years
Matthew Patton, SMO & FTO—
LEO—8 years
Matthew Peacock—LEO, 10
years—First Responder,
22 years
Matthew Seftick—First Responder
Matthew Slatkovsky—LEO
Matthew Steen, Sgt.—LEO
—24 years
Matthew W. Center—LEO
—42 years
Matthew West—First Responder
—10 years
Max Graves—LEO—34 years
Megan Adams—LEO—2.5 years
Megan Clark—First Responder
—5 years
Megan Rilee Jones—First
Responder
Melissa Coursin—First Responder
—15 Years

Melvin Claxton—LEO, 19
years—End of Watch 2/17/99
Melvin D. Lytle, Jr. COP—LEO
—28 years
Memphis Baker—First
Responder—3 years
Menke Franzen—LEO—Retired
Micah McDowell—LEO
—18 years
Micah Nobles—LEO—4 years
Michael A. Hodgson—LEO
—28 years
Michael Adkins, Jr.—LEO
—15 years
Michael Allen—LEO—24 years
Michael Brumley—LEO
Michael Calvert—LEO—15 years
Michael Cesare—LEO—30 years
Michael Couey—LEO—10 years
Michael D. Harris—LEO
—42 years
Michael Decker—LEO—12 years
Michael Dillon—LEO—17 years
Michael Dunn, Sgt.—LEO
—22 years
Michael E. Friday—LEO—37
years
Michael Eickmann, MPO—LEO
—26 years
Michael Fallon—LEO—25 years
Michael Guy—First Responder
—16 years
Michael Humes—LEO—1 year
Michael J. Carrasco—LEO—21
years
Michael Kircher—LEO—20 years
Michael L. Eubanks—LEO
—25 years
Michael Laurendeau—LEO
—9 years

Michael Lucas, Lt.—LEO
—30 years
Michael Matelski—LEO, 7 years
—First Responder, 8 years
Michael Maverly, Sgt.—LEO
—21 years
Michael Melione—LEO—4 years
Michael Monts—LEO—21 years
Michael Morris—LEO—6 years
Michael Peery—First Responder
—25 years
Michael Pollard—LEO—7 years
Michael R. Morton—LEO
—23 years
Michael Richardson—LEO
—26 years
Michael Row—LEO—9 years
Michael S. Brandt—LEO
—17 years
Michael VanHook—LEO
—26 years
Michael W. Faust—LEO
—32 years
Michael Ward—First
Responder
—2 years
Michael Weigand, COP—LEO
—12+ years
Michael Weigand, Jr. Sgt.—LEO,
6 years—End of Watch
9/14/08
Michael Williams—LEO—3
years
Michelle Palladini, Sgt.—LEO
—15 years
Michelle Strawser—LEO
—24 years
Mickey Yentes—LEO—19 years
Mike Auricchio—LEO—
31 years

Mike Barbian, In Memory Of—
LEO—19 years
Mike Fredrickson—LEO
—17 years
Mike Marine—First Responder
—25+ years
Mike McDowell—LEO
—32 years
Mike Moore, In Memory Of—
LEO—19 years
Mike Puig—First Responder
—30 years
Mike Ryall, Dep. Dir.—LEO
—43 years
Mike S. McAuliffe—LEO
—30 years
Mike Salazar—First Responder
—32 years
Mike Yawn—LEO—42 years
Miles Long, Sgt.—LEO
—20 years
Mitchell Hannon—LEO—5 years
Mitchell Martinez—LEO—7 years
Molly Roller—First Responder
—6 years
Morgan Mehlert—LEO
—10 years
Myles Scott—LEO—7 years
Nate Farr—LEO—10 years
Nathan G.—LEO—4 years
Nathaniel C. Chester—LEO
—4 years
Nathaniel Hoover—LEO
—13 years
Neil Fernander—First
Responder—11 years
Nicholas Engle—LEO—
3 years
Nicholas Maguire—First
Responder—4 years

Nicholas Oftedahl—LEO
—2 months
Nick Raddant—LEO—9 years
Noah Koss—LEO—2 years
Odette Daigle Dougherty—First
Responder—8 years
Omar A. Khan—LEO—14 years
Oral Banta—First Responder
—34 years
Oscar Mills—LEO—13 years
Parker Scruggs—LEO—3 years
Patrick Brady—LEO—6 years
Patrick Dillon—LEO—28 years
Patrick Randolph—LEO—2 years
Patrick Torek—LEO—30 years
Pattrick Selby—LEO—1 year
Paul Green—LEO—25 years
Paul J. Dore—LEO—23 years
Paul M. Dorman—LEO
—25+ years
Paul Schoder—LEO
Paul Sunday—LEO—11 years
Paul Vandenburg—LEO—
4 years
Paul Weller—LEO—13 years
Peter Sutton—LEO—30 years
Phil Chambers—LEO—30 years
Phillip J. Wolters III—LEO
—22 years
Quin Beers—LEO—16 years
R. Steve Collier, Maj.—LEO
—36 years
Rachel Anderson Greene—LEO
—11 years
Rachel Campbell—First
Responder—12 years
Randal McKinney—LEO
—11 years
Randall D. Cashatt—LEO
—23 years

Randall Watts—First Responder
—18 years

Randy Neely—First Responder
—26 years

Randy Pratt—LEO—21 years

Ray Downey, BC—First
Responder, 39 years—End of
Service 9/11/01

Rebecca Preibus—First
Responder—15 years

Rebecca Sizemore—First
Responder—8 years

Reggie Ray—LEO—37 years

Reid Stacy—LEO—23 years

Rex Newton—LEO, 7 years—
First Responder, 1 year

Ric Petersen—LEO—16 years

Richard Garayua, Sgt.—LEO
—18.5 years

Richard Hiles—LEO—14 years

Richard Kindle—Volunteer First
Responder—30 years

Richard Wood—LEO—30 years

Rick Dowling—LEO—43 years

Rick Farnsler—LEO—31 years

Rick Salsedo—LEO—30 years

Rickey Dandridge, Maj.—LEO
—39 years

Rob Burdess, COP—LEO
—23 years

Rob Shook—First Responder
—5 years

Robert Cave—LEO—3 years

Robert F. Noland—LEO
—39 years

Robert G. DeBok, In Memory
Of—LEO—33 years

Robert H. Randle—LEO
—21 years

Robert Hack—LEO—32 years

Robert Holland, Sheriff—LEO
—30 years

Robert Howard—First Responder
—11 years

Robert Kalinowski, Jr.—LEO
—33 years

Robert Kammerer, Sgt.—LEO
—32 years

Robert Kennedy, II—LEO
—23 years

Robert O.—First Responder
—25 years

Robert Phillips—First Responder
—4 years

Robert Stout, Sgt.—LEO
—12 years

Robert Thompson—First
Responder—13 years

Robert Vigil, In Memory Of—
LEO—16 years

Robin Sarrasin—LEO—17 years

Rod Costillo—LEO

Rodney Barrett—LEO—28 years

Rodney Eubanks—LEO—26 years

Rodney Whallon—Volunteer
First Responder—8 years

Roel Flores—LEO—25 years

Roger Dail—First Responder
—30 years

Roman Patricio Gonzales—LEO
—13 years

Ron Brown, Sheriff—LEO
—30 years

Ronald A. Kelly, Jr.—LEO
—14 years

Ronald Nord—LEO—34 years

Ross Peterson—LEO—27 years

Rudy Galvan—LEO—19 years

Russel Allen, MO—LEO
—16 years

Rusty Hill—LEO—18 years
Ryan Aasum—Volunteer First
Responder—5 years
Ryan Bent, PC—LEO—13 years
Ryan Fritz—LEO—24 years
Ryan G.—LEO—9 years
Ryan Keener—LEO—1 year
Ryan Long—Volunteer First
Responder—23 years
Ryan Manning—LEO—2 years
Ryan Quinn—LEO—5.5 years
Ryan Rupp—LEO—18 years
Ryan White—LEO—3 years
Sally Roller—First Responder
—6 years
Sam Bowles—First Responder
—9 years
Sam Crosley—LEO—23 years
Samuel Gallen—LEO—41 years
Samuel Hosea—LEO—8 years
Sara Smith—LEO—1 year
Sarah Finley—LEO—1 year
Scott Baird—LEO—30 years
Scott Carter—LEO—29 years
Scott Cook, DS—LEO—22 years
Scott Drugo—LEO—20 years
Scott Dykman—LEO—21 years
Scott Eugene Britton—LEO
—25 years
Scott H.—LEO—3 years
Scott Hall—LEO—16 years
Scott Neves—LEO—30 years
Scott Summers—LEO—20 years
Scotty Vestal, Cpt.—LEO
—20 years
Sean R. Cox—LEO—21 years
Sean Showalter—LEO—18 years
Seth Parsons—LEO—5 years
Shane Ash, Lt.—LEO—20 years
Shane Isaacs—LEO—23 years

Shawn P. Hauck—LEO—19 years
Shawn R. Haken—LEO—27 years
Shon Matthews, In Memory Of—
First Responder—15 years
Skyler Sisk—LEO—2 years
Spencer Chance—LEO—1.5 years
Stan Livingston—LEO—26 years
Stan Standridge—LEO—26 years
Stephen Eason—First Responder
—7 years
Stephen H.—LEO—10 years
Stephen Jeffrey "Jeff" Dunn—
LEO—22 years
Stephen O'Dell—LEO—4 years
Stephen Summers—LEO
—3 years
Steve Abbe, Chaplain—LEO
—26 years
Steve Cryan DS—LEO—35 years
Steve Disbennett, Cpt.—First
Responder—25 years
Steve Hutchens, In Memory Of—
First Responder—31 years
Steve Lemmen—LEO—19 years
Steve Sellers—First Responder
—38 years
Steve Strawser—LEO—36 years
Steve Tate Chattanooga—First
Responder—25 years
Steve Waltman—First Responder
Steven Alaniz—First Responder
—12 years
Steven Cliff, PC—LEO—15 years
Steven Cody—2 years
Steven Shelton—First Responder
—9 years
Sue Flowers—Volunteer First
Responder—10+ years
T.R. Branch—LEO—20 years &
K9 Macho—5 years

Tanner Wilson—LEO—1 year

Taylor Zirk—LEO—6 years

Terrell Ogilvie—First Responder —21.5 years

Terri NeSmith—First Responder —28 years

Tex Huffman—LEO—5 years

Theodore McGinley—LEO —6 years

Theresa Sue "T.K." King—LEO, 14 years—End of Watch 6/16/18

Thomas Bateson—LEO —32.5 years

Thomas Bell—LEO—18 years

Thomas Corbin—LEO—34 years

Thomas Haas—LEO—29 years

Thomas Hudak—LEO—25 years

Thomas J. Woodward—First Responder—6 years

Tiffany Bauereisen, DC—LEO —15 years

Tim Billingsley—LEO—24 years

Tim Davis—LEO—28 years

Tim Jackson—LEO—2 years

Tim Perry, Sgt.—LEO

Tim Schmidt—LEO—22 years

Tim Simon—LEO—5 years

Timothy D.—LEO—6 years

Timothy F. Davison—LEO —3 years

Timothy MacFawn—LEO —30 years

Timothy O'Connor, In Memory Of—LEO—3 years

TJ Favero—LEO—22 years

Todd Dabbs—LEO—9 years

Todd Gribbons—LEO—19 years

Todd L. Spillers—LEO— 14 years

Todd McConnell—First Responder—24 years

Todd McCoy—LEO—15 years

Tom Abbamonte—LEO —20 years

Tom Kenngott, In Memory Of— First Responder—35 years

Tommy Larison—LEO—3 years

Tommy Simms—First Responder —10.5 years

Tony Chisenhall—First Responder

Tony Lemke—LEO—10 years

Tony Widner—LEO—38 years

Travis Guidry—LEO—10.5 years

Travis Leslie—LEO—16 years

Travis Meadows—LEO—10 years

Travis Smith—LEO—20 years

Trent Anthony—First Responder —4 years

Trent Newman—LEO—10 years

Trevor Jolly—LEO, First Responder—10 years

Troy Clem, Jr.—LEO—4 years

Troy Magers—LEO—32 years

Tyler Beers—LEO—1 year

Tyler Dean—LEO—1+ years

Tyler Eller—LEO—2 years

Tyler Hess—LEO—8 years

Tyler Hummel—LEO—2 years

Tyler Lee—LEO—7 years

Tyler McCommons—First Responder—10 years

Tyler Schultz—LEO—2 years

Tyler Sheppard—LEO—6 years

Tyler Tilson—LEO—5 years

Tyler Turner—LEO—5.5 years

Tyler W. Martin—LEO—2 years

Ulrich O. Schulze—LEO

Urban Rodriguez—LEO—5 years

Verl Setler, Sgt.—LEO—20 years

Vern E. Fisher, II, Lt.—LEO
—27.5 years
Vicky Hollowell—First Responder
—20 years
Victor Camp—LEO—30 years
Victoria York, Cpl.—LEO
—12 years
Vince Kempf—LEO—29 years
Virginia Goodman—First
Responder—25 years
Wayne Chalker—LEO—40 years
Wayne Llewellyn—LEO
—15 years
Wayne Meyenberg, Lt.—LEO
—28 years
Wayne Wymer—First Responder
—24 years
Wesley Gargis, Lt.—LEO
—17 years
Wesley Turner—First Responder
—4 years
Wesley Wood—First Responder
William 'Bill' Brooks—LEO
William B. Payne—LEO
William B. Thomas—LEO
—20+ years
William C. Knepp—LEO
—35 years
William Cook—First Responder

William D. Hamby—First
Responder—42 years
William Flowers—First Responder
—25 years
William Goetluck—LEO
—44 years
William H. "Mel" Medlin, III—
LEO—27 years
William H. "Wil" Medlin, IV—
LEO—7 years
William K. Smith—LEO
—31 years
William Lewis, Sgt.—LEO
—9.5 years
William Maynes—LEO—
3 years
William Schutt—Volunteer First
Responder—60 years
William Thomas—LEO
—2+ years
Wilson Sutton—LEO—26 years
Wyatt Holdman—LEO—1 year
Zach Reilly—First Responder
—3 years
Zachary A. Jenkins—LEO
—12 years
Zachary A. Van Horn—LEO
—10 years
Zachary Tarrant—LEO—5 years